P9-DHK-703

ALSO BY JENNIFER CHIAVERINI

The Quilter's Apprentice

Round Robin

The Cross-Country Quilters

An Elm Creek Quilts Novel

THE RUNAWAY QUILT

JENNIFER CHIAVERINI

SIMON & SCHUSTER
New York London Toronto Sydney Singapore

SIMON & SCHUSTER
Rockefeller Center
1230 Avenue of the Americas
New York, NY 10020

This book is a work of fiction. Names, characters, places, and incidents either are products of the author's imagination or are used fictitiously. Any resemblance to actual events or locales or persons, living or dead, is entirely coincidental.

For information about special discounts for bulk purchases, please contact Simon & Schuster Special Sales:
1-800-456-6798 or business@simonandschuster.com

Designed by Leslie Phillips

Manufactured in the United States of America

1 3 5 7 9 10 8 6 4 2

LIBRARY OF CONGRESS CATALOGING-IN-PUBLICATION DATA

Chiaverini, Jennifer.
The runaway quilt : an Elm Creek quilts novel / Jennifer Chiaverini.
p. cm.
1. Underground railroad—Fiction. 2. Female friendship—Fiction.
3. Quiltmakers—Fiction. I. Title.
PS3553.H473 R86 2002
813'.54—dc21
2001057567

ISBN 0-7432-2226-1

To Marty and Nicholas,
with all my love.

ACKNOWLEDGMENTS

This book would not have been possible without the expertise and guidance of Denise Roy, Maria Massie, Rebecca Davis, and Tara Parsons. Thank you for your wisdom and your friendship.

I am grateful to author Barbara Brackman for providing me with important historical information regarding Civil War–era quilts and the use of quilts as signals on the Underground Railroad.

Thank you, Christine Johnson, for reading the manuscript of *The Quilter's Apprentice* so many years ago and posing the question that became this novel.

I thank my friends and family, especially Geraldine Neidenbach, Heather Neidenbach, Nic Neidenbach, Virginia and Edward Riechman, Leonard and Marlene Chiaverini, Martin Lang, Rachel and Chip Sauer, Anne Spurgeon, Vanessa Alt, the Mad City Quilters, and the members of RCTQ, for your encouragement and support.

Most of all, I am grateful to my husband, Marty, and my son, Nicholas, who inspire me every day with their humor and their love.

THE RUNAWAY QUILT

When her sister, Claudia, died childless at the age of seventy-seven, Sylvia Bergstrom Compson became the last living descendant of Hans and Anneke Bergstrom and the sole heir to what remained of their fortune. Or so she had thought. She had certainly searched long and hard enough for someone else who could assume responsibility of Elm Creek Manor, for as difficult as it was to believe now, at the time she had thought the estate in rural central Pennsylvania too full of unhappy memories to become her home again. Her lawyer had told her she was the sole heir, an opinion corroborated by her private detective.

Now she wondered if they had overlooked something, a familial connection lost to memory but documented in a threadbare antique quilt.

She had never seen the quilt before; that much she knew to be true. She saw it for the first time after a speaking engagement for the Silver Lake Quilters' Guild in South Carolina. One woman had stayed behind to help Sylvia and her companion, Andrew Cooper, pack up Sylvia's lecture materials. As the three folded

Sylvia's quilts and placed her slides carefully into boxes, the woman introduced herself as Margaret Alden and said that they had met before, for she was a former camper.

"Of course I remember you," Sylvia declared, but after a skeptical look from Andrew, she confessed otherwise. Margaret laughed and said she understood completely. So many quilters attended Elm Creek Quilt Camp each year that it was impossible to remember every one, although Sylvia felt that she ought to at least try. The campers were, after all, guests in her own home.

They chatted about quilt camp as they carried Sylvia's lecture materials to Andrew's motor home, but even after Sylvia thanked her for the help, Margaret lingered. "If you could spare me another few minutes," she said, "I'd like to show you a quilt. It's been in my family for generations, but I think it might have some connection to Elm Creek Manor."

"I beg your pardon?" said Sylvia. "What sort of connection?"

"That's what I hoped you might know."

Andrew and Sylvia were eager to begin the first leg of their long drive back to central Pennsylvania, but Sylvia rarely passed up the opportunity to see a quilt, and certainly couldn't resist seeing one so intriguingly described. Margaret hurried to her car and returned carrying a bundle wrapped in a cotton bedsheet. With Sylvia's assistance, she unfolded it to reveal a quilt—or rather, what remained of one.

The pattern caught Sylvia's eye first: Birds in the Air blocks, each a square divided along the diagonal, a solid right triangle of medium or dark fabric on one side, three small right triangles surrounded by lighter background fabrics on the other. The blocks were arranged on point so that all the right angles of the triangles, large and small, pointed in the same direction. The fabrics themselves seemed to be primarily muslins and wools, so faded and worn that Sylvia could only guess their original colors. Water stains and deterioration suggested age as well as rough handling, as did the muted colors of the once bright dyes and the worn binding, through which the cotton batting was visible. Fine stipple quilting held the three layers together—where they *were* still held together. Elsewhere, the thread had been removed or torn out by accident, and the middle batting layer it should have held in place was long gone.

Only a reluctance to appear hypocritical prevented Sylvia from scolding Margaret for risking further damage to the quilt by bringing it to the quilt guild meeting, for Sylvia was very glad to see it. "It's lovely, dear." She bent closer and peered through her bifocals at the quilting stitches. There was something unusual about them, something she couldn't yet place.

"Lovely?" Margaret laughed. "Most people look at it and say, " 'Hmm. Interesting.' "

"You can tell Sylvia's a true quilter," said Andrew. "She never fails to see through the wear and tear and find the beauty."

"True beauty stands the test of time," said Sylvia, straightening. "Although I must say it's a pity its previous owners did not take better care of it."

"I know," said Margaret apologetically. "But my mother says it was just one of many quilts her grandmother had around the house. They didn't realize they were sleeping under a family heirloom."

"Of course not. I'm not faulting you or your ancestors. I'm not one of those who believes quilts should be showpieces kept safely away from anyone's bed." Sylvia returned her gaze to the quilt. "It's a simple pattern, pieced from scraps. It wasn't intended as the family's best quilt. I'd say by using it so well, your family was acting well within the quiltmaker's wishes."

Margaret smiled, pleased. Then Andrew caught Sylvia's eye, and she was suddenly aware of how her lecture had wearied her and how long they planned to drive before stopping for the night. She couldn't imagine what possible connection the quilt could have to Elm Creek Manor, unless Margaret hoped Sylvia would buy it and display it there. Briskly, she said, "Now, were you looking for an appraisal of the quilt or an estimate of its age? If so, I'm afraid I can't help you. I could place it in the mid- to late nineteenth century, but you'll need to consult a textiles expert for a more precise answer. As for what it's worth in terms of dollars and cents—"

"Oh, I could never sell it," said Margaret, shocked.

"I'm pleased to hear that." Sylvia wished all families would show such appreciation for the heirloom quilts their foremothers had so lovingly made. "Then tell me, what did you mean by a connection between this quilt and my home?"

Margaret turned the quilt so that only the solid muslin backing was visible. "When you look at the quilting stitches, what do you see?"

Pursing her lips, Sylvia carefully scrutinized the quilt. Without the distraction of color and pattern, the stitches were more clearly visible. "The stippling pattern isn't consistent," she said. "Some of the stitches are long, others quite small, and the small ones seem to be grouped together."

Margaret's nod told Sylvia she had responded just as the younger woman had hoped. "When I told my mother I had attended quilt camp at Elm Creek Manor, she told me that she had an old family quilt her grandmother had called the Elm Creek Quilt."

Sylvia looked up in surprise. "Did she, indeed?"

"At first I thought its name came from the quilting pattern used in the border. See the elm leaf motif, and how these wavy lines look like running water?"

"I suppose." Sylvia saw the leaves now that they had been pointed out, but in her opinion, the wavy lines resembled a common cable pattern more than a creek.

"It had another name, too. The Runaway Quilt."

"Runaway?" Andrew chuckled. "I've heard of quilters getting carried away with their work, but I didn't know a quilt could actually run away."

"Perhaps the quilt turned out much larger than its maker had intended," said Sylvia. "Perhaps she felt it ran on and on, with a life of its own."

"Maybe, but my mother says it was most often called the Elm Creek Quilt," said Margaret hastily.

Sylvia nodded and exchanged an amused glance with Andrew. Margaret seemed most eager to prove her point, but she had said nothing yet to persuade Sylvia.

"Now look at these designs." Margaret pointed out groups of stitches that she said resembled, in turn, a tobacco leaf, a star, a mountain pass, a group of horses—

"And these," said Margaret, watching Sylvia expectantly, "form a picture of Elm Creek Manor."

Sylvia could no longer nod politely at the woman's wild imaginings. "I'm sorry, dear. I just don't see it."

"Remember the quilter was working from the other side," said Andrew, more mindful of Margaret's feelings than Sylvia had been. "The designs would be in reverse."

Sylvia carefully unfurled the quilt before the motor home's full-length mirror and studied one small section near the top. To her amazement, the reflection revealed a perfect outline of a pass between several low mountains.

She stared at the quilt, speechless. "My goodness," she finally managed. "I must admit, that bears a striking resemblance to the pass into the Elm Creek Valley." She held up another section. "This could indeed be the west wing of Elm Creek Manor."

"You told us at camp that the west wing predates the rest of your home," said Margaret.

"It would have been the only part standing at the time this quilt was made." Sylvia traced the design with a fingertip. "The original entrance is in the proper place."

"So it's a side view now," said Andrew. "But back then—"

"This would have been the front view of the house." Sylvia shook her head, is if to clear it of nonsense. "I admit I'm tempted to believe there's some connection, but I'm afraid it's all a bit too fanciful for me. Many houses share a similar design, and elm trees and creeks are hardly exclusive to my family's estate . . ." Her voice trailed off in disbelief.

Not far from the image of Elm Creek Manor appeared the outline of another building, one so unique and remarkable that there could be no mistaking it: a two-story barn, partially concealed by the slope of the hill into which it was built, exact in proportion and scale to the barn on the grounds of Sylvia's estate.

* * *

Andrew photographed the quilt, front and back, with close-ups of the quilted images, while Sylvia recorded Margaret's memories. Margaret surmised, based upon family stories, that her grandmother's grandmother had sewn the quilt, but the five years Margaret had spent researching her family's genealogy had turned up little information from that era, since many important documents had been destroyed during the Civil War. Then Margaret added, almost as an aside, "If my grandmother's grandmother didn't make the quilt, I suppose one of her slaves could have."

"Her slaves?" echoed Sylvia. "Goodness. Your family owned slaves?"

"Yes," said Margaret, "but you don't have to look at me like that. I never owned any."

"My apologies, dear. I didn't mean to be rude." Sylvia composed herself. Of course, she had probably met the descendants of slave owners before, just as she had certainly met the descendants of slaves. It was just unexpected to hear someone admit to one's ancestors' moral failings with such nonchalance, especially since Sylvia's family had treated their forebears with respect bordering on reverence.

"It seems to me, the person who made this quilt must have seen Elm Creek Manor," said Margaret.

"Could be she was recording memories of a visit," said Andrew.

"I suppose there's no way to know for certain." Sylvia gazed at the sections of the quilt where the thread had been removed. What patterns would they have found within those stitches?

"Sylvia," asked Margaret. "Did any of your ancestors leave the family estate and move South?"

"Do you mean to say you think our families might be related?"

"I think it's possible. I had hoped your family records would be more complete than mine."

"I suppose it's not entirely unlikely. My cousin Elizabeth left Elm Creek Manor when I was a young girl, but she and her husband went to California . . ."

"Anything else?" prompted Margaret. "Someone earlier?"

Sylvia searched her memory as best she could under the circumstances. Hans and Anneke Bergstrom had come to America in the middle of the nineteenth century, but Sylvia did not know the precise date. She knew they had had several children, but she could not recall how many had survived to adulthood. Surely some of them must have left to start families and households of their own, but if one of them was indeed Margaret's ancestor—

"I'm afraid I just don't know," said Sylvia, and lowered herself into a nearby seat.

Andrew must have seen how Margaret's questions had affected her, for he left her to her thoughts. He and Margaret exchanged addresses and phone numbers; then, with a promise to share whatever they discovered, Andrew showed her to the door. A few moments later, Sylvia heard him start the engine. Only then did she rouse herself and move to the front passenger seat beside him.

They drove in silence for nearly an hour before Sylvia spoke. "Do you suppose Margaret and I could have an ancestor in common?"

"It's possible." He kept his eyes on the road. "What do you think?"

"I think I was much more content before I learned I might have slave owners in the family."

"All families have members they're not so proud of."

"Yes, but slave owners?"

"Don't be too hard on them. They were people of their times."

"Plenty of other people of their times didn't own slaves. Hans and Anneke, for example. Elm Creek Manor was a station on the Underground Railroad, did you know that?"

He gave her a sidelong glance. "You might have mentioned it once or twice."

"If I've bragged, it's because I'm proud of them. I should be proud. That was brave and dangerous work. And now I'm supposed to accept that some of my relatives—well, I don't accept it." She folded her arms and glared out the windshield at the lights of other cars speeding down the freeway. Night had fallen, but the sky was overcast. She wondered where the North Star was. It ought to be directly overhead, or nearly so. So long ago, it had shown the way to freedom, and her family had offered sanctuary to many of those who had braved the hazards of the path it illuminated.

But Elm Creek Manor was so secluded, the North Star alone would not have been enough to guide a stranger to its door.

"Andrew," said Sylvia, "I don't believe the quilt preserved memories of Elm Creek Manor. I think it was meant to show the way."

She had heard of such things before, quilts with coded messages or even maps revealing safe pathways along the Underground Railroad. The very name of Margaret's quilt suggested it might be one of those legendary artifacts. But in all of Sylvia's decades as a quilter and lecturer, she had never seen one of these quilts, only heard lore of them around the quilt frame. Her friend Grace Daniels, a master quilter and museum curator, had once told her that not only had no one ever documented a map quilt from the era, no slave narrative or Abolitionist testimonial she had read mentioned one.

Sylvia respected Grace's expertise, and yet, in the stillness of her own heart, she yearned for the folklore to be true. Within her own family, a tale had been handed down through the generations about a quilt used to signal to fugitive slaves. Folklore carried a stronger ring of truth when one loved and trusted the person who spoke it.

But now, torn between her memories and the questions Margaret Alden's quilt raised, Sylvia would need more than folklore and family histories to discern the truth. She needed evidence only Elm Creek Manor could provide.

* * *

Andrew and Sylvia preferred to drive at a leisurely pace, so it wasn't until several days after the encounter with Margaret Alden that they pulled off the freeway and headed down the two-lane road past picturesque farms and rolling, forested hills toward home. Sylvia sighed with happiness when they turned onto a gravel road that wound its way through a familiar leafy wood. Before long, Elm Creek came into view, marking the southern border of the estate.

When the road forked, Andrew stayed to the left, following the road that led to the parking lot at the rear entrance of the manor. The right fork would have taken them over a narrow bridge and across a vast lawn up to the front entrance—a more grand approach, especially for visitors, but impractical for Andrew's ocean liner on wheels. Before long the creek wound north and disappeared from sight, but the road continued west for a little way before turning north.

The wood gave way to a clearing. To the left was the orchard, where several women strolled among the apple trees. They waved as the motor home passed, and Sylvia waved merrily back. Ahead and to the right stood the two-story red barn built into the side of a hill. Sylvia's gaze locked on it.

"It's an accurate picture," said Andrew, meaning the pattern of stitches in Margaret's quilt. His words echoed Sylvia's own thoughts, but she merely nodded, unwilling to commit herself.

Just beyond the barn, the path crossed a low bridge over Elm Creek and widened into a driveway lined by tall elms. Then, at last, the manor itself came into view, its gray stone walls solid and welcoming. It was three stories tall—not counting the attic—and L-shaped, with black shutters and black woodwork along the eaves. Four stone stairs led to the back door, and as the motor home pulled into the parking lot, Sylvia watched as women bustled in and out.

"My goodness," said Sylvia. "It certainly is busy around here this morning. Isn't anyone in class?"

"You forget how many more campers you have these days," said Andrew.

"Only fifty each week."

"Yes, but your first year, you had only twelve. No wonder it looks like you have a crowd milling around."

No wonder, indeed. What would her sister think if she could see how their family estate had been transformed? More than fifty years before, grief and anger had driven Sylvia away from her family home and into estrangement from her elder sister. Only after Claudia's death had Sylvia returned, intending to prepare the manor for sale rather than live there haunted by reminders of departed loved ones. She never imagined that hiring Sarah McClure as her assistant would force her to face all those old resentments and painful truths about her own mistakes. Elm Creek Quilts had been Sarah's vision and Sylvia's lifeline, for turning the estate into a retreat for quilters had made the halls ring with laughter and happiness as they had not for decades. Now Sylvia knew that, except for her occasional jaunts with Andrew, she would live out her days on the estate her ancestors had founded. She knew this was exactly as it should be, and her heart was full of gratitude for the friends who had made this second chance possible.

Eager for the company of these friends, Sylvia kissed Andrew on the cheek and hurried inside while he remained behind to look over the motor home. Sarah met her at the back door and greeted her with a hug. Sarah launched into a description of the week's events, but Sylvia's news would not wait. "Sarah, dear," she interrupted, "I have a special favor to ask of you. Would you join me in the attic, please?"

* * *

They began the search that afternoon.

Throughout the drive from South Carolina to Pennsylvania, Sylvia's thoughts had returned again and again to her great-aunt Lucinda's stories and the trunk she had described more than seventy years before. Somewhere among the dust and clutter of four generations there was a cherry hope chest with engraved brass fastenings, and in it—if Lucinda's stories were true—was a quilt Great-Grandmother Anneke had made.

Sylvia had always meant to find that quilt, but her long exile had made the search impossible, and upon her return, the improbability of finding it had been so daunting that she had put off the task. Even Grace Daniels's persistent requests to study the quilt had not been motivation enough. Now everything had changed. She did not know if Anneke's quilt could prove or disprove a connection between Margaret's quilt and Elm Creek Manor, but if it existed—and Sylvia refused to believe it did not—it might at least provide evidence that the manor had been a station on the Underground Railroad. Sylvia would be willing to acknowledge whatever other, more distant relations had done if she could first be certain her own direct ancestors had played a more noble role.

But after climbing the narrow, creaking staircase and surveying the attic, Sylvia knew that finding the trunk would be difficult, if not impossible, even with Sarah's help. The shorter, older west wing lay to her right, and the longer, newer south wing stretched out before her. Up here the seam joining old and new was more evident than below, the colors of the walls subtly different, the floor not quite even. Little visible evidence betrayed that fact, as the belongings of four generations of her family covered nearly every square foot of floor space.

"Four generations, and not one individual could be spared to tidy the attic," said Sylvia, her voice lost in the vast space. "Until me." Still, she was pleased her ancestors had left so much of themselves behind. She only hoped Great-Grandmother Anneke had not been the one exception to the family rule.

"We'll find it," said Sarah. She chose the nearest pile of

stacked items and began. "But we'll save time if we leave tidying up for later."

Sylvia agreed and set herself to work. They could spare only a couple of hours before camp duties summoned them downstairs, but after the evening program, they resumed the search. Matt, Sarah's husband and the estate's caretaker, joined them, moving heavy loads Sylvia and Sarah had been unable to budge, but promising leads turned repeatedly into dead ends. By the time Sylvia went to bed that night, she had been begun to suspect that the search could take much longer than she had anticipated.

All week Sylvia and Sarah stole moments from their busy days to ransack cartons and uncover old furniture, all in vain. They found trunks, to be sure—dozens of them, full of historic mementos, or so a cursory examination hinted, but Anneke's hope chest eluded them. Sylvia had never been a particularly patient woman, but each day's frustrations only made her more determined to keep looking.

It didn't do her temper any good that Sarah squandered valuable time digging through trunks that didn't meet the description, marveling over an antique toy or portrait, uncovering the hidden treasures Sylvia, too, was tempted to study. Nor did the tenacious July heat, or the dust they stirred up as they worked, or Sarah's shrieks at the discovery of yet another spider.

On one particularly humid Friday afternoon, Sarah dared to voice the same question that had been nagging Sylvia. "Are you sure the trunk is even up here?"

Sylvia refused to hear her discouragement. "If you want to quit, go ahead."

"It's not that—"

"No, go on. I'm sure you have more important things to do than help me."

Without a word, Sarah left, rebuking Sylvia with her silence.

Sylvia continued on alone, ashamed but too proud to go downstairs and apologize for her short temper.

Sensing progress in the increasing age of the artifacts she uncovered, for another hour she resisted thirst and fatigue until she was forced to admit that even her strong will was no match for the stifling conditions. She decided to return after the campers' evening program, when nightfall would bring restful quiet and cool breezes to Elm Creek Manor.

She left the attic assuring herself she would find the trunk that night or some day soon thereafter, but darkness seemed to foster doubt. Perhaps her memory had failed her, or Great-Aunt Lucinda's had failed *her.* Or maybe Lucinda's tale had been nothing more than a fiction meant to amuse a young girl. Of all the possibilities, that was the one Sylvia dreaded most. She couldn't bear it if the stories of Elm Creek Manor that had sustained her throughout her long absence turned out to be false. At one time, they were all she had had to remind her of home and the family she had left behind.

She picked up the search where she had left off earlier that day and soon forgot her exhaustion and the late hour. Only a small portion of the attic remained to be searched, a far corner of the west wing where the ceiling sloped so low Sylvia could not stand upright. Her grandparents might have used the chair that now sat covered in dust before her; some unknown aunt or cousin might have sewn a wedding gown on the treadle sewing machine now rusted and missing its belt. Melancholy colored her thoughts, and she forced herself to admit that even if Lucinda's story was true, the chest with its contents might have been lost to the fire that had destroyed part of the manor in her father's youth, or sold off like so many other heirlooms when the family's fortunes waned. So many misfortunes could have befallen it—

But perhaps none had after all, she thought, as she glimpsed beneath a film of dust a trunk made from cherry and brass.

She braced herself for the resistance of weight, but the trunk was surprisingly light. Quickly she pulled it into the open and brushed off as much dust as she could, for if a quilt was inside, she would not wish to soil it. Then she seated herself on the floor and studied it, reaching into her pocket for the slender key Great-Aunt Lucinda had given her decades before. Sylvia had saved the key more in remembrance of her great-aunt than from any certain plan to find the lock it fit, but now she knew there was only one way to discover if Great-Aunt Lucinda's stories were true.

After a moment's hesitation, Sylvia fit the key into the lock.

It turned easily, but the lid was more reluctant to cooperate, and only after several minutes of wrangling did it open with a groan. Sylvia scarcely noticed the odors of stale air and aged cloth, for within the trunk she spied a folded bundle wrapped in a sheet of unbleached muslin. Carefully she picked it up, and knew at once from its texture and thickness that it was a quilt.

Her breath caught in her throat. The protective sheet bore signs of age and decay. She never should have neglected the trunk so long. If she had come sooner she could have stored the quilt properly. She could blame only herself for a good half-century of its deterioration.

Praying that the quilt itself was in better condition than the muslin cover, she gently unwrapped it and unfolded it upon her lap.

And there it was, the Log Cabin quilt she half-feared existed only in Lucinda's imagination.

The blocks looked to be about seven inches square, arranged in fourteen rows of ten blocks each. Sylvia's first glance took in shirting flannels and chintzes, calicoes and velvets—the scraps of worn clothing, no doubt. The scraps had been cut in rectangles of various sizes and pieced in an interlocking fashion around a central square, light fabrics placed on one side of a diagonal, dark fabrics on the other. The blocks were arranged in a Barn Raising setting so that the overall pattern was one of concentric diamonds, alternately light and dark, just as Lucinda's description had foretold. And to Sylvia's amazement and gratitude, the central squares of each Log Cabin block were black.

Sylvia stroked the quilt reverently, hardly daring to believe what she held in her arms. According to tradition, the central square in a Log Cabin quilt should be red, to symbolize the hearth, or yellow, to represent a light in the window. According to folklore, however, in the antebellum United States, a Log Cabin quilt with a black center square was a signal to slaves escaping north along the Underground Railroad, a sign indicating sanctuary. As a child Sylvia had listened eagerly to Lucinda's story of how Great-Grandmother Anneke Bergstrom's Log Cabin quilt with the black center squares had welcomed fugitive slaves into the safe haven of Elm Creek Manor. This quilt provided the evidence she needed to document this important part of her family history.

"Not quite," said Sylvia aloud, pursing her lips and scrutinizing the quilt. For all she knew, this quilt had been completed decades after the Civil War. Lucinda had always had an odd sense of humor. She could have pieced the quilt herself and left it in the attic for the young Sylvia to find, never imagining Sylvia wouldn't discover it until Lucinda was beyond explaining the joke. The fabrics resembled those Sylvia had seen in other quilts of that period, but until a knowledgeable appraiser inspected the quilt, she had no more proof than before she opened the trunk.

She folded the quilt with care and, setting it aside, was about to return the muslin sheet to the trunk when she saw that the Log Cabin quilt had concealed two other muslin-cloaked bundles, one considerably smaller than the Log Cabin quilt, the other approximately the same size.

Sylvia immediately took up the smaller bundle, hardly daring to hope that she would find more quilts sewn by her great-grandmother Anneke's hands. In a moment the muslin sheet was on the floor beside her, revealing the age-weathered back of a second quilt. "Such an embarrassment of riches," said Sylvia as she turned it over. Then, as the pattern appeared, she sat back against a stack of cartons, stunned.

"Birds in the Air," she murmured. It was impossible, but she couldn't deny the evidence she held in her own hands. The quilt that lay before her used the exact same block pattern as Margaret Alden's quilt. Only the arrangement of the individual blocks on the quilt top differed; whereas the blocks in Margaret's quilt were placed on the diagonal, this quilt used a straight setting, with the squares arranged in neat horizontal rows. This quilt was much smaller than Margaret's, too, and although it certainly looked antique, with the wear and tear of hard use and lye soap all too evident, it was in far better condition. Still, Sylvia could not dismiss the use of the Birds in the Air pattern as mere coincidence.

She studied the quilt for a long moment before carefully folding it and setting it on top of the Log Cabin. Then, with great deliberation, she reached into the trunk for the third bundle. Slowly, as if to prepare herself for yet another unsettling surprise, she unwrapped the muslin sheet, unfolded the quilt within—

—and stared in astonishment at what fell from the folds and tumbled to the attic floor.

"My goodness." It was a book, its unmarked brown leather cover cracked with age. Mystified, she carefully opened the slim volume, wary of worsening the damage, only to discover pages covered in graceful script.

Without her glasses, and in the dim light of the attic, she could not make out the words so elegantly written, but the shorter lines and numerals heading some of the pages suggested dates.

A journal. It had to be. A journal, most likely Great-Grandmother Anneke's, hidden away within the folds of her most precious quilt. Sylvia clasped the book to her chest, forgetting her concerns about the Birds in the Air pattern in the growing awareness of her good fortune, and feared, for just a moment, that she was dreaming.

Quickly she gathered up the quilts and carried them down two flights of stairs to her bedroom suite on the second floor. She placed her treasures on the large chair beside her bed, put on her glasses, and took the journal into her sitting room, where she turned on the bright lamp beside her sewing machine and sat down. She caught her breath, then opened the journal to the first page.

October 2, 1895

Autumn has come again to Elm Creek, and I, too, am in the autumn of my years.

My history has barely begun, and already my pride has bested me, for I know all too well that I have long since passed into winter. If I cannot be honest about such a small matter of vanity, how can I hope to be forthright about the harder truths, which few but I remain alive to remember? Yet I must be honest, not merely for the sake of my own soul, but to honor the memory of those whom I love—those whom I loved even as they betrayed me, and she I came to love as she deserved only after she was betrayed.

I do not know for whom I write these words. They cannot be for my own eyes, which are failing me, for the memories burn too strongly in my heart for me ever to forget them. They cannot be for my descendants, for I have none living. Even so, the Bergstrom family endures in America, and shall endure, both in name and in truth. Anneke has seen to that.

If she knew I spoke within these pages, she would beg me to be silent, to protect her children, and their children. She would say the future generations of Bergstroms will not thank me for my frankness, and if others discover the truths we have all pledged to conceal, they would surely destroy us. But I remain hopeful, despite all I have witnessed since coming to this land of freedom, this land of contradictions, and I hold fast to the belief that we owe a greater duty to Truth than to our own earthly comfort. They are not my children or grandchildren who will suffer, so perhaps it is true that I do not fully comprehend the burden my tale will place upon them. But who among us knows how our choices will affect generations yet unborn?

Reader, if you bear the name Bergstrom, know first that you came from strong, proud people, and that it is for you I write, for if we can bequeath you nothing else, we must make you the heir of our truths, for good or ill. Know this first, and read on.

ꕥ

Sylvia read the passage again, slowly, underlining it with her finger. The graceful script had faltered near the end, as if written by a hand trembling with fear or anger. Or did she only imagine it so, shocked as she was by the words themselves?

Anneke could not have written those lines, that much was clear. But who, then, was the author? Surely not Hans; surely he would not have written such things about his beloved wife. The handwriting seemed feminine. Gerda, then? Was this the journal of Hans's sister? But it seemed more like a memoir than a journal, something written after the outcome of events was known rather than recorded day by day, as they were happening. The author had had time to reflect, to consider the effects of her words, and of her silence.

Then Sylvia had a disturbing thought: The family histories

said little of Gerda after her arrival in America and the laying of the cornerstone of Elm Creek Manor. Was it possible that Gerda was the hypothetical ancestor who had left Elm Creek Manor to become the owner of slaves in the South? Was Margaret Alden's quilt her handiwork? How, then, did her journal come to be here, in the attic of Elm Creek Manor with Anneke's quilts, rather than in South Carolina?

Those whom I loved even as they betrayed me, Gerda had written. Whom did she mean? Not Hans and Anneke. It was incomprehensible that they would have betrayed her, and yet, if they had been on opposite sides of the Civil War . . .

Future generations of Bergstroms will not thank me for my frankness.

Sylvia closed the book and set it on her sewing machine. Her pleasure upon finding Anneke's trunk had transformed in a matter of moments into foreboding.

* * *

Gerda's words haunted Sylvia as she tried to sleep. She woke at daybreak, restless and troubled, and her gaze fell upon the quilts she had left on the chair beside her bed. She had not even bothered to examine the third quilt, so captivated had she been by the journal.

She rose and made her bed, then spread the Birds in the Air quilt upon it. In the bright light of day, the deterioration seemed worse than she remembered. Some of the triangular pieces had entirely disintegrated, and the binding around the edges hung loose, where it remained at all. The quilting stitches were straight and even, pleasing though unremarkable in their layout, a simple crosshatch of diagonal lines in each block.

"I should look as good after a century and a half," remarked Sylvia, amused at her instinct to critique. This was obviously a utilitarian quilt, well used and no doubt well loved—and by a child, judging by the quilt's small dimensions. The faded colors had been vibrant once, the worn pieces whole and sound and strong. Sylvia found herself admiring the little quilt, and liking the long-ago quiltmaker whose matter-of-factness and pragmatism appeared in every frugal scrap and solid stitch.

Compared to the Birds in the Air Quilt, the Log Cabin seemed remarkably well preserved. A few small holes along several seams appeared to be the result of the quiltmaker's large stitches rather than the consequence of heavy usage, and the blurring of the fabric print seemed due to time rather than frequent washing. Frowning, Sylvia studied the quilt from different angles, wondering if it had ever even covered a bed. Families often set aside a special quilt to be used only infrequently by guests, but those quilts were typically the finest in the household. While this quilt had probably been quite comfortable in its day, it was simply not as elegant or as finely made as one would expect for a quilt reserved for company. Perhaps the quiltmaker had rarely used it because she had been disappointed with it—or perhaps she had used it often but had taken especially good care of it because it was her first effort, and thus had great sentimental value. Sylvia didn't suppose she would ever know for certain.

Her curiosity whetted, Sylvia carefully unfolded the third quilt and laid it beside the others. It was slightly larger than the Log Cabin quilt, and Sylvia soon found fabrics identical to those in the Birds in the Air quilt. That suggested the same hands had pieced both, but Sylvia wasn't convinced. The pattern, four patches in a vertical strip set, seemed no more complex than the Birds in the Air or Log Cabin, but only at first glance. By alternating the background fabric in adjacent rows, the quilter had created dark and light stripes, as well as a more difficult project, one with more seams to match and bias edges that might have stretched out of place if she had not been careful. And while the three layers were held together by simple concentric curves, the stitches themselves were smaller and finer, often seeming to disappear into the surface, as if the quilt had been etched with a feather.

Perhaps the Log Cabin and Birds in the Air quilts had been made earlier, and the third years later, after the quiltmaker had improved her skills. There was no way to say for certain, unless Gerda had written about the quilts in her journal.

Behind her, a knock sounded on the door leading to the hallway. "Sylvia?"

"Just a moment." Sylvia couldn't resist a quick glance in the mirror as she pulled on her robe. Her hair needed combing, but Andrew knew what she looked like, and he seemed to like her anyway. She opened the door to find him dressed in neatly pressed slacks and a golf shirt. "Well, don't you look dapper this morning."

The compliment clearly pleased him. "And you look pretty, as always."

Sylvia laughed as he kissed her cheek. "You say that because you aren't wearing your glasses."

"I say it because it's true." He looked past her to the quilts on her bed. "What's that you have there?"

"Anneke's quilts." She beckoned him inside. "Or so I believe. I'll need Grace to examine them before I know for certain."

Andrew nodded, studying the quilts. "But she can't know for sure who made them, right? She'll only be able to tell you how old they are."

"Hmph." Sylvia gave him a sharp look, which she knew he noticed, although he pretended not to. "Spoilsport. If I know how old they are, then I'll know who made them. Why would Anneke keep someone else's quilts in her attic? Honestly, Andrew."

He merely shrugged and grinned, used to her moods and her

sharp tongue. Sometimes she suspected he baited her for the enjoyment of watching her temper flare, but she liked him too much to stay indignant long. "I suppose you're right," admitted Sylvia. "But perhaps Anneke's sister-in-law will identify the quilter."

She returned to the sitting room for the journal, and as Andrew examined it, her eagerness to read the book rekindled. All her life she had wondered about Hans and Anneke Bergstrom, the first of her ancestors to come to the United States. Now part of their history—Gerda's thoughts in her own words—had been given to her. She told Andrew how she had found it, and was about to show him the troubling passage she had read the previous night when she noticed the time. She ushered Andrew from the room, promising to meet him downstairs for the Farewell Breakfast.

She readied herself quickly, unwilling to be late for one of her favorite parts of quilt camp. Since Sunday afternoon, the latest group of quilters had enjoyed classes, lectures, and fellowship with new friends and old, and it wouldn't do to simply send them packing when the week of camp concluded. Instead the campers and staff gathered on the cornerstone patio for one last meal together. After breakfast, they would sit in a circle, as they had seven days earlier for the Candlelight welcome ceremony. This time, each quilter would show off a project she had worked on that week and share a favorite memory of her stay at Elm Creek Manor. For Sylvia, their stories were one of the most gratifying rewards of the business. The campers' stories never failed to amuse or surprise her, and she was pleased to discover anew how much Elm Creek Quilt Camp meant to her guests.

Listening to their stories out on the gray stone patio made Sylvia treasure them even more. Surrounded by evergreens and perennials, the patio lay just outside what had once been the main entrance to Elm Creek Manor, back in the days of Hans and Anneke. Tree branches hid the cornerstone engraved "Bergstrom 1858" that had given the patio its name, but Sylvia thought of the marker each time she came there, and remembered how the patio had been her mother's favorite place on the estate.

By the time she arrived, the fifty campers and some of her teachers and other staff had already begun breakfast, laughing and chatting one last time together. *One of these years we're going to outgrow the patio,* reflected Sylvia as she returned the quilters' greetings. They might have to move to the north gardens or eat in shifts. The business had grown more rapidly than any of the Elm Creek Quilters had imagined, and what once had been a small camp operated by eight friends had become a thriving company with more than twice the employees and four times the campers of their inaugural year. Sylvia had retired from the day-to-day operations after her stroke nearly two years before, but she knew Sarah and her codirector, Summer Sullivan, valued her opinion and would continue to include her in the major decisions the company encountered.

Sylvia valued their opinions as well, which was why she couldn't explain her reluctance to tell them she had found Anneke's hope chest. Instead she joined in the Farewell Breakfast activities and later bid the campers good-bye as if her only concern was that they had enjoyed themselves, would tell all their friends about Elm Creek Quilt Camp, and would return next year.

When the manor was empty of all but its permanent residents, Sylvia returned to her room and studied the quilts. Then, abruptly, she decided to put them away, making the excuse that it was to minimize their exposure to light. She carefully refolded the quilts along different lines rather than return the stress to the seams and patches that had borne the burden for more than a century.

She then placed the quilts and the journal deep in the back of her closet and shut the door on them as if she could blot Gerda's words from her memory.

* * *

That evening, Sylvia had an unsettling dream about Lucinda. In it, she was a little girl again, sitting on the footstool beside her great-aunt's chair as Lucinda pieced a LeMoyne Star block.

"Your great-grandmother Anneke wanted the fugitives to know they would be safe here," said Lucinda as her needle darted in and out of the fabric, joining two diamond-shaped scraps. "They needed a signal, one that the escaping slaves would recognize but the slave catchers would ignore."

"So she made a quilt?" prompted Sylvia, who had heard the story many times.

Lucinda nodded. "A Log Cabin quilt with black squares where the red or yellow squares belonged. You see, slave catchers thought they knew what signals to look for, so they paid no attention to a quilt hanging out to dry. But the escaping slaves did. They would cross Elm Creek to throw the dogs off their scent, and hide in the woods until Great-Grandmother Anneke hung this special quilt on the clothesline. That told them it was safe to come inside."

Suddenly Lucinda set down her quilting and said, "I have something to show you." She took an object from her pocket and lifted Sylvia onto her lap. "Something secret, something you mustn't share with anyone, not even your sister or your cousins. Will you promise?"

Sylvia quickly did, and Lucinda placed a slender brass key in her hands. "Somewhere up in the attic," said Lucinda, "in the hope chest she brought over from Germany, Great-Grandmother Anneke hid her Log Cabin quilt. This key opens the trunk."

"Why would she hide her quilt?" asked Sylvia, turning the key over in her hands.

"To keep its secrets safe."

"From who? The slave catchers?"

"From whoever might use them to hurt the people she loved." Her great-aunt fell silent for a moment. "One day it will be safe to tell those secrets. Maybe you will be the one to tell. Or maybe your granddaughter. I don't think my mother wanted those secrets kept forever."

"Do you know what the secrets are?"

"If I did, I wouldn't tell you."

"Why not?"

But Lucinda merely smiled and busied herself with her sewing.

That was where the dream ended, the dream that was really a memory. But the memory had never unsettled Sylvia until she read the troubling words in Gerda's book. Sylvia had assumed the secrets were about the Underground Railroad, but now she suspected something more lay behind Gerda's decision to hide the quilts away and to record her secrets in a journal. Why had Lucinda trusted only Sylvia with the key to the trunk? And why had Gerda's journal not found its way into Lucinda's stories?

She woke several hours before dawn, brooding and unable to fall back asleep.

She dragged herself downstairs to breakfast in the kitchen, for on Sunday mornings, in the absence of the campers, they preferred the more intimate space to the banquet hall. She seated herself, bidding good morning to Sarah, Matt, and her own dear Andrew, who knew at a glance something troubled her. She patted his hand, a silent message that she was all right and would explain later, and fixed a smile to disguise her inner turmoil.

But she couldn't fool Sarah. "What's wrong?" asked the

younger woman in an undertone as they left the kitchen after the meal. "You seem upset."

Sylvia regarded her fondly. In the years Sylvia had known her, Sarah had changed so much, but that core of compassion and frankness had always been present, and had grown with the passing of time. It was difficult now to remember that when they first met, Sylvia had found Sarah self-absorbed and unduly dissatisfied with her life. Elm Creek Quilts had been good for Sarah, allowing her to truly shine, to learn the great extent of her gifts. Ever since Sylvia's stroke, when Sarah had been forced to shoulder the greatest burden of day-to-day camp operations, she had transformed from an awkward, somewhat flighty girl into a confident, self-possessed woman.

Sylvia loved Sarah like a daughter. She owed her nothing less, as Sarah had befriended her after her long, self-imposed exile from her family home, and had saved Elm Creek Manor by proposing they create a quilters' retreat there. But she had come to love her fellow Elm Creek Quilter Summer Sullivan, too, and when Sylvia compared the two young women—which she knew she shouldn't do—she couldn't help thinking of herself and her elder sister. Claudia, the prettier and more pleasant of the two, had been admired and adored by all, unlike Sylvia, with her moods and tempers. Recalling her and Claudia's bitter sibling rivalry, Sylvia had feared jealousy might ruin the friendship between Sarah and Summer, especially when Summer had assumed a position nearly equal to Sarah's with Elm Creek Quilts. To her relief, Sarah and Summer proved themselves to be of stronger character than the two Bergstrom daughters. Sarah preferred to operate behind the scenes, working tirelessly on countless financial and managerial tasks, and never minded that Summer, with her more public role directing the teachers and activities, became the appealing face for the company. Neither envied the other her role or thought her own—or herself—superior.

"I'm not upset," answered Sylvia finally, regretting, as she had for most of her life, that she and her sister had not been friends. Gerda's cryptic remark in the journal hinted that Anneke had known her share of familial conflicts, too, although all the family tales of her and Hans portrayed them with virtues bordering on heroism. It would not be easy to relinquish those golden tales for the truth, but Sylvia wanted her real family, not idealized heroes.

The longer the ideal remained, the easier it would be to let it linger.

"What's bothering you, then?" asked Sarah.

"Come upstairs with me," said Sylvia. "I have something to show you."

Once Sarah got over her surprise, she berated Sylvia for not telling her about the discovery immediately. Sylvia endured the complaints, figuring she had earned them, but as soon as Sarah paused to catch her breath, Sylvia said, "Are you going to scold me all day, or would you prefer to see the quilts?"

Immediately Sarah chose the latter, and after Sylvia retrieved them from the back of the closet, the two women carefully unfolded the quilts on Sylvia's bed.

Sarah exclaimed over the Log Cabin quilt, for Sylvia had shared Great-Aunt Lucinda's story with her, and she knew the significance of the black center square. She said nothing as she examined the Birds in the Air quilt, but stole quick glances at Sylvia as if attempting to judge her reaction to it. When Sarah turned her attention to the third quilt, she first noted the fabrics common to all three quilts, then asked, "Do any of these fabrics match those in Margaret Alden's quilt?"

Surprised, Sylvia said, "I honestly hadn't thought to look."

She brought out the photos Andrew had taken and gave them

to Sarah, who scrutinized them carefully against the quilts on the bed. "Some of them look alike," said Sarah, "but the scale is so small, I can't be certain."

Sylvia retrieved a magnifying glass from her sewing kit and handed it to Sarah. "If you see something, don't think you're protecting me by pretending otherwise."

Sarah held the magnifying glass to the photos and studied them at length, but eventually she shook her head, still uncertain. Some of the fabrics looked similar, but as Sarah pointed out, that didn't necessarily mean Margaret Alden's quilt had any connection to the quilts in Anneke's trunk. Quiltmakers of her time did not have the wide variety of prints modern quilters enjoyed, and the fading of the dyes could make even dissimilar fabrics seem alike in a photograph.

"Maybe we can find another connection," suggested Sarah.

"Isn't the choice of the Birds in the Air block a clear enough connection for you?"

Sarah dismissed that with a wave of her hand. "It was a common enough pattern. How many thousands of Birds in the Air quilts have been made throughout the years? I'm not going to assume anything based upon that, especially since the blocks don't even use the same setting."

Sylvia was glad to hear it, because she had been trying to convince herself that the same pattern choice was, at best, circumstantial evidence. "Very well, what *would* you base an assumption on?"

"Something that would be unique to a particular quilter's style. Piecing quirks, for example. You know, like how your sister used to chop off all the points of her triangles."

"Many quilters do that," said Sylvia. "Our own Diane is a master of the truncated tip. You've chopped off a point or two yourself."

"It's a shame we don't have Margaret's quilt here to compare to Anneke's quilts," said Sarah. "What about theme or symbolism? The Log Cabin block was supposed to represent the home, with the center square being the hearth or a light in the window, with the light and dark fabric representing the good and bad in life. Using the black center square gave it a special meaning on the Underground Railroad—"

"Except some say the Log Cabin block was designed to honor Abraham Lincoln," interrupted Sylvia. "If so, it couldn't have been used as a signal on the Underground Railroad."

"Why not?"

"Heavens. Didn't they teach you any American history at Penn State? The Underground Railroad operated much differently after the Civil War broke out, not long after Lincoln was elected. Quilts would have been useful as signals only before the war."

"You're the one who told me about Log Cabin quilts with black center squares," Sarah pointed out. "Are you saying you were wrong?"

"I'm saying there are alternative theories, and we can't have it both ways."

"I accept that, but my point is still valid. We might find some similarities in pattern choice to suggest that the same person made all four quilts."

Sylvia folded her arms. "I'm not even convinced that the same person made the three from the attic."

"Let's assume they were made by the same person, since they were together in the trunk," said Sarah. "Did Birds in the Air have any significance in the years leading up to the Civil War?"

"None that I know of." But then Sylvia reconsidered. "Well, birds migrate. Perhaps that pattern was a code telling slaves to follow the migrating birds as they flew north."

"Except birds only migrate north at a certain time of the year. In autumn—"

"Yes, I see. Escaped slaves would follow the birds farther south. That wouldn't do, would it?"

"If it's a code, it's not a very helpful one."

"Unless most escapes took place in springtime, to take advantage of fair weather."

Sarah nodded to the strippy quilt. "What pattern is this?"

"It's just a simple four-patch, as far as I know. I haven't seen it before."

"Maybe one of the other Elm Creek Quilters would recognize it."

"Grace Daniels certainly would." And if the unknown pattern or Birds in the Air carried any special significance, Grace would know that as well. Sylvia needed answers, but she doubted she could wait for Grace's visit in mid-August.

When Sarah left to return to her camp director's duties, Sylvia took up Gerda's memoir and carried it downstairs to her favorite room in the manor, a small sitting room off the kitchen. She settled into an armchair beside the window and, summoning her inner resolve, opened the book and read on.

Spring 1856—
in which my adventure begins

The dowry that proved insufficient to impress the parents of my childhood sweetheart was more than enough to purchase second class passage aboard the *Anabelle Marie,* bound for New York from Germany. My heart was broken, and as I was already twenty-five and plain, my mother agreed that I was unlikely to find another suitor in the Old World, and might as well try the New. I wanted to journey not to become a wife, however, but to put an ocean between myself and the only man I thought I would ever love.

My brother, Hans, who had preceded me to America, agreed

that I should come to him and help establish his claim out West. He sent me handbills about Kansas Territory, describing the fertile soil, the mild climate, and the industrious people who had already begun civilizing the wild frontier. Hans's letters glowed with the promise of the good fortune awaiting us, and since he never once suggested he planned to marry me off rather than allow me to participate fully in his ambitious plans to achieve prosperity, I was all too glad to go.

I will never forget my first experience of my new homeland after the long sea voyage—the disorienting humiliation of processing, interrogation by men full of their own importance, the babble of languages, the smells of unwashed bodies and unfamiliar foodstuffs. I spoke English passably well, and yet had to correct their spelling of my surname twice before they recorded it correctly. My heart went out to those who could not make themselves understood and waited in queues, fearful and uncertain. At least I could follow instructions, and knew that somewhere outside that vast room, my brother waited. I had thought myself adventurous, a woman traveling so far alone, and yet there were children in my queue far more daring than I.

Hans found me in the throng. "Gerda," a shout rang out, and before I knew it, I had been swept into the air by a man I was certain I had never seen before. Dumbstruck, I then recognized in this vigorous, laughing man the younger brother who had left the shelter of his family seven years before. Though my own height still exceeded his, Hans was at least three inches taller and forty pounds heavier than the boy I remembered, but his smile was the same, as were his eyes. His manner was cheerful and confident, as if all the treasures of the world lay before him.

I never wept, not even when E. had told me whom he would marry in my stead, and yet I nearly wept with joy then to see my brother so healthy and happy.

We collected my trunk—stuffed full of more books than

clothes, which I assumed I could obtain in Kansas, once I knew better what a farm woman needed—and were making our way through the crowd to the exit when we discovered a beautiful young woman desperately arguing with a uniformed bureaucrat. She pleaded in German, he drowned her out in English, and around them gathered a crowd of men, enjoying the spectacle.

Hans, as I knew he would, halted and questioned some of the men. I started at first to hear Hans speaking so well; his accent was now better than mine, though he had spoken not a word of English when he departed our home. We learned that the beautiful young woman was supposed to have been met by her fiancé three days before. She had never met this man, and did not know how to reach him except by the address on the letters he had sent her father, but she was determined to wait for him until he arrived.

I suspected she would be waiting a very long time indeed, and was telling Hans so when another man added that the bureaucrat, having failed to convince the girl to move along, intended to hand her over to the police or, better yet, send her home to Germany.

Hans did not approve of either option. She had come so far to seek her fortune in America, as had they all. Why should she be punished for the failures of her betrothed? He gave me a sidelong look and said, "There's room in our wagon for one more."

I said, "Do you intend for her to accompany us all the way to Kansas Territory?"

"She can stay as long as it suits her."

I must say I was shocked. The very idea of an unmarried woman traveling with a strange man, even when that man was my dear brother, scandalized me. Then, suddenly, it occurred to me that my own mother had planned something very similar for myself, that Hans should marry me off to the first eligible man he could persuade to take me. At least in me, Hans and the young woman would have a chaperone.

And I will confess something else.

The beautiful young woman had brought with her a sewing machine, and I, who detested sewing, who thought working with needle and thread the most tedious and unendurable of a woman's domestic duties, saw in this young woman and her sewing machine the means of escaping the detestable chore indefinitely.

So I intimated that Hans was welcome to invite her to join us, which he did, in German, so the official would not comprehend. His arguments were charming, if unromantic; he pointed out that one man she had never met was as good as another, and that she was welcome to stay with us until she found her fiancé, or someone else, or decided she would be fine alone, or chose to return to Germany. He hoped, however, that she would decide to marry him.

She stood there speechless for a long while, and who could blame her for that, so unusual the offer and so enormous the consequences of her reply. But soon she agreed to depart with us, and I had the sense that she was conceding defeat in doing so. If Hans also suspected this, he gave no sign, but cheerfully escorted us outside, where his wagon awaited us.

That is how I made my acquaintance with Anneke, my brother's future wife.

ꕤ

Sylvia clasped the book to her chest, exultant. Her suspicions that the memoir was Gerda's had been confirmed, and better yet, Gerda's account of how Hans and Anneke had met echoed the story she had heard as a young girl. Enough details matched perfectly to convince her of the authenticity of the memoir, and enough were dissimilar to further heighten her curiosity. She had never heard of Gerda's unrequited love, the mysterious E., or of plans to settle in Kansas. Had she forgotten those elements, or had they been culled from the history by the intervening generations of storytellers?

"Sylvia?" said Andrew from the doorway between the sitting room and the kitchen. "It's almost time for the new campers to arrive. The Elm Creek Quilters are waiting."

Sylvia stowed the book in the drawer of her writing desk and tucked her arm through Andrew's as he escorted her to the manor's grand foyer. "How's the *Queen Mary*?" asked Sylvia, referring to Andrew's motor home, still parked behind the manor where they had left it upon their return from South Carolina.

"She's ready to sail with the tide." He pulled out her chair at the registration table. "Are you?"

"Of course," said Sylvia, surprised. "You don't think I'd let you make this trip alone, do you?"

"I thought you might prefer to cancel the trip so you could bury your nose in that old book of yours. Or look at those old quilts a few hundred more times."

"I can read Gerda's memoir while you drive."

When Andrew merely shrugged, Sylvia was struck by the thought that—no, it couldn't be. Andrew, jealous? Of three quilts and a book? Guiltily she thought back upon her behavior ever since meeting Margaret Alden, and had to admit she had been distracted. Too distracted, perhaps, to pay as much attention to him as he liked. She would make it up to him, she promised herself. She would start by including him in the unfolding tale of her ancestors rather than hoarding Gerda's memories to herself.

After their newest guests arrived and Sylvia saw the week off to a good start, she asked Andrew to help her pack for their trip.

As they did, she told him what she had learned from Gerda's memoir, and was pleased to see that by the time her suitcase was full, he was nearly as eager to learn the rest of the story as she was. Then, to show him she was as interested in his family as she wanted him to be in hers, she changed the subject. They chatted about their upcoming visit to Andrew's daughter, Amy, in Connecticut. Amy's husband planned to take Andrew fishing, and Sylvia had promised Amy her first quilting lesson.

* * *

Once they were on the road, Sylvia found herself delighted to be traveling again. As much as she enjoyed passing the summer days at Elm Creek Manor, reminiscing about the summers of her girlhood and enjoying the lively activity of quilt camp, she was glad to spend time alone with Andrew. His quiet companionship was as comforting as a favorite quilt, and she grew fonder of him the more they shared memories of years they had spent apart. She liked to tease him that they got along so well because they never ran out of stories to share, and considering that they had more than fifty years' worth of catching up to do, they ought not to run out of conversation anytime soon.

Andrew had bought the motor home after his wife's death to make traveling between his daughter's house on the East Coast and his son's on the West more comfortable. "I don't mind having no permanent address," he had told Sylvia once. "It beats moving in with the kids." Sylvia agreed, but she noticed he took on a permanent address readily enough when she invited him to live with her in Elm Creek Manor.

After Sylvia began her partial retirement from Elm Creek Quilts, she had more time to join Andrew in his cross-country travels. His children had been startled to meet her. Apparently they never imagined Andrew would find a lady friend only three years after their mother's death, so devoted had he been to her throughout their more than fifty years together. But among her own friends Sylvia had seen that those who had known happy marriages were more likely to find love again than those who had been miserable. Granted, Sylvia had needed an interim of half a century, but she hadn't been looking.

Lately, unless they had merely learned to hide their feelings better, Andrew's children and their spouses had come to accept her, and it seemed that their father's newfound happiness pleased them. So Sylvia and Andrew passed much of the summer on the road, stopping by Elm Creek Manor for only a few weeks at a time, visiting the best fishing holes and quilt shops in the country and having a grand time.

At her insistence, Andrew had stopped fretting about appearances, and what other people thought of an unmarried couple traveling together. Sylvia thought his worries were nonsense. Most people were too busy managing their own lives and problems to give the private lives of a couple of senior citizens a second thought. Besides, since they both still wore the wedding bands of their first marriages, people probably assumed they were married to each other.

"If that's what people assume," Andrew would say, "then why not—"

"Don't even suggest it," Sylvia would reply firmly before he could finish the thought. Andrew would scowl grumpily for a while, but eventually his good humor would return. In recent months, he had learned to stop hinting at marriage, and thank goodness for that. Honestly. To become a bride again, at her age. The very idea made her laugh. What Andrew's children thought of their father remarrying, if they thought of it at all, Sylvia refused to conjecture.

The visit kept both of them so busy that Sylvia couldn't find a moment to take up Gerda's memoir, so as much as she enjoyed playing with Andrew's grandchildren and teaching Amy how to piece a Sawtooth Star block, she was glad to return home, unpack, catch up on all the camp news, and settle into her armchair with the book.

ꕥ

For days we journeyed from New York City west across the state of New Jersey and into eastern Pennsylvania. At first, Anneke spoke little, perhaps intimidated by her unfortunate circumstances or ashamed that her fiancé had abandoned her. She had won my sympathies, however, as I understood something of what it felt like to be cast adrift by a man.

For his part, Hans conducted himself as a true gentleman, and before long he had charmed Anneke's story out of her. We learned that she was from Berlin, the third youngest of seven daughters. She had never met the man she was to marry, although she possessed a daguerreotype of him. I thought his physiognomy suggested a crafty, duplicitous nature, but Hans told me I was imagining things, influenced by what I knew of his behavior. Still, Hans looked none too pleased when Anneke carefully tucked the portrait away in her satchel instead of discarding it by the side of the road.

That small satchel contained a few dresses, some undergarments, two wool blankets, a Bible, and twenty dollars, all her worldly goods, save the sewing machine. Cumbersome though it was, she had brought the sewing machine with a singular purpose: to earn her keep, since she had no dowry, and did not wish to be a burden to her new husband. She had planned to purchase bolts of fabric in the East and take them out West to her husband's homestead in Missouri, where an enterprising woman could earn a modest fortune by sewing shirts for the unmarried men who populated the West. Anneke's thrift and practicality made me ashamed of the many books tucked in my hope chest among the coverlets my mother had made, as I disliked sewing too much to create anything useful myself. I was more embarrassed still that I, a spinster of twenty-five, had brought a hope chest in the first place, while Anneke, younger than I by at least six years and traveling to America to meet her husband, had not. In comparison I no doubt seemed vain and foolish, me with my plain face and unwomanly stature beside Anneke's dainty beauty.

We stayed at inns along the way, Anneke and I sharing the bed while Hans slept on the floor. Once, when there was no inn, Anneke and I slept by the hearth of a kindly farmer and his wife, while Hans slept in the barn near his horses.

And now I must tell you of these horses, for they play an important role in this history.

Castor and Pollux were the two most perfectly matched pair of Arabian stallions it had ever been my privilege to look upon. Coal black, each with a white spot on the forehead, they pulled the sawboard wagon with an air of patient dignity, as if they knew they were meant for greater things. They were not workhorses, and although the wagonload was light, I could not bear to think how they would endure hauling it all the way to Kansas Territory, and I told Hans so.

"They won't have to," said he. "We aren't going to Kansas."

I was so dumbfounded I could only echo, "We aren't going to Kansas?"

No, he told me, and then explained that the region was in turmoil, something his handbills had never mentioned. According to law, the settlers themselves would determine whether Kansas would be a Slave State or Free, and even as Abolitionists were helping opponents of slavery to settle there, others from neighboring Slave States, especially Missouri, were doing the same for people who would vote in their favor.

"All the more reason we should go" was my stubborn reply. "Even your one vote might make the difference."

But my brother shook his head gravely and said that people in Kansas had been injured and even killed in the violence as those on one side of the issue tried to drive out their rivals, and not even innocent women and children had been spared. Until matters of statehood and slavery were resolved there, Hans said, we would be better off in a region where the matter had already been settled, on the side of freedom.

I agreed this would be wise, but was compelled to inquire, "And where, precisely, is that?"

"Pennsylvania," came his reply, a farm on the outskirts of a town called Creek's Crossing. Now my brother became ebullient, and described in glowing terms the two-story stone house awaiting us, the fertile land nourished by the waters of Elm Creek, the corral, the paddock, and the stable full of horses just like the dazzling pair pulling our wagon.

Anneke, thinking of her plan to sew shirts for the bachelors of the West, perked up then and inundated my brother with questions about the town. No, he didn't know the population of Creek's Crossing; no, he wasn't sure how many churches it possessed; no, he wasn't aware if they had a lending library—each question made him squirm more than the last, and his answers became more evasive until I finally burst out, "Good heavens, Hans, have you seen this town or not?"

No, to be precise, he had not.

Anneke and I looked at each other, and then at him, and thus confronted by two bewildered and alarmed women, he was forced to reveal the truth. He had not seen Creek's Crossing, or Elm Creek Farm, or even a single leaf on a single tree in the region where these places were reputed to exist. All these many years, when I and my family back in Germany believed him to be a merchant's son turned gentleman farmer, working on his own thriving land, he had been wandering from pillar to post, working for one farmer and then another, living for a time in the city, earning a small fortune and losing it just as quickly in one business enterprise after another.

"Then how," asked I, as calmly as I could manage under the circumstances, "did you come to be master of Elm Creek Farm?"

By winning it, he confessed with more pride than I thought proper, in a horse race.

The previous owner, a horse breeder with a taste for whiskey, had come to New York to sell some of his prize horses. He was new to the business and trying to make a name for himself selling thoroughbreds to the new generations of gentlemen sprouting up like weeds from the soil of their peasant forebears. He had overestimated the market and, his funds nearly exhausted, found himself with four horses and little to show for his journey. Naturally, as men do, he decided a drink would help him see a solution to his quandary, and as one drink turned into many, he took to wandering the streets, belligerently ordering passersby to examine his horses and admit they had never before seen their like.

Most ignored the man, but Hans humored him and said the horses were impressive to look at but were not, ultimately, a well-matched team. The man sputtered in rage and demanded that Hans explain himself. Hans indicated one horse, Castor, and said his gait was longer than the other three horses', so his superior speed would throw off the team.

"You're wrong, sir," said Mr. L., and to prove it, he would have Hans ride Castor while he himself rode one of the other three. If Hans lost the race or if the horses crossed the line at the same time, Hans must buy two of the horses; if Castor won, Mr. L. would give Hans all four horses free of charge.

Hans did not have the money to buy one, much less two, of the horses, but he knew that Mr. L. in his drunken state would not be able to sit a horse well enough to win the race. Sure enough, after witnesses were assembled and a course determined, Hans sailed across the finish line and found himself the proud owner of four horses.

Mr. L. promptly demanded that Hans allow him to win back his horses. At first Hans refused, but when Mr. L. called it a matter of honor and staked his farm in central Pennsylvania against Hans's newly acquired thoroughbreds, Hans consented. After another brisk run around the course, he found himself the owner of everything but what Mr. L. carried upon his person. Before Mr. L.'s pocket change and clothing should fall into his possession as well, Hans returned to him two of the horses and encouraged him to forgo additional gambling until a day when his luck was better.

Anneke, eyes shining, praised Hans for his cleverness and admired his generosity in giving Mr. L. two of the horses he had lost fair and square, but I was shocked—stunned and appalled that my brother would take such advantage of his fellow man. I reminded him what our father would have thought of his deportment, but Hans merely laughed at me and said, "Father's ways don't work in America, dear sister. That is why he remained at home, and I came here."

I did not like this, but lest the two of them think I, too, should have remained at home, I kept my arguments to myself and vowed to see that the Bergstrom family would not abandon all dignity and righteousness in this wild land.

"How far is this farm?" said I instead, thinking that though it was nearer than Kansas, our destination might yet be too far for the horses. Hans showed me on the map, and it seemed a more isolated place than I had ever imagined, although logically I realized it could not have been any worse than Kansas Territory, far to the west, and likely it would be better. There, Hans declared, he would raise crops to support us and the livestock, but he would make his fortune in horse breeding.

"Make your fortune as Mr. L. made his?" inquired Anneke, thinking, as I did, of how Mr. L. had been unable to sell the four horses he had brought to New York.

"I hope you did not intend to breed Castor and Pollux," said I, "since they are both males."

"And gelded," added Anneke.

We dissolved into laughter at Hans's scowl, and soon he joined in, reminding us of the other horses awaiting us at Elm Creek Farm. "A stable full," said he, including the very horses that had sired and foaled the regal animals before us.

Our laughter faded, and I could see in my companions' faces that mirth had been replaced with anticipation and eagerness. As for myself, I thought of the unfortunate man who had lost those beautiful horses, along with his farm and his entire livelihood. I imagined him returning to Creek's Crossing in defeat to break the news to his family, if he had one, and to his workers, who perhaps even now were caring for the horses and wondering if they, too, would be driven from their homes or if the new owner wanted for stablehands.

However, my pity for Mr. L. was short-lived.

When at last we reached Creek's Crossing, we were pleased to discover a quaint, pleasant village built along the banks of Elm Creek, which, in my estimation, should have been named a river. We had driven our wagon beside it for many miles, and only here did runoff into lakes and marshland north of the town cause the creek to narrow and slow enough for ferries to provide not entirely hazardous passage across the waters.

We traversed the town and discovered several churches, and saloons enough to equal their number, as well as various thriving businesses, including a general store. Here Hans stopped to obtain basic provisions, planning to purchase more once we learned what, if anything, Mr. L. had left behind.

In the meantime, Anneke and I made an errand of our own, to a tailor's shop across the street, where I pretended to inquire about prices but in truth was helping Anneke study the competition. We exited the shop armed with the knowledge that another tailor as well as a dressmaker were already well established in town, but Anneke was untroubled, confident that her plans would yet succeed.

Hans was waiting in the wagon, frowning in a bemused fashion. When we inquired what was the matter, he said, "Maybe nothing." Then he paused and added, "The men inside have never heard of Elm Creek Farm."

Anneke and I looked at each other but said nothing. We could not bring ourselves to tease him, as we had about the horses. His manner was too pensive to elicit our laughter.

But the deed to Elm Creek Farm awaited us at the bank as Mr. L. had promised, and once it was in Hans's possession and the transfer of ownership was in order, our concerns faded. We headed out of town, following the road and the directions Mr. L. had provided. The creek accompanied us for a time as we passed other, well-established farms, then wound away from us and disappeared into a thick wood. Soon afterward, at a path through the trees barely wide enough to accommodate our wagon, the road and Mr. L.'s directions diverged.

On any other occasion I might have enjoyed the sublime beauty of the forest and delighted in the sunbeams as they broke through the leafy boughs, but that day I felt only trepidation. Then Elm Creek emerged again, which brought us some measure of relief, as Mr. L. had said the water crossed his property.

But although he spoke truthfully in this regard, nearly every other detail proved false.

Even now, knowing how we prospered in the end, it pains me

to recall the sorry sight that greeted us. Of the forty acres Hans now owned, just four were cleared. The two-story stone house was nothing more than a cabin a stone's throw from the creek, barely twelve feet by twelve, with two oilcloth windows, a dirt floor, and sunlight streaming though the logs where the chinking had fallen out. The stable of horses was empty, which perhaps was just as well, since it was but a ramshackle lean-to, with just enough room for Castor and Pollux.

When we had surveyed our domain, Hans seemed furious and humiliated but resigned. Anneke looked as if she might weep; when Hans held out a hand to comfort her, she stormed away and climbed aboard the wagon to sit beside her sewing machine. She looked as if she heartily regretted her decision to leave New York in our company, and I cannot say I blamed her. When she thought herself unobserved, she brought out the portrait of her intended and regarded it with a strange look in her eye. Perhaps she wondered if she had not waited long enough for him in New York, and if she should seek him out. With the awareness of all that befell us since, I cannot help contemplating how different my life and Hans's would have been if at that moment she had summoned up the courage to leave us and make her way on her own.

The sun was beginning to disappear behind the trees, we were tired and hungry, and all our happy prospects seemed to lie in ruins. This, I told myself, is what comes of such ill-gotten gains. But I lacked the cruelty to say so aloud, so instead I said, "We have less than what we thought we had, but we still have the land, and two horses, and our own fortitude. That is far more than we had upon our arrival in New York. So Mr. L. did not do the work of clearing the land and planting the crops and building us a fine house. Very well. We shall do it ourselves."

My brother still looked discouraged, so I added, "Did we not intend to work in Kansas? Was someone to have done everything for us there?"

Anneke sighed and rested her head in her hands. Hans idly brushed straw from the horses' coats. They were moments away from giving up and turning back, and we had only just arrived!

I was no less disappointed than they, but suddenly I grew angry. "It's just as well we didn't go any farther west," I declared, snatching up a parcel Hans had purchased at the general store and marching over to the cabin with it. Alone I unloaded the wagon of all but my trunk and the sewing machine, which were too heavy for me to lift. Then I built a fire in a circle of stones that Mr. L. had arranged not far from the entrance to the cabin, filled a cook pot at the creek, and soon had potatoes on the boil. As the sun set and my companions' appetites grew, they left their isolated places and joined me at the fireside. Wordlessly I handed them their tin plates and cups and served them potatoes and dried beef as I had on the road. We ate in silence, with only the noises of the forest to welcome us home.

Then, suddenly, my brother spoke. "Tomorrow I'll find the borders of our property. There must be neighboring farms. They will tell us where our acres end, or I'll find a surveyor in town." He poked the fire with a stick. "There might be some crops in, somewhere. He's been feeding his horses something."

"I'll ready the cabin," said Anneke in a soft voice. "When I have enough daylight to see by."

"I'll help you," said I, and that was how we decided to stay at Elm Creek Farm.

ꕥ

"A horse race," said Sylvia, shaking her head.

Andrew looked dubious. "It could have been worse."

"I suppose. Hans could have held the man at gunpoint and robbed him that way."

"It wasn't robbery," said Sarah. "It was gambling."

"A horse race with a drunken man who was certain to lose is no gamble." Sylvia rose and carried her empty coffee cup into the kitchen, but instead of returning to the sitting room and her friends, she exited the manor through the back door. She crossed the empty parking lot and followed the back road to the bridge over Elm Creek, where she sat down on a bench and gazed at the water.

She wondered where that old cabin had stood. Gerda described a four-acre clearing a stone's throw from the creek, which narrowly ruled out the location of the manor. Any area cleared in Gerda's time could have become overgrown since, so Sylvia doubted she'd ever find the right place, if in fact any trace of it remained to be found. A cabin so decrepit in 1856 most likely would not have lasted into the next century.

Sylvia knew she should sympathize with her ancestors' predicament, but instead she found herself more than a little pleased that no two-story stone house had awaited the three travelers at the end of their journey. A run-down cabin was more than Hans deserved after swindling a man out of his home and livelihood. All her life she had admired Hans and Anneke for building the Bergstrom estate out of nothing—which, admittedly, they apparently had done, but not without trying to take the easy way out first.

She brooded until Andrew joined her. "Are you all right?"

She moved over to make room for him on the bench. "I'm fine. Merely . . . disappointed."

"Why so?"

"Why so? Why not? All my life, Hans and Anneke have been held up to me—to all of their descendants—as the epitome of the courageous immigrant fulfilling the American dream. And now I find out—"

"That your heroes are merely human?"

Sylvia knew any word she uttered would sound petulant, so she said nothing.

"You have a choice, you know," said Andrew. "You don't have to keep reading."

"Of course I do. I have to see how everything turned out."

"You already know." With his thumb, Andrew pointed over his shoulder at the manor.

Sylvia's gaze followed the gesture, and as she studied the gray stone walls that only weeks before had seemed so strong, so secure, she wondered if she knew anything at all about how things had turned out.

3

Summer and her mother had lived in Waterford since Summer was nearly eleven, but neither had ever heard Waterford referred to as Creek's Crossing. The details Sylvia had shared about Gerda Bergstrom's journal had piqued Summer's curiosity, so she arranged to have Sarah cover for her at Elm Creek Quilt Camp so she could investigate.

She crossed the street to the campus of Waterford College and walked up the hill to the library, where the Waterford Historical Society kept its archives. After scrutinizing her alumni association card, a library assistant led her to a remote room, indicated the location of various books, databases, and maps, and allowed her to search undisturbed. If not for one dark-haired man sequestered in a corner carrel, she would have been completely alone.

Just a few minutes with the map cabinet made Summer realize that she should have allotted more time. It took her nearly half an hour to locate the proper drawer, only to discover that the maps weren't sorted according to any logical order she could discern. *Sylvia's ancestors must have designed this filing system,* she thought ruefully, thinking of the manor's attic. With a sigh, she pulled open the first drawer and began paging through the maps.

Fortunately, by the time she had to leave, she had found two maps of the county that merited more scrutiny. One, dated 1847, showed only a town called Creek's Crossing, much smaller than present-day Waterford but at the very bend of the creek where the oldest district of the downtown now existed. The second, dated 1880, depicted the entire state, but Waterford was clearly labeled in its appropriate location. Sometime between 1847 and 1880, the name of the town had been changed.

Remembering the reportorial technique she had learned in her journalism seminar at Waterford College, Summer identified the town's name change as the "what"—now she needed to learn when and why. The "who," of course, were the Bergstroms.

Whether the family had played any role in the transformation of Creek's Crossing into Waterford, she could only guess, but her instincts—and her knowledge of how Sylvia's family had influenced the town's fortunes in later years—told her she was not pursuing a false lead.

Summer through winter 1856— in which we become farmers, and I am unwittingly courted

So passed our first evening at Elm Creek Farm. By morning's light, my companions had gained more resolve, while I felt my own weakening, as I began to realize how very far I was from home and everything familiar. But, I reminded myself, that was precisely what I had wanted, and since I could not bear to return to Germany in defeat even if I could afford the passage, I had to make the best of it.

By the end of the day, we discovered that our circumstances were not quite as dire as we had imagined. Mr. L. had put in a kitchen garden, so we would soon have fresh vegetables. We learned that an acre of corn had been planted, and this news cheered us immensely. Since much of our land had not been improved, our woods were full of game, and thus we celebrated our second night at Elm Creek Farm with a feast of venison and seed potatoes, eaten by the fireside under the stars.

As the weeks passed, we set the cabin to rights as best we could; Anneke and I filled the spaces between the logs while Hans repaired the roof enough to keep out the rain. Each day I marveled anew at the changes in my brother. He had left my father's house seven years before knowing a great deal about the textiles trade in Baden-Baden but little of horses and nothing of farming. Now he put in late crops and drove the team as if he were born to it.

Castor and Pollux did not pull the plow, of course. One of Hans's first acts as master of Elm Creek Farm was to trade them with the owner of a livery stable for a team of till horses, a pig, and a flock of chickens. We were all downcast to part with the elegant creatures, especially Anneke, who grew teary-eyed whenever she saw them prancing before a carriage in town. Hans promised her that one day, when his business was established, he would give her far superior horses, born and bred on our own land. Anneke didn't quite seem to believe him, but the promise pleased her just the same.

When our immediate needs were seen to, Anneke asked Hans to turn his attention to improving our little cabin. He had made us each a bed by stringing rope between oak posts, upon which Anneke placed straw ticks she had sewn, but only a curtain separated our beds from his, and we had no fireplace, which would surely be a problem come winter. I added my voice to Anneke's, but Hans instead set himself to work on the barn.

He had met a neighbor, a Mr. Thomas Nelson, whose land abutted ours to the north. His wife, Dorothea, befriended me, and in later years became my dearest friend and confidante—closer to me in many ways than Anneke ever was. Anneke thought Dorothea too solemn and bookish, but I admired her keen mind and sensible temperament. After the day's work was finished, we enjoyed many evenings discussing literature and politics, and I learned a great deal about our new country from her. Often we gathered at the Nelsons' home, which despite its simplicity seemed a palace compared to our cabin, but I had too much pride not to reciprocate their kind invitations, and we entertained our neighbors nearly as frequently as they did us.

We spoke English with the Nelsons, since they did not speak German. Anneke would have preferred to sit silently with her sewing rather than have Hans or me translate the conversation, as her inability to speak English shamed her, but Hans said, "You will never learn if you don't try, and you need English in America." He was right, of course, and though Anneke's attempts at conversation were at first reluctant, she gradually acquired a rudimentary knowledge of English. But in those first years, she spoke rarely to strangers, a behavior that some of the women in town misinterpreted, considering her aloof and unfriendly. Later these same women were to decide that they had been mistaken: Anneke was the friendly and charming one, while I was arrogant and full of strange notions. Their opinions might have troubled me if I had not made other friends through Dorothea, but since I had, I cared not what Anneke's acquaintances thought of me. Perhaps I was a bit arrogant after all.

Hans and Thomas often exchanged work, and after Hans helped Thomas bring in his harvest, Thomas helped Hans lay the foundation for the barn, about twenty paces east of our front door, between ourselves and the creek. I did not think this a wise location, for although the winds typically blew from the southwest, placing the cabin upwind of the animals' odor, I did not relish the thought of passing the barn several times a day to fetch water. I did not mention this, of course, as I knew this to be a ridiculous complaint from someone who fancied herself a settler. It was not until the men began to raise the walls that I understood my brother's thinking and realized what a marvel of architecture he had designed. He ingeniously built the barn into the hillside with one entrance at the foot of the hill and a second at the crest, so that one could drive the team into either story with equal ease.

The occasion of our barn raising drew the aid of other neighbors: the Grangers, the Watsons, the Shropshires, the Engles, and the Craigmiles. How warmly I regarded them as I saw their carriages and wagons emerging from the forest onto Elm Creek Farm. Some I still hold in high esteem, but to others, my heart has turned to cold stone.

But, of course, I did not know then how I would come to feel later. Neither, I daresay, could they have imagined what scandal we Bergstroms would bring into their midst. If they had suspected, some of them would have brought down that barn upon our heads. It amazes me now, gazing back into the past, that nothing distinguished future friend from foe, and that I never would have imagined who would later shun us and who would prove true.

I race ahead in my eagerness to unburden myself, but I must not allow my urgency to muddle this history.

After the barn, Hans put in a corral, intending, to my surprise, to pursue horse breeding after all. I had thought he had abandoned this idea with the loss of Castor and Pollux, but if anything, his interest had grown. "Mr. L. did not make such a good go of it," ventured I, when I saw that Hans was determined.

Hans merely grinned at me and said, "Sister, I think I've shown you I'm much more clever than Mr. L."

So I said nothing more to dissuade him, although to this day I do not believe Hans gained Elm Creek Farm through cleverness.

As for Anneke and me, in addition to assisting Hans with the crops as needed, we divided our women's work in shares that suited us both. Anneke, with her gift for needle and thread, took care of all the mending and sewing. Relieved to be rid of those detested chores, I was glad to care for the kitchen garden. In those days I was happiest working outside, the bright sun on my cheek, the fresh soil between my fingers. Anneke washed and tidied the cabin, while I cooked our meals. We took turns caring for the chickens and, after Dorothea instructed us, milking the cow.

Daily we improved Elm Creek Farm, and daily, too, did Anneke and Hans grow more fond of each other. Theirs was a peculiar courtship, indeed, conducted while they lived in the same small house, with only an elder sister as chaperone. I had always imagined true love to be as mine was for E., evolving slowly over time as friendship transformed from the sweetness of childhood affection into steadfast and respectful devotion. But Hans and Anneke seemed to admire each other from the start, with only a token reluctance on Anneke's part to abandon thoughts of her first intended. They married six months after their meeting in New York, before the first snow fell.

As a wedding gift for his bride, Hans added to our cabin a fireplace, a root cellar, and a second room. Not long after her own marriage, perhaps because she wished me to know a happiness like that she had found with my brother, or perhaps because she sought greater privacy than my presence would allow, Anneke began entertaining thoughts of finding a husband for me.

Among those who had come to help us those early days was Mrs. Violet Pearson Engle, the twice-widowed dressmaker, and her grown son from her first marriage, Cyrus Pearson. Mrs. Engle was a stout woman, domineering and loud-voiced, whose main contribution to the barn raising had been to bark orders at we women laboring over our outdoor cooking fires to prepare enough food for all those men. As for Mr. Pearson, upon our first meeting I found him polite, if somewhat disdainful, with a quick grin that some might have called a smirk. But that impression might have been merely my own prejudice, as I never fully liked or trusted handsome men, perhaps because they rarely expressed interest in plain girls such as myself. Still, since he seemed pleasant enough, I thought nothing of it when Anneke suggested we invite him for supper.

On the appointed evening, Mr. Pearson arrived, bearing an apple tart his mother had baked for us, and a bouquet of wildflowers which he presented to me—in error, I thought, assuming he had meant them for the lady of the house. I promptly handed the flowers to Anneke and took his coat, while Hans offered him a chair by the fire. Since the fireplace was also my cookstove, I necessarily passed between it and the table several times as the men talked about their horses and crops. Before long, I noticed that every time I approached the table, Mr. Pearson bounded out of his chair. At first I thought it charming, but when he persisted in the ridiculous formality, I entreated him to remain seated for fear he would be bouncing in and out of his chair all evening like a jumping jack. He agreed with a smile that did not completely conceal his displeasure, but he no longer rose when I did, although he tensed in his chair as if it took all his strength to remain seated.

"I did not notice it before," I murmured to Anneke in passing, "but Mr. Pearson has a haughty temperament, don't you agree?"

"He's a perfect gentleman," hissed Anneke, glancing at him to be sure he had not overheard. "And he's a guest, so mind your manners."

"I have no intention of doing otherwise," I protested in a whisper, but Anneke merely glared at me.

The meal itself was an even more baffling affair, with Hans the only one of us perfectly at ease. Anneke interrogated Mr. Pearson about his education and prospects with a directness that would have seemed rude if not for her charming manner and lack of fluency in English, but Mr. Pearson did not seem to mind. In fact, he seemed to relish the opportunity to talk about himself, but instead of responding to Anneke, he directed his replies to me. I was embarrassed for him, that he should slight Anneke and Hans so, when suddenly it occurred to me that he was behaving exactly as eager suitors did in novels.

This realization so astounded me that I could not reply when Mr. Pearson remarked for at least the seventeenth time how wondrously sublime my cooking was. Perhaps I should have perceived Mr. Pearson's intentions sooner, but E. had been my first and only love, and we had known each other since childhood. Our courtship had possessed none of the silly rituals with which adult men and women torment each other. I was not accustomed to the language of romance, nor did I ever expect it to be directed toward me. Nor, I knew with great certainty, did I wish to hear any more of it from Mr. Pearson. I looked from Anneke to Hans and back again, pleading silently for their aid, but Hans appeared oblivious to my distress, and Anneke seemed to enjoy it.

"You're so accomplished, Mr. Pearson," said Anneke then, disarmingly, "that I must wonder why there is no Mrs. Pearson."

"I have not yet found a woman deserving of that title."

"Oh, you must keep looking," said I, thinking, *But not at Elm Creek Farm.* "I'm sure you'll find her."

Some of the brightness faded from his smile, and he looked

to Anneke for an explanation. Before she could speak, Hans said, "Tell me, when you find your Mrs. Pearson, will you give her a home of her own or bring her into your mother's house?"

"My mother's home will be her home, as it is mine."

"Come now," persisted Hans. "You know how women are. Asking two to share a kitchen is like throwing two wet cats into a sack and tying it shut. Asking them to share a home is asking for trouble, unless it is clear from the start who will be mistress of the household."

Anneke gave her husband a slight rebuke, but Mr. Pearson chuckled. "Mother will not be dictated to in her own home."

"So your Mrs. Pearson will have to know her place?"

"Indeed."

"You couldn't have her speaking her mind or acting contrary to Mrs. Engle's judgment."

"Of course not, but I do not anticipate any conflict. The only woman I could love would be of such purity of heart and generosity of spirit that she would love my mother as if she were her own. She would tend to my mother's needs with the same tender, unselfish eagerness as she would to mine."

Anneke twisted her pretty features into a frown. "You sound as if you are looking for a nurse or a housekeeper, not a wife."

"It would only be for a little while," said Mr. Pearson, with a hasty glance at me. "Once Mother passes on, my wife will be the mistress of the household, but until then—"

"Until then she is to be a servant in her own home?" said I, indignant on behalf of this unfortunate bride, forgetting, for the moment, that Mr. Pearson hoped I would be she. "My goodness, but you require a great deal of patience and forbearance in a wife. I do not think half the women of my acquaintance could manage it."

"It would not be as bleak as I have made it seem," said Mr. Pearson.

"I should hope not," said I. "If I were to marry into such circumstances, I might be tempted to hasten your mother's demise."

"I hope your future bride lacks my sister's temper," said Hans to Mr. Pearson in a confidential tone. "If not, you'd better find someone else to do the cooking."

Mr. Pearson glanced down at his plate in alarm as if expecting to find some deadly poison amid the mashed turnips. As Hans and I laughed merrily, he grew red-faced and said, "Yes, I'll be sure to do that."

"Your bride will be a lovely woman," said Anneke soothingly, glaring at Hans and me in turn. "Do not let their silly jokes trouble you."

Mr. Pearson let out a thin laugh as if to show us he understood our joke. Anneke steered the conversation to other matters, but for the remainder of the meal, Mr. Pearson spared no opportunity to avoid looking in my direction. Afterward, he thanked Anneke for her kind hospitality, shook Hans's hand, gave me a curt nod, then made some excuse about needing to tend to a sick horse.

As soon as the door shut behind him, Hans and I burst into laughter again.

"I fail to see what is so amusing," said Anneke.

I tried to speak. "The thought of that man—"

"—and my feisty, opinionated sister," finished Hans. "Married!"

Anneke folded her arms and pursed her lips, but eventually she, too, allowed a small smile. "Perhaps they would not be such a good match after all."

"Perhaps not, my love," said Hans, smiling tenderly. "But I can't blame you for trying."

"I can," said I. "I cannot imagine why you thought we were well suited for each other."

"You're both unmarried."

"True enough, but I would hope to base my future happiness on something more substantial than that."

"I agree," said Hans. "But I thought it would be easier for Mr. Pearson, and for our friendship with his family, if he realized on his own that you would not make him a good wife rather than hearing it in your refusal."

Only then did I understand that my brother had deliberately prodded Mr. Pearson into revealing his weaknesses as a husband for me so that I might better reveal my inadequacies as a wife for him. All the while I had thought Hans oblivious to the drama of manners playing out before him, he had been directing the action from behind the scenes. I studied him with new respect. Hans Bergstrom of Baden-Baden was not known for subtle calculation, but this man was Hans Bergstrom of America. I resolved not to underestimate him again.

"Mr. Pearson might not make Gerda a proper husband," declared Anneke, "but someone will."

Thus I learned, to my dismay, that Anneke was not easily daunted, and that despite the evening's failure, she was resolved to see me happily wed.

❧

"The more things change," said Sylvia, "the more they remain the same."

Andrew looked up from his newspaper. "What's that?"

"Gerda's sister-in-law wants to marry her off." Sylvia slipped off her glasses and stretched her neck, which had an painful kink in it, so intently had she been reading. "Honestly. It is a truth universally acknowledged that a woman without a husband is eager to find one, no matter what she says to the contrary, and that all her married friends and acquaintances are obligated to help her nab some poor fellow before he knows what hit him."

Andrew peered at her over his bifocals. "You know, not everyone is as opposed to marriage as you are."

"I'm not opposed to marriage in principle. I was very happily married myself once, I'll remind you. Marriage is fine for youngsters with their whole lives ahead of them, who want to build a future with the one they love. I have no objection to that, if that's what they want."

Andrew returned his gaze to the newspaper and said, "If you ask me, people ought to build their futures with the ones they love no matter how old they are, even if that won't add up to as many years as the young folks get."

Sylvia was about to concur, but she thought better of it and said nothing. If she agreed with his principles, one of these days she might find herself accidentally agreeing to a proposal.

Winter 1856 into summer 1857— in which we complete our first year at Elm Creek Farm and begin a second

I had not told Anneke about E., and although Hans might have told her I had been disappointed in love, I was certain he had not explained the intensity of my sorrow. He could not have, since I do not believe he thought his sensible elder sister capable of such depth of feeling. How could either of them, entranced as they were with each other upon first sight, know what it was to have a love slowly blossom over time, only to have it crushed beneath the heel of parents who cared more for class distinctions than for the happiness of their son?

In those years, I wanted to believe E. the cruel victim of his parents' contempt for my family's lack of rank. Now I realize that if he had truly wanted to be my husband, he would have followed me to America. That would have meant abandoning the wealth and social position that had prevented us from marrying, and apparently he had no wish to do so, or the thought never occurred to him. Either way, his inaction proved that either our love was not true, or it was, but he was unworthy of it.

Time, hard work, and the newness of my life in America eased the pain of my grief, and I reconciled myself to being no more—and no less—than Hans Bergstrom's spinster sister. As our first autumn passed in a frenzy to make Elm Creek Farm livable for the coming winter, I realized I did not mind the role as much as a properly brought up girl ought to have done. Anneke and Dorothea were fortunate in their choice of husbands, but other women of my acquaintance were not, and I soon learned that an unmarried woman can do and say things a wife cannot. In any event, I envisioned a future doing my part to make Elm Creek Farm prosper, looking after Hans and Anneke and their children yet to be born, being a part of their family, and never desiring one of my own.

Winter snows had cut us off from contact with all but our closest neighbors, but the coming of spring brought a renewed liveliness to the town. Our dependence upon the kindness and generosity of others had impressed upon Anneke the importance of friends, and she became determined to establish the Bergstroms in Creek's Crossing. Being well regarded in society would help Hans's business, she said, and she prodded me to do my share to socialize with the wives and daughters of important men who might be in a position to help Hans later. At first I shuddered at the very notion of society, remembering how it had cost me my dearest love, but society in Creek's Crossing bore little resemblance to that of my homeland. As one would expect, however, it remained the province of the oldest and wealthiest families, but in a land where anyone willing to work hard could prosper, no obstacle remained to prevent the meanest immigrant from elevating his status.

"Unless the immigrant is colored," observed Dorothea, when I remarked upon this.

I could not refute the obvious truth in her words, and her reflection soured the appeal of the town for me. While Pennsylvania was a Free State, and most of us took pride in our righteousness and disdained the Southern slaveholder, freedmen were not, it must be said, any more welcome here than elsewhere, except among themselves and, perhaps, the Abolitionists. As for myself, although I was a staunch opponent of the institution of slavery, I had never actually befriended a colored person, former slave or freeborn.

This troubled me, but when I repeated Dorothea's comment to Anneke, she merely laughed and said, "Only Dorothea would say such a thing."

"What do you mean?"

"Well, of course the coloreds can't rise in society. I don't condone slavery," she added with great haste, because she knew my views, "but we want to keep to ourselves just as they want to keep to themselves. Only Dorothea would look upon this as a crime."

I did not think Dorothea was thinking of parties and balls when she talked of elevating one's status, but rather of bettering oneself through hard work and education. The latter interested her far more than the former, as she attended few society gatherings, instead dedicating her spare hours to charity and the women's suffrage movement.

I must admit, the issue of women's suffrage sparked a passion within me as well, and as time passed, and I read more of the books and newspapers Dorothea shared, I became her equal in desire for the right to vote. I even endured sewing to learn more about the movement, because as the weather improved, Dorothea welcomed to her home numerous prominent speakers of the women's rights movement, acquaintances from back East. Invariably, since they could not drum up enough interest in our little village to fill a meeting hall, these women would speak at Dorothea's quilting circle.

One would suppose, perhaps, that a woman from a family of textile traders would have known of the art and craft of quilting, but I had never heard of it until emigrating to America. Dorothea and the other women of Creek's Crossing discussed their needlework with great interest and exchanged new patterns with delight. I could not muster up such enthusiasm, but even I could see the appeal in the cunning designs Dorothea and her fellow quilters created in patchwork, and I respected the frugality of not wasting a single hard-earned scrap of fabric. I will admit, however, that I gritted my teeth as Dorothea taught me to make my first quilt, and I accomplished little when I was meant to be piecing a Shoo-Fly block, but instead hung on every word of the speakers' passionate lectures on the Rights of Women.

Anneke did not attend the quilting bees, for as I said, she was not so fond of Dorothea as I, was embarrassed by her poor English, and thought politics unwomanly. Hans found Dorothea's ideas amusing and her visiting friends harmless—a view which, I must confess, annoyed me a great deal, though I suppose it was preferable to that of some of the townsmen, who forbade their wives to join Dorothea's sewing circle. However, I suspected some in Creek's Crossing objected not so much to Dorothea's position on women's suffrage as to the Nelsons' firm and unabashed Abolitionist views. While there were those in Creek's Crossing who silently agreed with them, far more felt that on the issue of colored people, objecting politely to slavery sufficed, but one needn't make such a fuss about it.

Every other week I attended Dorothea's sewing circle, where I forced myself to take up needle and thread so I could engage in enlightening discourse. I returned home glowing with visions of a future justice, but Anneke saw only the patchwork block in my hand, inattentively and reluctantly pieced. On one such evening, she took the Shoo-Fly block, smoothed it on her lap, and studied it, back and front. "Your hands were not meant to sew," said she mournfully, as if I would be grieved by the pronouncement. Then, to my astonishment, she asked if she might join me at the next meeting.

So Anneke and I began to attend the sewing circle together, I for the edification of my social conscience, Anneke for the lessons in patchwork. A gifted needlewoman, she took to the craft immediately and became Dorothea's most eager apprentice. Within weeks she had mastered setting in corners, sewing curved seams, and appliqué, and completed an entire sampler in the time it took me to finish a few haphazard Shoo-Fly blocks.

But I did not care. My days were full of hard work and the satisfaction of seeing Elm Creek Farm flourish with our labors; my evenings full of borrowed books and lectures and interesting people. Dorothea's guests included many whose activities would later make them famous—or infamous, some would say: Mrs. Sarah Grimké, Mrs. Susan Anthony, Mrs. Elizabeth Cady Stanton. Not all of our speakers were women—nor were their interests limited to suffrage. Frederick Douglass spent the night on his way from one speaking engagement in Philadelphia to another in Ohio, and other prominent figures such as William Lloyd Garrison, editor of the Boston Abolitionist newspaper *Liberator,* also graced the Nelson household. Nor were all of those in attendance women. The men did not deign to join us for sewing, of course, but they often appeared after our meetings and drew our guests aside for brandy or cider, the Nelsons being teetotalers.

A most frequent visitor was Jonathan Granger, Dorothea's younger brother, whose farm lay to the northeast of Creek's

Crossing. He often found occasion to visit Dorothea and occasionally accompanied her to Elm Creek Farm. His somber, direct manner reminded me of his sister. Like Thomas, he did not believe woman's intellect inferior to man's, but spoke to me as if he expected an intelligent reply. Hans, for all his fine qualities, was not infallible in this regard, and I admit I found Jonathan's company refreshing.

At first, however, I had mistaken him for the postman.

From overheard conversations, I learned he traveled around the county quite a bit, and when he attended the gatherings at his sister's, he occasionally distributed letters to her guests. I wondered that someone with his keen mind had chosen to become a postman instead of attending university, but shrugged off my puzzlement, choosing instead to admire him for delivering the post as well as managing his father's small farm. Only after he was called away from a lecture on the troubles in Kansas to deliver Mrs. Craigmile's third child did I discover that he was the town's physician, and carried letters as a favor to his neighbors, who did not travel as much as he. I grew very red in the face, for thankfully I had been spared much embarrassment, as I had in my pocket a letter that I had planned to ask him to carry to Philadelphia. I suspect he might have done it and thought nothing of the request, as he was a generous, unassuming sort.

We spoke often, discussing philosophy or the politics of the day; Jonathan recommended books to me, and I to him. Through my discussions with him, as well as with Dorothea, I began to see how inextricably intertwined were the Rights of Women and the Rights of the Slave, simultaneous battles in the same war.

I write so much of our evenings one would think I was a woman of leisure and did nothing all day but read and anticipate conversations with engaging companions. That would be far from the truth, for never had I worked so hard as I did in those first few years in America. And not only for my brother's happiness was I glad for Anneke's presence, for I cannot imagine how we would have managed without her. Our work began before dawn, and although we never allowed ourselves an idle moment except on Sundays, we fell into bed at night having completed only the most necessary of our chores. Sometimes, I admit, exhaustion and the relentless flood of duties needing my attention threatened to overwhelm me, but something spurred me onward. Perhaps it was the knowledge that our neighbors had managed, proving that it could be done. Perhaps it was the fear of disappointing Hans and Anneke. All I know is that I persisted, undaunted, sustained by Hans's vision for Elm Creek Farm and those precious times with Dorothea and Jonathan.

By the end of our second summer in Pennsylvania, Hans had purchased two thoroughbreds, a mare and a stallion, thus fulfilling part of his promise to Anneke, that she would once again have horses as lovely as Castor and Pollux.

"Those must have been the first Bergstrom Thoroughbreds," said Sarah. She had read the passage aloud as Sylvia worked on her latest project, an English paper pieced Tumbling Blocks quilt in homespun plaids. It was Sunday morning, in the last peaceful time they would enjoy together that week, the interval between breakfast and the arrival of the new group of quilt campers.

"I suppose so." Sylvia wondered that she did not feel more intrigued at the thought. Bergstrom Thoroughbreds, the business founded by Hans and Anneke—and Gerda, she added, amending the family history—had made the family's fortune. Later generations had sustained and expanded the business, but it had all been lost in Sylvia's time, when her sister, Claudia, and Claudia's husband had sold off the horses and parcels of land to pay the debts of their lavish lifestyle. Sylvia did not blame them alone. If she had not abandoned her family home, she would have continued to run Bergstrom Thoroughbreds. If the war had not claimed her husband and brother—and indirectly, her father and unborn daughter—she never would have left, and perhaps she would have passed the business to the next generation. But instead she had left it to her sister, knowing full well Claudia could not manage on her own, but too proud to return home and seek reconciliation, even to preserve Hans's and Anneke's legacy.

And Gerda's, she added silently, for based upon what Sarah had read, Sylvia could not believe that Gerda had left Elm Creek Manor to become a slave owner in the South. Perhaps she had left to marry Jonathan, but it sounded as if his farm was relatively near, certainly near enough that Gerda's strong will and temperament would have continued to influence the family. Sylvia had become certain that Gerda had been as instrumental as Hans and Anneke in shaping the Bergstroms' history.

"Gerda has never been given enough credit for what she contributed to this place," said Sylvia.

"Neither have you."

"You must be joking. Our campers would have you believe I laid each stone of Elm Creek Manor with my bare hands."

"Our campers give you plenty of credit, but you don't. You shoulder all the blame for the demise of Bergstrom Thoroughbreds, but you don't take enough credit for Elm Creek Quilts." Sarah gestured, indicating not only the sitting room but the entire manor. "Take a good look at this place. Think of what we've accomplished here."

"Our success has been your doing. Yours and Summer's and the other Elm Creek Quilters."

"You're the heart and soul of Elm Creek Quilts, and you know it," declared Sarah. "Or you ought to."

But I'm merely paying back a debt, Sylvia almost said. Her ancestors had created something great, and she had allowed it to be destroyed. She was merely trying to earn back what she had squandered. The burden had weighed heavily upon her heart for the more than fifty years she had been estranged from her sister, but although the success of Elm Creek Quilts had alleviated it a great deal, when she read in Gerda's own words how they had struggled to establish Elm Creek Farm, she felt her failures to her family anew.

Suddenly Sarah took her hand. "Come on."

"Where are we going?" asked Sylvia, as Sarah helped her to her feet and led her from the room.

Sarah guided her through the kitchen and out the back door. "We're going to find the cabin."

Sylvia laughed. "If the cabin were still around, I think I would have noticed it."

"There might be something left." Sarah tugged her arm to get her moving again. "Gerda said Hans built the barn twenty paces east of the cabin. So let's go to the barn and pace."

Despite her doubts, Sylvia felt a stirring of anticipation. The barn still stood, so perhaps something of the cabin remained after all. Of course, Hans, a far more able carpenter than the hapless Mr. L., had built the barn, and the structure had been carefully maintained. And yet . . .

She quickened her steps as she and Sarah crossed the bridge over Elm Creek.

Sylvia watched from the shade of the barn as Sarah measured off twenty paces west and carefully searched the ground. Since her steps had taken her to the edge of the well-worn dirt road, Sylvia was not surprised when, after a moment, Sarah rose and shook her head. She returned to the barn and tried again, heading off at a slightly different angle. Again she searched the ground, and once more she found nothing.

"Gerda describes herself as tall," said Sylvia. "Maybe you should lengthen your strides."

Intent on her task, Sarah nodded and tried again, stepping in exaggerated, long paces through the grass, leaving the barn from different places and varying her angles slightly, but always heading west. One attempt finally took her to a small rise at the edge of the orchard, and this time, when she stooped over to search the ground, she suddenly grew very still. "I think I've found something. It's wood."

"Likely it's just a tree root."

"No, I don't think so." Sarah scuffed the ground with her shoe, then looked up with wide eyes. "There's a log here, embedded in the ground."

"Trees look remarkably like logs," scoffed Sylvia, but she felt a tremor of excitement as she went to look for herself. Kneeling on the ground, Sarah pulled up clumps of dead grass and brushed aside dirt around what appeared to be a faint depression in the ground. At first Sylvia thought it was nothing more than darker soil, but as she drew closer, she perceived the fibrous splinters of what could only be wood and that the portion Sarah had uncovered lay in a nearly perfect straight line.

"My word," breathed Sylvia. She kneeled on the ground and gingerly began brushing aside decades' worth of accumulated soil. Sarah ran off to find some tools and returned with Matt and Andrew, carrying whisk brooms and trowels. Sylvia extrapolated a straight line extending in both directions from the exposed part of the log and directed her friends to positions along it. Quietly and quickly they worked, their eagerness to uncover the find tempered by wariness that they might damage whatever lay beneath.

"Look here," called out Andrew from his place at the end of the line. "I think I've reached a corner."

The others hurried over. Andrew had indeed reached a place

where the first wood line ended and another commenced at a slightly obtuse angle. As Matt helped Andrew dig around the bend, Sylvia saw to her amazement that there the direction of the wood grains varied, first tending horizontal, then vertical.

"The pieces dovetail," said Matt, and then Sylvia could envision perfectly the corner of a cabin, perpendicular logs interlocking.

They had found it. The cabin where Hans, Anneke, and Gerda had first lived, the place where they had dreamed and planned and built their legacy, lay within arm's reach. She could touch the very walls that had first sheltered them.

4

Sylvia grudgingly acquiesced when Matt suggested they break off their excavation until they could consult a specialist who would help them preserve their find. If not for the concern that she might ruin what remained of the cabin, she almost thought she could dig it up with her fingernails, so exhilarated was she by their discovery. Somehow the cabin made Gerda's story real in a way her words had not. It was proof, something tangible, that made the memoir ring true.

In their excitement, they had lost track of the time. The morning had waned, and the sun shone almost directly overhead. Sarah raced off to shower and change before the new quilt campers arrived while Matt gathered their tools. Sylvia was perspiring and out of breath from excitement and labor, but she tried to hide her fatigue as she and Andrew returned to the manor, knowing Andrew would worry if he thought she had overexerted herself.

By the time she had tidied herself, the other Elm Creek Quilters had arrived and were preparing for registration. Summer and her mother, Gwen, a stout woman with hair the exact shade of auburn as her daughter's, were placing chairs behind a long table to one side of the manor's elegant foyer. Gwen was a professor at Waterford College, as was Judy, who was arranging forms on the table with the help of Bonnie, the owner of Grandma's Attic. Diane, a strikingly pretty blonde who, along with Summer, occasionally assisted Bonnie at the quilt shop, had just entered with Agnes on her arm. As much as she delighted in all her friends, Sylvia's heart warmed most at the sight of Agnes, the closest thing to an actual relative Sylvia supposed she had. Long ago, Agnes had married Sylvia's younger brother, and long ago both women had been made war widows on the same day. Friendly fire, the officials called it, the senseless accident that had taken their husbands' lives on a remote Pacific island. The euphemism, meant to protect them, hurt worse than the truth, for it mocked their grief.

How Sylvia regretted that she and Agnes had not come together in their mourning and made the burdens of their grief lighter by sharing their losses. Instead Sylvia had fled Elm Creek Manor, unable to live there haunted by memories. She had returned home only after the death of her estranged sister, Claudia, but at least she and Agnes had forgiven each other—more than that, they had become friends. Still, as much as this consoled Sylvia, whenever she thought of Claudia, she tasted the bitterness of reconciliation sought too late.

With a sigh, Sylvia pushed aside her regrets. She could not change the past. She could only make her future as happy and worthwhile as possible. That was how to best honor those she loved and had lost.

She honored them a great deal, she thought, on Sundays when quilt camp was in session, when she and the other Elm Creek Quilters opened the manor to their guests. Sarah rushed downstairs, her hair still slightly damp, just as the first campers arrived. Soon the foyer was so full of activity that Sylvia hardly had a moment to catch her breath, much less share the discovery of the cabin with her friends. She and Diane shared the task of distributing the class schedules, a job that always involved last-minute adjustments as campers decided their interests had changed or requested a switch so they could be with people they already knew. Sylvia was reluctant to make changes for the latter reason, for one of the most important points of camp was to make new friends, and how could they if they went around in little cliques? Honestly. But since she wanted her guests to be happy, and being comfortable accomplished that for most of them, she adjusted their schedules. The evening programs would get them mixing properly.

The flood of new arrivals eventually slowed to a trickle, then ceased. It was time to clear away the registration tables and prepare for the welcome banquet. As Sarah went off to supervise the kitchen and banquet hall, Sylvia was finally able to share the news. Her friends' surprise and delight rekindled her eagerness to excavate the cabin, but she remembered Matt's warning and promised herself she would get the job done in due time with the proper supervision.

Gwen offered to contact a professor of archaeology she knew at Penn State, explaining that she knew of no one at Waterford College with the expertise they needed. Sylvia thanked her and wished she and Andrew weren't leaving first thing in the morning. But Andrew was itching to get on the road again, and she could not ask him to withdraw from the trout fishing competition he had entered, not when he was the defending champion in his age group. Besides, she had scheduled two speaking engagements for the return trip.

Sylvia could hardly swallow a bite of the delicious meal served at the welcome banquet, so distracted was she by thoughts of the cabin. When she glanced out the window and fretted aloud about the likelihood of rain, Matt assured her he had covered up the logs with a tarp, adding, "That should do until we hear from Gwen's expert."

"The cabin's lasted this long," said Sarah to Sylvia, with a teasing smile. "It will last through the night."

"It's the next night and the next that concern me," retorted Sylvia. "I won't be here to keep an eye on it."

"We'll be here," said Matt.

"Yes, but who's going to keep an eye on you?"

Matt clasped a hand to his chest and winced as if she had wounded him. "I'm the caretaker," he said with an exaggerated woe that provoked laughter from the others at the table. "I'll take care of it."

"But it's my responsibility. I can't let anything happen to it."

Sarah remarked, "You say that as if you wish we hadn't found it."

Sylvia found herself speechless. "Don't be ridiculous," she managed at last, and was glad when Andrew quickly changed the subject. How close were Sarah's words to the truth? Sylvia was pleased they had found the cabin; the thrill of its discovery nearly had her racing outside just to be sure she had not imagined it. Still, she worried and wondered if they should have left the log alone as soon as Sarah uncovered the first portion. She couldn't bear destroying yet another part of the Bergstrom legacy, not when so much had fallen into ruin on her watch.

After the banquet, she returned to her room to pack, but she was so accustomed to filling her suitcase that she quickly finished. As twilight fell, she knew she ought to go to bed—Andrew wanted to get an early start the next day—but she decided to attend the welcome ceremony instead. It seemed appropriate to visit the cornerstone patio on the same day she had discovered an even earlier foundation of the Bergstrom family at Elm Creek.

The quilt campers had already finished their dessert and had gathered in a circle on the gray stone patio when Sylvia arrived, but they eagerly made room for one more chair. The murmur of excited voices hushed as Sarah rose and lit a candle in a spherical crystal holder.

"At Elm Creek Quilt Camp, we always conclude the first evening with a ceremony we call Candlelight," said Sarah, meeting the eyes of each camper from her place in the center of the circle.

Sylvia smiled, remembering how nervous Sarah had been the first time she took a turn leading the Candlelight. Now Sarah spoke with serene confidence, her voice somehow both comforting and inspiring.

"Elm Creek Manor is full of memories," continued Sarah, with a look that told Sylvia the younger woman intended a special meaning for her. "Some we know well, but others, like the memories you will make here this week, have yet to be discovered. The Elm Creek Quilters are enriched by your experiences here, and we thank you for sharing your stories with us."

As Sarah explained the ceremony, Sylvia sensed the quilters' conflicted emotions. The campers would pass the candle around the circle, and one by one, each woman would hold the candle and explain why she had come to Elm Creek Quilt Camp and what she hoped to gain from the experience. They had been asked to bare their hearts to people they hardly knew. Some of the women around the circle, Sylvia knew, would not be entirely honest; some would choose to keep their secrets, as was their right. But those who shared the truth, those who were *ready* to share the truth, would find themselves accepted and affirmed more than they could have imagined possible. This was what Sylvia had learned after so many Candlelight ceremonies, that the truth, however painful, though sometimes hard to say and difficult to hear, had to come out.

Suddenly she was struck by the realization that this, surely, was how Gerda had felt, bearing the weight of the family history alone, determined to see that the heirs to the Bergstrom legacy should know more than just a partial truth about themselves and their origins. No matter how difficult those truths were for Sylvia to learn, she owed it to Gerda to read with an open heart, as accepting and nonjudgmental as the women who now sat around the circle, their faces illuminated by a single candle.

And, finally, as the women around her shared their secrets, she admitted to herself what she was too proud to say aloud: She feared herself inadequate to the responsibilities Gerda demanded of her. She who had always prided herself on her strength now doubted the one quality that had always sustained her. But Great-Aunt Lucinda had trusted her, even though Sylvia had been only a small child when she had been given the key to the hope chest. In her way, too, Gerda had trusted her, by having faith that a future descendant to whom she could confide her secrets would one day find the memoir. If Lucinda and Gerda both had found Sylvia a worthwhile heir, Sylvia would not fail them.

Besides, she had no choice. There was no one else. For good or ill, these heirlooms belonged to the Bergstroms, and she was the last remaining.

Autumn 1857—in which we have unexpected visitors

Our first harvest season arrived, and though we would reap but a modest bounty, we were exceedingly proud of our first efforts in farming. The corn had done well, and by Hans's estimation we would have plenty of hay and oats to see our stable of horses through the winter. My garden had thrived, and I worked long days putting up stores and selling what I could in town. I had an agreement with the owner of the general store Hans had first visited upon our arrival in Creek's Crossing: He would display my wares in exchange for a share of the profits. He sometimes chose to take my wild raspberry jam instead of money, but that suited me fine.

Anneke had not forgotten her original scheme to open a seamstress shop, and I believe she envied me my mercantile success, modest though it was. When we were in town together, I spied her gazing wistfully at the rows of storefronts; once she remarked in an offhand manner that extra income would permit Hans to obtain more horses without hurting our efforts to economize. Silently I agreed that any money Anneke might earn would not go to waste in our household, but I did not see how she could afford to bring in outside sewing when we had so much work to do already. As for opening a shop, Hans had neither the capital nor, I fear, the inclination to help his wife find employment outside the home. He never said so aloud, but I suspect he wanted every cent of his dream to be funded by his own efforts. My earnings were acceptable, since I was a spinster sister and ought to contribute to my keep. It was another matter entirely to send his own wife out to work.

Jonathan and I discussed this, and he agreed that I would not be interfering too much if I tried, discreetly, to encourage my brother to put Anneke's wishes ahead of his pride. Sometimes I would bring to Hans's attention the other women of Creek's Crossing who helped support their households:

"Mrs. Barrows runs the inn on First Street," said I.

"Only because Mr. Barrows is a shiftless lout."

And another day: "I hear Miss Thatcher and Miss Bauer run the school exceptionally well."

"As soon as they get married, they'll have their own children to look after."

And yet another occasion: "Mrs. Engle may expand her dressmaking shop, or so I hear."

Too late I realized Mrs. Engle was the worst possible example

I could have mentioned. Not only did Hans remark that it was a shame that Mr. Engle had died without leaving her better off, because a widow with three young children and a grown son should not have to work so hard, but he also pointed out that a town the size of Creek's Crossing hardly needed yet another seamstress, now, did it, and wasn't it fortunate that Anneke would not feel obligated to provide that service to the community?

How fortunate, indeed.

"Anneke should just tell Hans she wants to open her shop," Jonathan told me.

But that was not Anneke's way. She demonstrated exceptional talent in subtle remarks and sidelong glances that conveyed deeper meaning than the words themselves contained, tools she used to bring Hans around to her way of thinking more successfully in other matters. I, as ungraceful in speech as I was in dancing and sewing and all other pursuits feminine (save cookery, in which I excelled), was the one for straightforward, blunt statements. But as I told Jonathan, Hans was as stubborn as his sister, and if he did not wish his wife to work in town, she would not.

They had been married not even a year, and already this pattern, which was to last throughout their married life, was well established. Watching them, I wondered what sort of husband E. would have been to me. Would he have expected me to submit to him in everything, obey him in everything? I could not have borne that yoke, not even for love. This was what I told myself when I remembered E., and when I saw how happy Anneke and Hans were together, and Dorothea and Thomas.

In the middle of harvesttime, an unfamiliar wagon came to Elm Creek Farm. I recognized the driver, a slight, sour-faced man with greasy blond hair and tobacco-stained teeth who worked odd jobs on the waterfront. Hans was in the fields, and the mistress of the house, embarrassed by her poor English, hid inside as always, so I greeted him.

He looked me over suspiciously before speaking. "This the Bergstrom farm?"

I assured him it was. "Do you have a delivery for us?"

"I'm supposed to give this to the Bergstroms at Elm Creek Farm."

"I am Gerda Bergstrom, and this is Elm Creek Farm," said I, with some impatience, because the large wooden crate in the wagon behind him had captured my interest.

"That's what I don't understand." He studied me with sullen belligerence. "I thought this here's the L. place."

I had not heard the name of Mr. L. in so long that the remark caught me off guard. "Indeed, Elm Creek Farm did once belong to Mr. L.," stammered I, "but it has since passed to my family."

"Passed how?"

I was suddenly conscious of Hans's absence. "Quite legally, I assure you. My brother has the deed, if you require proof."

"I'm only askin' because . . ." He shrugged. "L. still has friends in these parts. They might not like it if they thought you 'uns took his farm out from under him."

"Certainly not," said I primly. "Though I must say, they must not be especially good friends if they have not missed Mr. L. before now. If there's nothing else—" I made as if to retrieve the large crate myself.

"I'll get it," grumbled he, setting the reins aside and climbing down from his seat. With great effort, he lifted the crate from the wagon, but rather than carry it into the cabin, he left it on the ground beside the front door. I paid him and gave him my thanks, but without another word, he drove away, casting one sullen backward glance over his shoulder before disappearing into the forest.

Anneke immediately joined me outside. "What did he want?"

"Only to deliver this," said I lightly, not wishing to worry her, and then excitement drove the surly man from my thoughts, for upon examining the crate, I discovered it had been sent from Baden-Baden. Anneke ran off to tell Hans, and they quickly returned, Hans bearing his tools. He brought the crate indoors and pried off the lid, and Anneke cried out with delight, for inside, tightly packed, were bolts of fabric—velvets and wools, even silks—as fine as anything I had ever seen in Father's warehouse.

There were letters, too, for all of us. Mother's to Anneke welcomed her into the family and informed her the fabrics were a wedding gift. Father's to Hans congratulated him on taking a bride and expressed hopes that Hans would be able to obtain a good price for the fabrics. Father's letter to me cautioned me to be sure my younger brother invested the profits into Elm Creek Farm rather than squandering them unwisely. Mother's to me was full of news of home; she provided the latest gossip on all of my acquaintances, except, of course, for E., who became the more conspicuous for his absence.

Our siblings had written as well, and as I hungrily read their letters, Anneke knelt on the floor and withdrew the fabrics from the crate, delighting anew with each bolt. Suddenly she looked up at me, stricken. "Oh, my dear Gerda. I'm so sorry."

"Whatever for?"

"Your parents sent me all these nice things, but they sent you nothing."

I indicated the pages in my hands. "They sent me letters."

"Yes, of course, but . . ." She hesitated. "Don't you feel slighted?"

Until that moment, I had not. "Of course not," said I, thinking a crate so large surely could have accommodated a small book or two.

Anneke forced a smile. "Likely when you marry, they will send an even finer gift."

Hans guffawed. "Likely they will, once they recover from their shock."

I poked Hans in the ribs as if we were children again and laughed with him, but Anneke merely shook her head at us, astounded and scandalized that we would treat my spinsterhood with such an inappropriate lack of shame.

"This is really a gift to us all," added Hans, in a nod to Anneke's concern for my feelings. "With what we can earn from the fabric, I can buy another two horses, and next spring, I can build us a real house."

Anneke rewarded him with a smile, but she ran her hand lovingly over each bolt as she returned it to the crate, and I could not help thinking that she would prefer to keep the fabric for herself, to create clothing for the townsfolk of Creek's Crossing in a shop of her own and piece quilts from the scraps.

But I soon forgot Anneke's thwarted ambitions as the most arduous labor of the harvest set in. By sharing work with Thomas, Jonathan, and other neighbors, Hans soon had our crops in, and they theirs. Elm Creek Farm had provided only enough to see us through the winter, and not a surplus to sell in town, as Hans had hoped, but at least we would not have to rely on the generosity of friends as we had the previous year.

Creek's Crossing was an industrious community, so our more experienced neighbors had fared even better than we neophytes on Elm Creek Farm. Everyone seemed content and satisfied, eagerly anticipating the Harvest Dance in mid-November, where, Dorothea said with a gentle smile, the women would wear their finest dresses and bring their tastiest recipes, which they would disparage until one would think they had worn rags and served slop, while the men would exaggerate the yield of their crops and the quality of their livestock until one was convinced the farmers of Creek's Crossing alone could provide for the entire Commonwealth of Pennsylvania. I, too, looked forward to the Harvest Dance, for Jonathan had danced with me at the previous year's celebration, and I was hopeful he would be my partner in even more dances this year.

Anneke, who was interested in finding me a more lasting partner, offered to make me a dress, in which, she said, I would dazzle the eye of all who saw me.

Scoffed I, "And after the dance, I'll wear it to dazzle the eye of the cow and the chickens?"

"You'll set it aside for special occasions." Her gaze went to the crate of fabrics, tucked away in a corner of the cabin until Hans could determine how to best sell them. "There's a lovely blue silk that will be very becoming to your eyes."

I laughed at the thought of scattering chicken feed clad in silk, but when she insisted, I said that if she must make me a dress, let it be a sturdy calico I could wear new to the Harvest Dance, and later as I did my chores. She grew impatient and pointed out that she knew much more about sewing than I did, and if I didn't want her lecturing me on politics or on the proper pronunciation of English words, I should not attempt to instruct her in dressmaking. Then her eyes took on a steely glint I had never before seen there, and have seen only rarely since. "Let me show you how to best dispose of your parents' gifts," said she. "Let me show you what I can do when permitted to follow my own judgment."

I knew it was not I she intended to impress. "What will Hans think of you cutting up a bolt of fabric? Won't he see it as the loss of at least the mane of a horse, or a wall of the new house?"

"Didn't your mother's letter say the fabric was a gift to me?"

So dumbfounded was I by her unexpected determination that I had no choice but to submit, especially as I suspected she had an underlying purpose. I will also admit that although I knew what obstacles my plainness presented to even the finest seamstress, I found Anneke's promises that she would make me look handsome dubious but perhaps not entirely outside the realm of possibility, because she was, after all, exceptionally talented with a needle.

One morning, a week before the dance, we rose early and raced through our morning chores so we could get to work on the dress as soon as Hans left to care for the horses. Thus I was standing in my corset as Anneke fit the bodice when a knock sounded on the cabin door.

"L.?" a gruff voice called from outside. "You there?"

Wide-eyed, Anneke scurried off to the other room, leaving me in my corset to welcome our visitor. I snatched up my calico work dress and threw it on over the pinned silk bodice, wincing as a pin found flesh. "Good morning," said I, pulling open the door, breathless.

Two men with rifles stood before me, one regarding me with his mouth in a grim line, the other taking in the exterior of our altered cabin with bemusement. Two weary horses nibbled at the thin shoots of grass behind them.

"I'm looking for L.," said the first man.

"He no longer lives here," said I. "I'm afraid I don't know where he is."

The second man gave me a hard look. "We hear tell you 'uns stole his farm."

I drew myself up, hoping he would not detect my nervousness. "You heard incorrectly."

At the sound of my accent, the second man nudged the first. "Dutch," spat he, in a most disparaging tone.

"We don't mind you Dutch," said the first man, addressing me, but speaking as if to remind his companion. "Not as much as some. Your man around?"

"My brother is in the barn." *Without his rifle,* I thought, feeling a pang of fear.

"We'll go talk to him there." The first man tugged at the brim of his slouch hat. His companion merely scratched his dark beard and glowered. As they turned to go, I saw over their shoulders that Hans was hurrying toward us from the barn. To my relief, Jonathan was at his side. He must have arrived only moments before the two men, as he had not yet come to the cabin to greet me.

"What brings you gentlemen to Elm Creek Farm?" Hans called out, with an easy smile.

The two men exchanged a look, then the first one said, "We're looking for a n——."

Someone else would have said "Negro" or "colored man." I have seen the injury caused by the word he did use, and I will not repeat it here.

"A runaway n——," added the second man.

Jonathan winced slightly at the word, but Hans's expression did not change. He merely shrugged and said, "Everyone at Elm Creek Farm stands before you, except my wife."

"He might be hiding in your barn." The second man took one step toward it before Hans put out an arm to stop him.

"I just came from there," said he, with that same easy smile. "There's no one hiding in my barn."

The first man said, "We might do well to check for ourselves."

"You might, if I were not a man of my word." Hans looked up at them steadily. "Is that your meaning?"

The second man swore impatiently, but the first man held Hans's gaze. "You're new to this country, and maybe you don't know the law. This may be a Free State, but anyone helping a n—— escape is breaking the law."

"We know the law," said Jonathan.

I prayed he would not choose this moment to distinguish for our visitors, as he had many a time at Dorothea's sewing circle, the difference between a just law, which ought to be obeyed, and an unjust law, which by a just man must be broken.

The second man squinted at Jonathan. "Ain't I seen you at the Nelson place?"

"Very likely you have, as Mrs. Nelson is my sister."

The second man spat on the ground and muttered to his companion, "G—— Abolitionists."

Jonathan stiffened, but restrained himself without need of the hand Hans placed on his shoulder. "That's no way to talk about a man's family," Hans said, and he held the second man in a gaze so firm that the man eventually looked away and muttered something resembling an apology.

The first man turned around in a slow circle, scanning the clearing surrounding our cabin. Suddenly he asked, "What happened to L.?"

"L. sold me Elm Creek Farm more than a year ago."

"We haven't been through these parts in some time," said the first man. He broke off scanning the horizon and, after an inscrutable glance at Jonathan, smiled at Hans in a friendly manner. "L. might have been a Yankee, but he was not unsympathetic to our employers. We could always count on him for a hot meal and a bed on the floor near the fire."

I felt myself balling my dress in my fists, and I forced myself to remain calm. Perhaps Elm Creek Farm had once extended its hospitality to slave catchers, but no more!

I was just about to declare the same when Hans said, "I'll have my wife fix you some eggs."

"Hans," I exclaimed, and Jonathan shot him a look of stunned amazement.

"Sister," said Hans in a level voice, "tell Anneke to fix these gentlemen some breakfast while they feed and water their horses."

I opened my mouth to protest, but when Jonathan gave his head the barest of shakes, I swallowed back my words and went inside. My thoughts were in turmoil as I delivered Hans's instructions. Anneke nodded wordlessly and obeyed, while I went to the window and watched as the slave catchers headed to the creek while Hans and Jonathan returned to the barn. I could not bear to witness the hay and oats we had harvested for our own horses going to feed those of slave catchers, so, fuming, I took off my dress and unpinned the blue silk bodice of my dancing gown, and flung the pieces onto Anneke's sewing machine.

"Don't be angry with me," Anneke said from the fireplace as I dressed. "Be thankful he didn't ask *you* to cook for them."

That was the first I realized he had not, which was unusual, since I did almost all the cooking for the family. But if Hans thought it would be enough for me that my own hands were unsullied, he was mistaken.

None too soon the men finished their meal and left, shaking Hans's hand and tugging their hats at me and Anneke. As soon as they were gone, I burst out, "Hans, how could you?"

"I could hardly feed their horses but not them, now could I?"

"Yes, you surely could have. Slave catchers are the lowest of men, and you have given them sustenance necessary to continue their pursuit. Better to send them away hungry, too weak and distracted to find this unfortunate slave."

"If they did not eat here, they would eat at another farm. Best not to make enemies of them."

Jonathan made a noise of disagreement, and I, disbelieving Hans could mean what he said, asked, "Do you want them to believe you're a friend to their cause?"

"I couldn't send those horses away before giving them a rest." Hans dropped onto a bench beside the fireplace. "They've been running them too hard. If they keep up that pace, I don't see how they'll survive the return journey. That's a long way to travel on horseback."

"That's a long way to travel on foot," said Jonathan, referring to their quarry. "Especially in this season. The nights are cold, colder still for a man hunted in a strange land."

"Likely he's found shelter along the way."

"More likely than not, he hasn't."

"If he's made it this far, he must be made of sterner stuff than you and I," said Hans, mustering up a grin. "I must say, his owner must sorely miss him to pursue him so far."

"Never underestimate the extent or the strength of a man's greed, especially when his pride is insulted."

Now Hans laughed. "You sound more like the minister every day."

"But Hans—"

Hans's smile vanished. "I will not be drawn into an argument."

"Into this argument," said Jonathan, "willing or not, we will all eventually be drawn."

As the entire nation would soon discover, he was correct.

ꕥ

Whenever she could spare time from Elm Creek Quilts and Grandma's Attic, Summer returned to the Waterford Historical Society's archives to pore over the maps and page through bound volumes of city resolutions and legal affairs.

One particularly fruitful visit had turned up two intriguing maps of the county. The first, dated 1858, identified the town as Creek's Crossing, but unlike the Creek's Crossing map from 1847 that Summer had found during her first library search, labels identified Elm Creek Farm as well as the farms of other families. A map from 1864, however, called the town Water's Ford, but it was clearly the same region as the one depicted on the first map, with the additional development not unexpected after a six-year interval. Although a dashed line still indicated the town boundaries, Elm Creek Farm was shaded to suggest that it lay outside the border proper. Furthermore, while other farms were labeled by name as before, Elm Creek Farm was not.

It looked to Summer as if someone wanted to pretend Elm Creek Farm did not exist.

On a later visit, with the date of the name change more narrowly defined, Summer had turned to the town government records. In the volume from 1860, she finally found an official proclamation renaming the town, but although the document cited the need to "restore dignity to the village and its people," it provided no specific reasons.

The town's name appeared as Water's Ford in every source from the decade that followed, but gradually Waterford came into greater use. Since Summer found no official proclamation noting the change, she surmised that Waterford was a corruption of Water's Ford. The archives became somewhat muddled after Waterford was used exclusively, since another town in Pennsylvania shared the name and some of the documents from it had been filed among those of the former Creek's Crossing.

After Sylvia told her friends about the Bergstrom's encounter with the slave catchers, Summer decided to extend her search to local newspapers published in Gerda's time. Even though the town proclamation had not provided any details, surely a scandal shameful enough to make them change the name of the town would have appeared in the Creek's Crossing newspaper.

After hours of studying microfiche, Summer remained convinced that some long-ago reporter would have broken the scandal in the paper, but to her dismay, she could not say for certain.

The archives of the *Creek's Crossing Informer* ended in mid-1859. When they resumed in 1861, the paper was called the *Water's Ford Register*.

Summer was no cynic, but she found it difficult to believe the paper wasn't published during the exact period something significant had occurred in the city.

She would have bet her entire fabric stash that either the Waterford Historical Society wasn't interested in preserving the newspapers from those years or someone had made sure no copies would remain to be preserved.

* * *

"How delightful," said Sylvia dryly when Summer told her what she had learned. As if it weren't bad enough that Hans had obtained the farm through less than honorable means, now it appeared that the Bergstroms had done something so scandalous that the town had had to change its name to divert the shame of it. "My family certainly made their mark on this town, didn't they?"

"We don't know for a fact that your ancestors were involved," said Summer. "It might just be coincidence."

Sylvia took off her glasses and rubbed her eyes. "Nonsense. On the map of Creek's Crossing, Elm Creek Farm appears, but on the map of Water's Ford, it's been all but expunged. Gerda herself writes of a scandal, and you call it coincidence?"

"Well . . ." Summer hesitated. "Until we have more proof . . ."

The poor girl looked as if she wished she had not told Sylvia what she had uncovered. "Now, dear." Sylvia patted her hand. "You mustn't worry about sparing my feelings. I have already come to terms with the fact that my ancestors were not the sterling characters I thought them to be."

"Maybe, but aren't they much more interesting this way?"

"Yes, I suppose they are." They were much more real, too, more like people Sylvia would enjoy chatting with than the remote figures from the family stories.

Still, the more she pondered Gerda's cryptic asides, the more she suspected there might be parts of her family history she would not wish to divulge, not even to her closest friends.

November 1857—the Harvest Dance

I never learned whether the two slave catchers found the man they pursued, but they did not return to Elm Creek Farm. I prayed often for this unknown, unfortunate man, and was encouraged by Jonathan's assurances that the longer he remained free, the greater his chances of escaping to Canada.

When I first came to Pennsylvania, I assumed that it and all Free States were havens for the escaped bondsman, and that once a runaway crossed the border into the North, he could not be compelled to return to his former masters. That was, sadly, not true. In 1850, as part of a compromise meant to placate Southern states angered by measures to check the spread of slavery elsewhere in the growing nation, Congress passed the Fugitive Slave Law. It proclaimed that runaways, even those who managed to reach Free States, must be returned to their owners, and that federal and state officials and even private citizens must assist in their recapture. Moreover, anyone—freeman or fugitive—suspected of being a runaway slave could be arrested without a warrant and, once apprehended, could neither request a jury trial nor testify on his own behalf.

This Jonathan told me, indignantly adding, "I cannot and will not submit to any law that compels me to act against the dictates of my conscience and my God."

I admired him for his convictions, for his sentiments were the same as my own. In comparison, Hans's reluctance to risk offending the two slave catchers troubled me. If the fugitive had been hiding in our barn that day, would Hans have delivered him into the hands of his pursuers? I did not wish to believe this of my brother, and I disliked that my admiration and faith in him had been so shaken.

Anneke, of course, believed that Hans had acted appropriately. They were a good match, I suppose, as neither would believe any evil of the other. She refused to discuss the matter with me, both out of loyalty to her husband and from her exasperation that I did not understand that citizens, especially immigrants, must obey the laws of the land—all laws, not merely those that suited one's own tastes. I, in turn, could not abide her blindness to one's moral obligation to disobey unjust laws. Anneke responded, "You would not say such a thing except to please Jonathan."

This flustered me a great deal, so much that I refused to speak to Anneke for the rest of the day, which suited her fine as she was not interested in conversing with someone who would criticize her husband. But by the next morning we were speaking again, more from necessity than choice, as it was impossible to avoid each other in our two-room house. It was Anneke who broke our silence, by offering to finish the task the two slave catchers had interrupted. I accepted her offer gratefully, and by noontime, she had finished the bodice of my new dress. The entire gown was complete the morning of the dance.

"You look enchanting," declared Anneke, and I heartily wished I could believe her.

Saturday dawned cool and crisp, and we completed our chores with glad hearts, looking forward to the evening's festivities. I baked two pies, one of apples Dorothea had shared with us from their trees, one of wild blueberries I had discovered growing near the creek, and I also made potato pancakes with soured cream. I did not know what our neighbors would think of the latter, but since numerous other families of German descent inhabited the town, I suspected few would remain on the platter, if only accounting for Hans's appetite.

We rode into town on the wagon pulled by two of Hans's horses—"Bergstrom Thoroughbreds," he liked to call them—to find the streets of Creek's Crossing full of other families, laughing and calling greetings to one another. We met Dorothea and Thomas at the grassy square in front of the City Hall, where already the picnic had begun. Four tables had been arranged in a long row to one side of the square, and the women of the town had covered them with all manner of mouthwatering dishes, to which I added my contributions. We filled our plates and set out quilts to sit upon. I was careful not to muss my blue silk dress, in which, I admit, I felt rather fair for a plain girl, and as we ate, I searched the crowd for Jonathan, disappointed that he did not join us. After Anneke's remark about how I sought to please him, however, I could not bring myself to ask Dorothea where he was, not within Anneke's hearing.

The dancing was well under way when Jonathan finally appeared. He told me I looked lovely, which, to my embarrassment, made me blush. I quickly replied, "It is the dress. Anneke has skill with a needle I will never know."

Too late, Anneke shot me a look of warning. Hans's eyebrows rose, and Anneke quickly took his arm. "Come, Hans. Dance with me."

He accompanied her without argument, but I knew from his expression that he had deduced where the fabric for my dress had come from. As Dorothea admired Anneke's handiwork, I watched my brother and his wife as they joined the line for the next dance, and was relieved to see that Hans did not seem angry.

Dorothea was not the only one to admire my dress, and I took every opportunity to sing my sister-in-law's praises, but never more so than when Mrs. Violet Pearson Engle, the dressmaker, passed by our quilt on the way for another serving of cake. She asked me to rise so she might better examine the drape of the skirt. "Fine silk," she announced as she had me turn around before her. "And the handiwork is finer still."

I knew Anneke would delight in the compliment, and wished that Jonathan would escort me to the dance so I might whisper it to her in passing, but as one song ended and the musicians called for another, Jonathan extended his hand to his sister instead. At the conclusion of that dance, Hans and Anneke returned to our quilt breathless and laughing, and since I would no longer be left there alone, Thomas left to claim his wife's hand from her brother. Jonathan did not return as I expected, and as the music resumed, I spied him whirling about with a bright-eyed, dark-haired young woman I had never met. Once more he danced with her, to my growing consternation—and then, to my astonishment, Cyrus Pearson approached and asked me to be his partner.

I did not wish to dance with him, but I could not refuse without good reason, so I gave him my hand and allowed him to escort me to the dance. He was a fine dancer, much better than I, but his lead was strong and confident enough that I managed to avoid treading on his feet. Rather than strike up a conversation with me, he directed his attention to his friends, who exchanged greetings and jokes in passing. I had no objection to this, for it was a complicated dance that required my full attention, and moreover I could not think of any particular subject I wished to discuss with him. He seemed satisfied that I smiled at his silly jokes.

I thought I was faring rather well, until he said, "You are accomplished in so many things. I had expected dancing to be one of them."

"I'm sorry to disappoint you," said I shortly. I had at that moment spotted Jonathan partnered for yet another dance with the pretty dark-haired girl.

"I would not call it disappointment, merely surprise," said he. "Perhaps in your youth you should have been practicing your dancing instead of sharpening your wit."

I halted at once and released his hand. "Perhaps you should have been practicing your manners." I meant to leave him there in the middle of the dance, but my grand gesture was spoiled by the musicians, who chose that moment to end their song.

I marched back to our quilt, fuming and wishing I had stayed home, when suddenly Jonathan appeared before me. "Are you free for this dance?"

"Oh, she's free," drawled Mr. Pearson, behind me. "Good luck, Doctor."

Jonathan watched him as he brushed by us, and then looked questioningly at me. Embarrassed, I took his arm and urged him toward the dance floor before he could ask me to explain.

In Baden-Baden I had learned to be amusing on the dance floor since I could not be graceful, and what I lacked in comeliness, I believe I more than made up for in wit. Jonathan seemed to enjoy himself well enough in my company; he smiled much more with me than with his previous partner, and I made him laugh out loud where the dark-haired girl had only made him smile. And yet, after two dances with me, he escorted me back to the quilt and requested a dance with Anneke, followed by one with his sister, and then the dark-haired girl was on his arm again.

"Her name is Charlotte Claverton," murmured Anneke as I watched them dance.

I had thought my observation discreet, and so Anneke's awareness of my interest bothered me. "Is it," said I, feigning indifference, but glad that Anneke had, in my absence, apparently asked the questions I could not.

"Her family's farm lies adjacent to the farm of Jonathan's and Dorothea's parents. He has known Charlotte all her life."

"We must endeavor to make her acquaintance, then," said I. "I would surely like any friend of Dorothea's."

"I did not tell you this so that you might become her friend," said Anneke. "I told you so you would not worry. If he has known her all his life, surely if he meant to marry her, he would have asked her by now."

My hopes, which until that day I had been unwilling to admit even to myself, rose. I nodded, unable to find words in my relief. Anneke smiled reassuringly, and just then, I caught Dorothea's eye. She smiled her serene smile and resumed conversing with Thomas, but I wondered how much she had overheard.

As afternoon turned into evening, I danced again with Jonathan, and with my brother, but I was happiest with Jonathan. Other men invited me to dance, too, but it was not until later that I realized I had been quite a popular partner that night. I would have enjoyed myself enormously if I had noticed, and if I had not been acutely aware that Jonathan seemed to be at Charlotte's side at least as often as mine.

The hour grew late, and one by one, the families from the most distant farms began to depart. At last Charlotte rode off in a wagon with her father and mother, and only then did Jonathan remain with me. He was an attentive and courteous escort, and so I repeated Anneke's reassurances to myself and tried to forget young Charlotte with her shining dark hair and graceful figure.

Not long after Charlotte's departure, the Nelsons bid us good night. Jonathan walked with Hans, Anneke, and me to our wagon before heading for his own home. Anneke gave me a look that implied this was of great significance, but I had to wonder if he would have helped me into our wagon if Charlotte had remained, or if he would have assisted her instead.

On the drive home, Anneke deliberately avoided Hans's eye and said to me, "I overheard many compliments of your dress."

I was ashamed that in my distraction with Jonathan I had forgotten my sister-in-law's problem. "I have you and your skill with the needle to thank," replied I.

"And our parents," remarked Hans. "Don't forget, they provided the fabric for that fine dress. Fabric I intended to sell in town to pay for our new house."

There was only a mild rebuke in his words, so I quickly added, "Mrs. Engle, especially, admired your sewing."

"I spoke with her myself," said Anneke. "She said she would have work for me in her dressmaker's shop, if I am so inclined."

"Did she," said Hans. "What about your work at home?"

"Whatever work she cannot do, I can, as well as my own," said I.

Anneke gave me a grateful look, and said to Hans, "We will get a much better price for your parents' fabric if I sew it into clothing first."

Hans looked thoughtful, and for a long while we rode in silence, Anneke and I watching him anxiously. By the time we reached home, he had decided that Anneke would be permitted to assist Mrs. Engle one day each week in her dressmaker's shop, and that she could dispose of the fabric however she saw fit. "I'm pleased you had the good sense to ignore me when I said to leave those bolts be," said he, smiling affectionately at his wife.

I was delighted for Anneke, and pleased that Hans had not let pride get the better of his pragmatism, but in my wistful heart, I wished that someone would smile so affectionately at me, too, and that that someone would be Jonathan.

❦

On the following Sunday afternoon, Sylvia greeted the new campers on the veranda, guiding them inside while impatiently eyeing the circular driveway for the shuttle bus that would bring Grace Daniels back to Elm Creek Manor.

Sylvia and Grace had been friends for more than fifteen years, united by their love for quilting. In addition to her work as a curator for the De Young Museum in San Francisco, Grace was a master quilter who had once specialized in story quilts, folk-art-style appliqué works that interpreted historical stories or themes, often with African-American subjects. Her passion for history had not diminished when multiple sclerosis forced her down a new creative path, and she had long wished to see the quilts from the manor's past. Grace attended Elm Creek Quilt Camp the same week every year, to reunite with friends she had made on her first visit as well as to see Sylvia. This time, at long last, Sylvia intended to fulfill her promise to show Anneke's quilts to Grace.

Another airport shuttle bus arrived, and finally Sylvia saw Grace emerge, supporting herself on two metal crutches. Matt spotted her, too, and bounded down one of the semicircular staircases to assist with her luggage. When Sylvia called to her and waved, Grace looked up and called, "When do I get to see the quilts?"

"As soon as you like," Sylvia promised, delighted to see her friend looking so well and in such good spirits. Grace rarely spoke about her illness over the phone, leaving Sylvia to wonder how much it had progressed between their visits.

After Grace completed her camp registration, Sylvia instructed Matt to deliver Grace's bags to her room. Then, before Grace's friends could whisk her off for their annual reunion, Sylvia invited her to the west sitting room off the kitchen, where she had laid out the quilts in anticipation of Grace's visit.

"What a find, Sylvia," exclaimed Grace when she saw the quilts. She studied them without speaking, occasionally lifting a corner up to the light or bending close to inspect a particular scrap of fabric. Every so often she jotted notes on a pad, then returned her attention to the quilts.

"Well?" prompted Sylvia.

"I don't suppose you'd consider donating these to the museum?"

"Absolutely not," declared Sylvia, then conceded, "Not yet, at least. I might consider leaving them to you in my will, since I know you'll take good care of them."

"In that case, I'm willing to wait a long time." With effort, Grace sat down on the sofa beside the Log Cabin quilt and turned it over, searching the muslin backing for an appliquéd tag or embroidery, just as Sylvia had done weeks earlier. She shook her head when she found neither. "I wish the quilter had documented her work."

"There might be a record of their history, even so." Sylvia retrieved the slim leather book from her writing desk and handed it to Grace. "My father's great-aunt Gerda's memoir. I believe my great-grandmother Anneke Bergstrom made the quilts, and I hope Gerda wrote about them."

Grace glanced at the first page. "That would definitely help determine their dates of origin."

"Can't you do that by inspection?"

Grace shook her head and returned the memoir to Sylvia. "Only to some extent. The pattern choices tell us something, and I can place the fabrics, but I can't determine when the quilts were pieced from them. Think about how long you've had some of the fabric in your stash. The material might be from 1987, but your quilt will be completed in the twenty-first century."

"Of course." Sylvia thought of the Tumbling Block quilt she had begun earlier that summer with hundreds of diamonds trimmed from scraps used over several decades of quilt making. Fortunately, she always embroidered her name and date in the border of her quilts, so no one would mistake who had made them, or when.

"There are some fabulous examples of the dye and discharge process in here," said Grace, touching several of the logs gently. Her finger lighted on a yellow fabric with a small, close print. "This was called a butterscotch print. They were popular in Pennsylvania from around 1840 through 1860."

Sylvia nodded, pleased that the dates corresponded so well to Gerda's time.

"Prussian blue," continued Grace, indicating several scraps in turn. "Here's a turkey red, and here's another. Oh, I've seen this purple print before, or one very like it. It's probably imported."

Sylvia frowned at the brown fabric. "That doesn't look very purple to me."

"The dye was fugitive. All of these"—Grace pointed to several different brown pieces, some dark prints on light backgrounds, others medium in value and embellished with small, white floral designs—"were purples once."

An awful feeling struck Sylvia. "Is it possible that the black center squares were not originally black?"

"No," said Grace, studying the quilt thoughtfully, "I don't believe so."

Relieved, Sylvia inhaled deeply to settle her nerves and asked,

"What about the other quilts? I've spotted some of the same fabric in all three."

"Yes, I noticed that, too." Grace looked from the Log Cabin quilt to the four-patch and then to the Birds in the Air, examining the quilting stitches closely. "They seem to be the same age, but I don't believe the same quilter made all three. Even accounting for a quilter's improvement with practice, the quilting stitches in the Log Cabin and the Birds in the Air aren't as accomplished as those in the four-patch. And, of course, the Log Cabin and Birds in the Air are machine-pieced. I'm surprised you didn't mention that."

"I didn't realize it."

Grace must have detected her dismay, for she smiled. "Don't worry. That doesn't mean they weren't completed in your great-grandmother's time. Quilters have been piecing by machine for as long as there have been sewing machines."

"One of my Elm Creek Quilters won't be happy to learn that," said Sylvia dryly, thinking of Diane, who insisted that only quilts made entirely by hand could be considered "true quilts."

"She's not the only one. Many people become uncomfortable when they discover their traditions are founded on shaky ground."

"My great-grandmother did own a sewing machine, but if different quilters made the three quilts, I suspect Anneke made the four-patch and Gerda made the Log Cabin." Family lore attributed the Log Cabin quilt to Anneke, but it seemed the most logical explanation. "I'm not sure about the Birds in the Air."

"The piecing quality is inconsistent," noted Grace, "as is the quilting. Maybe they worked on this one together."

"Of the two, Anneke was the better seamstress. Gerda—Hans's sister—quilted only because she had to. She despised sewing."

"She must not have despised it too much. Whoever made the Log Cabin put a great deal of care into it."

"I should think so." Sylvia gave Grace a pointed look over the top of her glasses. "I've told you my great-aunt Lucinda's story about this quilt."

"And I've given my professional opinion about that story," replied Grace. "It's highly unlikely that Log Cabin quilts with black center squares were used as signals on the Underground Railroad. The block didn't even come into widespread use until the 1860s, years after the Underground Railroad functioned as it did in the time leading up to the Civil War. I've looked, and the earliest published description of the Log Cabin block I could find was in 1869."

"That hardly matters," scoffed Sylvia. "Patterns were transmitted from quilter to quilter long before they were printed up in magazines and newspapers. Have you ever been to the Carnegie Natural History Museum in Pittsburgh?"

The apparent change in subject clearly baffled Grace. "What?"

"The Carnegie Natural History Museum in Pittsburgh. The Egyptian exhibit, to be precise. I saw the mummy of a cat there once, and its wrappings were made up of tiny folded Log Cabin quilt blocks."

"I don't deny that the design itself might have existed, but I'll guarantee you the Egyptians didn't call it a Log Cabin block."

Grace's painstaking distinctions made Sylvia impatient. "But why, then, do so many stories—not merely my great-aunt's—describe Log Cabin quilts with black center squares used on the Underground Railroad?"

"Unfortunately, most of these stories are based upon misdated quilts." Grace sighed. "Look. I'm a quilter, I'm an African-American, and I'm someone who loves a good story, but I'm also a historian, and I have to go by the evidence in the historical record. Until now, there haven't been any surviving quilts of that era meeting that description."

"Until now?"

Grace hesitated. "Well—"

"I distinctly heard you say, 'Until now.'"

"I admit I'm puzzled. The pattern suggests that the Log Cabin quilt is Civil War era or later, but the fabric predates the war."

"Which suggests the quilt was made before the war."

"Or that the quilter saved her scraps for later use," Grace reminded her. "Still, the quilting pattern also displays characteristics of the antebellum period. And when I consider the four-patch quilt . . ."

"Yes?" prompted Sylvia.

"Well, the picture becomes even less clear." Grace frowned and fingered the edge of the four-patch. "I believe Anneke would have called this the Underground Railroad pattern."

"That couldn't be. I would have recognized it. The Underground Railroad pattern was merely the Jacob's Ladder by another name, was it not?"

"Again, we have to go back to the historical record. The earliest quilts containing the modern Jacob's Ladder pattern date back to the end of the 1900s, no earlier. If the Jacob's Ladder block we know today was renamed Underground Railroad, it happened long after the events that inspired the name."

"Dear me." Sylvia sat down, hard, on the ottoman of her armchair. "I've been perpetuating a myth."

"At least one, maybe more."

"Thank you, Grace," said Sylvia dryly. "You don't need to make me feel worse. Why did you say you think Anneke's quilt was called Underground Railroad, then?"

"These strippy quilts were very popular in Anneke's time." Grace placed her hands on the quilt, isolating five of the four-patches and the setting triangles surrounding them. "Imagine these as one nine-patch block. Do you see how it resembles our Jacob's Ladder pattern?"

Sylvia studied the pieces for a moment before she could see the similarity. "Goodness, yes. Do you mean to say that a quilt such as this was called Underground Railroad, but a later quilter saw the secondary pattern within the arrangement and determined that the block's name had been changed?"

"It's possible. I'm afraid it's another theory."

"You and your theories."

"I wish I could give you definitive answers, but I can't. I don't even know for certain if this quilt was called Underground Railroad. I'm surmising that since it was found with the Log Cabin." Grace frowned and returned her gaze to it. "Which, I'll admit, does puzzle me."

Sylvia hated to let go of the folklore that had enchanted her for so many years. "Allow me to play devil's advocate, if you please."

"Certainly."

"Based on all the other evidence, but excluding Anneke's choice of the Log Cabin pattern, when would you have dated these quilts?"

"I can't ignore the pattern. It's one of the most important clues."

"Indulge an old woman's fancy, would you, please? Just this once?"

Grace smiled wryly and conceded, "I'd say somewhere between 1840 to 1860."

"Now, just because no one has ever found a Log Cabin quilt predating the Civil War, that doesn't mean they never existed, correct?"

Grace hesitated. "Well, no, but lack of evidence to the contrary isn't reliable evidence."

"But it is possible, however improbable, that Anneke's quilt does predate the Civil War, and that it could have been used as a signal on the Underground Railroad? Here, at Elm Creek Manor, if nowhere else?"

"I suppose it's possible, but—"

"Thank you," said Sylvia, triumphant. "You can stop there."

Grace laughed and shook her head. "Okay. You win. Your quilts pose an interesting puzzle, and I'll need more time to figure it out."

"More time and more evidence," said Sylvia. "I do wish you could have seen Margaret Alden's quilt in person. All I have are photos."

"I can look at those, at least."

Sylvia went to fetch them, unable to keep the smile off her face. Grace had done all she could to caution her, and Sylvia knew she ought to reserve judgment until they had more evidence, but she couldn't help feeling elated. Despite all the qualifiers and contradictions, Grace had admitted that Sylvia might have stumbled upon the one remaining Log Cabin quilt that had served as a signal on the Underground Railroad.

Surely Gerda's memoir would prove the folklore true.

December 1857 through January 1858—in which I encounter hints of future unhappiness and signs of ill times to come, and ignore them all

Within a month of the Harvest Dance, Anneke began working for Mrs. Engle at her dress shop in Creek's Crossing. Once a week I drove her into town, delivered my preserves and bread to the general store and collected my earnings, and completed whatever errands the farm required before rewarding myself with a visit to friends from Dorothea's sewing circle. The mornings flew by as we exchanged books and gossip, and all too soon

I would have to hurry away to fetch Anneke home again, her newest sewing projects in a neat bundle on her lap, in time for me to make Hans his dinner. He did not mind his wife's enterprising spirit as long as it did not postpone his mealtimes.

The first snow of the season fell around that time, but the worst harshness of winter held off, and so we enjoyed cold but sunny days until the end of December. Our Christmas was an especially joyous one; Hans's business had begun to grow, Elm Creek Farm was flourishing from our attentive labors, and all around us were signs of our imminent prosperity. We Bergstroms were well liked by our neighbors, and we never suffered from loneliness, despite the relative isolation of our home.

The Nelsons remained our closest friends, and to this day I thank the Lord for blessing us with such generous neighbors. Dorothea was such a practical, capable woman, and in countless ways she helped Anneke and me better manage our household. Although Creek's Crossing was not the Kansas wilderness I had planned for, it was frontier enough for women of Anneke's and my inexperience. Without Dorothea's gentle guidance, we would not have fared nearly half so well.

Anneke made other acquaintances, too, by virtue of her days spent at Engle's Draper and Fine Tailoring. The young ladies of the finest families in town frequented the establishment, and while some snubbed Anneke as an "illiterate immigrant," their more practical friends, who recognized the wisdom of an alliance with such a gifted seamstress, befriended her. Mrs. Engle grew quite fond of her and introduced her to her circle of friends, the matrons of the town, and before long each had exacted a promise from her husband that he would consider purchasing one of Hans's Bergstrom Thoroughbred foals come spring.

I was so pleased that Mrs. Engle had given Anneke employment that I felt guilty when I could not bring myself to like her more. I did try to like her, at least at first: I ignored the small jokes she made about immigrants and clenched my teeth when she spoke of the necessity of slave labor to the economy of the South, especially cotton, the cultivation of which directly affected her business; I told myself that if Anneke could bear the tone of self-important condescension with which Mrs. Engle addressed her, surely I could as well. But I lost my temper when she published a letter in the *Creek's Crossing Informer* denouncing the vote for women and beseeching men to guide their daughters with a firm hand lest they, too, succumb to corrupting influences. "Women's suffrage and the desire for the right to vote render our young ladies argumentative, unfeminine, and unsuitable for marriage," wrote she. "We doom our precious daughters to embittered spinsterhood if we do not teach them humility and obedience."

"She was not speaking of you," said Anneke when I grumbled over this. "She knows you tried to marry."

"And how would she know that?" asked I, too astounded to say that whether Mrs. Engle referred to me personally was irrelevant.

"I told her how you came to be unlucky in love."

Thus I had embarrassment to compound my outrage.

Mrs. Engle's letter concluded on a note that would have been ominous if it had not been so prim and ridiculous: "Certain Factions, especially those which bring in outsiders to inflame our minds and hearts, ought not to imagine they speak for all the Ladies of Creek's Crossing, or they may find themselves without Friends."

Her letter set the sewing circle all abuzz with indignant calls for us to compose a rebuttal for immediate publication in the *Informer,* and we all clamored for Dorothea, the obvious target of Mrs. Engle's last rebuke, to author it. "I will write to explain my position and the righteousness of our cause," replied Dorothea, "but I will not engage in petty argument simply for the sake of defending my injured pride."

"We cannot allow her insults to go unanswered," protested one of our circle. "She should not have been allowed to write such things."

We others chimed in our agreement, but Dorothea merely smiled and said, "Remember, we also fight so that Mrs. Engle may vote."

That sobered us. We had assumed that all women, once secured the right, would naturally vote as we would have them do, and that together we would bring about a new renaissance of justice and peace in our country. But when we could not forge solidarity even among ourselves, how could we hope to transform the entire nation?

A few of our sewing circle vowed never again to patronize Mrs. Engle's shop, a decision that pained me for Anneke's sake until I discovered this would account for the loss of only two dresses a year. Still, I was relieved that Anneke had not joined us that evening, and my heart was troubled when I thought of how she would react to news of the resolution. But some of my good humor was restored by our second declaration, which was unanimous: We would henceforth call our little group the Certain Sewing and Suffrage Faction of Creek's Crossing, Pennsylvania.

After that, I could not bring myself to enter the dressmaker's shop out of fear I would tell Mrs. Engle exactly what I thought of her and cost my sister-in-law her employment, but left and collected Anneke at the door without stepping inside even to warm myself for the drive home. "Without Friends," indeed. Dorothea and I had friends enough among the Certain Faction, and would scarcely notice the absence of Mrs. Engle and her cronies.

Only then did I realize how rarely the two circles mixed. I, who prided myself on my powers of observation and inference, had not noticed until prompted by Mrs. Engle's letter the schism that divided the women of the town. Anneke alone seemed capable of traveling freely in both circles, earning the respect of one with her perseverance and determination to learn, charming the other with her beauty, skill, and eagerness to please.

When I remarked on the divide to Hans and Anneke, Anneke claimed, rather sharply, that it was nothing a little pleasantness and restraint on Dorothea's part wouldn't mend.

Said Hans, more soberly, "It's worse among the men."

The following week, Dorothea's reply appeared in the *Informer;* Anneke reported that it was not well regarded in the dressmaker's shop, nor was Dorothea. But with the coming of Christmas, the women of Creek's Crossing set aside acrimony in the spirit of the season, and the tensions between us settled once again beneath the surface, unspoken and unnoticed.

As they had the previous year, the Nelsons invited us to spend Christmas Day with them, and what a joyous holiday it was indeed. Jonathan came, as I had hoped he would; he brought his and Dorothea's parents in the senior Mr. Granger's sleigh, which pulled up to the house soon after ours with a jingling of merry bells. Mrs. Granger treated me with such kind affection that I allowed myself to hope that her opinion of me had been formed as much by Jonathan's reports as by Dorothea's.

After a delicious meal, Dorothea and her father entertained us with the music of organ and fiddle, respectively, and we sang Christmas carols. I recollect that evening as the most joyful I had yet spent in America, and it was to remain one of my happiest memories. We laughed and joked and shared stories of Christmases past in lands far away. No one regretted the evening's end more than I, but Mr. and Mrs. Granger needed to return to their farm, so Jonathan and Hans went to the barn to hitch up their horses.

They observed storm clouds gathered in the southwestern sky, so urged us not to delay our departure. As Anneke and I rose to don our winter cloaks and scarves, Jonathan murmured in my ear that he should like to speak with me alone for a moment.

My heart seemed to tremble, but I nodded, and we slipped into the kitchen while the others said their farewells. I was too nervous to speak, so I stood in silence and waited.

Jonathan did not meet my eyes as he fumbled in his pocket and said, "I had hoped for a better moment to give you this." He withdrew a small paper-wrapped parcel and placed it in my hands.

Speechless, I looked from the parcel to Jonathan.

"Please open it," said he, glancing over his shoulder.

Mindful that our time alone might be brief, I quickly unwrapped the gift and discovered a beautiful hair comb embellished with mother-of-pearl. "It's lovely, Jonathan. Thank you." He smiled to see me so pleased with his gift, as I truly was. I did not have many fine features, but my hair was thick and dark, and fell below my waist when unbraided, and I admit to being a trifle vain of it. I thanked him for the gift, and warmly wished him a merry Christmas.

He wished me the same, and I thought he might say more, but behind us, someone cleared her throat. Dorothea stood in the doorway, watching us. "I thought I might send you home with some of my dried apples, Gerda, if you think you might use them?"

"Of course I would," said I. "Thank you."

She nodded and passed between us on her way to the root cellar, glancing at her brother as she went, but Jonathan did not look at her, and instead excused himself to help his parents prepare for the trip home.

By the time Dorothea returned, I had composed myself and had hidden Jonathan's gift in my pocket. We both remarked on how delightful the evening had been, but then Dorothea fell silent, her expression troubled. "Gerda," said she at last, "I do not wish to speak out of turn, but . . ."

"But?" prompted I, when she hesitated.

"I hope you are not setting your cap for my brother."

The colloquialism puzzled me. "Setting my cap?"

"She means, do you think to marry him," said Anneke, who had entered the room in time to hear the exchange.

"I don't mean any offense," said Dorothea.

"Of course not," said I. "I assure you, I don't plan to set my hat for anyone."

"You needn't worry about my sister," said Anneke, grinning naughtily. "She's often said she will never trade her freedom for the bondage of matrimony. She does not wish to become old married women like us, and subject to the whims of a man."

Dorothea's eyebrows rose.

"I did not say it in quite that manner," said I with haste, embarrassed. "Anneke misrepresents me."

"Your words, perhaps, but not the sentiment," said Anneke.

"Sometimes the yoke is not so difficult to bear," said Dorothea with a small laugh. "It depends upon the husband."

I wondered, did Dorothea think Jonathan would make a poor husband? Or did she think I would make him a poor wife? I was so conflicted by her unexpected remarks and Anneke's teasing that I could not bring myself to give voice to my questions. Dorothea and I were friends. If I had indeed set my cap for Jonathan, why would Dorothea find this objectionable?

Suddenly I was relieved that we were leaving. The mother-of-pearl comb felt heavy and conspicuous in my pocket, even when concealed beneath my outer wraps. I couldn't meet Jonathan's eye as Hans, Anneke, and I bid our friends good-bye and climbed into our wagon. I buried my chin in my scarf to ward off the cold and said not a word as Hans drove the horses back to Elm Creek Farm, and when we reached home, I hid the comb in my hope chest before Anneke could see it.

When at last I showed it to her, a few days later, she squealed with delight and commanded me to tell her every word Jonathan and I had exchanged. This I accomplished soon enough, as we had had little time alone. Dorothea's interruption had been so troubling that I had forgotten the pleasure Jonathan's gift had first brought me, but Anneke's enthusiasm soon rekindled it. That he had given me any gift was a promising sign, she insisted, but such a beautiful ornament surely indicated he wished to increase our intimacy.

As always, I feigned disinterest. "Jonathan is my friend's brother, and so naturally he is my friend as well, but you mustn't imagine he is anything more."

"Hans and I are his friends, too, but he didn't give us Christmas presents."

This I could not deny, but I did my best to assure her I had no interest in Jonathan beyond friendship.

You may wonder why I insisted on this deception, which was in all likelihood becoming transparent, or perhaps you will have guessed the reason to be my disappointment with E. I was determined not to become an object of pity in my new country as I had in my homeland. If my heart were to be broken a second time, my one consolation would be that no one save myself would know it. True, I cherished our conversations, looked forward to our meetings, and noted with pleasure the signs of Jonathan's increasing affection for me, but until he made some declaration of his intentions, I must assume he had none.

The New Year came, followed by a series of January snowstorms that for several days kept us confined to Elm Creek Farm. Hans had his endless chores and Anneke her sewing for Mrs. Engle, but I longed for the companionship of the Certain Faction. When Anneke complained at my stalking about the cabin, I took up my sewing basket and worked on my Shoo-Fly quilt to appease her. To my surprise, the hours passed quite pleasantly as Anneke and I sewed side by side in the firelight. She told me stories of her childhood in Berlin, and I told her about my family's life in Baden-Baden. By the time the storms broke, I had nearly finished enough blocks for a quilt top, and Anneke and I had deepened our understanding of each other. I reflected then that I had known my younger sisters all my life, and I missed and loved them dearly, but Anneke and I had shared hardship and hope in a strange land, and that bound us closer than any ties of blood or affection ever could.

In later years, only by recollecting the closeness we shared in those days was I able to set aside my hatred and remember that once I had loved Anneke. If not for my resolution to try to love her again, I might have left my family forever rather than share a home with her.

But I must remember to record this history in the order in which it transpired, or it will make no sense at all to my reader, even if by your day, these events are well known to every Bergstrom.

Our first visitor after the weather cleared was Jonathan. He met Hans in the barn, to discuss a horse he intended to buy, but then he came to the cabin. I was pleased to see him, and glad that I had worn the hair comb; though I had intended to save it for special occasions, seeing the sun again had made the day special enough. He accepted the tea I offered him and joined me and Anneke by the fire, but his attempts at conversation were uncharacteristically awkward.

Eventually Anneke made some excuse and left us, and soon we heard her sewing machine whirring as she worked the treadle with her foot. "I'm glad you ventured out to see us," said I. "I wished to return the book you lent me. It was quite good. Thank you."

He nodded and took it absently. "Gerda, I must speak with you on a difficult subject."

In the other room, the treadle ceased abruptly. "Not until I give you your Christmas gift," said I, quickly. My heart pounding, anticipating his words, I retrieved and presented his gift. "It's belated, but I think you will like it all the same."

Slowly he unwrapped the book and read the title. "Franklin's *Autobiography*."

"You've often said you admired him, and you enjoyed the French version," said I, wondering why he did not smile. "This is the English version his grandson published later, with additions to the manuscript."

"Thank you," said he. "I'm sure I will enjoy it." Only then did he look up and meet my eye, but just as quickly his gaze alighted on the ornament in my hair. "You're wearing the comb." Involuntarily I touched it, my cheeks growing warm, and I nodded. "It suits you."

"It suits my hair," said I, attempting a laugh. "It keeps it out of my eyes, which is a great benefit when one is trying to sew, I assure you."

"Or to dance." His voice grew distant. "At the Harvest Dance, that lock above your ear kept slipping out of place and tumbling across your cheek."

"I did not think you had noticed," said I, nervous, and trying once again to tease him out of his serious mood. "As I recall it, we saw little of each other that night. You danced with your sister and with Charlotte Claverton as much as with me."

"Yes." He looked up at me gravely. "I suppose I did." Then he took a deep breath and stood. "Gerda, there are things I must tell you, but perhaps you have guessed them already."

I shook my head.

At that moment, someone pounded on the door. "Dr. Granger," a young voice shouted. "Dr. Granger, are you there?"

Alarmed, I flew to the door and opened it. In tumbled a boy of about thirteen, gasping for breath, his face red and frightened.

"Daniel?" said Jonathan.

"Mrs. Granger said you would be here," said the boy, panting so hard I could barely make out his words. "It's my pa. He's been shot."

Jonathan was already throwing on his coat. "Where is he?"

"Home. Susanna's looking after him."

Susanna, I was to learn later, was the boy's ten-year-old sister. Daniel's mother had died two years before while giving birth to his youngest brother.

"When did this happen?" asked Jonathan, as he followed the boy out the door.

"Same day the storms hit. He was out in the barn—" Daniel swallowed hard. "They hit him in the stomach. He was bleeding real bad, but I couldn't get to your place any sooner. The snow—"

"It's all right, son. We'll get back to your place in no time." Suddenly Jonathan looked at me. "There's no time to stop for Dorothea—"

"I'll come." Quickly I threw on my wraps, my mind racing. The same day the storms hit, Daniel had said, which meant his father had been suffering for four days.

Anneke, who had returned to the room at the pounding upon the door, fled to the barn, where Hans saddled a horse for me and one for Daniel, whose mare was spent from the long run first to the Granger farm and then to ours. In minutes we were on our way.

As we rode, Daniel gasped out the story. When the storm worsened, his father had gone to the barn to check on the livestock, and discovered two men engaged in stealing his horses. Unarmed, Daniel's father attempted to flee, but before he could escape, one of the pair fired upon him.

"Did your father recognize the men?" asked Jonathan.

"He said he didn't, but I know who they were," said the boy, his voice full of hate and exhaustion. "Only one kind of people shoot a man for his horses then run off without the horses."

But the road and our pace prevented him from saying more.

We raced on, north through the woods to the Wilbur farm, which lay to the northwest of Creek's Crossing. At last we arrived, expecting the worst, only to find a familiar wagon in the yard. Jonathan's parents had come.

His mother met us at the door, relieved to see her son but still anxious. Her husband, she reported as Jonathan hurried inside, was upstairs, distracting the other children. Nodding, Jonathan requested soap and two basins of water, which his mother quickly made ready. "Wash your hands," he instructed me, and did so himself before racing to his patient's side.

I obeyed, then quickly joined him in the other room. Mr. Wilbur lay on a bed, eyes closed and pale, a blood-soaked dressing covering his abdomen. He moaned in pain as Jonathan lifted the bandage to inspect the wound. I glimpsed raw, seeping flesh and felt my head grow light, but Mrs. Granger held me steady and whispered that I should not think of what I saw, but must steel myself and provide what assistance Jonathan required of me.

I gulped air, nodded, and followed Mrs. Granger to the bedside, where we helped Jonathan as he fought to preserve Mr. Wilbur's life. My memory is a blur of blood and flesh, but I know I followed Jonathan's instructions automatically, rapidly and without thinking, numb and frightened. I had cared for ailing relatives, I had assisted in childbirth, but never had I witnessed a struggle to repair so great a wrong done to the human body, and my mind was numb with disbelief that any man could knowingly inflict such agony on another.

It seemed hours until Jonathan stepped away from the bed,

exhausted, and said that he had done all he could. He withdrew to wash himself and rest, while his mother and I tried to make Mr. Wilbur more comfortable by changing his soiled bed linens. Mr. Wilbur little noticed our efforts, as he had long ago fallen unconscious from the pain.

Mrs. Granger offered to watch by his bedside. I thought then of the children whom I had not yet seen, and since I could do nothing else, I went to the kitchen to prepare them something to eat.

Jonathan was in the kitchen, slumped in a chair, his head in his hands.

"You saved his life," said I, quietly, as I scrubbed my hands clean.

"I did nothing of the sort." His voice was oddly emotionless. "I came too late."

"He's alive. We'll care for him until he recovers."

"No. He's lost too much blood. The bullet remained in him too long. The wound was not closed, nor was it covered well enough to prevent infection. He will not live out the week."

I could not bear to think of those children left without their only remaining parent. "He has survived four days already. He may make it."

Jonathan did not reply. I knew he disbelieved me but was either too tired or too kind to contradict.

When the meal was ready, Mr. Granger brought the children downstairs to eat. They wanted to see their father, but Jonathan told them he was sleeping, and they must be good little children and let him rest. They ate somberly, even the youngest, still just a baby. Jonathan beckoned to his father, and quietly they slipped outside to the barn, where I imagined them looking over the scene of the terrible act.

Later, I put the three youngest children to bed and returned downstairs to find Jonathan gently asking Daniel to tell them all he remembered about the two men. Daniel repeated the story, adding little to what he had told us earlier, but I listened intently to each detail, certain he would confirm what I had already decided: The two men must have been the two slave catchers who had visited Elm Creek Farm the previous autumn. The greatest evil I had ever heard of and the greatest evil I had ever seen had become intermingled in my mind, so that I could not picture the crime without seeing those two slave catchers in the place of the horse thieves.

I waited for Daniel to provide the details that would prove my convictions true, but once more he said although he had run outside at the sound of the gunshot, he had glimpsed only the men's backs as they rode off, heading west, away from Creek's Crossing.

"Did your father have any enemies?" asked Mr. Granger.

"Yes," said Daniel venomously. "Those g—— Abolitionists."

Shocked, I looked to Jonathan, who gave me the barest shake of his head to warn me to be silent. "Why would Abolitionists wish to kill your father?" asked Jonathan.

"Because they know what Pa thinks of them, and they came to quiet him, just as Pa always said they would. They always want to kill a man who thinks different than them." Suddenly he exploded with anger. "I know why they wanted our horses, too. So those g—— Abolitionists could ride 'em to Kansas. My pa says all the g—— Abolitionists should go the h—— to Kansas if they want and leave us alone, and I wish they would, I wish they would!"

The words choked out of him as he struggled not to cry. I wept inside to see so much hatred and pain in such a young boy, but I stood frozen, helpless, unable to comfort him and afraid that he would learn Abolitionists were in his house that moment, and that his father's life was in their hands.

But Jonathan knew exactly what to do. He clasped the boy's

shoulder and said, "We do not know who committed this terrible act, but you were very brave to try to help. You tended your father well during the storms, and you came for me as soon as you were able. I'm sure your father is very proud of you, and he'll tell you so himself, when he wakes up."

He said this, I knew, believing Daniel's father would never wake.

Mr. Granger had to return home to care for his livestock, but Jonathan, Mrs. Granger, and I remained, tending to Mr. Wilbur through the night and watching over the children. By the next morning, Mr. Wilbur had been taken with a fever. He lived two days more, but then, as Jonathan had foretold, he perished.

Mr. Granger and other men from town saw to the burial. Jonathan saw me back to Elm Creek Farm. It seemed as if months had passed since last I had been there.

We did not speak as we rode along. I do not know what thoughts occupied Jonathan, but I worried about the young Wilbur children, now orphaned, and wondered what would become of them. And although I tried to tell myself the two men were surely long gone, my heart quaked with fear knowing that two murderers had come among us and might yet lurk nearby.

"Why did Daniel believe them to be Abolitionists?" I heard myself ask.

Jonathan was silent for a long moment before he spoke. "It is no secret that Wilbur supports the Southern cause. I know he earned at least one bounty by informing upon a family that helped escaping slaves." He paused again. "L., the man who owned Elm Creek Farm before your brother—he and Wilbur were friends, and of like minds in this."

I nodded to show that I understood, but I felt bile rise into my mouth, picturing our barn the scene of the recent crime, and Hans bearing Mr. Wilbur's fatal wound. "Do you think Daniel was right?" asked I. "Could Abolitionists have done this?"

"I do not and cannot believe that," said Jonathan. "Likely the men were common horse thieves. What troubles me is that young Daniel is firmly convinced otherwise. His father taught him hatred well, and I do not know if such a deeply planted belief can ever be uprooted."

"You knew Mr. Wilbur hated Abolitionists, and yet you helped him."

He looked at me, surprised. "Of course."

I said nothing more, and yet I marveled at him. Creek's Crossing and all the country had begun to whisper of a conflagration to come, in which Free Staters and slaveholders would fight in every corner of the nation as they were now fighting in Kansas Territory and Missouri. And yet Jonathan had struggled to save the life of this man who was already his enemy, and who might one day desire to kill him. He had fought with all his strength and skill, persisting even when he knew all hope was lost. He had tried to save the man even when he knew he would fail, because it was right, because it was necessary, because to Jonathan even the life of an enemy was precious.

Mrs. Engle, who had known Mrs. Wilbur well, wrote to her family informing them of Mr. Wilbur's passing. Mrs. Wilbur's sister replied, requesting that the farm be sold and the proceeds used to send the children to her and her husband. Within weeks the matter was settled and the children were on their way to Missouri.

I do not know what became of them after that.

6

Grace examined the photos of Margaret Alden's quilt under a magnifying glass, but although she did not find any fabrics that definitely matched the three at Elm Creek Manor, she could not rule out the possibility. One cotton print in particular, an overdyed green print of leaves scattered on a black background, seemed to appear in all four quilts, but without actually seeing Margaret Alden's quilt, Grace could not say for certain.

Sylvia was so confounded by the newly revealed contradictions between folklore and historical fact that she did not know how to react to Grace's conclusions. She felt that she had come to know Gerda quite well, and she was certain Gerda could not have left Elm Creek Farm to become a slave owner—and Margaret Alden's ancestor—in South Carolina. Still, although the responses of her quilt campers proved that Elm Creek Manor could make a strong impression on its residents, she could not believe a mere casual visitor would have stitched such a tribute to it. If not for the quilted picture of Hans's unique barn and the overdyed green cloth possibly linking the four quilts, Sylvia could convince herself the so-called Elm Creek Quilt had nothing to do with the Bergstrom estate, despite the nickname Margaret's grandmother had applied to it. One thing was certain, however: Whatever location the quilt immortalized, the quilter had more than a passing acquaintance with it. The unknown quiltmaker's desire to remember that place forever was evident in every stitch.

Before her week of camp concluded, Grace photographed Sylvia's quilts and promised to further investigate the fabrics and patterns. "In the meantime, keep reading that memoir," said Grace, as she bid her friend good-bye Saturday after the Farewell Breakfast.

"I most certainly will," Sylvia assured her, but that was not all she had planned. She would write to Margaret that very day and ask her for more information about her family history, including any other family quilts possibly sewn by the same quilter. And a week hence she would welcome a professor from Penn State to Elm Creek Manor. She had invited him to study the half-buried log that might be what remained of the Bergstrom's cabin, and was pleased by his enthusiastic acceptance.

As the weekend passed, Sylvia frequently took up the memoir with the intention of reading on, but instead she found herself returning to the passage in which Gerda described how she and Anneke had passed the bitter January storms by sharing stories of their lives back in Germany. Sylvia wished with all her heart that Gerda had recorded those stories. She ached to know what Gerda and Anneke had learned about each other in those four days. Instead her ancestor teased her with glimpses into the past—Anneke's childhood, the daily life of Hans's immediate family—and left her with a thirst for knowledge she doubted even Gerda's memoir could fully quench.

But on Monday, before the evening program, Summer provided her with a small but satisfying taste.

Surmising that Mr. Wilbur's murder would have shaken the town, Summer had returned to the Waterford Historical Society's archives and searched the *Creek's Crossing Informer* microfiche. Sure enough, news of the murder occupied a prominent position in the January 15, 1858, edition, but Summer also found several smaller articles in subsequent issues, which she printed out and proudly delivered to Sylvia.

"'Local Man Murdered in Cold Blood,'" said Sylvia, reading the headline aloud. "Dear me."

"The story mentions Jonathan," said Summer, and Sylvia needed no further inducement to read on:

LOCAL MAN MURDERED IN COLD BLOOD!

FOUR CHILDREN ORPHANED

Mr. Charles Wilbur, a longtime resident of Creek's Crossing, was shot in his barn by persons unknown six days ago. He was said to have interrupted two men as they were engaged in stealing his horses, and though he was unarmed, they fired upon him as he made to depart. Mr. Wilbur's eldest son responded to the sound of gunfire in a brave attempt to defend his father, but arrived too late to see who committed this cowardly and heinous act. The youth sustained his father's life for four days with only his younger siblings to assist him, their mother being dead, but he could not summon help, for like many of us his family was snowbound during the most recent spate of storms. Dr. Jonathan Granger arrived to find the victim yet drawing breath, but despite prodigious skill, the doctor was unable to preserve his life.

It is said that the two murderers and would-be horse

thieves left the Wilbur farm heading west and that they will probably not return, but all citizens should keep a sharp eye out for suspicious strangers entering the town and take care to lock up their horses at night.

Mr. Wilbur will be laid to rest on Sunday at the First Lutheran Church with a sermon by Reverend Lawrence Schroeder. The Ladies' Aid Society is seeking contributions for the unfortunate children orphaned by this outrageous crime.

Another article, dated January 20, announced a "Covered-Dish Supper" at the First Lutheran Church to raise money for the four Wilbur children, and a second, published a few days later, reported that the event had raised thirty-two dollars and praised the residents of Creek's Crossing for their generosity. The last of Summer's articles, dated February 2, stated that the culprits had not been caught, although a trail of horse thefts and attempted murders suggested that the two men had headed west and south, on a meandering course "to escape justice in the lawless West."

Sylvia read the articles again more carefully, not surprised that neither Hans nor Anneke appeared in any of the stories, but disappointed that Gerda, who might have been mentioned for her role in caring for Mr. Wilbur before his death, was not named either.

As far as the *Creek's Crossing Informer* was concerned, Gerda might have spent those harrowing days secure within her own home—which only strengthened Sylvia's reluctance to rely on the official historical record alone.

Spring and autumn 1858— in which we build our new home

The murder of Mr. Wilbur transformed our town, making even the bravest wary of strangers. It also widened the ideological divide between the Abolitionists and those sympathetic to the slaveholder. The Abolitionists were convinced the two would-be horse thieves had been slave catchers, seeking fresh mounts upon which they would pursue their unfortunate prey. Most anti-Abolitionists, among them Mrs. Engle, insisted the murderers were Abolitionists, stealing horses for escaped slaves to ride to Canada. Others believed as her son did; Cyrus Pearson wrote an editorial in the paper declaring that the two men wanted to steal the horses for Abolitionists planning to settle in Kansas Territory, where they would skew the electorate and make Kansas a Free State. He called for "all just Men of our Virtuous City" to donate money and arms to send to "our Brethren whose blood has watered the fair fields of Missouri."

"If the Engles care for Missouri so much, they would do well to move there," I grumbled, "and spare the just people of our virtuous city any further diatribes."

"If you don't like what they write in the newspaper, don't read it," snapped Anneke.

"How will I know whether I like what is in the newspaper," said I, "unless I first read it?"

I should not have baited her, but each time she defended the Engles, I grew more irritated. I understood that Mrs. Engle was her friend and employer, but Anneke owed them no loyalty in matters of politics and virtue. In my opinion, which I would have given if asked, Anneke should have left Mrs. Engle to start her own shop, or obtained a position with the tailor, whose wife was one of the Certain Faction and whose dislike of slavery was well known. Anneke would have done so immediately if Hans had asked, but he did not, and I knew he would not. Hans would neither condemn the Engles and their ilk nor support them, preferring to deal equitably with all. This was not merely a businessman's pragmatics on his part; he had told me once that the argument over slavery was not his fight, and that he had no desire to make it so. I believed that his silence lent his tacit support to the Southern cause, but I could not persuade him of this and eventually gave up trying.

Hans did have one decided opinion: Abolitionists or slave catchers, the men were clearly dangerous, and having killed once, they might kill again. Thus did my brother, who had since our arrival at Elm Creek Farm sheltered his horses better than his family, become determined to build us a house with firm stone walls. With the help of Thomas and Jonathan, he broke ground as soon as the soil thawed enough to give way to a pickax.

As other farmers prepared for the spring planting, Hans helped them clear away stones from their fields, exchanging his labor for the stones. He hauled some from riverbanks and creek beds, many from our own land, and others from the countryside for miles around. One large limestone boulder he delivered to a stonecutter, and when it was returned to us, it had been squared off and engraved with the words "Bergstrom 1858." Hans, Anneke, and I each placed our hands upon it and together laid it in place at the northeast corner of the foundation.

Upon this cornerstone, we built our home.

It was a magnificent house by the standards to which we had become accustomed. Two stories and attic, four rooms downstairs and five above, with a kitchen and a fireplace and all the comforts we had longed for throughout those cold winter months in Mr. L.'s cabin. Anneke had saved all her earnings since going to work for Mrs. Engle, and now she poured them into the house, ordering glass windows and a cunning new cookstove, as well as other furnishings. By day I helped Hans in the fields so that he could have more time to work on the house; by night I took on Anneke's share of the housework so that she might accept more work from Mrs. Engle. My brother and sister-in-law devoted themselves to this grand project knowing they would live out their days within those walls; I worked with no less fervor, but with an increasing hope that I might yet have a home of my own someday, and not be dependent upon their kindness forever.

Still, with a superstitious fear that yet embarrasses me, I furnished my own room with special care, as if anticipating my departure would delay it forever. To the bed Hans had made me I added a desk with a comfortable chair, a bookcase, and a table for my washbasin and lamp. Anneke taught me to braid a rag rug for the floor, and sewed curtains for me rather than allow me to waste precious fabric attempting to make them myself. My hope chest I placed at the foot of my bed, and the bed itself I covered with my Shoo-Fly quilt, at last completed.

I had hastened to finish that quilt so that I might sleep under it our first night in the house. That is the only excuse I will make for the glaring error I discovered in it once it was fully spread out upon the bed. In one block, rather than sew the four corner triangles with the vertices touching the central square, I had arranged them pointing out. Naturally, I had not placed this errant block on an edge where it might have been easily hidden, nor in the exact center, where I could pretend I had intentionally contrived a variation on the design, but off to one side near the top, as conspicuous as could be.

At first, I thought I must promptly fix the mistake, but then I recalled all the hours I had spent cutting and piecing and quilting, and I could not bear to undo any of that labor, even to fix an obvious mistake. At last, exasperated with myself, I decided that no one would see the quilt but myself, and since I would rather have the quilt finished than perfect, I decided to leave it as it was. If I did happen to invite a friend into my room, the artful placement of a pillow would disguise the flaw.

But for Dorothea's first visit I did not hide my error but left it in plain sight, knowing she would enjoy a good laugh with me about it. To my amazement, however, Dorothea did not notice the mistake until I prompted her to search for it! Once alerted, her experienced eye found it immediately, and she consoled me with assurances that the quilt was nonetheless lovely. I retorted that it was warm, and it was done, and that was all that truly mattered to me, although it would have been nice to show off my handiwork at the next meeting of the Certain Faction as was customary whenever a member completed a project. Now I considered my quilt unworthy of such a display.

Dorothea told me I must bring it anyway, mistakes and all. "No one needs to know you did not intend to alter the pattern," added she with a gentle smile. "Tell them it is a humility block."

I had never heard of such a thing, and so Dorothea explained that some would consider it a sin of pride if one attempted to create something without flaw, for only God can create perfection. Therefore, a quilter might deliberately place an error in her quilt as a sign of her modesty and humbleness.

I found this quite amusing and promised Dorothea that my quilt would be in no danger of achieving perfection even if I had not sewn that particular block incorrectly. In fact, it seemed to me an even greater sin of pride to assume that one needed to add intentional flaws to one's handiwork lest it approach the perfection of the Divine. I told Dorothea so, and she laughed and agreed that perhaps the humility block was invented by a quilter less able to admit her own mistakes than I, and was used more frequently to explain unintentional mistakes than for its ostensible purpose.

Still, even with the glaring error in my quilt, I was pleased with the simple comforts of my room, but it seemed Spartan in comparison to the room Anneke and Hans shared, with its frilly bed curtains, dainty pillows, and double-ruffled draperies. I choked on silent laughter, imagining my brother surrounded by such pretty things so unsuited for him, but he did not mind, or if he did, he did not complain. Of course, he usually collapsed into bed at night thoroughly exhausted and rose before dawn, so perhaps he never saw the furnishings by the light of day.

But it would be unfair to make light of Anneke's handiwork without giving her credit for assuring our comfort as she increased her sewing skills. The designs she practiced on her own home later appeared in items she created for her customers. There was nothing created by thread and cloth that Anneke could not duplicate, simply by viewing it, without benefit of a pattern or instruction. She could make an elaborate gown after glancing at a drawing in a magazine, or piece a quilt block from memory, having seen the original hanging out to dry as she rode through town.

As much as I then admired my sister-in-law's talent, I cannot now think back on it without a curious mixture of pride and remorse. If not for her gift, we would have been spared the trials that awaited us—and yet, remembering the good we did, I cannot wish she had never picked up a needle. I would not have changed what Anneke's talent and fate conspired to bring our way; I would banish only the fear that led to our undoing.

At the time, of course, I knew only the comfort Anneke's gift brought to our home. She transformed simple calicoes into curtains and tablecloths; with the scraps from her dressmaking she pieced quilts enough to warm every bed in the house several times over. I saw her piecing smaller quilts, too, from the most delicate cottons and softest wools, but since she made no announcement and I saw no change in her manner, I concluded that she and Hans had not yet been blessed with a recipient for these tiny quilts.

I was stumbling along on my second quilt, a Variable Star, when Anneke began piecing what must have been her twentieth, or so it seemed to one as clumsy with a needle as I. Unlike her previous quilts comprised of individual blocks, this one was fashioned of squares and triangles arranged in vertical stripes. "What do you call this pattern?" asked I, curious.

She looked up from her work, startled, and only then did I realize she had thought me lost in a book and herself unobserved. "I do not know the name."

"It's quite pretty. Is it a design of your own invention?"

"No. I saw the block in one of Dorothea's quilts. She did not say it was an original design, so I saw nothing wrong in duplicating it."

"I'm not accusing you of stealing her patterns," said I, surprised by her defensive tone. "Beside, even if it were an original design, I'm sure Dorothea wouldn't mind your using it. She would probably be flattered."

"I suppose so," said she, more conciliatory. "But she behaved so oddly when I asked her about the quilt. When I remarked that the pattern was different from the styles she usually prefers, she simply smiled at me, and when I asked her the name of the pattern, she pretended not to hear me and began a conversation with someone else."

This sounded very unlike Dorothea. "Perhaps she truly did not hear you. Or perhaps you misunderstood her."

Anneke regarded me skeptically. "My English is not *that* bad."

I said nothing more on the subject, uncomfortable hearing criticism of my friend. In all likelihood Anneke had misunderstood Dorothea, but even if she had not, I could think of many reasons why Dorothea would not divulge details about her quilt. Perhaps it was in fact an original design she did not wish to share, or perhaps the quilt was intended as a surprise gift for Thomas, and Dorothea feared Anneke would carelessly give away the secret.

As time passed, and I saw no further evidence of discord between my sister-in-law and my friend, the conversation slipped into the back of my mind. By the time Anneke's quilt was complete, I had forgotten about the exchange entirely, until later events promptly evoked the memory. There were so many other things to think about: the unrelenting work around the farm, the Certain Faction, Jonathan, and our new home, which was taking shape stone by stone.

In hindsight I do not know how we managed it, but by autumn both abundant crops and a new house had risen from the soil of Elm Creek Farm. The first Bergstrom Thoroughbred foals had sold for better prices than even Hans had expected. Anneke's reputation as a seamstress had spread beyond Creek's Crossing, so that Mrs. Engle raised her wages rather than risk having her become a competitor. We rejoiced in the fruits of our labor and assured ourselves that only prosperity and happiness awaited us, just over the horizon.

We did not hear the distant thunder.

ꕥ

"This can't be right," murmured Sylvia.

Andrew looked up from the fly he was tying in preparation for his next fishing trip. "What can't be right?"

"Gerda's memoir." Sylvia hardly knew what to make of it. "She writes that they built the original house in 1858, which I knew, since that's the date engraved on the cornerstone. However, my grandfather was supposed to have been present when they placed the cornerstone, but Gerda expressly states that Anneke and Hans had not yet had any children."

"Are you sure Gerda is the one who has it wrong?"

"I'm not sure of anything anymore," said Sylvia. "Gerda's is most likely the correct version." She wondered why the incongruity troubled her so much. It was hardly the first or even the most drastic she had encountered in the memoir.

"It's probably only a matter of a few years," said Andrew. "It's no surprise a few details got garbled over time."

"That's precisely the problem. I can't help wondering what else has been garbled." Sylvia could feel the first stirrings of a headache, and she rubbed absently at her temples. "It's bad enough to discover that Hans was indifferent to the Abolitionist movement, and Anneke—well, she was far worse, wasn't she? If I didn't know better, I wouldn't be surprised to discover she is the ancestor Margaret Alden and I have in common."

"Don't forget, you're only getting Gerda's side of the story," said Andrew. "The memoir's from her point of view. If you read Hans's memoir, or Anneke's, things might look a lot different."

Sylvia knew Andrew was trying to help, but his observation made her feel worse. The only factual evidence she had was what Anneke had stitched into her quilts and what Gerda had recorded in her memoir, but Grace had made her doubt the authenticity of Anneke's handiwork and now Andrew wanted her to question Gerda's. "If only I had some other record, something to fill in the gaps as well as corroborate what Gerda wrote."

"Summer could search the historical society's archives again."

"But only if I knew what to tell her to look for." She sighed, frustrated. "Why *didn't* Hans and Anneke cooperate by leaving journals of their own? I'd settle for a page or two from Great-Aunt Lucinda, as fanciful as her stories were."

"Was Lucinda your grandfather's elder sister or younger?"

"Younger, although by how much, I don't recall." Suddenly

inspiration struck. "Oh, my word. Why didn't I think of it before?"

"Think of what?"

"My mother's Bible," Sylvia called over her shoulder as she hurried out of the sitting room and through the kitchen, startling the cook and his assistant as she passed. By the time Andrew caught up with her, she was halfway down the hall. "It's the family Bible," she explained as they crossed the grand foyer on their way to the carved oak staircase. "Claudia and I were allowed to look at it, but only as my mother held it open for us as we sat on her lap. It was her grandmother's, an heirloom from her side of the family, and she forbade us to touch it without permission. After she died—well, I suppose it sounds foolish, but even as a grown woman I never felt comfortable handling my mother's Bible." Not since that day soon after their mother's death, when Claudia had found her reading it in her refuge, a large, smooth stone beneath a willow tree on the bank of Elm Creek. Claudia had snatched the Bible away and scolded her for taking Mother's treasured possession outside. Sylvia had not touched the Bible since then, but she knew where it would be, if Claudia had not sold it as she had so many of the family's other prized possessions.

Andrew followed Sylvia upstairs to the second floor and down the hallway to the library, where, always the gentleman, he quickened his pace so he could open one of the double doors for her. "So this Bible kept a record of the Bergstrom family milestones—births and deaths and what have you?"

"Births and deaths, marriages and baptisms, all the usual things," said Sylvia. "But as it was my mother's family Bible, the records preceding her marriage to my father are for her family, the Lockwoods."

"Then how will it help?"

"It might not," admitted Sylvia. "But my mother was a conscientious woman, and she would have wanted us to know about our father's ancestors as well as her own. I trust she would have left some record of them."

Sylvia went to the center of the room, which spanned the width of the far end of the south wing. Bright morning sunlight streamed in through the tall windows on the south and east walls, while those on the west wall still had curtains drawn over them. Between the windows stood oak bookcases, their shelves lined with books. Not long after Sylvia's return to Elm Creek Manor, she had hired Sarah to help her prepare the estate for auction. Sarah's first assignment—aside from sweeping the veranda, which didn't really count—was to clean this very room. Sylvia had told her to save what looked worthwhile and toss the rest, dismissing Sarah's hesitant suggestion that Sylvia ought to decide that for herself rather than risk her discarding something important out of ignorance. Surely Sarah would have known to save a Bible, a fine, leather-bound Bible. But there had been so many books, and the library had been so cluttered then, and Sylvia so hard-hearted and uncaring about anything to do with the estate . . .

She went to the first bookcase. "It had a black leather cover," she told Andrew, who had gone to a bookcase on the opposite wall. "Old, but not worn."

"We'll find it," said Andrew reassuringly, as if he sensed her apprehensions. Which, of course, he almost certainly did. Sylvia paused to watch him fondly as he studied the spines of the books before him, head tilted slightly, brow furrowed in concentration. Then she set herself to work.

Minutes passed in silence as they scanned the shelves, occasionally removing a thick volume with no markings on the cover in order to examine the pages. When one bookcase was finished, they moved on to the next, working down their opposite walls toward the fireplace at the far end of the room. When only one bookcase remained on her side, Sylvia heard Andrew say, "I think I've found it."

She quickly joined him. "Where?"

He nodded to the top shelf. "Up there."

Sylvia followed the line of his gaze to find a black leather book embellished with two thin gold lines above and below the words "Holy Bible." The sight called forth a distant memory, and she suspected they had found it, although it looked much smaller than she remembered.

"I believe that's the one," she said. "Would you get it down for me, please?"

Andrew reached for the book, then hesitated and let his arm fall to his side. "No."

Sylvia stared at him. "No?"

"Not unless you say you'll marry me."

"Andrew, please. I'm in no mood for games."

"This is no game. I mean it."

Sylvia scowled at him and strained to reach the book, but her fingertips only brushed the leather cover. "Stop teasing me and get the Bible down. Please," she remembered to add.

But Andrew merely folded his arms. "You can stretch all you want, but we both know you're not tall enough."

"I'm plenty tall," she retorted, straining for the top shelf once more, hating to admit Andrew was right. "Well, Matthew is taller than you. I'll get him to help me, if you're going to be difficult."

She began to march out of the library, but Andrew called after her, "Don't bother. When Matt gets up here, I'll talk him out of it."

"And what makes you think he'll listen to you instead of me?"

Andrew shrugged. "I think most folks around here would like to see us get married."

"Well, *I* think most folks would agree you've finally lost your marbles."

Andrew allowed a smile. "Maybe I have. Or maybe I'm just taking a lesson from Hans. When he wanted something, he took charge, didn't he? Look how he got Anneke to marry him."

Sylvia cast her gaze to heaven. "Oh, certainly, he's a fine example to follow."

"I love you at least as much as he loved Anneke, and we've known each other much longer than they did." He reached for her hands, and grudgingly, she allowed him to take them. "Come on, Sylvia, say yes."

"I can get the book down myself, you know. All I need to do is fetch a chair."

"I know. But I hope you won't."

"You wouldn't really want me to accept under these circumstances, would you? Knowing you had to blackmail me into marrying you?"

"At this point, I'll take what I can get."

"Andrew . . ." She studied him, dismayed to see that he was in earnest. "What if I promise that I won't marry anyone but you?"

He was silent for a long moment, but then he asked, "Is that the best you can do?"

"I'm afraid so."

"Then I guess I'll have to settle for that." Abruptly he released her hands, then reached up for the Bible. Without meeting her gaze, he handed it to her and strode quickly from the room.

Sylvia watched him go. He ought to know better; he *did* know better. Why would he ask her again, when he had agreed not to, when he knew she would refuse? Had he been dishonest with her when he had made that promise, and had he been hoping all along that she would change her mind, or had he simply found his promise impossible to keep?

What would she do if he decided he could no longer continue as they had been? If the alternative was to lose him, something she did not think she could bear . . .

"I would manage," she said, determined. She had managed alone for decades, and now, with Elm Creek Quilts and her friends, she would not be alone even if Andrew drove away in his motor home and never returned. She would not marry him out of fear or guilt. If he was willing to take her on those terms, then he was no man she wanted as a husband, or even as a friend.

Resolute, she seated herself at the large oak desk on the east side of the room and examined the cover of the book Andrew had handed her. Yes, it was certainly her mother's Bible, and it looked almost exactly the way she remembered it, little changed despite the passage of time. She turned to the first page, to the records of births and deaths and marriages written in several different hands. The last entries were her mother's.

Sylvia's heart welled up with sadness as she gently ran a finger over the lines her mother had written so many years before. The last entry recorded the birth of Sylvia's brother, Richard; no one had thought to record her mother's own death a few months later. If she had lived seventeen more years, she would have written of her son's passing, and that of her husband, her son-in-law, and her only grandchild, born too early to survive.

Sylvia sighed and closed her eyes. Too many of her memories were of people she loved dying too soon. Perhaps that was why she cultivated so many friendships among the young; she was hedging her bets that she'd be the one mourned rather than the mourner for a change.

It was a morbid thought, but she couldn't help a wry chuckle. She opened her eyes and turned the page, promising herself she would return to study her mother's side of the family more carefully another time. Neglecting the Lockwoods' history in favor of the Bergstroms' had been an inevitable consequence of growing up at Elm Creek Manor, but Sylvia could and would remedy that situation.

Today, however, she had another mission. She turned several pages of blank lines where her mother had expected her descendants to continue the family record, until she came to the last space. The facing page would have been blank, except for a few words written in her mother's careful script at the bottom. Between the two pages was a folded sheet of paper.

Sylvia slipped on her reading and quilting glasses, which hung by a fine chain around her neck, and scanned the page. The first words were her parents' names and birthdates; beneath them and connected to the line above by a vertical line were Sylvia's own name and birthdate and her sister's.

A family tree, Sylvia realized, except her mother had never completed it.

She carefully unfolded the piece of paper inserted between the book's pages. Again her mother's handwriting caught her eye, but this time the script seemed less precise, as if the words had been hastily written:

> My Freddy (the eldest), his younger brothers Richard, Louis, (both killed in Great War) and William, sister Clara (died age thirteen in influenza epidemic).
>
> Their parents: David Bergstrom, Elizabeth Reece (Reese?) Bergstrom
>
> David's siblings: Stephen, Albert, Lydia, George, Lucinda (definitely youngest), David the eldest or 2nd? Was Stephen or Albert his twin?

Their parents: Hans Bergstrom and Anneke (maiden name?) Bergstrom

Anneke's family?

Hans Bergstrom's siblings: Gerda Bergstrom (married name?) Others? Freddy unsure—ask Lucinda.

"Didn't you ask?" exclaimed Sylvia in dismay, turning over the page in case the list continued on the other side. It was blank, leaving Sylvia with a brief list of names that failed to provide her with the information she had sought, and also posed new questions. How was it that the names of David's five brothers and sisters were known, but not their birth order? Did the parenthetical remark after Gerda's name indicate she had eventually married—and had she married Jonathan? And what was this about David—Sylvia's grandfather—having a twin?

No wonder her mother had not completed the Bergstrom family tree, when so little was known of its branches. Sylvia leafed through the rest of the Bible, hoping in vain to find another page of notes or some other clue, but she found nothing more. Sighing, she closed the Bible and was about to return it to the shelf, but she couldn't resist one more look at her mother's handwriting.

My Freddy (the eldest), her mother had written, and later, *Freddy unsure.*

Tears filled her eyes, but Sylvia smiled. She did not remember ever hearing anyone call her father Freddy instead of the more dignified Frederick. It warmed her heart to think of her mother using the endearment, and for a moment she could imagine her parents a young couple in love, celebrating the intertwining of their two family histories in the births of their children. How her mother must have delighted in each detail of her Freddy's heritage, hungering, as young people in love have always done, to know the child her beloved had been, and wishing that they had met as children, so that their love, which she hoped would extend many years into the future, could also be extended into the past, and thus enjoy an even greater duration.

For a lifetime with the man you loved was never long enough—and a mere few years without him, interminable.

Sylvia slowly closed the Bible upon her mother's notes again and returned the book to its shelf.

7

After the Farewell Breakfast the following Saturday, Gwen Sullivan brought her friend from Penn State's archaeology department to Elm Creek Manor to investigate the half-buried log that Sylvia and her friends hoped had been a part of the Bergstrom cabin. Dr. Frank DiCarlo and the two graduate students who had accompanied him examined the site and, to Sylvia's relief, did not criticize them for uncovering it. Instead, the students photographed the log from several angles while DiCarlo quizzed Sylvia about the cabin. She told him the little she knew, pleased to see his interest pique when she mentioned Gerda's memoir.

The students had brought enough tools for themselves and several helpers, so Matt and Sarah offered their services as work began to unearth the rest of the log. Before long Gwen joined in, and when Andrew took a break from working on the motor home's engine and wandered over to check on their progress, he, too, took up a short-handled brush and began sweeping away at the base of the log. Sylvia doubted her back and knees were up to all that crawling around on the ground, so she contented herself with supervising and keeping the archaeology team supplied with water and lemonade, and seeing to it that they took breaks for meals.

As the hours passed under the hot sun, DiCarlo and his assistants gradually uncovered the rest of the first log and another that met at the corner Andrew had discovered the first day. Then, as the light was beginning to fade, one of the graduate students announced that she had found another log directly beneath the first one.

DiCarlo decided it would be best to end for the day on a high note, so after they secured the site, Sylvia invited everyone inside for supper. Gwen alone begged off. "I'm going home to bed," she said with a groan. "I'm too tired even to lift a fork to my mouth."

"I've never seen you that tired," teased Sylvia, but Gwen bid them all good night and walked—slowly and stiffly—back to her car. The others followed Sylvia inside, then upstairs to the rooms she had prepared for them to shower and change. By the time they returned downstairs and joined her in the banquet hall, she and the cook had set a table with a delicious fried chicken dinner with all the trimmings, pitchers of lemonade and iced tea, and a steaming pot of coffee made from fancy beans Sarah had purchased at a café downtown. It seemed too hot for coffee to Sylvia, but Sarah had insisted that graduate students drank pots and pots of the stuff at all hours of the day, in any weather, so Sylvia permitted it.

As they ate, relaxing and enjoying the satisfaction of a day's work well done, DiCarlo entertained them with stories of other archaeological digs they had undertaken. His projects had taken him to so many exotic locales, investigating sites of such historical importance that Sylvia was taken aback, embarrassed that such important research had been set aside for Mr. L.'s humble shack. She tried to apologize, but DiCarlo assured her he was glad to assist. "This is good training for my students," he said, then grinned and added, "Besides, I owe Gwen a favor."

"Well, I feel I owe you a favor," said Sylvia, nodding to his students to indicate she included them, too. "And to think you're doing all this work for what might be nothing more than a pile of old firewood."

The others laughed, and DiCarlo added, "But that's the mystery that makes this job so exciting. You never know what you're going to turn up. Maybe treasure—"

"Maybe trash," interrupted Sylvia.

The two students exchanged a quick look. "Don't get him started," the one seated beside Matt begged, too late, as DiCarlo launched into an earnest description of what could be learned about a culture by studying its long-buried garbage dumps. Some of the details Sylvia would have preferred to hear another time, preferably when she was not eating, but she was fascinated nonetheless.

"If we could find where your ancestors disposed of their trash," DiCarlo concluded, "you'd learn more about them than you ever dreamed possible."

Sylvia winced. "I don't know if I want to know them *that* well."

The others laughed, and Sylvia joined in, pleased to have such enthusiastic new friends to help her uncover the Bergstroms' past—and equally glad that the next morning they would return to unearthing the cabin, not a landfill.

Unfortunately, by noon Sylvia began to suspect that the archaeology team had exhausted all their good luck the previous day. No amount of searching revealed any adjacent logs that might have formed the third and fourth walls of the cabin, nor did there appear to be anything beneath the logs they had already uncovered. DiCarlo thought he found evidence of a fire, but could not say for certain if it was the cabin itself, some object it contained, or merely logs in a fireplace that had burned. One of the graduate students found a tin spoon and what appeared to be a shard from a teacup, which Sylvia cradled in her hands, wondering who had last used them. Aside from those small treasures, the day ended with nothing new to show for their efforts.

"I almost wish we could find the Bergstroms' garbage heap after all," said Sylvia to Sarah as they helped stow DiCarlo's tools in the back of his truck. "But I couldn't imagine where to look for it."

Sarah shrugged and brushed dirt from her hands. "If Matt had been with them, they would have made a compost pile near the garden."

"The garden," gasped Sylvia. "Sarah, you're a genius." Quickly she returned to the dig, where DiCarlo and his students were securing the remains of the cabin. "Professor, it seems I have another archaeological find to show you."

Mindful of the fading light, she led the excavation team back across Elm Creek, past the manor, and into a thick grove of trees to the north. If Sarah had not prompted her memory, Sylvia would have forgotten entirely to show the professor Hans's gazebo.

The story of the gazebo in the north gardens was one of the first she had shared with Sarah about the history of Elm Creek Manor, as they were taking their first tentative steps toward friendship. The octagonal gazebo with the gingerbread molding had been in near ruins then, but the Log Cabin blocks fashioned from wood veneers fitted into its seats were still visible. One of those seats had a block with a black center square, and if pushed in just the right way, the wooden slats folded into a hidden recess beneath the bench like a rolltop desk, revealing a hiding place beneath the gazebo. According to family lore, fugitive slaves would conceal themselves in the hiding place until nightfall, when one of the Bergstroms would escort them into the safety of the manor.

Sylvia repeated the tale to her companions as they walked, but when the gazebo came into view, DiCarlo's expression shifted from intrigue to polite interest. She showed him the Log Cabin blocks and enlisted Matthew's help in pushing back the top to the secret bench, hoping to whet his eagerness again, but before long DiCarlo shook his head.

"I don't know anything about quilt blocks," said DiCarlo. "But I can tell you this gazebo couldn't have been built in your great-grandfather's day. It's far more recent."

"How recent?" asked Sylvia.

Carefully, as if reluctant to disappoint her, he indicated several features that helped him date the structure, including everything from the good condition of the wood to the type of concrete in the foundation to the bolts holding the benches together. "In my estimation, the gazebo doesn't predate the twentieth century."

"It's been refurbished," said Sylvia, unwilling to believe him. "Matthew, tell the professor how you repaired it so he can focus on the original structure."

Matthew complied, but as he listed his alterations, Sylvia realized that DiCarlo had detected the recent work and had accounted for it in his evaluation.

"I don't understand," said Sarah. "If the story about the gazebo isn't true, then—" She broke off at a warning look from Matthew.

"No, go on. You might as well finish the thought." Sylvia sank heavily onto the nearest bench. "If that story isn't true, how can we believe anything my great-aunt Lucinda told me?"

"She described the trunk accurately and gave you the key," said Andrew.

"There is that. Pity. Now I can't simply dismiss her as a pathological liar," said Sylvia dryly. "Then at least I would know everything she told me was false. Now she forces me to sift through her stories, hoping the lies slip through my fingers and the truth remains in my hands."

"I can't believe she would be so malicious as to deliberately deceive you," said Sarah. "Maybe she thought the story about the gazebo was true."

"I suppose." Sylvia sighed and rose. "But that means someone lied to her."

"Or they told her the truth, but she misunderstood," said Andrew.

Despite her disappointment, Sylvia had to laugh. She reached up and patted Andrew's cheek, then smiled at her friends. "You all do try to keep my spirits up, don't you? I appreciate your loyalty to my ancestors, but you don't need to defend them so ardently." She caught Andrew's eye. "I've accepted that the Bergstroms were mere mortals after all."

And one of them had built the gazebo with a hiding place indicated by a Log Cabin block with a black center square—but who, and more puzzling still, since it could not have been done to conceal fugitive slaves, why?

After supper—a more subdued affair than the previous night's meal—DiCarlo and his students vacated their rooms and loaded their belongings into DiCarlo's truck. Before they left, DiCarlo told Sylvia how to properly preserve the site. "You might want to continue the excavation on your own," he suggested. "You might find something we missed."

"Such as a garbage heap?" said Sylvia. "Thank you, Professor, but if you and your students couldn't find anything, I doubt we amateurs will have any better success."

"I know you're disappointed we didn't find more, but don't forget, you did find a cabin exactly where that journal of yours said it would be."

As DiCarlo and his companions drove away, her pride in their discovery rekindled. The professor was right. It did not matter how much of the cabin they had found, only that they now knew with confidence that they *had* found it, and not some mere woodpile or fallen tree. It was enough to know she had found Gerda's first home in America, the first home on Bergstrom land.

Late autumn through December 1858—in which I reap a bitter harvest

The first crisp evenings of autumn meant that harvesttime would soon be upon us, and Elm Creek Farm bustled with activity as we prepared for the coming winter. Anneke offered to make me another dress for the annual Harvest Dance, and this year I promptly accepted, determined to look as lovely as a plain woman could. Jonathan and I had known each other for more than two years, and there was no mistaking his growing affection for me, nor mine for him, although we never spoke of it. I thought any day he might ask me to become his wife, and when he did, I planned to accept with all my heart. The days when I ached for the loss of E. seemed dim and far away.

Anneke sewed me a gown of beautiful lavender silk brocade, and when I tried it on, even Anneke was amazed by my transformation. I felt myself blushing like a young girl as I envisioned the pleasure in Jonathan's eyes when he first beheld me, and when I drifted off to sleep at night, I imagined his hand at the small of my back as he pulled me close to him in a dance. It would not be long, I knew, I hoped, until I would call him husband.

But a week before the Harvest Dance, when I met Anneke at the door of Mrs. Engle's dressmaker's shop, my sister-in-law seemed troubled. "Gerda," said she as she climbed onto the wagon seat beside me. "I have dreadful news."

"Mrs. Engle and Mr. Pearson are finally moving South?"

"This is not a joking matter."

Only then did I see how pale she had become, and how reluctant she was to speak. "Tell me," said I. "Whatever it is, it cannot be that bad."

Anneke took two deep breaths and placed a hand to her stomach before speaking. "Charlotte Claverton came to be fitted for a dress today."

"Did she, indeed?" I had not forgotten the beautiful, dark-haired girl who had been Jonathan's dance partner far too often for my taste the previous autumn, but Jonathan and I had become such intimate friends that I no longer feared her as a rival. "I suppose she wants to cut a fine figure at the Harvest Dance, like the rest of us." Perhaps a tiny spark of jealousy remained. "I don't suppose you'd be willing to sew a few crooked seams just this once?"

"Gerda. It wasn't a dress for the dance. It was her wedding gown."

"She's getting married? How delightful for her."

"She's marrying Jonathan."

Through the ringing in my ears I heard the steady clop, clop, clop of the horse's hooves on the road. I heard wind rustling in the trees as we passed, and the splash of water in Elm Creek.

"Gerda, did you hear me?"

"You must be mistaken." My voice sounded high and thin in my ears, falsely nonchalant. "She can't be marrying Jonathan. Not . . ." *Not my Jonathan,* I almost said.

"She is. I heard her tell Mrs. Engle. They will have a Christmas wedding."

"You must have heard wrong." It took every bit of my strength to get the words out. "Jonathan would have told me himself. He, or Dorothea."

"Gerda—"

"It cannot be true." I shook the reins and urged the horses onward at a faster pace, overcome by the need for home. "I refuse to listen to such nonsense."

Anneke said nothing more, but I could sense her fighting back tears. My mind was a blur of confusion and worry. Anneke believed what she told me; that was certain. She could have been mistaken—but that seemed unlikely. What was there to misinterpret about a woman being fitted for her wedding gown?

At home I began to prepare our supper without a word for Anneke or my brother. She must have told Hans the news when I was outside in the kitchen garden, for all evening he spoke to me with gentle kindness rather than the brotherly teasing to which I was accustomed. I retired early, but I was too sick at heart to sleep. Never in all my conversations with Jonathan had he even hinted that he planned to marry Charlotte Claverton. However, I was forced to admit that neither had he said he wished to marry me.

As the night passed and my apprehensions grew, I subjected my memories to unflinching scrutiny. Had I read too much into Jonathan's attentions? Had I perceived love where there was only friendship? But as I reviewed the past two years once, and again, and again, I could not believe that he did not care for me as much as I cared for him. His words, his actions, the smiles that lit up his face when we greeted each other—no, I concluded, I had not deluded myself. It was improbable that Anneke had misunderstood Charlotte Claverton, but equally so was the idea that Jonathan was in love with someone other than myself.

I held fast to that dim hope and somehow managed to drift off to sleep. I woke a few hours later, the pain in my heart having faded to a dull ache, and remembered it was a Saturday. Jonathan would arrive by midmorning, and we would stroll along Elm Creek together until lunchtime, as we had done every Saturday morning for months. Usually we discussed books or politics or matters of faith, but today I would have no choice but to speak plainly to him regarding ourselves.

But the morning passed, and then midday, and still he had not arrived. With each hour that crawled by, the sickening knot of dread in my stomach tightened. Each moment of his absence made Anneke's rumor seem more credible. I completed my chores for the day, and yet he still had not appeared. Finally I took up my Churn Dash quilt and tried to forget my distress in the rhythm of the stitches, telling myself he would surely arrive before I finished piecing a single block.

Two completed blocks had joined the others in my sewing basket when I finally heard a horse approaching, and then the sound of Jonathan calling out a greeting to my brother as he rode past the barn. I waited for his knock on the door before I set my sewing aside and rose to meet him.

I opened the door, and when I saw Jonathan's expression, all my hopes were destroyed.

"I'm sorry I'm late," said he, his face white and remorseful. "The Watson boy fell from his horse and broke his arm."

"Will he be all right?"

"Yes . . . yes, he'll be fine." He hesitated. "Gerda, may I come in?"

I nodded, not trusting myself to speak. My legs felt so weak that I quickly returned to my chair. I picked up my sewing again, hoping to disguise my grief by feigning normalcy, but my hands trembled so badly that I simply held the pieces in my lap, my eyes fixed upon them. I did not know what to do. I knew that the moment Jonathan spoke, my illusions that I would ever become his wife would vanish for good.

"I understand . . ." He tried again. "I am told you visited Mrs. Engle's dress shop yesterday."

"In a manner of speaking. I waited for Anneke in the wagon. I did not go in."

He nodded and looked around distractedly. "But Anneke—she told you who was inside?"

I could not bear his careful maneuvering as he tried to determine how much I knew. "She did mention one customer. Charlotte Claverton. I believe you are acquainted."

"Gerda, you must let me explain."

"Tell me first if it is true."

"Gerda—" He paced to the fireplace and back. "Yes. It is true. Charlotte Claverton and I will be married in six weeks."

It seemed an eternity until I could speak. "I see."

In a moment he was on his knees beside my chair, his hands grasping mine. "Gerda, I never meant for you to find out this way. I wanted to tell you myself. I tried to tell you so many times, but—"

"But?"

"I found I could not."

I strangled out a laugh. "In the course of all our conversations, you could not find one appropriate moment to mention you were going to be married?"

"I could not—" His voice broke off, and he seemed to struggle to find the words. "I did not, because I knew it would mean the end of our friendship, and I could not bear that."

"You were no true friend to me," said I, coldly.

"I know." He rose and raked a hand through his hair. "I regret that more than you will ever know. But Gerda, you must understand. Charlotte and I have known each other since we were children. Our parents' farms are adjacent properties. We were promised to each other before we knew what that meant. It was always understood that we would marry one day."

I could not believe what I was hearing. "You will marry because your parents arranged it? You, with all your modern ideas, would agree to such a marriage?"

"It is not that simple. When I came of age, I asked for her

hand and made my parents' promise my own. It was expected of me, and I did not know . . ."

"What?"

"That one day I would meet you."

I held his gaze long enough to read the remorse and frustration tearing him apart. "Break off the engagement," I heard myself say.

"It is too late for that."

"No." I shook my head and flew from my chair to his side, where I grasped his hands. "You have not yet exchanged marriage vows, so it is not too late. She has an unfinished gown and a promise made long ago. There will be a small embarrassment, but it will be forgotten soon."

"She thinks she loves me."

"She is a young woman. She will find someone else. If she cares for you, she will not begrudge you your happiness."

"Gerda, I will marry Charlotte." He caressed my cheek with the back of his hand. "I made her a promise. I gave her my word, and I am a man of my word."

I choked back tears. "Your honor is more important than our happiness?"

"I thought you knew me," said he, his voice a quiet rebuke. "Breaking my word would result in the injury of an innocent young woman. You could not expect me to do that merely to satisfy my own desires."

And what of my desires? I wanted to shout, but I knew this would not move him. "Tell me you do not love me and that you do love Charlotte. Tell me this and I will say nothing more on the subject."

He regarded me for a long, silent moment. "I cannot say that."

"Why not?"

"Because it would be a lie. You know I love you."

My heart swelled with grief. At last he had told me what I had so longed to hear, but the words meant nothing now. "Then you do Charlotte no favor by marrying her. She deserves a husband who loves her. If she knew the truth, she would release you from your promise."

He shook his head. "She suspects my affection for you, and yet she still wishes to marry me. As long as she holds me to my promise, I will honor it. And as long as I live, I will be a good husband to her. If I do not in time come to love her as a husband should, she will never know it."

I shook my head vehemently, unable to believe what I was hearing. I wanted to tell him that they were both fools, but I was afraid that if I spoke, I would burst into sobs. And I had too much pride to show him the depth of my grief.

"Gerda, I would not have you despise me for the world. Tell me I have your blessing."

The pleading ache in his voice dissolved my remaining composure. "I wish you and Charlotte every happiness," I choked out, and fled to my room.

I did not hear Jonathan leave, but before long, Anneke came and tried to comfort me. I would not be consoled. I grieved not only for the loss of Jonathan but also in anger and shame, that I should again be humiliated by a man who claimed to love me. I had fled my home in Germany to escape that embarrassment, but this time I could not leave my grief behind. I would remain in Creek's Crossing until the end of my days, where the sight of Jonathan and Charlotte together would again and again tear open the scar over my wounded heart.

Later that evening, Hans took me aside and asked me somberly if Jonathan had ever made any promises of marriage to me. I shook my head, and Hans nodded in relief. "If I thought he had misled you," said he, "I would not allow him to set foot on my farm again."

"It is I who misled myself." At that moment I vowed I never would again.

Naturally, after that, Jonathan refrained from visiting Elm Creek Farm, and I could not bear to call on the Nelsons. I missed the Certain Faction and longed for Dorothea's company, and yet I could not help but bear a smoldering anger for her, my dearest friend. She must have known about her brother's engagement, and yet she had said nothing, despite witnessing the growing affection between Jonathan and me. I could not understand her silence, and I resented her for it.

A week passed, and the day of the Harvest Dance arrived. I had no intention of going, but Anneke entreated me. "You must not let anyone see that you have been hurt," said she. "You will wear the lavender silk brocade and look lovely in it, and you will hold your head high. Don't cower at home as if you are the one who acted shamefully."

Her bitterness surprised me, and only then did I realize she had not mentioned Jonathan's name the entire week. "He never lied to me," said I, unwilling to hear him criticized.

"No, but he knowingly deceived you, and that is just as bad."

I was unused to Anneke's anger, so I agreed to attend the dance rather than argue. And as difficult as it was, I obeyed her instructions. I danced with other men as if I did not long for Jonathan's embrace. I expressed delight when the news of the engagement spread through the gathering, and wondered aloud with everyone else how they had managed to keep it a secret so long. When Anneke and I crossed paths with Jonathan and Charlotte as they left the dance floor, I gave them my best wishes for a long and happy marriage, conscious of the watchful eyes upon me.

Only with Dorothea could I not disguise my true feelings. I knew this as soon as I saw her arrive on Thomas's arm. She called out to me, but I pretended not to hear, and for the rest of the evening, I avoided her.

I would have happily avoided Cyrus Pearson as well, but to my chagrin, he sought me out. Three times I managed to snatch another partner before he could ask me for a dance, but the fourth time, he shouldered some other fellow aside and grabbed my hand. "Well, if it isn't the lovely Miss Bergstrom," said he. "At last I have the honor to escort you to the dance floor."

"The honor is mine, Mr. Pearson," said I. Anyone listening would have thought it a cordial exchange, but we knew differently.

"Did you hear the good news?" asked he as we began to dance.

"What news is that?"

"Dr. Granger and Miss Claverton are going to be married." He assumed a look of mock sorrow. "Oh, I suppose you wouldn't consider that good news at all, would you?"

"Of course I would. I'm delighted for them."

"Some people say you aspired above your station and sought to become the doctor's wife."

"Aspired above my station?" I regarded him with feigned astonishment. "My goodness, is this not America, where all are created equal? Did I return to Europe without realizing it?"

His mouth twitched in a scowl, but he persisted. "My mother told me Anneke was quite disturbed when she learned of the engagement. And since you and Dr. Granger's sister are such intimate friends, one naturally assumes—"

Scornfully, I said, "Between your assumptions and my sister-in-law's matchmaking, I should have been married a long time ago."

"Indeed, Miss Bergstrom," said he. "With your great beauty and charming manner, it is a miracle you remain a spinster."

He had guided us to the edge of the dance floor as he spoke, and with those last words, he bowed, released my hand, and left me there. My face flaming, I spun around and returned to the quilt where Anneke and Hans were resting between dances. In a low voice, I begged them to allow us to leave, but Anneke was resolute that I should remain and continue to behave as if all was well. When Hans echoed her, I reluctantly acquiesced, but only after they promised to keep Cyrus Pearson away from me. Anneke frowned, as she always did when reminded how poorly I got along with her employer's eldest son, but they agreed. As it turned out, there was no need; his mission to wound me accomplished, Mr. Pearson spared me no more than a passing glance the rest of the evening.

For the next two weeks, neither Anneke nor I attended the meetings of the Certain Faction. Apparently she did not feel I needed to maintain my facade of indifference before Dorothea, whom she held partially responsible for my disappointment. I assumed I would have to learn to live without Dorothea's friendship as well as Jonathan's love, but Dorothea was unwilling to sacrifice our friendship to her brother's foolishness.

In those days, as a part of their training for married life, young ladies would learn to sew by piecing quilts. It was the custom among some families in our region that a young woman of merit would have completed twelve quilt tops by the time she reached marriageable age. The thirteenth quilt was to be her masterpiece, a sign that she had learned all the womanly arts of needlework she would need as a wife and mother, and these quilts were often elaborate works of appliqué, embroidery, and stuffed work called trapunto. When the young woman became engaged, all the bride-to-be's female friends and relations would gather for a quilting bee, where the thirteen pieced and appliquéd tops would be quilted. These were festive occasions, full of merriment and congratulations for the future bride, and I had attended several since arriving in Creek's Crossing. As the sister of the groom, Dorothea appropriately offered to host Charlotte Claverton's bee, and since the Clavertons were well regarded in society, and Jonathan well respected as the town's only physician, it was seen as the most important social event of the year for the women of the town, even more important than the Harvest Dance.

When Anneke and I received two of those sought-after invitations, my instinct was to throw them on the fire, but Anneke stayed my hand. "If we do not attend, it will confirm the rumors that you resent Charlotte and want her betrothed for yourself."

I did resent Charlotte, and of course I wanted Jonathan, but since I could not have him, I could not bear for the entire town to know it.

Hans considered that reason enough for me to avoid the gathering. "As many people will be watching you as the bride," said he. "You have never been one to conceal your emotions. Your true feelings will be plain for all to see."

It seemed no matter what I did, the people of Creek's Crossing were likely to see a scandal simply because they wished to. Since I could not win, I took Hans's caution as a challenge and decided to attend the quilting bee.

Anneke, whose imperfect English remained a source of embarrassment for her, asked me to respond to the invitation, and so I did, feeling a curious mixture of eagerness and dread with each stroke of my pen. I missed my friends, even Dorothea, who had betrayed me with her silence, and longed for the warmth of their company. I grew weary when I imagined maintaining a pretense of contentment all day under the scrutiny of gossips, but I convinced myself that once that day had ended, the whole sad business would be in the past. And, although many women in my situation would have wished to avoid their rival in her moment of triumph, I hungered to see Charlotte Claverton. We had never spoken except for our brief exchange at the Harvest Dance, and I wanted to take my measure of her. I was convinced that everything I learned about her would confirm that she was a selfish child and a poor match for Jonathan, and that he would have been infinitely happier with me. I needed to confirm this—and I wanted Charlotte Claverton to know me, so that she would reach the same conclusion.

At last the day of the quilting bee arrived, so Anneke and I rolled up our thimbles, needles, and spools of thread in clean aprons and rode to the Nelson farm. I wondered how Dorothea would address me—if she would act as if nothing ill had passed between us, if she would pretend as I was forced to pretend that her brother meant nothing to me. Thomas greeted us when we arrived and took care of the horses while we went inside to join the ladies. I did not realize until that moment how much I had hoped to find Dorothea so eager to apologize that she had waited on the front porch or, better yet, had come halfway down the road to meet me.

Inside, Anneke and I were greeted by joyful embraces of the Certain Faction and friendly welcomes from what seemed to be all the womenfolk living within twenty miles of Creek's Crossing. How like Dorothea, I thought, to invite so many that the house seemed full to bursting, rather than hurt anyone's feelings by excluding them. And not long after, I discovered how inclusive Dorothea's invitation had been: Not only was Mrs. Engle present, but so, too, was Mrs. Constance Wright, a colored woman whose family owned a farm about fifteen miles southwest of ours, as well as a number of other colored women I did not know. I forgot my own turmoil for a moment in looking forward to making their acquaintance—but I will confess, instead of contemplating how I could make these women feel welcome when some present would surely scorn them, I instead looked forward to enjoying Mrs. Engle's discomfort at their presence.

Fortunately, Dorothea treated them with more than enough friendly intimacy to compensate for my defects of character.

The two front rooms of the Nelson home had been given over to the party, and in each a large quilting frame had been set up and chairs arranged alongside. "We seem to have far more willing hands than necessary," I murmured to Anneke, secretly pleased that I might be spared the insufferable chore of helping Charlotte Claverton complete her wedding quilts.

"We will take turns," retorted Anneke, knowing my thoughts, "and you will do your fair share."

I frowned and scanned the crowd in vain for Dorothea or Charlotte. Over the din I heard laughter coming from the kitchen, and I knew at once that I would find Dorothea within. Just then I saw Mrs. Engle approaching, full of smiles for my sister-in-law. Given the choice between confronting Dorothea or forcing polite conversation with the mother of Cyrus Pearson, I decided to brave the kitchen.

Dorothea spotted me as soon as I entered; she immediately broke off a conversation, dusted her hands on her apron, and approached me. "I'm so sorry, Gerda," said she in a murmur so that we would not be overheard.

"You could have told me," said I, shortly, for I still resented her. "You would have spared me a world of pain."

"It was not my secret to tell." She placed a hand on my arm, and her eyes were full of tears. "Gerda, so many times I urged him to tell you the truth. So many times I tried to convince him to reconsider his engagement. He is a fool to marry Charlotte when his heart belongs to you. I told him so, but he would not listen."

Her words—and the heartfelt sorrow with which she spoke them—melted my anger. I had lost Jonathan, but I would not allow my dearest friendship to perish because of it.

Somehow I endured the day. Despite the many eager workers,

there was a great deal of quilting to be done, and although the more experienced quilters set a pace far more brisk than I was accustomed to, I was determined to keep up. I meant to show with every stitch I put into those quilts that I did not covet Charlotte Claverton's husband-to-be.

And although my bitterness had eased with Dorothea's apology, as we finished all thirteen of Charlotte's beautiful quilts, I could not help appraising Charlotte's every word and action. She was obviously my superior in beauty; I provided not the least competition in that regard. She was charming and seemed kind, and everyone from Dorothea to Mrs. Engle was fond of her, although of course Mrs. Engle's esteem hardly held much merit with me. She was, thankfully, an Abolitionist in spirit, although her behavior more closely mirrored Hans's isolationist stance than Dorothea's activism. However, she was unlearned, and reluctant to express an opinion differing from whomever she happened to be speaking with at the moment. With Jonathan's help she could learn, if she was willing, and if she applied herself, but her unwillingness to speak her mind would be more difficult to overcome. I thought of all the conversations—heated debates they were, sometimes—Jonathan and I had shared, and when I pictured him attempting to draw out the same intellectual passion from Charlotte, my heart grew troubled. By the end of the evening, I concluded that indeed Jonathan and I were of like minds and would have made a far more excellent match. But this realization, which I had thought would bring me satisfaction if not peace, instead made me sadder yet.

In the interim between the quilting bee and the wedding, I prayed that the engagement would be called off, that Jonathan would sacrifice his honor to my happiness, or that Charlotte Claverton would release him from his ill-made promise. I wished no harm to befall either one of them, but I sometimes prayed to die before they exchanged wedding vows, for witnessing that, I was certain, would kill me.

It did not, of course. Such ill strokes occur only in romances or in song.

Jonathan and Charlotte married on Christmas Eve, before all their happy friends and one plain woman from Germany who closed her heart around her grief and tried to wish her beloved happiness with the fate he had chosen. Instead, she hoped—I hoped—that he would come to regret his decision, and that he would be as desperately unhappy in marriage as he had made me in my spinsterhood. Today I am ashamed of my bitter thoughts, but on his wedding day, which should have been ours, I could not feel otherwise.

Jonathan took his bride into his parents' home, and when the couple's parents passed on, Dr. and Mrs. Jonathan Granger's inheritances combined to form the largest farm in the county, just as their parents had wished. They fared well, and had four children, and many grandchildren as well, although I do not remember exactly how many. There is no reason why I should remember, since it had nothing to do with me.

Perhaps you wonder, Reader, why I bothered to record these events here. Since I did not marry Jonathan and he did not join the Bergstrom family, it would seem his life had little bearing on the Bergstrom legacy. I assure you, I do not relive those painful days for my own amusement, but because it is important that you know what sort of man he was. Anneke made the choice that condemned us, but with Jonathan's help, she brought about what I hope will be our redemption.

Sylvia sat lost in thought, the memoir resting open on her lap. She longed for some magic that would allow her to reach back into the past and comfort Gerda, whose pain she understood all too well. Their circumstances differed, of course, but both she and Gerda had been forever separated from the men they loved: Sylvia by death, Gerda by marriage.

Memories of her own husband suddenly sparked Sylvia's indignation. Gerda wished the Bergstrom descendants to know what sort of man Jonathan Granger had been—and Sylvia knew, all right. He was a spineless, selfish fool. Even in her anger Gerda seemed to want to excuse his behavior, but Sylvia wasn't buying. He should have told Gerda about the engagement the moment he sensed the growing attraction between them. And what utter nonsense, to marry because one's parents wanted to join two farms together! Gerda was better off without such in-laws, and certainly better off alone than linked for life to a dishonest rascal. Sylvia couldn't imagine why Gerda thought it would be important for future Bergstroms to know about Jonathan, except to warn the young ladies of the family about deceitful young men.

She glanced down at the last page she had read, and frowned when she read the final sentence in the entry. More cryptic allusions that Anneke had done something dreadful. Wondering what on earth her great-grandmother had done to provoke Gerda's harsh judgment was enough to drive Sylvia to distraction.

"Then why don't you just flip through the book until you find the section where she explains?" asked Sarah later that week. The Elm Creek Quilters had gathered in the formal parlor for their weekly business meeting after the Wednesday evening camp activities, and as usual, after these matters had been discussed, they caught up on their personal news.

"She doesn't want to spoil the suspense," said Gwen.

"It would be like peeking at her presents before Christmas morning," added Agnes with a smile.

"That's not it," said Sylvia. "I'm also looking for information about the quilts, something Gerda might have mentioned in passing or something that can only be deduced based upon the context. If I don't read carefully, I might miss the one piece of evidence I need."

"You can always read it more thoroughly later," said Sarah. "Won't you at least skim through it until you find out how Gerda and Jonathan ended up together?"

"Yes, do it," urged Diane. "I mean, was the ceremony invalid for some reason? Did Charlotte die, or what?"

Sylvia studied them. "What makes you think Gerda and Jonathan eventually married?"

They exchanged a look. "I don't know," said Sarah. "I just assumed they did."

"Well, I think it's quite evident they did not." Abruptly Sylvia rose. "Honestly, Sarah. These were real people living real lives, not characters in a storybook. Don't expect a happy ending."

Without another word, she left the room, leaving her friends gaping in astonishment. Halfway to her bedroom, Sylvia regretted letting her temper get the better of her. She considered returning to apologize, but she was in a foul mood, and whatever she said was likely to come out wrong and make matters worse. Fortunately, the Elm Creek Quilters weren't ones to hold grudges. After all, they'd forgiven her for far worse.

Sure enough, the next morning at breakfast, Sarah acted as if nothing had happened. Sylvia was glad her young friend didn't ask her to explain her outburst, because Sylvia wasn't sure what had made her temper flare. She was angry at Jonathan and frustrated that she could do nothing to help Gerda—and she felt foolish for allowing events of the far distant past to affect her so.

Later that afternoon, she returned to her sitting room determined to read on as objectively as she imagined Professor

DiCarlo approached an archaeological dig. She had just picked up the memoir and had settled into her favorite armchair when Summer knocked tentatively on the door frame. "Is it safe to come in?"

"Of course, dear. I've vowed not to act like an ogre today."

Summer grinned. "That's a relief. I left my ogre repellent at home." She sat down on the footstool and placed her backpack on the floor between her feet. "I stopped by the library today."

"And what did you discover?"

In reply, Summer removed a manila folder from her backpack and handed it to Sylvia. Inside was a document, a certificate of some sort, reproduced from microfiche. Quickly Sylvia slipped on her glasses and scanned the page. "Oh, my word."

"It's their marriage certificate, isn't it?" asked Summer, eager. "It has to be them."

"I don't see how it could be anyone else." Sylvia ran a finger along each line as she read aloud. "Dr. Jonathan Granger, Miss Charlotte Claverton—the date is correct, too. December twenty-fourth." Sylvia set down the folder and beamed at Summer. "My dear, you are a wonder."

"You say that, and you didn't even see what else is in the folder."

Quickly Sylvia looked under the first sheet and found a second. "Mr. Hans Bergstrom, Miss Anneke Stahl—" She gasped. "You found my great-grandparents' marriage record!"

"It wasn't difficult, once I found Jonathan's and figured out the filing system." Summer grinned. "But you can go ahead and call me a wonder again, if you like."

"You are certainly that, and many other delightful things as well." Sylvia gazed at the paper and suddenly gasped again. "Anneke Stahl—my goodness, I know her maiden name now. Even my mother didn't know that."

"Now you can add it to your family Bible."

Sylvia nodded as if she had intended to do so all along, but Summer's suggestion caught her by surprise. It had not occurred to her to finish the record her mother had begun, and she could not explain why. Was it a sense of prohibition lingering from childhood, or did she wish to preserve the Bible exactly as her mother had left it? Sylvia had no descendants who would chastise her for failing to fill in the gaps in the family history, and yet leaving the record incomplete didn't feel right.

"I think my mother would have wanted that," said Sylvia slowly. Yes, she was sure of it.

"Sylvia . . ." Summer hesitated. "Because of what Sarah and Diane said, I looked for a marriage record for Gerda and Jonathan. I didn't find one."

"Of course not, dear. I would have been astonished if you had."

"But just because I didn't find the record, that doesn't mean they didn't marry eventually," added Summer hastily. "They could have married after the years I searched, or they could have married somewhere other than Creek's Crossing, or maybe the record was lost—"

"Now, now, Summer. You don't need to keep my hopes alive." Sylvia closed the folder and set it on the table beside her armchair. "Jonathan married Charlotte and that's that. Gerda said quite explicitly that she did not marry Jonathan and he did not join the Bergstrom family. I don't know why Sarah and Diane assumed otherwise."

"Maybe because they wanted it to be true. I know I did." Again Summer paused. "I thought you should know, I also looked for a marriage record for Gerda and Cyrus."

"What?" Sylvia stared at her. "Why on earth for? They despised each other."

"They did in 1858, anyway."

"What do you mean? What did you find?"

"Nothing," said Summer quickly. "I didn't find a record for them."

"Well, my heavens." Sylvia tried to compose herself. "Goodness. You could have said so at the beginning."

"I only meant that their feelings could have changed with time," said Summer, looking as if she was choosing her words carefully in order to avoid alarming Sylvia again. "Would it really be that extraordinary if they fell in love? He did try to court her once. Now Jonathan has abandoned her, she's lonely, and you have to admit, she and Cyrus do have rather intense feelings for each other."

"Yes, intensely negative. Don't you remember what Mr. Pearson wrote in the Creek's Crossing newspaper? How could an Abolitionist like Gerda marry someone like that?"

Summer shrugged, uncomfortable. "Remember that Jonathan and Dorothea were the ones who first introduced Gerda to the Abolitionist movement. They betrayed Gerda. Maybe in anger she turned against everything they believed in."

"I don't accept that." Sylvia frowned and shook her head. "Remember, she was writing in 1895, so she knows how things turned out, even if we don't. There would have been some sign of it in her memoir."

"You're right. It was just a thought. Anyway, it turned out not to mean anything, because I couldn't find a record for them."

"And thank goodness for that," declared Sylvia, as if that put an end to the matter.

But in her heart she knew the question was far from settled. Sylvia's mother had written a comment in the Bible that could mean that she was uncertain of Gerda's married name, unsure whether she had married at all, or both. Cyrus Pearson and his mother had apparently expressed interest in moving to the South. If they had done so, and Gerda had left Elm Creek Farm to marry Cyrus, she might have made a quilt in memory of the home and family she had left behind . . .

No. Quickly Sylvia closed her mind to such thoughts. Even in her disappointment, Gerda would not have turned her back on her principles. Sylvia would not believe it, despite the many inconsistencies and questions a marriage between Gerda and Cyrus would explain.

Sylvia closed the book and shut it firmly away in her desk drawer. If Gerda had married Cyrus, Sylvia would rather not know.

8

If Sylvia's friends noticed she left the memoir untouched the rest of the day, they said nothing about it. Only Andrew mentioned the book, when he reminded Sylvia to pack it for an extended weekend trip to Door County, Wisconsin. They were well into Ohio before Andrew suggested she read aloud from it as he drove, and when Sylvia told him she had left it at home, he merely nodded and turned on the radio instead. Sylvia didn't tell him she had left it behind on purpose, but she suspected he knew.

They spent two days in Sturgeon Bay, where they enjoyed a traditional fish boil and boating on Lake Michigan as the guests of one of Andrew's army buddies and his wife. Then they drove north and west to a campsite overlooking Green Bay, not far from the quaint shops and charming restaurants of Egg Harbor and Fish Creek. Andrew persuaded Sylvia to join him on a tandem bicycle for a jaunt through Peninsula State Park. Sylvia half feared she was in for a teeth-chattering ramble over rocky hiking trails, but Andrew knew all the paved routes from previous visits and only occasionally made her shriek with alarm by steering too close to a tree.

They woke Tuesday morning to the sound of rain pattering on the motor home's roof, but they did not mind the change in the weather, since they had planned to head back that day anyway. Only as they crossed the Illinois border did Sylvia feel melancholy creeping into her thoughts. Although every bit of the heat and humidity felt like summer, the northern Wisconsin forest they had left behind had already begun changing into autumnal hues. She didn't like the reminder that within weeks summer would soon end, and Elm Creek Quilt Camp would conclude for the season. Although Sylvia wasn't as involved with the day-to-day operations as she had once been, she would miss the campers' presence, and the way they filled her home with their laughter and energy.

Andrew spread the drive home to Waterford over three days, giving them plenty of time for sight-seeing along the way. They pulled into the parking lot behind the manor just in time for supper on Thursday evening. In honor of their return, all the Elm Creek Quilters stayed for the meal. It was almost like old times again, back when their business was new, when each day of camp presented unexpected challenges and they were never quite sure if they would survive until the campers left after breakfast on Saturday. Back then they had assured one another that eventually they would fall into a smooth, well-functioning routine, but now that they had, Sylvia occasionally felt nostalgic for the odd calamity that forced them to create solutions out of little more than inspiration and hope.

After supper, she agreed to act as master of ceremonies for the campers' talent show. Of all the evening entertainment programs, this was Sylvia's favorite, for it allowed her guests to express their interests beyond quilting. The shows never failed to be highly entertaining, with musical acts, skits, and other performances that defied classification, delivered with widely varying degrees of talent and polish. New campers put together their acts on the spot, while veterans of previous years often prepared ahead of time. Four members of a quilting guild from Des Moines dramatized a scene from *Little Women,* while three veteran campers, who had discovered a shared interest in the accordion at last year's camp, brought their instruments and performed a medley of Bach cantatas. Best of all, however, was a new camper whose gift for mimicry rendered them helpless with laughter at her impersonations of some of the camp's more vivid personalities. The evening was the best welcome-home present Sylvia could have imagined.

But the talent show was not all that had awaited her.

When she finally bid her friends good night, kissed Andrew, and retired to her room, she found her mail stacked neatly on her bedside dresser. She crawled into bed, snuggled beneath her blue and gold LeMoyne Star quilt, and thumbed through the envelopes. A return address from South Carolina caught her eye, and she realized it was a letter from Margaret Alden.

Apprehensive, Sylvia set the other letters aside and opened the envelope.

August 13, 2001

Dear Sylvia,

I hope this letter finds you and your friend Andrew well. Your program for the Silver Lake Quilters' Guild received rave reviews. We all hope you'll consider returning someday to share more of your quilts with us.

Since we spoke that evening, I've increased my efforts to learn more about the Elm Creek Quilt. While I still haven't conclusively determined who made it, I have learned a few details about its history that I thought might interest you.

My aunt Mary, my mother's younger sister, says she believes

the quilt was completed shortly before the War of Secession began. This would follow what my mother told me, that during the war itself, the women of the family rarely made any new quilts, but made do with what they had. They could no longer obtain fabric from the Northern mills, and since Southern cotton gins and textile mills were frequently attacked as military targets, thread sometimes became scarce. Eventually they resorted to spinning their own thread on a spinning wheel and conserving it for the most necessary sewing projects, such as blankets, bandages, and other items for the soldiers.

According to my aunt, it's something of a miracle the quilt survived the war at all. The plantation was frequently overrun by troops from both sides, depending upon who controlled the territory at the time, and the soldiers scavenged food and supplies from people whose resources were already scarce. Sometimes the troops offered receipts for what they took, but more often they did not, though there was little likelihood of redeeming the receipts, anyway.

In order to protect their valuables, my grandmother's grandmother hid the family silver and other heirlooms under her daughter's mattress. When the family heard soldiers arriving, her daughter would dash upstairs, climb into bed, and pull the Birds in the Air quilt over herself. Then she would groan and toss about as if suffering from some terrible illness, while her mother pretended to care for her. When the soldiers entered the house and were told that the daughter was afflicted with typhus, they would not enter the room. My grandmother's grandmother made sure to leave items of lesser value elsewhere in the house, so the soldiers would not suspect they had a hidden cache, and grow angry and destructive at the prospect of leaving empty-handed.

This scheme preserved their property for nearly the entire duration of the war, but when their region was finally overwhelmed by Federal troops, the family was forced to flee. They took what they could carry and bundled the rest in the Birds of the Air quilt, which they buried on their property. Previous attempts to hide their valuables had taught them that scavenging soldiers knew to look for recently overturned soil, so again my grandmother's grandmother devised a deception. She placed the quilt at the bottom of a deep hole, covered it up with several feet of dirt, then on top laid the remains of her beloved dog, which had been shot only days earlier by a scavenger. After filling in the hole, she remarked that her faithful friend was a loyal guardian for the family even in death.

When they finally were able to return to the plantation months later, they found most of the house an utter ruin. The soil over the hiding place had been disturbed, but their valuables were still there at the bottom of the hole. Whoever had searched the site in their absence must have struck the dog's bones and decided they had found only a grave, and gone no further.

I think this at least partially accounts for the quilt's dilapidated condition, wouldn't you agree? It certainly explains the water stains in the middle of the top row.

When I told my aunt it was a shame they buried the quilt, though, she told me that was the only reason the quilt remained within the family at all. When they fled their home, they took the fancier quilts with them, including a broderie perse wedding quilt and a whole-cloth trapunto coverlet they used only for company. At some point during their flight, they were robbed on the road, and the thieves took the quilts along with everything else. So only because the Elm Creek Quilt had been considered utilitarian rather than fine did it survive the war—and if you ask me, those fancy silk quilts wouldn't have survived burial as well as the Birds in the Air quilt did, with its sturdy linsey-woolsey and muslin. I wonder, though, if those two stolen quilts became some other family's heirlooms. More likely they were used as horse blankets or cut up to patch worn shoes. It's unlikely a thief would appreciate all the time, effort, and affection that went into those quilts.

I hope this new information will shed more light on the history of the Elm Creek Quilt, although we must keep in mind that it's only as accurate as my aunt Mary's memory of old family stories. Why didn't more women document their quilts with a tag or at least their signature? I suppose they never imagined the frustrations they were creating for their descendants.

Please keep me posted about your own research. I'm eager to hear from you, whether you have good news or bad, or no news at all.

Sincerely,
Margaret Alden

Sylvia read the letter a second time, then folded it carefully and returned it to its envelope. Why, indeed, didn't women document each and every quilt they made? As the Alden family story proved, sometimes the everyday quilts rather than the painstakingly stitched masterpieces were the ones to endure for future generations.

But of course, quilters didn't often think their creations deserved documentation. In Sylvia's opinion, they valued themselves—and the work of their hands—too lightly. If a quilt was worthy of the thread that held it together, it was surely worthy of a simple appliquéd tag identifying the quilter, her geographic location, and the date of completion. More details would be even better, but Sylvia would settle for those.

She placed Margaret's letter on top of the others and returned the stack to the top of her dresser, then switched off the light and settled into bed. She closed her eyes and tried to still her thoughts, but images from the Birds in the Air quilt's perilous journey through the years played in her mind.

Suddenly a phrase from the letter jolted her memory. Quickly Sylvia groped for the lamp switch and snatched up the letter and her glasses. She scanned the lines until she reached the third to the last paragraph, where she spotted the familiar words. Linsey-woolsey. Grace had mentioned that type of fabric years ago in one of her lectures. Sylvia could not remember the exact context, but she knew it was significant.

She glanced at the clock and had a moment of dismay before remembering the three-hour time difference between Pennsylvania and California. She threw back the quilt, pulled on her dressing gown and slippers, and within moments was hurrying down the hallway, Margaret's letter in hand. Too many telemarketers had spoiled perfectly good naps for her to consider keeping a phone in her room, and the nearest was in the library.

Grace answered on the second ring. Sylvia barely gave her friend a chance to say hello before she launched into a summary of Margaret's tale. "Linsey-woolsey," Sylvia repeated when she finished. "When I saw the quilt, I assumed it was wool and muslin. I didn't think to inquire if it was something else."

"It would be easy to mistake them if you didn't know what to look for," said Grace. "Linsey-woolsey was woven using a cotton warp and a wool weft. It was a rough and uncomfortable cloth, but cheap and durable."

"That's what I thought," said Sylvia, triumphant. "There's our proof that this so-called Elm Creek Quilt has nothing to do with the quilts I found in my attic. Not a scrap of linsey-woolsey appears in any of them. They were pieced from silks, cottons, chintzes—just about everything but linsey-woolsey. Anneke used scraps from her dressmaking, remember? And much of that fabric was the fine imported material Hans's parents sent as a wedding gift."

"Sylvia," said Grace, "the presence of identical fabric in all three quilts could have proven a connection, but the absence of identical material doesn't disprove one. Do all of your quilts contain one common fabric?"

"What a silly question." But Sylvia hesitated and admitted, "No. Of course not."

"The quiltmaker could have resorted to linsey-woolsey when her better fabric scraps ran out. During the Civil War, many Southern families resorted to homespun when other fabric became too difficult to obtain. On the other hand . . ."

"Yes?" prompted Sylvia.

"Homespun was a common fabric used for slaves' clothing."

Sylvia could not speak.

"I'm sorry, Sylvia. I knew you wouldn't like to hear that. But since Margaret Alden believes the quilt was finished before the Civil War began . . ."

"Someone must have been wearing that homespun, and it probably wasn't the mistress of a plantation." Sylvia took a deep breath. "So. You believe my ancestors were slave owners."

"Not necessarily *your* ancestors. Margaret Alden's, and we knew that about her already. We don't know that one of your ancestors pieced Margaret Alden's quilt. We still don't know that the Bergstroms have any connection to the Aldens. The presence of homespun in the quilt changes nothing."

"I simply cannot imagine Gerda the mistress of a plantation, wearing fine silks and ordering people about." And then, with a sudden flash of insight, Sylvia nearly laughed aloud from relief. "And that's not all she wouldn't do."

"Meaning?"

"Gerda hated to quilt. She hated anything to do with sewing, but she did understand fine fabric. She wouldn't have spent all that time and energy quilting elaborate images from Elm Creek Farm into a top pieced from homespun."

"It does seem rather incongruent, for any quilter," mused Grace. "Any quilter who had access to better fabric, anyway."

Sylvia hardly heard her, so pleased was she with her new realization. "Thank you, Grace. You've put my mind at ease."

Grace laughed. "You're quite welcome, although I don't think I really did all that much."

Sylvia laughed, too, her heart light. Gerda could not have made Margaret Alden's quilt. Anneke surely had not, either, because family stories after the Civil War placed her right where she should have been, at Elm Creek Farm. And Hans, too, could be ruled out, for that same reason, and because he probably never lifted a needle in his life.

Whoever made the Alden family's heirloom, the unknown quilter could not have been a Bergstrom.

* * *

When Sylvia returned to the memoir the next morning, it was with renewed confidence that her ancestors' reputation for courage and goodness would yet be proven true.

January 1859— what the New Year brought

By the first days of January, Anneke could no longer hide what I had suspected: She and Hans were expecting a child.

I embraced Anneke with great joy when my persistent questioning at last compelled her to reveal the truth. I was nearly overcome with delight to know that a tiny baby boy or girl would be joining our family, although I admit I pitied Anneke the pains of childbirth she would experience, and considered myself fortunate to be spared them. If Jonathan had married me, however, I am sure I would have felt differently.

As the winter snows fell outside the windows of our happy home, Hans fashioned a cradle from trees felled on our own land, and Anneke pieced tiny baby quilts from the soft fabrics my father had sent from Germany. Perhaps I need not explain how Anneke's glad news brought me comfort from my own grief. The promise of new life brought me hope, and I knew I would find solace in the hard work that would be required of me as Anneke's confinement approached and my niece or nephew entered the world.

It seemed that nothing would diminish the pleasure of our anticipation, but troubled times awaited us.

For one, Anneke was loath to give up her position at Mrs. Engle's dress shop, which brought her not only wages but also work she enjoyed and friends. She was certain Mrs. Engle would dismiss her when her condition became too obvious. She put off telling Mrs. Engle the news as long as she could, and when she finally summoned up enough courage, she begged me to accompany her.

Only for Anneke's sake, and that of my niece or nephew, would I agree to voluntarily subject myself to that woman's company. I even promised to be cordial. But we had not even entered the shop when I realized I would not be able to keep my vow.

For nailed to a post just outside the door was a handbill, which I preserved, since naturally I tore it down, and have enclosed here.

ꕥ

Sylvia turned the page, and in the fold of the book she discovered a brittle, yellowed piece of paper. It was torn along one edge, and it seemed so fragile that Sylvia almost didn't dare to unfold it, but she couldn't resist. As carefully as she could, she laid it on top of her desk and gingerly peeled back the corners.

$20 REWARD!

For the capture and return of a Negro woman, runaway or stolen from me two days after Christmas. She is of medium height and build; she may attempt to pass as White or Free but you will know her by the fresh mark of a flatiron, which I made on her right cheek. She is an expert with the needle and may have in her possession a silver thimble and needle case, which belonged to my late Mother and which the Negress has stolen. The above reward of twenty dollars will be given upon return of the said Negress to me or my agents, and an additional ten dollars will be provided for the restoration of my stolen goods. Josiah Chester, Wentworth County, Virginia, December 29, 1858.

A shiver ran down Sylvia's spine. She set the handbill aside and quickly returned to the memoir.

ꕥ

As I gazed upon the deplorable announcement, my indignation quickly turned to white-hot outrage. The nerve of Mrs. Engle, to permit such a posting on her property!

"My goodness." Beside me, Anneke was staring at the handbill with shocked intrigue. "The mark of a flatiron upon her cheek. Can you imagine it?"

I could imagine it all too well. "If I burned a woman's face with a flatiron, I would not be so quick to boast of it." And with that, I snatched the handbill right off the nail and crumpled it into my pocket.

Anneke looked around, fearful someone had seen. "You can't do that."

"I most certainly can, and I believe I just did," said I. "Twenty dollars for a woman. Ten for a thimble and a needle case."

"They're silver," explained my sister-in-law.

I was too angry to reply, so I returned to my seat on the wagon, determined to wait for Anneke outside despite the cold. After a moment Anneke entered the shop, and after a frigid half hour passed, she returned outside carrying a bundle of sewing.

"She said I may continue to work for her as long as my condition is not apparent to the customers," said Anneke in a subdued voice as we rode off. "After the child is born, if I wish to, I may resume my work."

I merely nodded. The anger that had reduced to a simmer now resumed a steady boil. How could Anneke even think of prolonging her association with Mrs. Engle now? I had faith that the decent people of Creek's Crossing would assist a fugitive slave if the opportunity arose, but there were others in our town of weaker character who would be tempted by the promised reward into betraying that unfortunate woman. If she were delivered to her owner because of that handbill, the shame and the sin would be Mrs. Engle's.

I yearned to discuss the matter with Jonathan, for I knew he would understand my outrage. Instead I confided in Dorothea, whose compassion for all sorts, even her enemies, left me unsatisfied. Rather than joining me in my denunciation of Mrs. Engle, she urged me to leave the matter to God, to pray that Mrs. Engle would see the light one day, and to ask the Lord to protect the fugitive woman, wherever she was.

I could do the latter, but regarding Mrs. Engle, I was unforgiving and unrepentant. "I simply cannot abide such handbills littering our main streets."

"Nor can I," said Dorothea, "but I fear we will soon grow accustomed to it."

"What do you mean?"

"Many routes north through Pennsylvania are obstructed by the Appalachians. The slave catchers know there are only so many passes through the mountains, and they watch them carefully. Gaps to the east and west of us are so well known to the slave catchers that the slaves have been forced to discover other, more hazardous mountain passes. One that still remains little known lies directly south of Creek's Crossing."

This knowledge gave me a thrill of apprehension. "This pass is becoming better known, I think, if slave owners know to post handbills here."

"I fear you are correct." Dorothea set down her sewing and gazed out the window. "This woman has avoided capture for several weeks. It is possible she may reach Canada soon, if she is not there already. We must pray for fair weather."

But I had followed her gaze out the window, and saw as she did that a dark cloud loomed in the southwest, which meant we would have snow before nightfall.

I hurried home, arriving only minutes before the first flakes fell. As the blizzard raged for two days and nights, my thoughts went often to the Negress of the handbill, and I wondered what would have compelled her to flee captivity in winter that could not be endured until spring. Then I recalled the horrors I had read of in Jonathan's books and heard of from Dorothea's speakers, and I believed I understood, as well as anyone who had never been a slave could.

At last the storms ended, and suddenly the weather grew as temperate as spring; the January Thaw was upon us. It was a peculiar quirk of the climate in the region that for a few days each January, we enjoyed a brief respite from cold temperatures and snow until winter resumed in full force. Energized by the precious sunshine, Anneke and I flung open the windows and decided to accomplish what spring cleaning we could in the time available. While Anneke scrubbed the floors and beat our few rugs, I washed our quilts and hung them out to dry as

Anneke had taught me: colors in the shade, and whites in the sunlight.

Since the days were not any longer despite this prelude to spring, twilight had descended by suppertime. Hans, Anneke, and I made merry over our supper, our spirits greatly elevated by the day's fair weather. We laughed and talked so loudly that when the knock came at our door, we could not be certain our unexpected guest had not been trying to get our attention for some time.

Anneke excused herself to answer the door, and when she returned, she looked pale and strange. "It's a woman," said she. "I don't know what she wants. I did not understand her English."

"Why did she stay outside?" ask Hans.

Anneke glanced over her shoulder and wrung her hands. "I believe . . . I think she may be a Negress."

Wondering which of our neighbors she had left standing on the doorstep, I said, a trifle sharply, "Why didn't you invite her in?"

Distractedly, Anneke brushed her right cheek with the back of her fingers. "She has a burn, like a flatiron."

Hans and I had time to exchange a quick glance before we bolted to our feet and hurried to the door. Just outside, where shadows yet hid her, stood a woman. In the poor light I might have thought her a white woman if not for her clothing, which was fashioned of coarse and soiled cloth, and the haunted look in her eye, which, when our gaze met, struck me with nearly physical force. Her shoulders slumped from exhaustion, and although she stood warily as if prepared to run, there was a determined set to her jaw that convinced me she could just as readily hold her ground if she must.

And upon her cheek blazed the mark of a flatiron, red and blistered and sore. It sickened me to look upon it.

Somehow I knew the woman had expected a much different reception from us. Just as she shifted her weight to hurry away, I called out, "Wait. Come in. You're safe here."

She seemed to weigh my words for a moment before she nodded and entered.

I closed the door firmly behind her, my heart pounding. "Draw the curtains," said I, but Hans had already begun to do so. I directed the woman to a chair beside the fire and hurried off to fetch a dressing for her injured cheek.

Anneke trailed after me. "We should send her on her way."

"We will. As soon as she is rested and fed, and I have tended to her burn, we will help her determine the best route north."

Anneke seized my arm. "I mean we must send her on her way now."

"Hungry and tired, and with no proper guidance north?" I brushed off Anneke's hands and snatched up clean linen for bandages. "What if she wandered to the Engles' farm and sought help there?"

"They would turn her over to the authorities."

"Precisely. What do you think would become of her then?"

Anneke looked as if the thought sickened her, but then she shook her head. "I don't like it, but it's the law. If we don't send her away, we could be discovered and prosecuted."

"No one saw her arrive."

"Are you sure?"

I was not, but I would not admit it. "Of course. No one can see the house from the main road because of the forest, and if a pursuer had followed her onto our property, he surely would have come to the door by now."

My voice sounded glib, but my knees were shaking with fright as I hurried back to the fireside. I heated water and tended to the woman's burn rapidly, without speaking, hardly aware of the movements my hands made. The burn was badly infected, and her skin radiated fever. Anneke brought her something to eat, and the woman wolfed down bread and cheese and meat without pausing to speak or barely to breathe.

Before she finished, Hans left the house, rifle in hand, to see if anyone had followed her. None of us women spoke; with my brother gone, the house felt cloaked in a fearful silence. I heated more water so the woman could wash and fetched her some of my own clothing to wear, the sturdiest I had, and the warmest. She was considerably shorter than I, but still a good deal taller than Anneke, so my things would have to do.

She thanked me as I offered her my things and set her empty plate aside. I averted my gaze as she tended to her toilet, but not quickly enough to avoid seeing the whiplash scars crisscrossing her back. I swallowed hard and could not look upon them again, but Anneke stared in horrified fascination.

"You're the slave," she accused. "The one who escaped from Josiah Chester in Virginia."

The woman gave her a hard look. "This here's Pennsylvania," said she, pulling my dress over her head, slowly, as if her every muscle ached. "I ain't nobody's slave now."

"This is Pennsylvania, but you're not safe here," said I. "You need to continue north to Canada."

"I know." She said it matter-of-factly, but something in her words conveyed an exhaustion so complete I could have wept for her, thinking how much farther she would have to travel.

I said, "You don't need to leave until you're rested."

"I go tomorrow, at nightfall," said she, thanking me with a nod. "But where I go from here? Where the next station?"

I stared at her, uncomprehending. "Station?"

She stared back at me, and gradually I saw something in her eyes transform from relief to confusion to fear. She glanced at

Anneke, then back to me. "Lord help me," she whispered. She struggled to her feet and tried to run, but she collapsed halfway to the door.

In a moment I was kneeling by her side, attempting to succor her, but she fought me off. "Calm yourself," said I, bewildered and frightened by her sudden desperation. "We want to help."

If she heard me, she gave no sign. "But I saw it," said she, over and over, nearly delirious. "I saw it."

I tried to soothe her, to assure her she was safe, but her outburst had drained the last of her strength, and she slipped into unconsciousness.

"We must get her to bed," said I, and Anneke rushed to assist me, without a word of protest.

The infection within her burned cheek had leached its poison into the woman's blood, and none of us thought she would survive until morning. I thought of Mr. Wilbur, slowly dying as Jonathan fought to preserve his life. I longed for Jonathan's skill, I longed for his presence, but we could not send for him, lest we force him to shoulder our own defiance of the law.

For two nights and a day the woman lay more asleep than awake in the bed we made up for her in Anneke's sewing room, murmuring and sometimes crying out, tormented by fever. I remained at the bedside, doing the little I could to see her through each hour, terrified that she would die before my eyes. Anneke's earlier objections were forgotten as she changed the woman's bed linens, soaked with perspiration, and tended to me as well, helping me keep up my strength. And although Hans had found no sign of pursuers, we expected the slave catchers to arrive at any moment.

Then, at last, on the second day, the woman's fever broke. She roused herself enough to drink a cup of broth, then slipped into restful sleep.

With the immediate threat of her illness now diminishing,

other worries began to plague me. We would have to find some means of concealing the woman until she could continue her journey north. She had seemed to expect us to know where she could next find respite along the way, so we must find such a place. How, I did not know. And how Anneke, who wore her emotions plain upon her face, would avoid raising Mrs. Engle's suspicions in the days to come, I could not imagine.

I sat at the woman's bedside as she slept, brooding, wishing that she had approached some other farm, and despising myself for such thoughts. I had learned something about myself in the short span of time since her arrival, something I did not like: I was a staunch enough Abolitionist when slaves were mere abstractions, far removed from my own hearth and home, but weak-willed indeed when a runaway had become a threat to my own safety and freedom and comfort.

I knew well that this threat would grow with every day she remained under our roof, and those days would number longer than I had anticipated when I had offered her shelter for the night. I had not yet told Hans or Anneke, but in the course of caring for her, I had discovered that she was afflicted with more than exhaustion and fever.

Although my dress hung loose upon her shoulders and limbs, it fit snug around the midsection. The fugitive slave was with child and, as best I could estimate, was nearly as far along as Anneke.

She would not be fit to travel for months, and knowing that, I could not bring myself to send her away—

ꕥ

The line ended abruptly, followed by one crossed out so heavily that whatever Gerda had originally written was almost completely obscured. Sylvia strained her eyes, trying to make out the words, but all she could perceive were a few letters, and these were a scrawl compared to the elegant precision she had come to expect from Gerda's writing.

It was the only cross-out in the book, which made Sylvia all the more determined to know what it said.

She hurried to her bedroom for her magnifying glass, but when it failed to help her, she went in search of Sarah. She found her at the library computer, working on the business's accounts. After Sylvia explained the problem, Sarah offered to examine the line herself.

"I can't bear not knowing what she wrote," said Sylvia as Sarah held the book up to the bright lamp on the desk. "When I think of the other things she did not cross out—some of them not very pleasant—I can't imagine what could have been so terrible that she had to obliterate it. No, I *can* imagine, and that's worse. What if she said, 'I could not bring myself to send her away, but I did anyway'? or, 'So Hans did it for me'?"

Sarah smiled, her eyes fixed on the book. "I doubt that's what it says."

"Well, we don't know, do we?" said Sylvia grumpily. "Can you make out anything?"

"I'm not sure."

"Try this." Sylvia handed her the magnifying glass. "I think perhaps this last bit refers to Gerda's mixed feelings. Could that say, 'heart was torn'? Do you think that means she's going to send the woman away?" She could not bear it if it was true.

"Where do you see 'torn'?"

"Here." Sylvia pointed.

"That looks too wide to be a 't.' I thought it was a capital letter."

"Isn't that the end of the previous word?"

"It could be . . ." Sarah turned the page and held it up to the light, looking at the obscured line from the back. "No, there's a space before the letter, not after. You can see the ink is lighter there, as if she didn't have to mark out anything." She returned to the previous page. "And I think this says 'born,' not 'torn.' You know the context; would that make sense?"

"Both Anneke and the slave woman were expecting."

"Maybe the line says, 'until her child was born.'"

Sylvia took the memoir and studied the line. She perceived no more than she had before, but Sarah's interpretation did seem to match the peaks and dips of the pen, if not perfectly. "Or perhaps instead of 'her child,' she wrote the child's name."

"That would make sense."

"Except for one small matter: Why would Gerda feel compelled to blot out such an innocent remark?"

Sarah frowned, uncertain. "Maybe because at that time, she didn't know what the baby's name was going to be. She knew when she wrote the line, of course, in 1895, but not at that point in the memoir, months before the baby was born. Maybe she crossed it out to avoid confusing the chronological order."

Sylvia shook her head. "That doesn't follow. In other parts of the memoir she leaps forward in time. We already know Jonathan and Charlotte are going to have four children, for example. If divulging future information doesn't bother Gerda elsewhere, why should it here?"

She could tell from Sarah's expression that her young friend could not think of a logical explanation, either.

9

February through March 1859—in which Elm Creek Farm becomes a station

By the time our guest had recovered enough to sit up in bed and talk, the January Thaw had passed, usurped by the brooding skies and bitter cold of February.

"How long I been here?" was her first question to me, as her eyes darted around the room, unnaturally darkened by the storm outside.

"Six days."

She pushed back the bedclothes. "I best be going."

"You can't leave now." I drew the quilt over her again. "You're not strong enough, and there's a storm."

"Slave catchers come after me if I don't keep on."

"The storm will slow them. But if anyone does come, we're arranging a hiding place. You'll be safer there than outside."

To my relief, she accepted this and sank back into bed again. I offered her a glass of water, which she drank thirstily, her dark eyes fixed on the window. "The last storm was worse than this one," said she. "I got lost in it, couldn't find the path. Don't know what I would've done if I hadn't seen the signal."

I nodded as if I understood, wary of alarming her as I had that first night. "Was it easy to find?"

" 'Course. Right there on the clothesline like they told me at the last place. Lady there drew the Underground Railroad picture in the dirt, showed me how the pieces go. I make quilts on the plantation, but never seen that pattern before. Missus likes fancy work." She glanced at the quilt covering her—my own humble first attempt at quilt making—and I could see she was trying not to smile. "This quilt here, now, this called Shoo-Fly. It plenty warm, but missus think herself too good for it."

"No one would ever mistake any of my quilts for fancywork," said I, dryly. "It keeps off the chill, and that's about all."

"That's plenty. Even missus be mighty grateful for it if she ever be cold as I was."

It was the highest compliment anyone but Dorothea had ever given my handiwork, and despite my distaste for needlework, including my own, especially this quilt with its humility block, I was pleased. "My name is Gerda," I told her. "Gerda Bergstrom."

Her name was Joanna, and as I tended to her that day, I pieced together how chance and misunderstanding had brought her to our door. After leaving her last place of refuge, she had become lost in the snowstorm that had struck the day after I discovered the handbill on Mrs. Engle's store. When the January Thaw brought fair weather, she had tried in vain to resume her previous course and, in her wanderings, encountered Elm Creek. She followed it, knowing she could cross the waters if need be to throw pursuing dogs off her scent, until it led her to an abandoned cabin near a barn. Too fatigued to go on, she slept the rest of the night and all the next day. When she rose at sunset, determined to continue her journey despite her increasing sickness, she spied a house on the other side of the creek. Near it was a clothesline, upon which hung several quilts, including one pieced in the Underground Railroad pattern—the signal her previous benefactors had told her would indicate the next station on her journey north.

I hid my astonishment as best I could and quickly deduced the rest: The signal Joanna referred to was the quilt Anneke had made of squares and triangles arranged in vertical stripes. In copying Dorothea's design, Anneke had inadvertently created an echo of the message. Now I understood why Dorothea had not responded when Anneke had asked her the name of the pattern—and I also discovered Joanna's intended destination.

The Nelson farm was a station on the Underground Railroad. Knowing the depth of their feeling for the Abolitionist cause, I was not surprised by this revelation, but I was astounded that Dorothea had managed to conceal the truth so well, and, I will admit, somewhat hurt that she had not confided in me. Upon further reflection, however, I realized that because of the inherent danger to both runaway and stationmaster, she could not have entrusted the truth to even the closest friend. The less others knew, the less they could reveal through accident or under duress. Even Mr. Frederick Douglass himself had faulted some stationmasters for concealing their activities so poorly that they allowed slave owners and slave catchers to discover their methods, thus helping to perpetuate the very institution they sought to undermine. Dorothea and Thomas would never allow themselves to be included in their number.

One deduction quickly led to another: Dorothea would know the next destination in Joanna's flight north. By the time Joanna was prepared to continue her journey, I intended to tease that information from my friend without revealing why I sought it, for I needed to maintain secrecy just as the Nelsons did.

Days passed, and as Joanna recovered from her illness, our expectation that the slave catchers would arrive at any moment began to ebb. Or so it was with Hans and me; Anneke seemed never to forget her anxieties. She took little consolation in knowing Hans had devised an ingenious hiding place in her sewing room, nor in his repeated assurances that no ill would befall our family.

"Hans does not wish to alarm us, but I know the truth," confided Anneke to me when we were alone. "Mr. Pearson says anyone assisting fugitive slaves will be prosecuted under the law. We may be fined, or even sent to prison."

"We will face no punishment," said I, "because we will not be detected."

Anneke looked doubtful, and my own heart was full of misgivings when I wondered how that particular subject had come up in a conversation with Mr. Pearson.

Joanna's care fell almost entirely to me, as Anneke was burdened by her duties for Mrs. Engle as well as the fatigue of her condition. Even when she did assist me, however, she shied away from Joanna, avoiding her gaze and speaking to her through me, if at all. I can only guess why Joanna made Anneke so uncomfortable: perhaps because she knew few colored people, perhaps because of the danger her presence put us all in, perhaps because her dialect, which I have but poorly reproduced in these pages, was difficult for Anneke to comprehend.

"She want me gone," said Joanna to me, unexpectedly, after Anneke stopped by the room on some errand and left as quickly as it was completed, with scarcely a word for either of us.

"She wants you safe in the North" was all I would concede. "As do we all." And then, as a way of making her seem more sympathetic, to show that the women shared a common experience, I added, "She, too, is in a condition. You know what it is to worry for the fate of your child."

"I don't know nothing about that."

"Of course you must," said I, confused. "Or am I mistaken? Are you not . . . expecting?"

From the shock and emotion that came into her eyes then, I first thought she had not surmised her condition, and then I knew she had indeed suspected it but had not allowed herself to believe it.

"You must be well into your fifth month, at least," said I, gently.

Her voice was dull. "Sixth, more likely."

I nodded, mute, for although Anneke was only a few weeks further along, her condition was significantly more apparent, for she had never lacked sufficient nourishment. "Your child will be born in a Free State, and you will raise him in freedom." I expected that to cheer her, but it did not, and I thought I understood the reason why. "His father, I assume, is still in the South?"

She snorted. "That where he likely be, all right."

I placed my hand upon hers, and said consolingly, "Do not despair. Perhaps someday your husband will follow you North to freedom."

She jerked her hand away. "I ain't got no husband."

"Well . . ." I hesitated. "Your man, then."

"No man of mine gave me this baby." Her voice stung with contempt. She rolled over on her side on the bed, putting her back to me. "I don't care if it live or die, so long as I get my freedom."

Shocked, at first I could only gape at her. "Be that as it may," said I, when I found my voice. "You should remain with us until after your time, when you and the baby are strong enough to travel again. For your sake, if not for your child's."

She said nothing, and with nothing more to say myself, I left her alone.

* * *

As Joanna gradually regained strength, she began to grow restless. She was still too weak to take any exercise but for slow walks the length of my room, but she could sit up in bed well enough. When she told me of her desire for something to occupy her time and distract her from her worries, in my thoughtless way, I offered her one of my books.

"I can't read," said Joanna. "Massa don't allow it."

My cheeks flamed, and I busied myself with the sock I was darning. "Oh. Of course."

"Don't matter none."

It matters a great deal, I almost replied, but instead said, "Perhaps I could read to you."

She shrugged, dubious, but said, "That be nice."

I set my mending aside, went to my room, and scanned the titles on the bookcase Jonathan had made for me. When my gaze lit on a certain volume, I pulled it from the shelf. "Here's one," said I, returning to my chair by Joanna's bed. "It was written by a man who was once himself a slave, but acquired his freedom, and has fought to win the same right for others."

At that, her interest was piqued, and thus I commenced reading the *Narrative of the Life of Frederick Douglass, an American Slave.*

I had almost finished William Lloyd Garrison's preface when Anneke entered, made curious by the sound of my voice. Not quickly enough, I set the book aside and snatched up the sock and needle, for I had promised Anneke to help with the darning and had long put off the task. When Anneke said, in a teasing manner, that she could always count on me to shirk my household duties, Joanna spoke up: "I can do the darning."

Anneke and I exchanged a stricken glance. "Anneke is only teasing me," said I. "You are our guest. We don't expect you to work for us."

"It ain't for you, it for me," said Joanna. "I go out of my head sitting here in bed all day and all night, nothing to do but listen for the slave catchers' dogs. You read, and I'll darn."

She insisted, so reluctantly I agreed, but I was greatly disturbed that this woman, so recently near death, and so recently forced to work for white people, now found herself darning white people's socks. I cannot commit to paper why this troubled me so; it simply felt wrong. But unable to articulate an objection, I wordlessly handed her the pile of stockings.

Joanna asked for her bundle, and Anneke, who was nearest, retrieved it from the corner, not quite able to conceal her distaste. Joanna untied the coarse blanket of homespun, upon which every mile of her hazardous journey had apparently left its mark in sweat and grime, and withdrew two shining objects. Anneke gasped, and I nearly did, too, so markedly did the elegant silver needle case and thimble contrast with the bundle that had carried them.

"You *are* the woman from the handbill," exclaimed Anneke. "You stole those things from Josiah Chester."

A dangerous glint appeared in Joanna's eye. "I didn't take nothing that wasn't owed me."

"Be reasonable, Anneke," said I, hurriedly. "The trifles are a poor recompense for the lifetime of suffering she endured at his hands."

"I didn't mean to steal nothing," said Joanna to me. "I was in the sewing room—I was a house slave. The missus have me do all her laundry and sewing and quilting. Massa Chester come after me when I alone there. He always come after me, but this time—that time I just couldn't. I hold the scissors, cutting silk for a dress, and when he grab at me, I point those scissors at him and tell him to leave me be, or I tell the missus he be coming to my cabin when he tell her he going riding. He bring his fist down on my hand, and I drop the scissors, and then he grab me and put his hand over my mouth and push me against the wall. I try to get free, and my hand touch something—I don't know what, but it hard, so I grab it and hit him with it. It scratch his face, his scalp, and draw blood. The blood run all down his face, down into his mouth, and he stand there screaming at me, the blood and spit flying. I try to crawl away, but he take the flatiron off the fire, and then he do this."

Her hand went to her scarred cheek.

"I be too hurt to fight him no more. I don't remember when he finish and go. My mind just went out my body, and when it came back, he was gone, and I still be on the floor. I didn't think about it, I didn't plan nothing, I just got up and left. Middle of the day yet, and me with no idea where I going. I just up and left. I pass other slaves working in the fields, I even walk right by Missy Lizabeth, the massa's daughter, on the road, but no one stop me. They all think I do an errand for the missus. She always have me going here and there, sewing for her friends.

"I walk all day. Only when night come and it get too dark to see do I stop. That when I realize what I done, run off, and how it too late to go back, unless I want a beating that like to kill me. So I hide in a haystack."

She looked down at the gleaming silver objects in her hand. "Before I fall asleep, I open my fist and find Mrs. Chester's needle case, with a little bit of blood on the corner. That what I grab without looking, that what I hit Massa Chester with." She looked at Anneke, unflinching. "So you see, I didn't mean to steal nothing. It just happen."

Anneke, white as a sheet, made no reply. Joanna calmly slipped the thimble onto her finger and began darning one of Hans's socks. Anneke watched her for a moment, then turned on her heel and left the room.

I wanted desperately to apologize for my sister-in-law, or to at least explain her way of thinking, but her condemnation of Joanna's thievery shamed me, especially when I compared it to her tolerance for Mrs. Engle's posting of the handbill. So instead I cleared my throat and resumed reading Douglass's *Narrative*.

* * *

Whether out of anger with me, or fear that she might reveal our secret, Anneke chose not to attend the next meeting of the Certain Faction. We met irregularly during wintertime, as the weather would permit, and thus I had spent two impatient, anxious weeks since Joanna's arrival longing to speak with Dorothea.

I was the first to reach the Nelson home, for I knew once the others arrived, I would have little opportunity to speak with Dorothea alone. As we set up her quilting frame, she shared the latest news from her household, and I bided my time until I could casually remind her of the handbill. She smiled and said, "Dear Gerda, are you still plotting some dire revenge against Mrs. Engle?"

"I cannot forgive her as easily as you, but no, I am not," said I. "I was merely wondering about the unfortunate runaway. She might have been driven from her intended path by the storms, or was forced to change direction when the slave catchers passed through town. They must have, don't you agree?"

"I suppose they must have," said Dorothea, "if only to deliver their handbills. We can only pray she was able to elude them."

I learned more from my friend's expression and the mournful note in her voice than she had intended to tell me: After seeing the handbill, Dorothea had anticipated the runaway would soon appear at her door, and when she had not, Dorothea had given her up for lost. Perhaps she thought Joanna had wandered the Pennsylvania countryside until she froze to death, or had been recaptured, or had suffered another equally dire fate, and perhaps Dorothea wrongly blamed herself.

My heart went out to her as I imagined her anguish. "I'm certain she did elude them," said I, ignoring, for the moment, the need for secrecy. "But perhaps circumstances forced her to seek an alternate refuge."

Dorothea's eyes darted to mine. "I suppose that might have been necessary."

I busied myself with smoothing the back layer of a new quilt in the frame, and said in a careless manner, "I do hope that isn't the case, however."

"Why not?"

"Her new protectors would hardly know where to send her next, would they? They could point north and say, 'Head in that direction and mind you don't stumble over any slave catchers on the way,' but that's not very helpful, is it?"

Dorothea gave me a long, searching glance and, after a long moment, finally said, "You're right. They would not know about others who would help the fugitive. There are many others, but more are always needed."

And then, in elliptical language that suggested more than it explicitly stated, Dorothea told me how Joanna would know the next safe house on her journey north. Our conversation was oddly restrained for two close confidantes, but necessarily so, for neither knew what one might someday be required to say under oath about the other.

Reader, you will forgive me, I hope, if I do not record those identifying details in these pages. That family's role in the Underground Railroad is their story, not mine, to share with their own descendants or not, as they see fit.

I told neither Hans nor Anneke what Dorothea had revealed to me, only that I knew where Joanna should go when she departed Elm Creek Farm. They did not press me for details, Hans because he was aware that as few people should know the route as possible, Anneke because she was relieved to be spared the burden of yet another secret.

Her relief was to be short-lived, I knew, for Dorothea's words lingered in my thoughts: *There are many others,* she had said, *but more are always needed.* One fugitive had found shelter within our home. If others happened to pass our way, I would not deny them our hospitality.

Naturally I could not proceed without Hans's consent, for although I was the elder sibling, he was master of Elm Creek Farm. It took some impassioned pleading on my part, and heartfelt appeals to the best parts of his nature, but eventually he agreed. He did not agree because knowing Joanna had influenced his opinion of the dispute between Slave State and Free; he persisted in the belief that what did not directly affect him did not concern him. What he did acknowledge was that as beneficiaries of America's promise of freedom and opportunity for all, we Bergstroms would be remiss if we did not assist others who braved unimaginable dangers and risked their very lives in the struggle to achieve what we now took for granted.

When he made up his mind, he told Anneke his decision. She shot me one accusing look, then returned her gaze to her husband and gave him a wordless nod of acceptance. I wished he had asked her for her consent rather than merely telling her how things would be, but it could not be undone, and I allowed myself to believe the result would have been the same regardless.

From that day forward, whenever we did not anticipate visitors, whenever the winter weather was such that a clothesline strung outdoors would not raise suspicions, we hung Anneke's Underground Railroad quilt and waited for a knock on the door in the night.

* * *

Joanna had been with us a month when the knock finally came.

It was shortly before dawn. I started at the sound, instantly awake with a pounding heart, and leapt from my bed. I threw on my dressing gown and hurried downstairs, pausing only to rap upon Joanna's door and warn her to hasten to the hiding place. Hans was not a second behind me as I opened the outside door to discover two figures shivering in the cold.

We beckoned them inside, and as I stoked the fire and prepared a meal for them, Hans took his rifle and went to search for pursuers. By the time he returned, Anneke had come downstairs to help me to tend to the newcomers, and Joanna, assured by the lack of uproar that it was safe to leave her hiding place, had joined us—but rather than take a place by the fire with the other guests, she began to help me with the cooking, without a word and as naturally as if she had been doing so for years.

The arrivals were two men, escaped from the same tobacco plantation in South Carolina. After they were warmed and fed, they told us something of their lives in captivity, and though I think they spared us the most gruesome details, their brief accounts were horrific enough to convince me that no risk was too great to help them toward freedom. Anneke's bleak silence, and the courteous manner in which she addressed the fugitives, so different from the skittishness she had first displayed toward Joanna, told me she agreed.

But something else also occupied Anneke's thoughts. "They think she's white," murmured Anneke when the others could not overhear, nodding toward the two men, and to Joanna, who wore my dress and worked alongside us as one of the family.

Taken aback, I studied the men surreptitiously and soon concurred with Anneke's observation. Perhaps because her skin was indeed quite light, or perhaps because the ugly scar on her face drew attention away from her features, the two newcomers did not see a fellow runaway in Joanna. Perhaps they did not look upon her long enough to discern her true heritage; upon her first appearance, each man had glanced at her scar, then quickly diverted his gaze as if he did not wish to appear rude. Once

Joanna's dialect exposed her, however, there was a subtle shift in the men's address—mild surprise, which they well concealed, was followed by a new warmth, a familiarity, that did not enter into their voices when they spoke to Anneke or me.

Throughout that day, as the men slept in the beds we made up for them in the nursery, I pondered Joanna's inadvertent duplicity and wondered if we might not somehow use it to help her elude capture when she resumed her journey north.

The men left shortly after dusk, clad in some of Hans's stout winter clothing and carrying bread and cheese enough to sustain them until the next station. Joanna watched them go, her longing to accompany them plain upon her face. Then her hand absently went to her gently swelling abdomen, and she turned away from the window.

* * *

Not a week later, another knock woke us in the night; two days after that fugitive's departure, another arrived to take his place. With each escaped slave who found shelter beneath our roof, our confidence grew, and the Underground Railroad quilt appeared more frequently on our clothesline.

We grew confident—perhaps overconfident. Thus one late night when a man and a boy of about eight years pounded frantically on the door, we were rudely restored to our senses. As we beckoned them inside, the man told us through labored breathing that the slave catchers were not far behind.

I stood stock-still for a moment, and so it was Anneke who sprung into action. "This way," said she briskly, guiding them upstairs. I quickly looked over the first floor for any sign of Joanna or the new arrivals, and followed the others upstairs. Anneke and I helped the fugitives into the hiding place, then returned to our bedrooms, to feign sleep.

Perhaps a half hour passed before the baying of dogs and a second pounding interrupted the quiet night. I prayed God would make me a good liar as I followed Hans and Anneke downstairs. My brother pulled open the door, and to my dismay and astonishment, we found ourselves facing the same two slave catchers who had disturbed us during our first autumn at Elm Creek Farm. This time, each held a yelping bloodhound by the collar.

Without waiting for us to ask their purpose, the first man demanded entry to our home. "We're in pursuit of two runaway n——s, a man and a boy," said he. "We know they came this way."

Annoyed, Hans said, "That's why you woke my family in the middle of the night? I thought the devil himself was after you."

"Let us in, g—— d—— it," snarled the other. The dogs barked and panted, and would have leapt past Hans and inside if they had not been restrained.

"Did you check the barn?" inquired Anneke, her eyes wide and innocent. "Last time, you said sometimes runaways hide in the barn." She turned to Hans, stroking her abdomen as if comforting the child within her womb. "These runaways won't hurt us, will they?"

Hans put his arm around her protectively. "Don't you worry, dearest." Then he glared at the men as if to shame them for frightening a poor defenseless woman.

But they were not deceived. "Yes, we surely did check your barn, and we checked L.'s cabin, too," said the first man. "And that is where we discovered this."

He held out a worn shawl of linsey-woolsey, filthy and torn.

"That's mine," said I, and took the slave cloth from him. "My goodness, when I think of how long and hard I searched for this—"

"We found footprints, too," interrupted the second.

"Of course you did," said Hans, with perfect bemusement. "We used to live there."

"Likely we left many other things behind, besides," said I.

The first man addressed Hans. "If you don't allow us to search your house, I'll come back with the law, and we'll force our way in."

"Not with those filthy curs, you will not," I declared. "I will not have them tracking mud all over my clean floors."

"Surely they wouldn't bring the dogs inside, would they?" Anneke shrank back, putting Hans between herself and the door. "Hans, please say they won't."

"As you can see, my wife is as terrified of dogs as my sister is of a dirty floor," remarked Hans dryly. "I suppose I could let you in if it will get rid of you, but the dogs stay outside."

The second man fumed. "See there?" said he to his companion. "They're afraid. They know what the dogs will find."

"Oh, come now," said I. "Be reasonable. Would your own wives allow those muddy paws in their homes? Surely our house isn't large enough to conceal someone from two experienced slave catchers, dogs or no dogs."

I do not know if my caustic remark injured their pride or if they thought of their own wives and decided my obsession with a clean floor was quite typical for my sex, but, muttering complaints and curses just loud enough to be heard, they tied the hounds' leashes to a post. Hans opened the door and waved the men in, and they wasted no time searching through the first level as we Bergstroms sat in the front room and pretended we feared nothing more than the loss of a few hours' sleep. "Don't track dirt into the baby's room," called Anneke after the two men as they trooped upstairs. Then we all fell silent.

We listened to their boots on the floorboards as they moved from room to room above us. We knew the precise moment they entered the sewing room. I could scarcely breathe, silently willing the fugitives to be as still as stone, waiting for a triumphant shout of discovery that would announce our undoing.

But the shout did not come.

The footfalls moved from room to room a second time, and then, after what seemed an eternity, we heard them coming slowly, reluctantly, down the stairs. Hans shrugged at the men as if to say he had tried to prevent them from wasting their time, but the two men were unmollified. So great was the first man's fury that he could scarcely strangle out a vow that he would be watching us, and that one day he would catch us helping runaways and see us hanged for it.

"Threaten my family again and I'll kill you," said Hans.

He said it as easily as if he had made killing men his life's work. The two slave catchers frowned, but they did not look as if Hans's threat troubled them. Still, they left our home in great haste, and soon even the sound of their horses' hooves on the road faded into the distance.

"Fools," said Hans. "They don't hang a man for helping slaves."

Anneke gave me a look that suggested she found little consolation in that fact, and she set herself down heavily in the nearest chair.

"Joanna," said I, remembering with a jolt her own condition, and how three fugitives were sharing a refuge meant for one.

I raced upstairs to the sewing room to find it in a shambles, as if two slave catchers had spitefully strewn fabric and quilts about when their search turned up nothing amiss. Picking my way through the mess, I went to Anneke's sewing machine and pulled it away from the wall, revealing a minuscule crack in the new plaster behind it. I slipped my fingernails into the crack and tugged, and away came the makeshift door. "They're gone," said I. "It's safe to come out."

Joanna was the first to emerge, looking faint. I helped her back to bed as the man exited, but upon my return, I found him sitting beside the hole in the false wall, earnestly appealing to the young boy to come out. The boy refused, and I cannot say I blamed him. In the end, we agreed to allow him to remain inside as long as he wished; we left the wood-and-plaster covering off, but nearby, where it could quickly be replaced if need be.

"I apologize for the cramped accommodations," said I as I made up a bed for the man on the floor beside the opening, where he wished to remain, to comfort the boy. "That space was once a closet, but even then it was little more than a nook. Hans plastered over the door remarkably well, but he had no way to enlarge the space."

"We hide out in worse places than that," said he. "Once we hide in a pigsty, another time an outhouse. Slave catchers be low types, but even they don't like that stink."

"Imagine that," said I, dryly. "I would have thought them perfectly suited for such a stench. Their souls reek of the filth of their occupation."

He chuckled grimly in agreement, and I felt my fear lifting, replaced by a relief so complete I felt light-headed. Our secret alcove had passed its first test, and I was greatly reassured that the fugitives who sought shelter with us would be safe within our walls.

But as I drifted off to sleep, I thought of the young boy who feared capture too much to quit the hiding place. If not for an inexplicable quirk of fate or the unfathomable caprice of God, he could have been born in the North and free. He could have been Anneke's child, and Anneke's child could have been born into slavery.

When I read over these lines they seem no more than ramblings, although at the time I felt I had touched on something profound. I cannot trace the path my thoughts traveled that night, but in my fatigue and my fear, I saw quite plainly a sameness linking all of us entangled in this great conflict, so that I felt at once both guardian and fugitive, both slave and freeborn. Slavery made slaves of us all, it seemed to me, imprisoning those with dark skin in the iron shackles of injustice, those who owned slaves in chains of sin, and those of us complacent in our freedom with the heavy yoke of obligation to help our enslaved brethren.

* * *

But while the events of that night brought me increased confidence and insight, they brought Anneke greater fear.

I did not know how she felt until later. If I detected anything unusual in her demeanor, any reluctance to help the fugitives or desire to forgo displaying the Underground Railroad quilt on the clothesline, I must have ascribed it to her condition. If she seemed fearful of our safety, I must have assumed hers was the ordinary preoccupation of a new mother nearing her time. Our days and nights were such a whirlwind of activity that I do not recall what I thought, or if, in fact, Anneke gave any noticeable sign of her increasing apprehension.

A certain occasion I do remember clearly: One afternoon, when I retrieved Anneke from Mrs. Engle's shop, she greeted me in a distracted fashion and responded with little more than monosyllables and shrugs to my attempts at conversation. I attributed her mood to disappointment, as Mrs. Engle had recently begun urging Anneke to rest at home rather than come in for more sewing work, but suddenly Anneke said, "Does it not trouble you that we are breaking the law?"

"It is wrong to obey an unjust law," said I. "Sometimes submitting to God's law means we must disobey those created by man."

"Yes, of course, but . . ." She hesitated. "Is it not possible that slavery is also the will of God?"

"Anneke," said I, astounded.

"I know what you and Dorothea say, but tell me, is it not possible? Slavery surfaces so often in the Bible—"

"So does sin, so does evil, but we are not meant to perpetuate them."

"But there are directives given for how one is to treat a slave. Why would such things appear in holy scripture if there were not some divine purpose for them? Mr. Pearson says that the African races are the descendants of Ham, condemned by Noah to live in bondage to his brothers. If this is true—"

"It is not true. It is utter nonsense." I hardly knew what to say, so bewildered was I by Anneke's questioning of obvious truths. "I do not think it is wise for you to discuss such issues with Mr. Pearson. You know his views. He is a rigid, blind rule follower with neither the sense nor the judiciousness to decide matters for himself. He would turn his own mother in to the authorities if he thought her in violation of some law."

"He might," countered Anneke, "if he thought it was for her own good. In any event, you needn't worry about me conversing with Mr. Pearson in the near future, for today Mrs. Engle told me quite firmly not to return until after my confinement."

And thus, I thought, the true reason for her contrariness was revealed. I abandoned our argument in lieu of consoling her, reassuring her that she would return to her sewing work in no time, and mocking Mrs. Engle for her silly notions that a pregnant belly was an abominable sight best kept locked indoors where it could not cause offense. Ordinarily Anneke sprang to her employer's defense, but that day, she was understandably receptive to my criticism, and to my great pleasure, she even joined in with a few pointed barbs of her own.

* * *

If Anneke conversed as often as I did with Joanna, she would not have entertained even for a moment the ludicrous idea that God intended any of His children to own another. The horrors Joanna described were beyond anything I could have imagined, and I marveled that she, that anyone, had been able to endure it. I yearned to ask Mr. Pearson if he had considered such brutality when concluding that slavery had been ordained by God.

As our intimacy grew, Joanna made it plain that, as I had surmised, her master was the father of her unborn child. Little wonder, I thought, that she displayed such indifference to it. Joanna had been taken by force more times than she could remember, the first when she was but a young girl. Her circumstances so differed from Anneke's, who carried a child conceived in love and awaited with eager joy, that I could not fault her for her feelings.

And yet, over time, I began to notice a subtle shift in her temperament. She began to respond to Anneke's tentative overtures to discuss the condition they shared; she asked for scraps to piece a baby quilt, which I gladly gave her. And as she sewed, if I had completed my chores or desired a respite from them, I would read to her.

I knew something had changed in her sentiments toward her child when she asked me to read again a passage from Douglass's *Narrative,* which we had completed several weeks before, wherein Mr. Douglass describes how he was separated from his mother in infancy, and saw her but a handful of times before her death, and how slave owners conspired to destroy the natural affection a mother feels for her child and the child for his mother.

She sat in silence after I finished, her silver needle darting swiftly through the fabric scraps in her hands. "If I didn't run off, they likely take my baby away," said she. "Sell him off farther South, maybe. The missus don't like seeing her husband's babies from other women."

"It's hardly the fault of the women," said I, indignant.

Joanna regarded me with amusement. "Don't you hear nothing I tell you about that place? You think it matter that we don't want him? It easy to blame us. She can't get rid of her husband, so she sell us farther South and get rid of the problem. Until the massa take a liking to another."

"This will not happen to you," said I. "You have escaped that fate. Your child will know you and love you, and your affection will make him thrive."

"Freedom make him thrive," corrected Joanna, but she allowed a smile.

Then she asked me to read a later, lengthier excerpt, the story of how Mr. Douglass learned to read and write. As I read his words aloud, I stole glances at Joanna. First she stopped sewing, then a faraway look came into her eye. When I concluded, she briskly took up the quilt pieces again. "This Frederick Douglass a clever man."

"Ingenious," said I. "There is perhaps no more powerful voice championing the Abolitionist cause than Mr. Douglass."

"Maybe it's true what he said, that learning to read spoil a slave, because it make him discontent and unhappy," said she, "but I plenty discontent and unhappy already, and I can't read."

"You could learn. I could teach you."

"Maybe a house slave don't need to read, but a free woman in Canada probably do." She placed a hand on her abdomen. "I'll want to read to my baby, read him the Bible and Mr. Douglass's book, so he know where he came from, and where he can go."

My heart swelled with admiration and affection, and we began our lessons that very day.

So Elm Creek Farm passed from winter into spring, with furtive activity in the night, growing anticipation for the two children who would soon be born, and danger always present, always lingering on the frontiers of our thoughts.

Only later did I realize our greatest threat lay much nearer, that it had crossed our threshold and lay curled up by the hearth, watching us unnoticed, and biding its time.

❧

10

Sylvia's sense of vindication that Elm Creek Manor had been a haven for slaves was tempered by the knowledge that her family had only unwittingly become stationmasters.

"But they did," said Sarah. "That's what matters. When Joanna knocked on the door, they sheltered her. They just as easily could have sent her away."

"I suppose so," admitted Sylvia. And even if they had felt they had no choice but to assist Joanna once she stumbled upon them, they had actively sought to help the later runaways. Sylvia ought to be glad for that, and that this newest revelation did not contradict any of the family stories passed down through the generations. The stories said only that the Bergstroms had run a station on the Underground Railroad, not how they had begun it.

"They continued even after that scare with the slave catchers," said Sarah.

"Yes, indeed. They certainly could think on their feet, couldn't they? Even Anneke. I must say that pleased me. From the way

Gerda described her, I feared she would fall apart and blurt out the secret the moment those two slave catchers arrived."

Sarah laughed but added, "In her defense, remember we're only seeing Gerda's interpretation of Anneke, not the real person."

Sylvia cast her gaze to heaven. "Our friend Gwen, the college professor, already gave me the lecture on 'reliable narrators.' Well, I for one believe Gerda is reliable, and I'm confident her portrayal of Anneke is accurate." She paused. "At least, accurate within a modest margin of error."

"I wonder," mused Sarah. "Where was this hiding place she wrote about?"

"I have no idea." Sylvia wasn't sure which room had been Anneke's sewing room. For that matter, Gerda had not even specified which room had been her own.

"Maybe she assumed her reader would be a more recent descendant, someone who would know whose rooms were whose."

Sylvia shrugged. "Perhaps." But if Gerda's preface was any indication, she had intended her words to be read long after the principal participants in her memoir had passed on.

Sarah gave Sylvia her hand. "Come on. Let's go find it."

"Now?" Sylvia allowed herself to be pulled to her feet. "Don't you think our campers will mind having their privacy invaded?"

"Are you kidding? They'll probably be delighted to be in on the mystery."

Sylvia conceded the point, and so she accompanied Sarah upstairs to the second floor, trying not to allow her hopes to rise too high. The manor had undergone so many changes since Gerda's time, from the addition of the south wing to the extensive remodeling after the fire that occurred in her father's day to the modernizations her sister, Claudia, had added a generation later. Not only might Anneke's sewing room be unrecognizable, it might be gone entirely, its place usurped by the hallway linking the original wing with the new.

They began with the unoccupied rooms, and since it was late August, there were more of these than there would have been earlier in the summer. But while the closets in the first four rooms were not very big, especially by modern standards, they were substantially larger than a "nook" or an "alcove," the two words Gerda had used to describe the hiding place.

"The closets could have been enlarged in the renovations," said Sarah.

Sylvia had no choice but to agree, and felt their chances of identifying the correct room dwindling.

She hesitated before entering the last vacant room. She allowed this suite to go unoccupied during all but their busiest weeks, and even then she had to resist the urge to ask campers to double up rather than assign someone to it. The pink, white, and yellow Grape Basket quilt remained on the wall where Sylvia had discovered it upon her return to Elm Creek Manor, but she and Sarah had long ago substituted a strip-pieced Trip Around the World quilt for the pink-and-white Flying Geese quilt that had once adorned the queen-size bed. Whether because of their estrangement or in spite of it, Sylvia could not bear the thought of someone else, even a friendly quilter, sleeping beneath the quilt her sister Claudia had used as her own.

Sylvia pursed her lips and opened the door. "This closet is certainly large enough," she said briskly, to disguise the hesitation she always felt upon entering her late sister's room. "Claudia wouldn't have settled for anything else. I'm surprised she chose rooms in the west wing, since the south-wing suites are larger and more comfortable."

Sarah led the way into the adjoining room. "I'm surprised there are any suites in the west wing at all."

"There weren't, originally. My father had doorways cut in

some of the walls to turn adjacent rooms into suites." She looked around the room. "Well, there's no closet here, large or small. I suppose we'll have to disturb our campers after all."

"Wait." Sarah placed a hand on her arm to prevent Sylvia from leaving. "What about the loveseat?"

Sylvia eyed the floral tapestry cushions. "What of it?"

"It's set into a nook. Don't you see?" Sarah crossed the room and measured the depth with her hand. "I'd say it's about a foot and a half deep."

"That's not a closet," scoffed Sylvia. "In the room on the other side of the wall, there are two closets, there and there." She pointed to the corners on either end of the concavity in turn. "They encroach on this room's space."

"All the more reason to believe there was once a closet on this side, too. This wall was a part of Hans's original design, right?"

"I can't say for certain . . ." Sylvia hesitated. "I suppose it must have been. My father had a predilection for enlarging spaces, not for making them more intimate."

"Gerda did say the hiding place was shallow, even for a closet."

"True." Sylvia joined Sarah and inspected the wall. Sarah's measurement was conservative, but even so, the alcove could not have been more than two feet deep and five feet long, and Hans's false wall would have taken up some of that space. It was difficult to imagine anyone hiding there for long, in stifling darkness, listening to the bewildering noise of the search, with nothing but a thin wall of plaster separating the fugitive from the pursuer. "I suppose its very narrowness makes it a better hiding place."

"And harder to detect by someone searching in the other room. If it had been any larger, the missing space would have attracted attention."

Sylvia ran her fingertips along the wall, then flipped back the braided rag rug on the floor, but if Hans's false wall had once occupied the space, no sign of it remained. "I'll reserve judgment until I see the other rooms."

They collected an eager group of assistants as they went from one camper's room to the next, explaining their errand and searching for an alcove resembling Gerda's description. Upon completing the last room, however, they concluded that Claudia's room was the most likely candidate.

"That doesn't mean it's definitely the one," cautioned Sarah, when she and Sylvia were alone again. "Gerda doesn't say that Anneke's sewing room was the only one in the house with a nook instead of a proper closet. There might have been others."

"Yes, either lost when the addition was put on or renovated beyond recognition." Sylvia shook her head, exasperated. "Why is it that every time I think we've obtained some evidence, something tangible to prove Gerda's story true, we end up with so many cautions and qualifiers that we're no better off than when we started?"

"It seems that way, doesn't it?" Sarah laughed. "Then you're really not going to like my next question."

Sylvia sighed wearily. "Pose it anyway."

"According to your family stories, the Log Cabin quilt with the black center square was the signal, but it turns out the Underground Railroad quilt was," said Sarah. "So how does the Log Cabin quilt you found in Gerda's hope chest figure into all this?"

April 1859—in which our waiting ends

Come springtime, talk around Creek's Crossing turned to the rising tensions between North and South as often as it did to planting and the weather. Kansas, where we had once planned to settle, had become soaked in the blood of courageous Free-Staters and hostile Missouri raiders, but although I am loath to admit it, the Abolitionists committed their share of atrocities as well. More than once I thanked God for delivering us to Elm Creek Farm three years before, thus sparing us from the violence we otherwise would have faced. I saw the good we did in helping fugitive slaves as but a small show of gratitude for His Providence.

With the return of fair weather came an increase in the number of fugitives who sought shelter with us, but it also increased the number of slave catchers poking about. Far too often I was forced to keep the Underground Railroad quilt inside because earlier that day a patrol had trespassed upon our property or had been bold enough to knock upon our door and inquire if we had seen any suspicious Negroes wandering about, who might be slaves passing as free. I would respond with a curt negative and send them on their way. But their questions did make me reflect upon the situation of the free coloreds around our town. It seemed to me they had been keeping to themselves even more than usual, and I cannot blame them for their wariness. Dorothea had spoken of treacherous slave catchers who, when unable to find their actual prey, would seize upon some poor freedman and pass him off as the runaway. Once spirited off to a Slave State, he could expect no one to believe his accusations against his deceitful white captors, and would be sold into slavery, leaving his family and friends ignorant of his fate and unable to rescue him even if they did know.

Sometimes the slave catchers mentioned Mr. L. and assumed we were on friendly terms with him, since he had sold us his farm (as they believed); they assumed, too, we would offer them the same hospitality he had. Hans provided as little as he could, as cordially as he could. He wished to avoid making enemies or raising suspicions, but he did not want to encourage future visits, lest our secret activities be discovered.

Then one night, I was roused not by a knock on the door but

by a groan of pain from down the hall. My first thought was that Joanna's time had come, but then Hans appeared in my doorway, carrying a light and beckoning me to help. It was Anneke's cries I had heard, though her baby was not supposed to come for another month.

I thought, at first, that it was a false labor, and that it would fade within an hour. I had seen that happen before, especially with a woman's first child. But as the birth pangs grew more painful and more frequent, we all realized that the infant's arrival was imminent.

Hans raced from the house to fetch Jonathan, for I was not so confident in my own abilities that I did not welcome his guidance, especially considering that none of us had expected this child quite so soon. I had assisted my mother as she cared for women in labor, but never had I been alone at the bedside, nor even in charge with helpers of my own. I did what I could to ease Anneke's sufferings, bathing her brow, speaking of the joys she would soon feel upon holding her child, but nothing I did could comfort her for long. She cried from pain and from fear, repeating again and again that it was too soon, that it had to stop, and that I must help her. My longing to do so brought tears to my eyes, but I was powerless.

Roused by Anneke's cries, Joanna soon joined us. When Anneke screamed from the shooting pains in her lower back, Joanna immediately had her go upon her hands and knees on the bed. To my astonishment, this did seem to relieve much of the pain, but when I complimented Joanna on her cure, she only shook her head, grim-faced. "That mean the baby's head the wrong way," said she in an undertone. "Gonna be hard to push him out, so hard."

My alarm growing, I prayed Hans and Jonathan would return soon. When they did, it was so sudden that there was no time for Joanna to conceal herself within the secret alcove. Instead, with a speed that belied her cumbersome belly, she crawled beneath Anneke's bed. I threw a quilt over her as the two men ran up the stairs.

Joanna lay there as still as stone throughout the night and into the day, when the first light of dawn pinked the sky, and Anneke's cries had grown faint and hoarse. It was as Joanna had said; the baby's head was turned directly opposite the way it should have been, which made for long, exhausting hours of pushing. But, thanks be to God, by the time sunlight shone in through the windows, Anneke had delivered a beautiful son.

Jonathan examined the baby and declared him apparently healthy in every way, despite his early arrival. I wept with joy when Jonathan handed him to me to bathe and wrap in a blanket. Afterward I kissed the babe's head and placed him in Anneke's arms, which were trembling from fatigue so that she could not clasp them about her son. Hans embraced her so that his arms supported hers around their precious bundle.

When Jonathan spoke to me next, to ask my assistance in tending to Anneke, I felt his words like a jolt. As foolish as it might sound, until that moment I had thought of him only as the doctor, not as Jonathan, who had once been *my* Jonathan. I tried not to meet his gaze as we cared for the new mother and her child, but my every nerve was raw and conscious of his presence. When our eyes accidentally met, I knew at once that he was thinking, as I was, that we would never together know the joy Hans and Anneke now felt.

But then my heart chilled against him. All that had prevented our mutual happiness was his stubbornness and a misguided sense of duty. He would very likely know the delights of fatherhood with Charlotte, while I would likely never know the joys of motherhood. Jonathan could have married me, if he had been courageous enough, if he had truly wished to. In that respect he was no different than, and no better than, E.

Jonathan remained with Anneke for a little while, but as soon as he departed, I hastened to assist Joanna from her hiding place beneath the bed. She seemed weary, and little wonder, but when I asked her how she felt, she assured me she was fine. Only after I had helped her back into her own bed did she confide that she had never witnessed a birth as difficult as Anneke's. "I hope mine go easier," said she, faintly. "Don't know if I could have done all she just done."

"You have endured more than I would have thought possible for any woman, or any man, for that matter," said I, stroking her head. "You are stronger than you know. You will do just fine."

My words seemed to reassure her, and as she drifted off to sleep, I marveled that a woman who bore such scars upon her back and heart could doubt her ability to endure childbirth.

❧

Summer tilted her head to the side, scanning the titles on the spines of the books. If she had known the Waterford College Library had so many books on block patterns and quilt history, she would have visited this wing a long time ago. Not that she had lacked quilt information—in addition to those she bought from Grandma's Attic with her employee discount, the Elm Creek Quilters routinely exchanged books from their personal libraries, and Sylvia was virtually a walking encyclopedia on the subject of all things quilt-related.

But her friends' resources weren't exhaustive, or she wouldn't be scanning the library shelves looking for more. Unfortunately, while she found many books about quilts from the Civil War era, books focusing on the years before the war were more scarce. Even those three that she had found did not mention signal quilts or the Underground Railroad in their indexes, but

Summer planned to check them out anyway, in hopes that a closer examination might turn up, if not the specific information she sought, other references worth pursuing.

She finished looking over the bottom shelf and moved on to the top shelf of the next case where the books on textile history continued. Most of the books were older titles, with enough dust to suggest they were rarely used. Her gaze lit upon a promising-looking volume, and as she rose on her tiptoes to reach for it, a man's voice said, "Here. Let me get that for you."

"I'm fine—" Summer started to say, but the man reached past her and snatched the book so quickly that her fingertips brushed the back of his hand. "Thanks." *I guess,* she added silently, since she had not needed his help.

"Anytime." The man grinned at her in such a cheerful manner that she found herself no longer minding his unnecessary assistance. He was about her age, with dark, tousled hair and wire-rimmed glasses, and he carried a stack of books under one arm. In the other hand, he still held Summer's book.

Summer suppressed a smile and held out her hand. "Did you want to read it first, or . . . ?"

"Oh." Quickly he handed her the book. "Sorry."

"That's okay." She turned back to the bookshelf and opened the book to the table of contents.

"Is this for your local history project or are you starting something new?"

Summer looked up, surprised. "How did you know about that?"

She might have been mistaken, but for a moment, she thought he looked disappointed. "I've seen you in the historical society's archives at least twice a week all summer."

Then Summer recognized him. "Oh, right. You're the guy who helped me find the court files. You're usually hunched over your books in the carrel by the window, oblivious to the world."

He grinned but said, "Not *that* oblivious." He craned his neck to read the title of the book in Summer's hands. "*Quilts and Their Makers in Antebellum Pennsylvania.* Sounds interesting."

Summer gave him an appraising look, wondering if he meant it. "It is," she said when she decided he was sincere. "It's related to my historical society research project."

"Can you talk about it, or"—he glanced over his shoulder as if to make sure no one could overhear—"are you afraid someone might steal your topic and publish the results before you do?"

Summer couldn't help laughing. "It's not like that." She explained the mystery that had brought her so frequently to the library archives. At first she provided only a sketchy narrative, but when she saw he was truly interested, she warmed to her subject and filled in more details. She concluded by telling him the focus of this particular library search: to find, if it existed, some mention of quilts used as signals on the Underground Railroad.

"I haven't found much," admitted Summer, "and what I have found mentions signal quilts only in passing, as if it's common knowledge that certain patterns were used to designate stations or to transmit directions. Not one book or article has provided a photo of one of these quilts or gives any other kind of concrete documentation that such quilts existed. It's as if the author heard of them from one person, who heard about it from another person, and so on."

"That must be frustrating."

"That's one of the milder words I've used."

He laughed, but then grew thoughtful. "You know, it's the nature of secret signals that they aren't published or even spoken about, or they lose their efficacy. There might not be any published records out there to be found."

"I realize that, but I thought by now diaries or other family records might have been published, since revealing the secrets so many years after the Civil War, wouldn't do any harm."

He shrugged. "More than fifty years ago, my grandfather and his parents fled from Nazi Germany to Switzerland with the help of the underground movement. He told me that even after they came to America, even when the war had been over for decades, his parents said very little about the secret signals and communications they used during their escape."

"Why?"

"They said they couldn't risk it, since one never knew if those signals would be needed again someday."

April into May 1859—in which we raise and attempt to dispel suspicions

Anneke and Hans's good news spread rapidly through town, and Elm Creek Farm was soon besieged with well-meaning well-wishers, bearing covered dishes and baby quilts, all eager for a peek at the beautiful little boy. Anneke delighted in the attention paid to her son, and I was grateful for the food, since I was so busy playing nurse I could scarcely find a moment to catch my breath, much less put together a meal for the new parents, Joanna, and myself. Hans and I had agreed we could not display the Underground Railroad quilt under such circumstances, and I was plagued by thoughts of fugitives spending the night in the woods within sight of our house, unable to receive food or clothing or the comfort of a reassuring word.

Joanna helped me as she could, but with visitors arriving unannounced at all hours of the day, she found herself scrambling for the hiding place so often she finally decided it would be most prudent for her to remain there throughout the day. Thinking of her shut up in that confined place drove me to distraction, and I yearned for the flood of neighbors to slow to a trickle.

Our most frequent visitor was someone who would have been chagrined to learn her presence kept Joanna shut up within the secret alcove: my dear friend Dorothea, who came over nearly every evening after her own chores were finished to assist me with mine. Would that every woman could be blessed with a friend possessing such a willing heart and generous spirit! Frequently during those weary days, when I was tempted to fall asleep on my feet or crawl under the bedclothes and stuff my quilt into my ears rather than help Anneke soothe her howling infant, Dorothea's unwavering serenity and quiet confidence cheered me, and helped me marshal my strength so that I could be the kind of aunt my family needed.

Two of the last guests were, in my view, the two least welcome. A fortnight after my nephew was born, Mr. Pearson and Mrs. Engle paid their respects to the new mother. They arrived at dinnertime, just as Hans returned hungry from the fields, so I was obliged to entertain them better than I otherwise would have done. While Anneke and Mrs. Engle sat in the front room, with Mrs. Engle holding the baby and cooing to him while Anneke looked on, radiant, I set out some of the dishes the neighbors had brought and hoped Mr. Pearson would not feel the need to assist me. He did not, apparently, for when he entered the dining room, he merely stood there smirking, as if I should be grateful he chose to keep me company.

"Anneke looks well," he remarked, leaning against the door frame and watching me set the table.

I made a noise of agreement but otherwise ignored him.

He followed me in a leisurely fashion as I went back and forth, carrying dishes from the kitchen to the table. "How fortunate is she to know the bliss of motherhood," said he. "It is truly the highest state to which women can aspire, don't you agree?"

All manner of retorts rose to my sharp tongue, but I withheld them. If he hoped to provoke within me even a spark of jealousy toward my sister-in-law, he was wasting his own time as well as mine. "Anneke has been richly blessed, and I am truly overjoyed for her," said I, and I meant it with all my heart.

He seemed disappointed by the lack of venom in my response, and his gaze turned away from me—and alighted on the Underground Railroad quilt, folded and forgotten on the sideboard. "What's this?" asked he, unfolding it.

"A quilt."

"Yes, of course, I see that," he snapped, but then he frowned. "I do believe I've seen this pattern elsewhere."

"Perhaps your mother has made a similar quilt."

"No, that's not it."

He studied the quilt with such intensity that I grew agitated. "Oh, indeed, Mr. Pearson, are you such a connoisseur of patchwork that you know every quilt block your mother has made?"

He looked up from the quilt, his eyebrows raised in mild surprise. "She would like it better if I did, but I confess I only pretend to listen when she chatters about her needlework." He folded the quilt and returned it to the sideboard. "If you'll excuse me, Miss Bergstrom." With his usual smirk in place, he returned to the front room.

I chided myself for my shaky nerves and resolved to conceal my emotions so well that I would be thought as serene as Dorothea. Knowing that Mr. Pearson could not possibly understand the quilt's significance steeled my confidence, and since he dared not bait me too much in front of the others, dinner passed without a mishap.

With so many other distractions to occupy my thoughts, I put the incident out of my mind. When another week passed, and it seemed safe again, I draped the Underground Railroad quilt over the clothesline and made ready for new arrivals.

There was, indeed, much to prepare, so much we did not

know about when Joanna first knocked upon our door. Food and rest were the most pressing needs, but after that, the fugitives often needed new clothing, especially shoes, for the men, and gloves and bonnets for the women, the better to pass themselves off as free if they were seen. They also needed papers declaring them free citizens, although I sometimes wondered what good these would do if they were apprehended by slave catchers. Still, if the documents spared only one runaway from the clutches of slavery, they were worth far more than the paper and ink and the work I put into them. I must say I became quite an accomplished forger. Once Hans said, in jest, that he knew people from his vagabond days who could help me turn a nice profit with my skills, but Anneke was decidedly not amused by the suggestion. She said we broke enough laws on Elm Creek Farm not to joke about violating more for mere lucrative gain. For someone who went about day and night beaming over her beautiful son, motherhood had rendered Anneke rather humorless.

In addition to clothing and forged papers, the fugitives needed food for their journey. I learned to bake hardtack and sent them off with that as well as dried apples and hard cheese that would not spoil quickly. They needed directions to stations farther north; Hans determined the most prudent courses based upon rumored slave-catcher activities. Most of all, our guests needed hope, and so we provided encouragement in abundance.

Sometimes our visitors shared news from the places they had abandoned, and their accounts confirmed what we had begun to read in the papers: that Southern animosity for the North was increasing as Northern condemnation of Southern slaveholding became louder and more insistent. Even Southerners who did not own slaves resented Northerners for their self-righteous attempts to interfere in Southern matters, which, they feared, could destroy the economy of the entire South. "Abolitionist" was a word spoken with venom by Southern whites, and slaves knew better than to utter it, even to ask in all innocence what it meant.

But most runaways who passed through our station were too exhausted and wary to converse much about the institution of slavery. Their strength they reserved for the difficult flight to Canada; their thoughts they saved for the family and friends they had left behind, and would almost certainly never see again.

Four weeks passed between the birth of Anneke's son and the restoration of the signal quilt to the clothesline; another five days passed with no knock on the door in the night. Then one morning shortly after dawn, when Hans was already in the fields and I was tending to my household chores, two quick raps sounded.

I opened the door and discovered a colored man dressed in farmer's clothes, the brim of his hat pulled down low over his eyes—and our Underground Railroad quilt folded over his arm. A flash of panic shot through me—did he not realize how he endangered himself and us, approaching the house so boldly in daylight, the signal quilt in hand?—so that I did not at first recognize him as Mr. Abel Wright, the owner of a farm lying roughly fifteen miles south and west of ours outside the boundaries of Creek's Crossing, whose wife I had met at Charlotte Claverton's quilting bee.

I stammered out a greeting and invited him inside, but he refused, saying that he had to return to his fields. Then he held out the quilt to me and said, "I just wanted to tell you not to use this quilt no more." When I told him I did not understand, he looked away, paused, and added, "Too many people know about it. Someone talked. Someone down the line, or someone captured—I can't rightly say who. But you ought not to use this anymore." Then he looked directly into my eyes and said, "Do you get my meaning?"

I did indeed, but I also found myself wondering why it had

not occurred to me before that free Negroes in the North might also be stationmasters. Even now it shames me to admit this, but until that moment, I had assumed the Underground Railroad was operated solely by benevolent whites. Though I had prided myself on being an enlightened sort, I had never suspected that Negroes might be perfectly able and willing to help one another, without the benefit of some white person's direction. What this said about me, with all my high ideals and rhetoric, it troubled me to ponder.

I thanked Mr. Wright and hurried off to find Anneke. She was in the baby's room, rocking and nursing contentedly, but when I repeated the warning to her, her eyes grew large with fright, as if she could already hear the pounding hooves of slave catchers' horses storming up the road toward us. Indeed, I had to struggle to maintain my own composure, for although I could not discern the connection, I knew our neighbor's warning was somehow linked to Mr. Pearson's odd musings about the Underground Railroad pattern. That despicable man would bring us trouble. He had not done so yet, and so I had no explanation for the intensity of my feelings, but I was certain he meant us harm.

"We shall have to contrive another signal," said I.

Anneke declared she knew exactly the thing: a quilt pattern common enough that it would not attract unwanted attention, and yet simple enough that even I could fashion it well. It was called Birds in the Air, and as it was fashioned of many triangles, we could, by the placement of the quilt upon the line, indicate in which direction the fugitives could find a safe haven.

At first I was dubious; I suggested a pattern of logs in the woodpile or an arrangement of buckets by the well, anything as long as it bore no resemblance whatsoever to the signal that had become a danger. But Anneke noted that slave catchers, being men, were likely to ignore clotheslines, and even if a slave catcher did take note of it, he would ignore other quilts in his search for the one pattern he knew Abolitionists favored. "They would not suspect we would substitute one quilt pattern as a signal for another," said Anneke. "That is why it is the perfect choice."

Thus she persuaded me, and thus we began our second signal quilt.

Since nearly every moment of Anneke's days and nights was given over to the care of her son, the task of completing the quilt fell to me, the least able quilter in the county. Anneke suggested that I make a crib-size quilt, both to hasten its completion and to contribute to our ruse: No one would think it odd to spot the same baby's blanket so frequently upon the clothesline, for as I had recently learned, infants rarely kept garments or bedding clean for long. Moreover, I finally consented to learn to use Anneke's sewing machine, something she had been pestering me to do since our arrival at Elm Creek Farm. Pumping the treadle and guiding the fabric through the machine was hardly work at all in comparison to the tedious drudgery of hand sewing. I worked swiftly, feverishly, whenever my other chores would permit, and as the days passed, one Birds in the Air block after another joined the rising pile beside the sewing machine. Now that Joanna did not need to hide continuously in the secret alcove, she, too, learned to use the sewing machine, and she completed as many blocks as I.

Working side by side, Joanna and I joined the blocks into rows, sewed the rows together, then layered the pieced top, cotton batting, and a muslin lining in Anneke's frame. We devoted one long stretch from dusk until dawn quilting, and in the morning when Anneke came downstairs with the baby in her arms, she found us putting the last stitches into the binding.

The three of us inspected the quilt. "It'll do," said Joanna matter-of-factly.

I nodded, too tired to do anything more, but Anneke took the quilt and wrapped it around her son. "It's beautiful." She cradled her son in her arms and kissed his brow.

My heart swelled with pride. Anyone else would have laughed in surprise to hear this quilt, sturdily though hastily made, pieced of scraps and quilted in simple lines, given such praise. But I understood my sister-in-law's meaning. The quilt was beautiful not for itself but for what it represented, and what it would accomplish.

It was the finest thing my hands ever made, then or since.

We sent word to stations south of us—as before, I shall not explain the particulars of how—so that fugitives would know to look for our new signal. Within days of the completion of the quilt, it had beckoned a runaway from Virginia into our home. The Elm Creek Farm station of the Underground Railroad was open once again.

11

The second time the librarian passed by to remind Summer that the Waterford Historical Society's archives closed early on Fridays, Summer nodded absently and glanced at her watch. She had five more minutes to search the database before the librarian would kick her out and lock the door, but with the pitiful luck she'd had so far that day, five minutes more or less probably wouldn't make much difference.

She sighed and shut down the computer, admitting to herself that she might be wasting her time. Lately she had turned up nothing related to the Bergstroms or Elm Creek Farm, so she had not even told Sylvia about her searches. She would rather have Sylvia believe she was too busy to investigate rather than dash her hopes that something remained out there, waiting to be found.

"That was one heavy sigh. You're supposed to be quiet in the library."

Summer looked over her shoulder to find the same dark-haired man who had tried to help her in the stacks smiling at her from his usual carrel. "Sorry," said Summer. "Does this mean you have to confiscate my library card?"

"I don't think that happens on the first offense." He rose and crossed the aisle, and nodded to the computer. "Are you having trouble finding something?"

"Are you kidding? I've been here for two hours and all I've found is frustration." Summer laughed ruefully. "I wouldn't mind if at least one of my possibilities would have led somewhere."

"Maybe I can help. What are you looking for?"

"Birth records, death records, documents relating to a family that immigrated here before the Civil War. I looked through the hard copies of the city government files already, but when I couldn't find what I wanted, I tried the database. Unfortunately, it's even less complete than the books."

"Did you look in the old local newspapers? The historical society has microfiche of issues going as far back as the 1800s."

"I looked, but the years I wanted are missing."

"Did you ask at the newspaper office?"

Summer nodded. "They said they might have the issues but they couldn't be sure, and they couldn't spare the personnel to help me look."

"That's rude of them. I think I'll cancel my subscription in protest."

"Don't do it on my account. It's not their fault." Summer checked her watch and, seeing that the archives were about to close, began gathering her notebooks and photocopies. "All I can give them is a last name and a time period. If I could be more specific about what I was looking for, they could probably be more helpful."

The man picked up his stack of books and followed her to the door, where the librarian waited, key in hand. "Have you checked the phone book?"

Summer raised her eyebrows at him. "They didn't have phones back then, so they didn't have much need for phone books."

"No, I mean our phone book. The family you're researching lived in this area, right? Maybe there are some living descendants who would be willing to talk to you. Even if they don't have the specific details you need, they might be able to point you in the right direction. They could give you additional names to research, like other branches of the family."

"Oh, I know there are living descendants," said Summer. One living descendant, anyway, but if Sylvia had that information, Summer wouldn't be searching for it. And as far as additional names were concerned—

"That's it," exclaimed Summer. She had to get home and get her hands on a phone book. "Thank you so much, um—"

"Jeremy. And you're?"

"Summer. Thanks, Jeremy. You've given me a great idea." She left the archive room and headed briskly for the stairs, Jeremy close behind. "I should have asked you for help before. I'm so glad I happened to be here during your shift."

"My shift?"

She glanced at him. "You don't work for the library?"

"Nope. And not for the historical society, either."

Summer stopped short and regarded him with a skeptical grin. "But you offered to help me search the archives."

He shrugged. "I'm just a good citizen." When Summer laughed, he added sheepishly, "I'm a grad student in history. I study in the Waterford Historical Society's room because it's quiet. Usually no one comes in there except for you. Not that I'm keeping track or anything."

He looked so embarrassed Summer couldn't resist teasing him. "Well, if I need any more research assistance, I'll be sure to ask."

He grinned, pleased. "You know where to find me."

May 1859—in which we enter our darkest hours

Our new signal quilt proved so successful that I allowed myself to believe we had eluded the dangers Mr. Pearson's apparent recognition of the Underground Railroad pattern had hinted at and our neighbor's warnings had confirmed. How foolish I was. I should have been more vigilant, but even in hindsight I do not know how I could have predicted from which direction the most dangerous winds would blow.

Fair weather brought a steady stream of runaways; they followed the creek north to our home, with slave catchers never far behind. Elm Creek Farm, which as recently as winter had seemed so remote, now was assured of a visitor at least every second day—and for every three friends we ushered inside to safety, we encountered one unfriendly stranger, full of suspicions and questions. And once again, the same two slave catchers who had searched our home in March came to contend with us.

They arrived amid a fierce thunderstorm, the sudden, violent sort we had learned to expect in that region each spring, but which awed us anew each season. Our first warning of the men's approach came in a respite between thunderclaps: the high, shrill whinny of a horse, so close and sudden we started. Barely a heartbeat later there was an urgent pounding upon the door.

Needless to say, our usual night visitors did not arrive on horseback. Joanna hurried as fast as she could from the fireside upstairs to the secret alcove, and as I assisted her inside, my heart raced with alarm. I wondered who was outside, and if they had glimpsed Joanna through the windows.

When I returned downstairs and found the two familiar and unwelcome figures dripping water in our foyer, I felt a lump in the pit of my stomach, which did not fade until I realized they must not have seen Joanna, for if they had, they would even now be dragging her from the hiding place. I longed to order them from the house, but we could not send them back out into the storm without raising their suspicions. Instead Hans took them to the barn where they could leave their dogs and tend to their horses, and I began to prepare them something to eat.

Suddenly Anneke clutched my arm, stricken. "Gerda," said she, and nodded out the window toward the clothesline.

I raced outside to snatch the Birds in the Air quilt from the line. I returned inside, thoroughly drenched, and hurried upstairs, where I wrung out the quilt in my washbasin and hid it beneath my bed. I had barely enough time to change into dry clothes and return to the kitchen before the men returned.

My own stomach was in knots, so that I hardly dared speak to them as I served their supper, lest they detect my turmoil. Anneke busied herself with the baby, as if too distracted by him to notice the men. To my relief, they conversed with Hans as if they did not notice anything out of the ordinary; or perhaps they noticed but had grown accustomed to odd behavior from the Bergstrom family, as we were never at ease when they were around. I prayed they would soon depart, but as the hour grew late with no abating of the storm, we had no choice but to invite them to spend the night.

They bedded down beside the fireplace, and as I climbed the stairs, I thought of Joanna crouching in darkness almost directly above her enemies. Upstairs, I paused outside the hidden alcove long enough to murmur a warning to Joanna, then crept off to my own room, where I lay in bed, too tense to sleep. If Joanna should cry out as she slumbered—if slumber was possible in such close quarters—or if she did not hold perfectly still and silent, the men below might hear her. We might be able to convince them that Anneke or I had made the sound, but what if—and this was my greatest fear—what if Joanna's child should decide to enter the world that very night?

Eventually snores drifted up the stairs, telling me the slave catchers were resting peacefully, but they were the only ones in the household to do so. Even the baby, who woke twice to nurse, did not rouse them with his cries. I heard Hans and Anneke whispering, but from the sewing room, there was not even the smallest noise. For my part, I held perfectly still in bed, clenching my quilt in my fists, praying that we would somehow manage to avoid detection a second time.

When finally the morning sun began to pink the sky, I dressed and went downstairs to the kitchen to prepare breakfast, making no attempt to work quietly and allow our unwelcome guests to sleep any longer than absolutely necessary. I heard them stirring in the other room, speaking in low voices, then one or both left the house briefly and returned. By the time I summoned everyone to the breakfast table, I had regained my confidence. The men had not demanded to search the house, and perhaps our hospitality would once and for all convince them we had nothing to hide.

We Bergstroms all but wolfed down our food in our eagerness to bring a swift end to the meal, and we could barely contain our relief when the first of the two remarked that they would need to set off immediately, to make up for time lost. Then he looked directly at me and said, "Miss Bergstrom, I don't wish to trouble you none, but if you could spare some of that bread, we'd be mighty grateful for it on the road." He smiled. "We never know when we'll come across a home as welcoming as this one."

"Of course." I hastened to the kitchen and packed a bundle as quickly as I could, and spinning around to return to the dining room, I ran right into the slave catcher. I gasped, startled, and stepped back. "Excuse me," said I, and tried to laugh. "I did not realized you followed me."

He stepped toward me. "Why so nervous, Miss Bergstrom?"

"I'm not nervous, not at all." I thrust the bundle at his chest, shoving him backward. "Here. Enjoy the bread."

He caught my arm. "Yesterday, when we arrived, you wore a blue dress," said he, stroking the fabric of my sleeve with his other hand. "When we returned from the barn, you were dressed in brown."

"You are mistaken," said I, and pulled myself free. "You have confused me and Anneke. I was dressed in brown. She wore blue."

"Miss Bergstrom, are you accustomed to hanging your laundry out to dry in the middle of a rainstorm?" He fixed his gaze on mine. "Or is that how you Dutch wash your bedclothes?"

I feigned embarrassment. "Oh, I fear you have discovered me. And I had so hoped no one had noticed. Please don't tell Anneke I forgot the baby's quilt outside. She'll be so upset."

He scowled, but before he could speak again, Hans entered and offered to help the two men with their horses. The slave catcher nodded, his gaze still upon me, but suddenly he turned and addressed my brother. "What are your plans for L.'s cabin?"

Hans shrugged. "I haven't yet made any plans for it."

"Seems strange to leave it unused, a good, solid building like that," said he. "Or maybe it doesn't go unused. Maybe you don't care if passersby sleep there, so long as they don't bother you up at the big house."

"That cabin is on my land. Anyone entering it is trespassing, whether they're sleeping or looking for someone who is."

"That's good to know. You don't want to encourage vagrants." The slave catcher slung the bundle over his shoulder. "Of course, it could be people stay there without your knowing about it."

"I'd know." Hans's voice was like ice. "Now it's time you were on your way."

The man had little choice but to challenge Hans or obey, so

at last he and his companion departed, leaving me shaken and afraid. The more I tried to alleviate the slave catchers' suspicions, the more I gave them reason to scrutinize us. They would not cease to observe us, I knew, whenever their searches took them near Creek's Crossing.

As soon as their horses disappeared into the forest, I hurried upstairs to free Joanna from the secret alcove. Faint and hungry, she asked me in a strained voice to help her to bed. I brought her water, which she drank thirstily, and something to eat, which she picked at but seemed unable to stomach. She kept touching her abdomen and wincing in pain, but when I asked her if she thought the baby was coming, she shook her head and told me the pains had been coming for days now, but they always faded when she rested.

I assured her that now that the slave catchers had departed, she would most likely not need to stir from bed for a while. She nodded wearily, and I prayed that my assurances would not be proven false.

Fortunately, as it happened, we had no visitors, friendly or otherwise, for three days and two nights. But on the third night, my slumber was interrupted as it had been a month before: not by a knock on the door, but by a woman's cry of pain.

Anneke heard it, too; she reached Joanna's room at the same moment I did. We entered to find Joanna on her feet and drenched with perspiration, one hand at the small of her back, the other on the bureau, supporting her weight. "The baby be here soon," gasped Joanna. "This been going on all night."

"You should have woken us earlier," I scolded, and tried to assist her back into bed, but Joanna brushed me off and said she felt better on her feet. With Anneke on one side and myself on the other, we helped her walk about the room, pausing when Joanna wished, which was when the pain was greatest. She paused more and more frequently as one hour passed, and then two, but by then her legs trembled with fatigue so that she could scarcely stand.

We helped her into bed and made ready to deliver the baby, and I said a silent prayer that my experience assisting Jonathan was fresh enough in my mind that Anneke and I would be able to manage without him. At first Joanna's labor progressed as we had expected based upon Anneke's experience, but just as Anneke assured Joanna she was nearly through the worst of it, Joanna screamed in pain. "It's coming," she gasped. "It's coming now."

I glimpsed Anneke's surprised expression, a mirror image of my own, before I examined Joanna. I discovered, to my horror, not the baby's crown but a tiny foot, already entering the world.

Again Joanna screamed, and Anneke, coming to see what I saw, drew a sharp breath. "Don't push," said I to Joanna. It was all I could think to say. We needed more time, time for me to figure out what to do.

"We need Dr. Granger," said Anneke in a low voice.

"We can't summon him," said I. Joanna's freedom, our own security, and the safety of future runaways seeking shelter with us depended upon our secrecy.

"We must. And quickly." Anneke left me to take Joanna's hand and mop her brow. Joanna looked from her to me, and I knew she had detected our alarm. "What's wrong?" she asked, then sucked in a breath and screamed in pain.

I needed no further inducement. I ran for my brother, and within minutes he was on his way to summon Jonathan. "How will I explain Joanna?" asked Hans before he left. "What should I tell him?"

"Tell him only that a woman is in labor and that she and the child are in distress," said I. That was all Jonathan needed to know to help her. I would worry about the consequences of divulging our secret after she was safe.

The wait seemed endless, but no more than an hour passed before Jonathan arrived. He attended at once to his patient, speaking to me and Anneke only to ask our assistance.

Once before I had witnessed Jonathan save a life, but on that night I believe I watched him save two. The child entered the world feet first, entangled in the cord that had sustained him in the womb, and when he made no sound upon feeling the cold air upon his skin, I thought for certain he was dead. But Jonathan worked upon him and rested him upon his mother's bosom, and as Joanna placed her arms around her son, I saw the little limbs move, the chest rise and fall. When at last he uttered an angry, indignant cry, tears of relief filled my eyes, and I whispered a prayer of thanksgiving.

Jonathan glanced up at me from caring for Joanna. "Anneke can assist me with the rest," said he quietly. "Hans might need you outside."

"Why? What's wrong?"

"The cabin is burning."

Only then did I detect the faint odor of woodsmoke upon Jonathan's clothing. I stared at him, my mind in a whirl, then bolted downstairs and outside.

The odor hit me full force the moment I left the house. Ashes drifted like snowflakes on the air, and through the trees on the other side of Elm Creek, something glowed a fierce red. I ran toward it, and before I even reached the bridge I saw the churning clouds of smoke and heard the roaring as the flames consumed our former home. My brother was silhouetted against the flickering light, motionless.

I did not realize I was screaming as I ran until Hans spun around and seized me about the waist. "Gerda, stop. Stay back."

"Why don't you fight it?" I shouted, but my voice was nearly lost in the din.

"I tried." His voice was low in my ear. "It was too far gone.

All I can do is let it burn, and be sure it doesn't spread to the barn or the house."

I watched as his gaze followed sparks rising from the fire, carried aloft to the treetops, brighter than the stars against the night sky. The fire cracked and popped, and a bright shower of sparks shot out, igniting a patch of grass several yards away. Immediately Hans was upon it, beating out the fresh flames with a gunny sack drenched in water.

Then I noticed the buckets scattered on the ground, only one among them still upright and full of water, and the smoldering sacks among them. Without another word I took a sack in hand and joined Hans in his vigil. We kept watch all night and into the day, sometimes one on guard alone as the other ran to fill the water buckets in the creek, sometimes both of us racing from one place to the next as several fires erupted at once. By midmorning our former home was nothing more than a smoking ruin, but the barn and the new house were undamaged.

Hans studied the ground encircling what remained of the cabin. A horse, perhaps two, had left deep impressions in the mud leading up to and surrounding the smoking timbers. "The slave catchers?" I asked him, examining the hoofprints.

"Could be, but they didn't make these prints the night they stayed with us. I watched them leave, and they didn't pass this way. If they were up here before coming to the house, the prints would have been washed away in the storm."

He walked amid the ruins, kicking rubble aside with his heavy boots. Suddenly he bent down and examined a half-buried object. "Sister, would you know if we forgot a can of kerosene up here when we moved to the new house?"

"I know very well that we did not."

"Someone else must have brought this one I see here, then."

Despite the heat radiating from the ruins, I shivered. "Who?"

"I don't know."

"I doubt any of the runaways left it."

"I'd bet my best horse they didn't." Hans stood and regarded me gravely. "You should know, the cabin wasn't burning when I left to fetch Jonathan."

I nodded, absorbing the full meaning of his words. Not only had someone set fire to our cabin, but whoever had done so had arrived when Joanna was in the worst of her travail. At that distance, he—or they—might very well have heard her screams of pain. The slave catchers, Mr. Pearson and his cronies—anyone who might have wanted to frighten us because of our Abolitionist sympathies would have known Anneke had already had her baby, and that I was not with child.

Soberly, we returned to the house. Anneke was in the kitchen, carrying her son in one arm and setting out breakfast with the other. Hans took the baby from her and stayed to explain what had happened with the fire, while I continued upstairs. I peered in the doorway of Joanna's room to find Jonathan packing his instruments and Joanna reclining in bed, nursing her child, who was swaddled in the quilt she had made.

Jonathan looked up and saw me but quickly looked away. "She has a fine, healthy son," he told me.

"And Joanna?"

"She needs rest, and something to eat." He returned to the bedside and spoke briefly with her before picking up his bag and joining me in the hall. "She should not travel for at least a week. I would have her wait a month for the baby's sake, if she can. If it is safe for her to do so."

"I understand."

"I'll return tomorrow to check in on them, but be sure to summon me immediately if either encounters any difficulties." Still he would not look at me. "You should have called for me earlier."

The rebuke, mild though it was, stung, perhaps because I had been chiding myself for the same lapse in judgment. "You know why I could not."

"Yes, I do."

We descended the stairs in silence, and I led him to the door. There I turned and regarded him defiantly. "Aren't you going to ask me who she is and what she is doing here?"

At last he met my gaze. "I have many questions. Someday, when it is not so unwise for you to answer, I will ask them."

We stood in the doorway, nearly touching, and for one frantic moment I thought he might kiss me, but then he tore his eyes from mine and bolted out the door. I shut it behind him, hard, and turned my back to it.

Hans entered and lowered himself into a chair beside the hearth, exhausted. Anneke followed close behind; she handed her son to me and went to her husband to remove his boots and wipe the soot from his face with a wet cloth. I was conscious then of my own fatigue, and my disheveled appearance. I cannot explain it, but despite all the terrible events of the previous night, at that moment I could think of nothing but how I must have looked to Jonathan compared to the graceful loveliness of Mrs. Charlotte Claverton Granger, and I felt coarse and ashamed.

But those thoughts lasted only a moment, for Anneke looked up at me, her mouth in a tight, angry line. "This time it was the cabin," said she. "Next time it might be the house."

I tried to retort but coughed instead. My eyes stung from smoke; my lungs felt thick and rough, my throat raw. "No one would dare."

"How can you know that?" demanded Anneke. "Are these such compassionate, scrupulous men that they will merely terrorize us and not murder us as we sleep?"

Wearily, Hans held up a hand. "Anneke, you are in no danger."

"Don't speak to me as if I am a child." Anneke rose, strode across the room, and snatched the sleeping baby from my arms. "I will not have it, from either of you. I will not be treated like a fool."

I was dumbstruck, but Hans said, "Very well. You're right, Anneke. We are all in danger, every one of us, even the baby. Every day Joanna and her child remain beneath our roof we risk discovery and prosecution. Every day we hang that quilt upon the line we risk our freedom and our lives. Is that what you want to hear?"

Anneke began to weep. "I cannot bear this anymore. I cannot endure this constant fear, this endless worrying. We have done our part to help. Now we have our son to think of."

"If we stop now," said I, "how many fugitives will we condemn to death or recapture?"

"If we do not stop, to what will we condemn my child?"

"How can you think only of your own child, when Joanna is upstairs with a child of her own? Would you like to see her back in chains? Would you like to see that helpless infant torn from her, sold off like a pig or a horse to the highest bidder? How would you feel if you could never see your son again?"

"Better her than us," shrilled Anneke.

My words choked in my throat, and I gaped at her, shocked into silence.

Anneke glared at me, defiant. "If we are captured, we will be thrown into prison, and my son will be taken from me just as Joanna's would have been taken from her had she remained a slave."

I found my voice. "You cannot truly believe that."

"Mr. Pearson assured me that is the law."

"Mr. Pearson," said I, scornful. "What does he know of the law?"

"Better yet," said Hans, "what does he know of our activities?"

His voice was hard, and Anneke blinked at him. "Nothing."

Hans regarded her, his gaze piercing. "You're certain."

"As certain as I can be," stammered Anneke. "Do you—do you think I would tell him we're part of the Underground Railroad?"

"Have you told him?"

"Of course not." Anneke's face was scarlet. "How could you accuse me of betraying you? Have I ever lied to you? Have I ever deceived you?"

"Anneke, my love." Within an effort, Hans rose from his chair and put his arms around his wife. "I did not mean to suggest you would intentionally tell him, but perhaps in a moment of fear, you might have accidentally—"

Anneke tore herself away from him. "I am neither that stupid nor that careless."

I knew Hans would not care for her disrespectful tone, but it was too late to warn her.

"Be that as it may," said my brother sternly, "we cannot take that risk. I forbid you to speak to Mr. Pearson as long as Elm Creek Farm is a station on the Underground Railroad."

Anneke stared at him. "You cannot mean that."

"I do." Hans returned to his chair, his back to us.

"And how am I to avoid speaking to him when I resume working for Mrs. Engle? He is her son, you recall, and he does upon occasion visit his mother at her shop."

"Then you will not resume working for her," said Hans tiredly. "You have too much to do as it is, with the baby."

Anneke stood motionless, the baby in her arms. Her mouth

opened and shut without a sound, as if she longed to argue but was too astounded by his demands to muster up a retort.

Hans was oblivious to her fury. "When we no longer harbor runaways, our lives will return to normal. Then, if you still wish to, you may resume working for Mrs. Engle without fear."

"How long will that be?"

"I do not know. Until the crisis passes. Until we are no longer needed."

Without a word, Anneke left us, the baby in her arms. I heard her steps light on the stairs and on the floor above as she went to the room she and Hans shared. "You have angered her more than you realize," said I. "Do you think forbidding her to work was necessary?"

"I thought you would have been the first to support my decision," said Hans, surprised. "Do you truly think allowing her near Mr. Pearson and Mrs. Engle is wise?"

Of course I did not, and I could not deny I was relieved Anneke would be protected from their influence. Still, the way Hans had ordered Anneke to accept his decision made me uneasy. He did not treat her as an equal, but as an inferior subject to his will. I did not doubt he loved her, and that he was a good man with a good heart—and yet he wielded his authority as the man of the household in a way that made me wonder what he would do or say if I or Anneke challenged him. Unlike Anneke, I would not be able to defer to him if his choices went against my conscience or good judgment.

Troubled, I excused myself, and after washing and changing into clean clothes, I went to see Joanna. She was sleeping when I entered, her tiny son nestled beside her beneath the Shoo-Fly quilt I had made, still swaddled in his own quilt. Joanna had told me the pattern was called Feathered Star, and that she had chosen it because often she had used the North Star as her guide out of the land of slavery. "When he old enough to understand," said she, "I show him this quilt and tell him how his mama brought him North to freedom."

Remembering the pride and love that had shone in Joanna's eyes as she had spoken of the babe within her womb, I stroked his head and marveled at the perfection of his features; I touched his little hand and felt my heart swell with delight as he seized my fingertip in a strong grip. This beautiful boy was a precious child of God, but if Josiah Chester of Wentworth County, Virginia, could see him, he would think only of his worth on the auction block. If he were to feel the baby's grip, he would think with smug satisfaction of how strong a field hand he would one day become.

Joanna stirred in her sleep, and I placed my free hand upon her brow, stroking her hair to soothe her, watching her as she slumbered. The scar from the burn of the flatiron would forever mar her face, but nothing could diminish the beauty of her spirit. She had shown more courage than any of her protectors, not only in fleeing her captors but also in finding the strength to endure sickness, fear, and unimaginable danger to win the freedom that should have been her right; and in finding the strength to love the child she had not wanted, the child who had come from herself but also from her greatest enemy.

Joanna slept peacefully now, sheltered at Elm Creek Farm, knowing no one could tear her child from her arms, confident that she would soon resume her journey north to Canada and freedom. As I looked upon them, I knew I could never consent to abandoning the good work we had begun by responding to Joanna's knock upon our door. Not only for Joanna and her child, but for every woman who had been raped by a man who dared call himself her owner, for every mother who had ever wept as her child was sold away from her, for every son who had been powerless to defend his mothers and sisters and friends who cried out in pain and grief—for them we must continue, despite the risks. What were our risks compared to those of the people who sought shelter with us? Let slave catchers suspect and challenge us. Let cowards burn our cabin in the night. They would not deter me from doing my small part to forward the cause of freedom and equality for all in this new land.

I had left the stratified society of the Old World behind only to find it, steadily and surely, being reproduced in the New. This was not the America I had envisioned as I crossed the sea; this was not the America I had learned to love as we Bergstroms tilled the soil and laid the cornerstone of our home. That America had not been waiting for us, so we must build it with the sweat of our brow and the work of our hearts, as surely as we had built Elm Creek Farm.

"Why can't you tell me where we're going?" asked Sylvia, clutching her purse in her lap and hoping she wasn't overdressed in her beige striped suit.

Summer kept her eyes on the road. "It's a surprise."

"Hmph. It will be a fine surprise indeed for our friends if we aren't back in time for our business meeting."

She glimpsed the smile Summer tried to hide, and couldn't help allowing some of her grouchiness to ease—but only some. A cloud of foreboding had hung over her thoughts ever since she had put down Gerda's memoir the previous day, and the agenda for the Elm Creek Quilters' upcoming business meeting only worsened her gloom. Granted, she didn't like to dwell on the bittersweet conclusion of the camp season, but she usually enjoyed helping plan the annual end-of-the-season party, where the faculty, staff, and their families would celebrate another successful year. This year, though, her mood was so melancholy she almost wished she could miss the whole affair rather than risk ruining everyone else's fun, but she was supposed to be the hostess, so she couldn't very well dodge her responsibilities.

She eyed Summer suspiciously. Maybe her friends suspected her misgivings and had contrived this little jaunt with Summer to keep tabs on her. "I have no intention of avoiding the meeting," she told Summer firmly, just in case. But Summer merely laughed and assured her she wouldn't miss it either, and she'd be sure to have them back in plenty of time.

The car turned onto a residential street near the downtown, into a neighborhood populated by the families of Waterford College faculty and administrators. "Are we going to Diane's house?" asked Sylvia, admiring, despite her mood, the changing colors of the maples and oaks lining the streets.

"No." Just then Summer pulled into the driveway of a neat white colonial house with black shutters. She shut down the engine and turned to her passenger. "We're here."

"Where's here?" demanded Sylvia, but Summer merely bounded out of the car and came around to open Sylvia's door. Sylvia grumbled under her breath as they walked up the stone path to the front door, but Summer's mystifying behavior had piqued her curiosity, and as her young friend rang the doorbell, she waited eagerly to see who would answer.

A woman in her middle years opened the door. "Yes?"

"Kathleen Barrett?" said Summer. "I'm Summer Sullivan, and this is my friend Sylvia Compson."

Kathleen smiled. "Oh yes. You wanted to see Mother." She opened the door wider and beckoned them inside. "She's been looking forward to your visit ever since you phoned. She doesn't get many callers. She's a little tired today, but when I asked her if I should postpone your meeting, she absolutely forbade it."

"We won't keep her long," promised Summer.

Kathleen nodded and led them into the living room, where a woman who looked to be in her late eighties sat in an armchair, an antique Dove in the Window quilt pieced from indigoes and turkey-red cottons draped over her lap. Her daughter introduced the visitors to her mother, Rosemary Cullen, then disappeared into an adjoining room.

"What a lovely quilt," exclaimed Sylvia, taking a seat beside Rosemary. "May I have a closer look?"

Rosemary beamed and held out the quilt to her. As Sylvia and Summer admired it, Kathleen returned with a tray of tea and cookies. After the women had served themselves, Summer at last revealed the purpose behind their visit. "Sylvia," said Summer, "Rosemary is the great-granddaughter of Dorothea Nelson."

Sylvia gasped. "I don't believe it." She looked from Summer to Rosemary to Kathleen and was delighted to find them all smiling and nodding. Sylvia clasped Rosemary's hand. "My word, dear. I feel like we're old friends."

"We ought to be," said Rosemary. "If what your young friend here says is true, my great-grandmother and your great-grandfather's sister were very close."

"They were the best of friends," declared Sylvia. "Gerda wrote of Dorothea quite often in her journal. Dorothea taught Gerda how to quilt—although Gerda was a reluctant student." Suddenly she gasped and clasped her hands together. "My goodness—I suppose this means Dorothea and Thomas had children. They had none at the time of the memoir."

"My grandmother was born shortly after the Civil War began," said Rosemary. She gestured to a sepia-toned portrait hanging above the fireplace. "She's the baby, there, sitting on her mother's lap. The man is my great-grandfather."

Returning the quilt to Rosemary, Sylvia rose and drew closer to the portrait. "This is Dorothea?" The woman looked kind but ordinary. From Gerda's description, she had expected Dorothea to be beautiful, her serenity and benevolence evident in every line of her features. Suddenly it occurred to her that she had no basis for that assumption. Gerda had never described Dorothea's appearance, only her spirit.

Sylvia's gaze shifted to the man, a slight, scholarly fellow who nonetheless had an air of steadiness and strength. "Now Thomas, on the other hand, looks exactly as I imagined him."

"We're fortunate to have any picture of them together," said Kathleen. "Not only because of their era, but also because Thomas died a few years after this picture was taken."

"He fought with the Forty-ninth Pennsylvania in the Civil War," said her mother. "He was killed in the Spotsylvania campaign, in May 1864."

"Oh, dear." Sylvia felt a pang, as if she had just heard of the recent passing of a dear friend. "I know it happened so long ago, but my heart goes out to Dorothea. From what Gerda writes, she and Thomas seemed devoted to each other."

"They were," agreed Rosemary. She stroked the fragile quilt on her lap gently but lovingly, and her gaze grew distant. "This was one of the quilts Dorothea pieced as a young wife. She sent it off with her husband when he went to war. After he died, the quilt was not among the possessions returned to the family. Dorothea assumed it had been lost."

"But it wasn't?" prompted Summer when the older woman's voice trailed off.

Rosemary roused herself. "No, indeed. It was stolen. Perhaps 'found' is a better word. Thomas lost it somehow—in the chaos as they retreated from the enemy, or it was taken from him after he died—we'll never know. But somehow it ended up in the hands of a Confederate soldier." She shrugged. "I can't blame him for keeping it once he had it. It is a lovely quilt, and it must have seemed a godsend to a weary soldier on a cold night.

"The soldier's conscience must have plagued him, though, for several years after the war ended, he sent the quilt back to Dorothea with a letter. He wrote that his wife was a quilter, and knowing how much love she put into every stitch of her creations, he couldn't rest until this quilt was returned to its proper owners."

"I think his wife must have made him write that," said Kathleen.

Rosemary smiled. "Be that as it may, Dorothea had her husband's quilt restored to her, and it has remained in our family ever since."

Summer looked intrigued. "How in the world did he know where to send it?"

"Well, I'll show you." Carefully Rosemary turned the quilt over to reveal a small section of embroidery. "Dorothea put her name right here."

"'Made by Dorothea Granger Nelson for her beloved husband, Thomas Nelson, in our sixth year of marriage, 1858. Two Bears Farm, Creek's Crossing, Pennsylvania.'" Sylvia sat back in her chair, pleased. "At last, someone who knew how to properly label her quilts."

"Too bad she didn't pass that lesson along to Gerda and Anneke when she taught them to quilt," said Summer.

Sylvia was about to agree when she saw that Rosemary's eyes had taken on a faraway look again. "My great-grandparents were true sweethearts. He wrote to her often from the front lines, very affectionate letters, and she saved them all." She shook her head. "The poor man. He was not meant to be a soldier. He was too gentle and good to ever become accustomed to killing his fellow man. But he believed completely in the Union cause, and he was determined to fight for what he believed in. That much is evident from his letters."

"I would like very much to read them," said Sylvia, without

thinking, and hastily added, "That is, unless you wish to keep them within the family."

Rosemary looked uncertain. "Well, I hate to let them out of the house. They're so fragile, you see. But I think I might be willing to share them with you in exchange for a peek at that memoir of your great-great-aunt's."

Sylvia hesitated, unwilling to promise to divulge Gerda's secrets before she knew what they were. Before their hostesses could have detected her discomfort, Summer quickly spoke up to cover for her. "What about Dorothea's brother, Jonathan Granger?" she asked. "Do you know what became of him?"

"Oh yes, Jonathan." Rosemary pursed her lips and thought. "I'm not certain whether he survived the war. He and Thomas weren't in the same unit, so Thomas had no news to pass along about him. Thomas mentioned Jonathan only to ask Dorothea if she had heard from him, and to say he was keeping Jonathan in his prayers."

"Jonathan became a soldier?" asked Summer in disbelief.

"He joined the army as a doctor, not to fight," explained Kathleen. "From what Thomas says, Jonathan was as passionate about the Union cause as he was, but it was his devotion to medicine that inspired him to enlist. Doctors were needed desperately, and so he went."

"I understand Jonathan and his wife had children," said Sylvia.

"Oh my, yes," said Rosemary. "Four or five, I believe. Anytime I hear the last name Granger, I always wonder if we're related somehow."

Sylvia nodded, because it would have been rude to scold her hostess for not maintaining better ties with her distant relations. Besides, Sylvia could hardly criticize Rosemary for losing track of a third cousin twice removed when Sylvia herself had allowed fifty years to pass without speaking to her own sister.

Instead Sylvia took a deep breath. "Did Thomas ever mention the Bergstrom family in his letters?" She prepared herself for a disappointing reply.

"I don't recall offhand," said Rosemary apologetically. "I'd have to go back and read them again. He did mention neighbors and friends occasionally, but since the names were unfamiliar, I always skimmed right past them."

"Dorothea would be the one to have news about the Bergstroms," said Summer to Sylvia. "What we really need are Dorothea's letters to Thomas."

Kathleen shook her head, regretful. "I'm afraid we don't have any of those. I'm sure Dorothea wrote to her husband at least as often as he wrote to her, but his letters were the ones to survive, since they were mailed to Dorothea at home. Dorothea's letters could easily have been lost or destroyed on the battlefield."

Sylvia nodded glumly, thinking of the precious information lost forever. "I suppose we ought to be grateful we have any of these fragile paper records to remember our ancestors by. My memoir and your letters aren't nearly as durable as most monuments to the past. It's quite a responsibility now that they belong to us, isn't it, to make sure they endure so that we can pass them on to future generations?"

Rosemary and Kathleen exchanged a look. "Did you hear that, Kathleen?" inquired Rosemary.

"I heard it," said Kathleen, with a laugh. To her guests she added, "You've stumbled upon a little family disagreement."

"In my will, I've left the letters and the Dove in the Window quilt to Kathleen. She's my eldest." Rosemary patted Kathleen's hand. "It's just as you said, Sylvia: I want to pass these treasures on to future generations, and I know Kathleen will be a faithful steward until it comes her time to pass them on." She leaned forward and confided, "Kathleen thinks I should leave them to a museum. Can you believe it? The very idea. Giving our family heirlooms to strangers."

"A museum would know how to properly care for them," said Kathleen. "Part of good stewardship is ensuring that something lasts so that it may be passed down. Those papers are getting more fragile every day, Mother, and the quilt is, too."

Sylvia decided it would be prudent to stay out of the argument, but Summer said, "I'll bet Waterford College would love to have them."

"That's exactly what I suggested." Kathleen turned to her mother. "Think of what the students could learn from Thomas's letters. And think of your great-grandparents' contribution to history and to the cause of freedom. Shouldn't some part of their memory be preserved, and in a way that would teach others about all they did?"

"You just want to brag about your family," admonished Rosemary. "Well, I think Dorothea and Thomas would be the last people to brag about themselves."

"I don't want to brag, but I am proud of them." To Sylvia and Summer, Kathleen explained, "They ran a station on the Underground Railroad."

"Yes, I know," said Sylvia, delighted to have another detail of Gerda's journal confirmed. "Gerda and my great-grandparents operated one, too, on Elm Creek Farm. The Nelsons and the Bergstroms each knew about the other family's station, but they didn't speak about it openly."

Rosemary looked puzzled. "Why not? I gathered that everyone knew about my great-grandparents' activities."

"Well . . ." Sylvia hesitated. "I don't believe that was so. Gerda only stumbled upon the truth about your great-grandparents by chance, and she mentioned several times that both stations were run with the utmost secrecy."

"But then . . ." Rosemary looked to her daughter for help. "How did everyone know about it?"

Kathleen shrugged. "Maybe the truth came out after the war started."

"No, no." Rosemary shook her head firmly. "That's not it. This was before the war, when they stopped running their station. I know it was before the war."

Surprised, Sylvia and Summer exchanged a look. "The Emancipation Proclamation and the war changed the way the Underground Railroad operated, but it was still needed until then," said Summer. "Your great-grandparents were devoted Abolitionists. Why would they stop running their station early?"

"Well—well, I must say I don't know." Rosemary gave her daughter a pleading look. "Do you remember, dear?"

"Did they close their station because they were discovered?" asked Sylvia.

"I—I suppose that could be how it happened," said Rosemary, distressed. "I'm not sure. I know I heard something about it somewhere, maybe in those letters. Or maybe my grandmother told me. I'm afraid I don't remember."

Sylvia could see that Rosemary had become troubled and anxious, so she was relieved when Kathleen rose, signaling an end to the interview. "It's all right, Mother. Maybe it will come to you later, but if not, that's fine."

"What really counts is that we were able to meet you," said Summer, rising. She reached over and took the older woman's hand. "I really enjoyed hearing your stories. Thanks for sharing them with us."

"It was my pleasure, dear," said Rosemary, but she seemed fatigued.

Sylvia thanked her as well, and she and Summer left. They drove back to Elm Creek Manor in silence, both mulling over Rosemary's words. Sylvia puzzled over the new details about the

Nelson family as well as Rosemary's strange insistence that their Underground Railroad station had ceased operation while it was very likely still needed, wondering what it all meant.

Suddenly Sylvia's thoughts returned to another part of Rosemary's story. "Summer, do you suppose Margaret Alden's Elm Creek Quilt could have a history similar to Rosemary's Dove in the Window?"

"How do you mean?"

"Perhaps Anneke made the Elm Creek Quilt for Hans to take into battle—I don't know if he fought in the Civil War, but let's say for the sake of argument that he did. Maybe she quilted those scenes of Elm Creek Farm into the cloth, to remind him of his home. Perhaps he lost the quilt, or traded it for a pair of boots or some other necessity, and eventually it fell into the hands of Margaret Alden's ancestor."

Summer was silent for a long moment. "It's as logical as any other explanation we've thought of."

"Hmph," said Sylvia. Summer meant well, but Sylvia recognized faint praise when she heard it.

12

June 1859—in which we are undone

A chill descended upon our household, but since I was certain it would eventually lift, I paid it less attention than I should have. To be sure, with two young babies in the house, we adults had no time to idly ponder one another's moods and tempers. Sometimes I felt as if I spent all day on the run, racing from one chore to the next, from wiping one infant's face to changing the other's diaper, from singing to one while Anneke rested to rocking the other so Joanna could sleep. It occurred to me once, when I was feeling overtired and self-pitying, that I had inherited all of the drudgery of motherhood but none of the joys.

I knew Anneke resented Hans's decision to forbid her from working for Mrs. Engle so long as we remained stationmasters. I could see it in the set of her jaw, in the abruptness of her conversation, in the way she brooded in her chair after her son had fallen asleep in her arms. The warmth that had entered her behavior toward Joanna cooled again, surprising me, for I had expected their shared experiences to draw them together.

I also knew Anneke was angry, but I did not know how angry until the storm that had been gathering on the horizon finally crashed down upon us, like a cloudburst from a clear blue sky.

I remember that it was a Friday, for the next day I had planned to attend a quilting bee at Dorothea's. Though I looked forward to the event with pleasure, all that week my heart had been filled with wistful anticipation, for Joanna and I had been planning her continuing journey north. She insisted she felt well enough to go, and her baby certainly seemed healthy and strong; in fact, though nearly a month younger than Anneke's son, he was nearly as big and at least as alert.

We planned her route carefully, knowing she would be carrying a precious burden, and would need certain shelter whereas other runaways could endure a night or two sleeping under the stars. For that reason—and because she had become so dear to us, and because her particular appearance encouraged us to believe our scheme could succeed—we devised an unusual means for her to journey on.

Anneke gave her two dresses, a hat, and a pair of gloves. I gave her forged documents identifying her as Caroline Smith, a widow from Michigan. Hans gave her the best present of all: a one-horse carriage and a Bergstrom Thoroughbred to pull it. Joanna and her son would travel in fine style indeed, and seeing her, not only would people assume she was a lady, but they would also take for granted that she and her child were white.

Joanna was the only one who doubted she could pull it off. "Soon as I talk, they know what I be."

"Then pretend you have an affliction of the throat," said I. "Pretend that the same accident that scarred your face robbed you of your voice, and that you must communicate through writing. You can do that."

"Yes, I can," said she. "Thanks to you."

I was so moved by her plainspoken gratitude that I embraced her. As thrilled as I was that Joanna would soon make a new life for herself and her son in freedom, I would miss her, for we had grown close over our lessons and chores. She promised to send word once she was settled, but I feared that I would never hear from her again, and would forever wonder what had become of her.

Those worries had settled into the back of my mind that Friday morning as Joanna and I took stock of her son's layette and made plans to sew more clothes for him before they set off on their journey. I was holding the baby, and we were laughing over something I can no longer recall when I heard the door burst open downstairs. "There's trouble coming," shouted Hans.

There was a terrible note in his voice that filled me with dread. Without a moment to lose, Joanna scrambled into the hidden alcove, and I replaced the false door and the sewing machine behind her. Then, just as I spun around and discovered to my horror the baby still on the bed where I had left him while assisting his mother, I heard the baying of dogs, the pounding of horses' hooves, then boots on our front porch and fists on the door.

"Bergstrom, open up," shouted a man, and then came a crash as the door burst open beneath the weight of many arms.

Without thinking, I snatched up the baby and fled to my room. He looked up at me, solemn and uncomprehending, as I wrapped him in a quilt and set him on the floor of my closet, praying he would not cry out for his mother. I pulled dresses down from their hooks and flung them upon him, then tore back the quilt from my bed. In the moments it took to make my room seem carelessly untidy so no one would think to poke through quilts on the floor of my closet, I heard an exchange of angry voices from below, and Anneke's scream. My heart quaked with panic as I shut the closet door and fled from the room to help her and Hans.

I made it only as far as the top of the stairs; from there I spied Hans sprawled unconscious on the floor, and Anneke kneeling by his side, weeping. Led by their dogs, the two slave catchers who had plagued us in the past were running up the stairs toward me, followed closely by two men from town I recognized but did not know by name.

I tried to block their way, but they easily shoved me aside and ran past me, down the hall and into the sewing room. I heard the sewing machine moved aside, then the cracking of plaster, and then the shout of triumph: "We've got ourselves a n——, boys!"

White-hot fury burned away my fear. I did not think; I ran into the sewing room and found those hateful men with their hands upon Joanna, and I lashed out at them with all the strength in my body. I do not know how I managed it, but somehow I freed her. "Run, Joanna," I screamed, but then a fist swung out and struck me hard in the face, and I collapsed.

Groggy, I watched as the men dragged Joanna from the room. Even now, when I close my eyes against my tears, I hear her low moan of despair, and my heart is rent once more, always in the same place, so no scar will ever form.

I gasped in pain as a boot connected with my side. "Got any more n——s here?" demanded the second slave catcher. I said nothing and rolled over to get away from him. "You answer me when I ask you a question, b——!" He kicked me again, harder, and I heard a rib crack.

I watched as he hastily searched the room, then stormed out. I heard him enter the vacant room next door and ransack it; by the time I stumbled into the hallway, he had moved on to the room Anneke and Hans shared. My instinct was to snatch Joanna's baby from his hiding place and flee into the woods, but I knew I would never make it. Instead, gasping from pain, I descended the staircase, praying that the little boy would be as still and silent as stone. My only hope came from knowing that the slave catchers' dogs could not have been given the baby's scent.

Behind me, the slave catcher entered my room with his dog at the ready, but I refused to watch, lest he become suspicious and search it more thoroughly. I forced myself to continue taking each stair one painful step at a time, until I reached the first floor. Dazed, I watched Anneke cradling Hans's head in her lap. Through the front door, I saw the other slave catcher bind Joanna's wrists and lash the other end of the rope to the pommel of his saddle.

He dug his heels into the horse's side, and as he pulled Joanna into a stumbling run, her head flung back and her eyes met mine. A desperate, silent plea passed between us, and then she was gone, yanked out of sight by the trotting horse.

Hans groaned and sat up, and the two men from town immediately dragged him to his feet. At that moment, the second slave catcher came downstairs, muttering curses. "That's the only one here now, but I swear they had others," he told his companions.

"One is enough to break the law," said one of the townsmen. With that, he declared that my brother was under arrest. As he took Hans's arm to lead him away, the other man placed his hands upon me.

Anneke followed us outside as my brother and I were taken into custody. "You were only supposed to take the runaway," said she, weeping. "Mr. Pearson promised me they would not be punished."

My captor made some retort about how Anneke ought to be grateful she was allowed to remain free, and if not for their kind hearts and her infant son, they might have acted otherwise. But I hardly heard him for the ringing in my ears.

Anneke had betrayed us.

Hans stared bleakly at her as we were forced onto the men's wagon and taken away.

They took us to the city courthouse, where, to my amazement, Dorothea and Thomas Nelson were already imprisoned. Dorothea's face was ashen, and Thomas's face was bruised and bleeding. A second posse of slave catchers and local lawmen had descended upon them at the same time we were assaulted; two runaways, a husband and wife, had been discovered hiding in their cellar. Not long after our arrival, another wagon brought Mr. Abel Wright—the colored farmer who had warned us about the Underground Railroad quilt pattern—his wife, Constance, and their two sons. The younger clutched his arm to his side, gritting his teeth from the pain. Later we learned it had been broken in two places.

They left us in a cell for hours with no food or water, and not a word about the charges against us. Perhaps they thought our crime so evident that the normal rules of law need not be followed. We spoke in hushed voices about what we ought to do when they finally did address us; Dorothea led us in prayer. And still we waited.

We slept as best we could on the cold stone floor and were awakened before dawn by a constable offering us water and bread. Later that morning, the chief of police arrived in an indignant fury, having heard of our arrests only upon his arrival. He had us brought a decent meal and separated Dorothea, Constance, and me from the men, thinking this nod to our modesty another act of kindness, though we would have preferred to remain with the others.

As afternoon turned into evening, Dorothea urged us to take courage. Her friends in the Abolitionist movement would see to it that we had the best lawyers to plead our case, and surely no jury would punish us harshly for disobeying the Fugitive Slave Law so reviled in the Northern states. "The worst they can do to us is break our spirits," said she. "And we will not allow that."

I nodded, but at that moment I believed my spirit had already been shattered. In my mind's eye I saw Joanna, her hands bound, being pulled behind the slave catcher's horse. I thought I heard her baby's muffled cries as he lay hidden in my closet beneath the quilt and my scattered dresses. Surely Anneke would have searched for him, knowing that he had not departed with his mother—but what would she have done upon finding him? Anneke, who would betray her own husband—what would she do with Joanna's child?

What, I wondered, would become of Joanna now?

My heart was filled with despair, despite Dorothea's attempts to comfort me.

In the evening, Jonathan was finally permitted to see us. Never had I seen him so angry, though outwardly he remained calm and promised us that everything possible was being done to arrange our release. It was through Jonathan we learned that Mr. Pearson had arranged the raids on all our homes, having enlisted the aid of powerful friends in the local government sympathetic to the Southern cause. But they were in the minority, Jonathan assured us; our allies included most of Creek's Crossing, including the chief of police and the judge who would most likely preside over our arraignment, should one occur. Even now the Nelsons' solicitor, a friend of Jonathan's from university, was demanding we be charged or released immediately, and he promised to bring to justice all who had violated our rights.

Dorothea seemed greatly reassured, and she asked about the men. Jonathan hesitated before responding. Thomas was fine, though angry and worried about his wife. Jonathan had set the youngest Wright son's broken arm and had persuaded the chief to release him into Jonathan's custody so that he might recuperate in better surroundings, but he might yet be compelled to return to prison. Jonathan paused and gave his sister a look that she immediately understood, for she put an arm around Constance to lend her friend strength.

Only then did Jonathan tell us worse news than we could have imagined: One of the slave catchers had declared that the Wright men were runaway slaves recently escaped from his employer's plantation.

"But Abel has been free all his life," cried Constance. "Both of my sons were born right here in Pennsylvania."

We knew, of course, that the Fugitive Slave Law rendered the truth irrelevant. The slave catcher's sworn testimony alone was sufficient to detain the Wright men, and once his employer corroborated the lie, the Wright men would be condemned to slavery.

"We cannot allow Abel and his sons to be put in chains," said Dorothea. "We cannot."

"We won't," said Jonathan. "They aren't allowed to testify for themselves, but there are people enough in this town who will speak up for them."

"People enough?" echoed Constance bitterly. "What people? My people? Since when does the law listen to my people? Or do you mean white people? Which white people do you mean? Which white people in this town are going to risk themselves for my family?"

Dorothea and Jonathan exchanged a glance, and Dorothea said, "You do have friends, Constance. White as well as colored."

"You will also have documented evidence even Cyrus Pearson cannot refute," said Jonathan. "I will have certified birth records at hand before the week is out, as well as an affidavit from the doctor who delivered your sons. Do not fear, Constance. They can threaten you all they want, but their lie will not persist."

Constance seemed little reassured by their words, perhaps because history had taught her to put more faith in actions, but there was a glint of resolve in her eye that told me the slave catchers would not take the Wright family without a fight.

We comforted Constance as best we could, then I remembered my brother and asked Jonathan how he fared. Hans had asked about me and about Anneke, Jonathan said, but otherwise he sat apart from the others, brooding in silence, his disbelief and shock impossible to conceal.

"I promised to send him word about you," said Jonathan to me. "What should I tell him?"

"Tell him I am fine." I was not about to give Hans reason to worry about me; he had enough to occupy his thoughts with Anneke.

"Gerda would not complain, but she is injured," said Dorothea.

I demurred, but Jonathan insisted upon examining my injuries through the bars separating us, whereupon he discovered my broken rib. If I had thought him angry when he arrived, he was truly furious now. He stormed off down the hallway from whence he had come, and I do not know what he said to the chief of police, but in a few minutes Jonathan returned with a constable, who meekly unlocked the cell and told me I was free to go.

I hardly knew what to think, but when Jonathan put his arm about me, protecting my injured side, I allowed him to lead me away. The constable swung the door shut again with a loud clanging of metal—and Dorothea and Constance still trapped inside. I stopped short. "What about my friends?"

"It's all right," said Constance firmly. "We'll be fine."

"Let's go before they change their minds," murmured Jonathan.

"No." I reached through the bars and extended my hands to Dorothea and Constance. "I will not leave you here alone."

"I only got orders to let you go," said the constable. "The others stay."

"Then I stay, too." I pulled away from Jonathan. "Unlock this cell, or give me the key and let me do it myself."

"Gerda, this is not necessary," said Dorothea.

"I said, I'm staying." I was nearly in tears. Dorothea, Constance, and Jonathan pleaded with me, but I was resolute. Joanna had just been dragged off to face her fate alone. I could not similarly abandon Dorothea and Constance.

Before he left, Jonathan treated my injury as best he could, but I still feel it, even to this day. If I had gone with him as he had entreated me to do, the bone might have knitted properly. For years afterward, whenever I complained of the stiffness, Dorothea would smile gently and remind me that it was my own fault.

The next two days were a blur, fear alternating with boredom, numb disbelief with despair. Sometimes we heard voices shouting outside, too faint for us to make out their words. Jonathan visited us daily, and the Nelsons' lawyer came once, accompanied by a newspaperman. With grim determination he took down our every word and assured us that once people read his story, there would be such an outcry against our imprisonment that our captors would be wise to change their names and move out West.

On the morning of the third day, Jonathan arrived with mixed news: We women were free to go, but the men must remain in custody. "The people of Creek's Crossing are outraged that women should be held for so long without any charges brought against them," said Jonathan.

"They ought to be outraged, not because we are women, but because we are citizens with the right to due process," said Dorothea. "A right that has been shamefully denied us."

I marveled at her composure and strength. The same ordeal that had cowed me had invigorated her, and while I wanted nothing more than to flee to the seclusion of Elm Creek Farm, Dorothea seemed ready to challenge any accuser. Her courage warmed me, and I grew determined to fear no more. Whatever became of us, I was not ashamed of our so-called crime, and I would face the consequences with head held high.

As the constable escorted us from the cell to the common area, the chorus of voices that had been barely audible grew louder. The room where we were discharged had windows facing the main street of Creek's Crossing, and through them, we beheld a large crowd, men and women alike, milling about and shouting, some with signs bearing slogans. The officer who processed us warned that despite our release, we would in all likelihood be brought to trial, and that we must not attempt to flee the county. As he spoke, he seemed harried by the noise outside and declared that if it were up to him, he would set free the lot of us if it would quiet that crowd.

Dorothea and I exchanged a look, and that was the first moment I realized the commotion was about us.

When we went outside, the deafening cheer of the crowd hit me with such force I might have stumbled if not for Jonathan's strong arm supporting me. There seemed to be more people in the street than in the whole of Creek's Crossing.

"They've been gathering for days as word spreads," said Jonathan. "People have come from several counties around."

Dorothea gasped and touched my shoulder. "Do you see that?" said she, nodding to a banner in the midst of the crowd.

I could not miss it. In foot-high letters, it demanded: RELEASE THE CREEK'S CROSSING EIGHT!

"Dear me." I felt faint.

"It appears the battle is joined," said Jonathan to his sister, wryly.

"Then we will fight," declared Dorothea, and she waved to the crowd, both arms stretched high above her head. They responded with a roar of approval.

"Do not be misled by this," warned Jonathan. "Pearson's cronies work in the shadows, but they are numerous, and they have powerful allies. We will have a fight on our hands, and you did break the law."

"I would break it again in a heartbeat," I heard myself say, thinking of Joanna. Dorothea squeezed my hand, eyes shining with pride and sympathy; Constance nodded solemnly but glanced back at the courthouse with misgivings, as if she could not bear to leave her husband and eldest son behind.

Jonathan had arrived that morning on horseback, not knowing we would be released, and so he had sent to the livery stable for a horse and carriage. None too soon for my liking, it carried us away from the throng, following the road out of town toward Elm Creek Farm.

Dorothea offered to stay with me until Hans came home or my injury ceased to pain me, but I told her there was no need. *Anneke will be there,* I almost said, and then my heart trembled. I could not bear to see her again. I thought of how she might greet me, with tears of remorse, with defiance, justifying her treachery, and I wished with all my remaining strength that I would return home to find her gone, the children placed in a neighbor's safekeeping.

Three years we had lived together, and I had come to love her as a sister, and yet I must not have known her at all. I could not comprehend her betrayal. Was it as simple as spite? I had forced her into sheltering runaways by hanging that quilt upon the line week after week; Hans had forbidden her to continue work that she loved. Was that why she had confessed to Mr. Pearson, to have her revenge upon us?

Beside me, Dorothea, Jonathan, and Constance talked of strategy for our defense, but I pondered the mystery that was Anneke. She had betrayed us, and yet it could be said that we Bergstroms had betrayed her time and time again, ever since our fateful meeting in New York. Hans had lied to her about what awaited us in Pennsylvania; I had shared her house instead of allowing her peace and privacy with her husband; we both had dismissed her fears that our clandestine activities would be discovered. And so they were at last, but only through her agency.

My heart swelled with anger, and silently I cursed the moment we rescued her from the bureaucrats in Immigration. How much better it would have been for all of us if we had left her there, alone. How well she had repaid us for our good intentions!

"Gerda?"

Dorothea's gentle voice interrupted my thoughts, and I realized the carriage had stopped at the front door of my home. My companions regarded me inquisitively, and Dorothea asked again if I would like her to stay. Once again I refused. Unless Anneke had indeed fled in shame, I would have to confront her eventually, and postponing the encounter would not make it easier.

But I was in no hurry. I remained outside and watched as the carriage drove off. Only when it had reached the bridge over Elm Creek did I realize why the livery horse had seemed so familiar. He was Castor, or perhaps Pollox—I never could tell them apart. He was older now, and less vigorous than he had been when Hans won him from Mr. L., but as proud and elegant a creature as he had ever been. As for me, I felt myself to be an entirely different woman from the one he had brought here three years before. How little that woman had known of what awaited her in this place.

Behind me, the door burst open. "Gerda!"

I stood frozen in place, eyes closed against my tears; I could not even turn around. Suddenly Anneke was on the ground at my feet, clutching my skirt and weeping. "I am so sorry," said she through her sobs. "It was never meant to happen this way."

My voice was cold; I could not even look at her. "Where are the children?"

"Inside."

I entered the house. Anneke had moved the cradle to the front room, beside her chair; in it, David and Stephen slept side by side. I cannot describe my relief upon seeing them safe and sound. As much as I had wanted to avoid seeing Anneke and wished her away, I had feared she would have taken the children with her or, worse yet, taken her own son and abandoned Joanna's.

Anneke had followed me inside. "Where is Hans?" Her voice was muffled as she fought to control her tears.

I told her, abruptly. She asked me if Hans would soon be freed, and I told her I did not know. Then Stephen woke and began crying; I reached for him, but Anneke darted in front of me and picked him up. I watched her as she comforted him. Her face was bleak. "Please, Gerda, let me explain."

I wanted to shut my ears to her voice, but my profound bewilderment at her betrayal needed an answer, so I listened. She told me how Mr. Pearson had frightened her with tales of the terrible punishments lawbreakers received in the American judicial system; he filled her with stories of the suffering of Abolitionists in Kansas. All the while she worked at Mrs. Engle's shop he worried her thus, playing the role of a concerned friend, aware of the Abolitionists among her friends and family. After the baby was born, he doubled his efforts; she did not tell him about our secret activities, yet he suspected nonetheless. Since Anneke rarely went into town, he came to Elm

Creek Farm when he knew Hans and I were away, insisting that unlawful behavior of one member of the family would condemn the entire household. For her own safety, and for the safety of her son, Anneke needed to come forward with the truth. The burning of the cabin ought to be sign enough that we were under suspicion, and we would want the law on our side if angry neighbors continued to show their disapproval in such a frightening fashion. If Anneke confessed, she would avoid punishment and would ensure better treatment for Hans and me, much better than if we were discovered, which Mr. Pearson made seem a certainty.

So at last she told him. She had not meant to mention the Nelsons or the Wrights, but once she let the secret out, Pearson pounced on it and forced the rest from her. His manner changed entirely, and whereas she had only moments before thought him her benefactor, she now feared him. She begged him to tell no one and to forget everything she had confessed, but he insisted he could not, lest he be drawn into our guilty conspiracy. All he would promise was that although any runaways found on our land must be taken, we Bergstroms would be permitted to remain free.

As Anneke spoke, my heart, which had been filled with icy contempt for her, began to soften. Guileless Anneke cared for her family more than anything in the world, and knowing this, Mr. Pearson had deliberately preyed upon her feelings. Anyone subjected to that constant barrage of fear and threats might have succumbed in time; I might have myself, if I did not so despise Mr. Pearson and suspect his every word.

But just as I was about to tell her so, Anneke added, "You and Hans were never supposed to suffer. I would need a lifetime to tell you how sorry I am. Will you ever forgive me?"

I chose my words carefully, to be sure I understood her. "You regret betraying us?"

"With all my heart."

"Because Hans and I were imprisoned."

"Yes," said Anneke passionately, taking my arm. "Only Joanna was meant to be taken."

My heart became like cold stone toward her again. "I cannot forgive you for what you did to Joanna. I cannot forgive you for what you have done to her son." I tore my arm away from her. "As for what you have done to us, if Hans can bring himself to forgive you, so will I. But only then."

And thus, I thought, I would never need to forgive her.

The next morning I went to Dorothea's to consult with her about freeing the men from prison. My injured side pained me with every step the horse took and my mind was a tempest of anger and grief. By the time I reached the Nelson farm, a plan had coalesced: I would contact Josiah Chester and find Joanna. If he had sold her farther south, as she had always feared he would, I would make him tell me who had bought her. Then I would buy her freedom. If it took every cent I had, if it took Elm Creek Farm itself, I would not rest until I saw her free again, free and reunited with her son.

When I arrived at the Nelson farm, Dorothea, her parents, and their lawyer were engaged in an urgent discussion of our legal entanglements. Breathlessly I announced my plan to Dorothea; she kindly did not warn me of the difficulty of the task, but allowed me to believe I could accomplish it presently—after our immediate concerns were resolved. I agreed and sat down as the discussion resumed, but as the others debated and planned, I was feverish with eagerness to begin my search for Joanna. I composed a letter to Mr. Chester in my head, determined to send it off that day.

But by the time I returned home, my side throbbed and ached so that I had to grit my teeth to keep from moaning. I cared for the horse and stumbled into the house, where Anneke immediately perceived something afflicted me. I confessed my broken rib, and although in my pride I wanted to disdain her help, when she hastened to assist me, I hurt too much to refuse.

I hardly stirred from my bed the next day; Anneke brought the babies in to keep me company, and I was so glad to see them I clung to them, sleeping and waking, barely allowing Anneke enough time to see they were kept with full bellies and clean diapers. Gradually my coldness toward Anneke thawed; she had become a sister to me, and I was too heartsore to hate her as passionately as I once thought I could.

The next morning I moved downstairs to the front room, where I wrote to Mr. Chester and exacted a promise from Anneke that she would post my letter that very day. My mind somewhat more at ease, I played with the boys while Anneke worked in the kitchen garden. Then, suddenly, I heard a horse upon the road, and Anneke cry out. I hurried to the window and, to my glad astonishment, discovered the rider was Hans.

Anneke had run out to meet him; they exchanged words I could not discern, but Anneke's impassioned plea for forgiveness was unmistakable. My brother replied tersely, stoic and unmoved by Anneke's tears. On and on they went, Hans proud and angry high atop his horse, Anneke remorseful and ashamed, clinging to his leg and to the bridle as if she feared he might ride off. The boys began to grow restless and hungry, but I stood frozen at the window, my heart in my throat, wondering how it would end, if this would be the end of our family.

Then Hans slid down from his horse and embraced his wife.

I drew back from the window and hugged both babies to my chest, not knowing whether I was glad or disappointed. I loved Anneke, but whenever I thought of Joanna, my heart hardened and I knew a lifetime of apologies would never compensate for how Anneke had ruined her.

Together Hans and Anneke entered the house. They said

nothing of what words or promises they had exchanged, but I knew eventually the chasm between them would close.

We entreated Hans to tell us how his release had been accomplished, for as recently as yesterday, the Nelsons' lawyer had said we were in for a long, difficult struggle.

For months tempers around town and across the county had been growing hard and brittle like dry grass in a drought, and the news of our arrests had been the spark to set off the conflagration. Neighbors who had lived together peaceably enough despite their disagreements on the slavery question now argued outright, and everyone had been forced to account for his position. As word of the conflict spread, the city officials who had endorsed the raids on our homes had been denounced in one Northern newspaper and public forum after another. One man's home had been burned to the ground; a second man had been badly injured when an argument turned into a brawl. One violent act sparked another, and as the ugliness grew and spread, one matter became clear: The faction approving of the arrests of the Creek's Crossing Eight found themselves increasingly on the defensive, forced to justify their support of the Fugitive Slave Law, which every decent Pennsylvanian abhorred.

"Creek's Crossing has earned the reputation of being populated with Southern sympathizers," said Hans. "Pearson and his ilk are nervous and getting more so."

My brother seemed righteously satisfied by this turn of events, but his face was gray with exhaustion and strain, and his voice was hoarse. Anneke insisted he go to bed immediately, and when he protested that he had to see to the farm, I added my voice to hers, and Hans had no choice but to comply.

By the next day he seemed nearly recovered from his physical ordeal, though an air of polite formality lingered between him and Anneke. Still, it was apparent he had forgiven her, but if Anneke remembered what I had said about extending my own forgiveness, she said nothing of it. Truly I wanted to forgive her, but Joanna's face haunted me, and every time I held her son I thought of how his mother could not. I grew more fierce in my determination to find her, and, impatient for a reply, I sent off another letter to Josiah Chester.

Two days after Hans's return, two men came riding up to the house while my brother worked in the fields. I needed only a moment to recognize them as the two men who had arrested us. If they were disturbed by the conflict Hans had spoken of, which seemed to me so distant from the peace of Elm Creek Farm that it was difficult to believe it was real, they gave no sign of it as they demanded entry to the house to search for evidence against us.

I knew nothing of whether I should or must let them enter, but saw no reason to hide in shame. They had found a runaway in our midst; if that was not evidence enough to convict us, nothing else they found would be.

I followed them as they poked about the front room, the kitchen, the dining room, and down into the cellar, making no effort to disguise my impatience. They ignored me and addressed only each other, carelessly handling our possessions and making rude remarks about "n—— lovers." I thought of what Hans had said, about theirs being a minority point of view, and held my temper in check. I would not do anything to worsen our position, not that I supposed it could have become much worse.

Their search took them upstairs, to Hans's room, then to mine; they spent a scant few moments in the spare room and lingered longest in the sewing room, where they scrutinized the hidden alcove inside and out and exchanged pointed and gleeful remarks about how damning that evidence would be at the trial. As if they knew what I was thinking, they warned me sternly against destroying it, assuring me that would do me no good whatsoever, since they were both witness to it.

Then they headed for the nursery, and with a stab of fright I realized Anneke was inside with the children.

Before I could think of how to prevent them, the two men had entered the room. Beyond them I saw Anneke turn in surprise. David was in her arms, while Stephen lay in the cradle where she had just placed him. Anneke's eyes darted to mine, and I saw them widen in shock, but her voice was calm when she said, coldly, "I cannot possibly imagine what more you two would want with us." She turned her back on the men and picked up Stephen again, cradling a baby in either arm protectively.

The two men studied her and exchanged a bewildered look. The first one said, "I don't remember there being two babies last time."

Anneke laughed sharply and regarded the men with scorn. "As I recall, you were occupied with other matters."

"How fitting that Creek's Crossing would send its most observant citizens to investigate us," I added, contemptuous. My heart pounded with fear, and I fought the urge, as I had before, to seize Joanna's son and flee to safety. "Were you searching for babies, too? Is it now against the law to shelter one's children?"

The second man's eyes narrowed, and he drew closer to Anneke. "Whose children are these?"

Her grasp about them tightened. "They are mine, of course."

"Both of them?"

"Yes."

"They look to be nearly the same age."

"They're twins," said Anneke, as if it were the most obvious thing in the world.

The second man looked dubious. "I only saw one baby last

time." He pointed at Joanna's son. "This here one. You were holding him, and he was crying."

Anneke's eyes were fierce. "Crying because you terrified him. You should be ashamed of yourself. It took hours to calm him."

"His brother was in his cradle," said I. "I know one of you must have seen him, because you snatched his quilt off him and threw it on the floor. It was torn in two places."

Anneke's voice was acid. "Did you think he was hiding a runaway beneath his quilt?"

"Let it be," the first man advised the second. "Anyone can see this child is white."

"And anyone can see he wants his mother," sniffed Anneke, handing her own son to me. "Gerda, would you help, please?"

Dumbfounded, I could only nod as Anneke took to her rocking chair and, full of contempt for the men watching her, began to nurse Joanna's son.

Embarrassed by the sight, the two men hastened to leave the room. I returned my nephew to his cradle and followed them as they quickly searched the last room, then departed our house with unwelcome assurances that they would be back if they thought it necessary.

Slowly I returned upstairs to the nursery. I watched from the doorway as Anneke finished feeding Joanna's son, then returned him to the cradle, picked up her own baby, and began to nurse him. "Anneke—" My voice faltered. I wanted to tell her she had certainly saved the little boy, but my heart was too full for words.

Anneke looked up at me. "How many people know I had only one baby?"

"All our friends," said I. "Anyone else they might have told."

"A great deal, then." Her gaze was far away, brooding. "We will have to get Joanna's son to safety before someone reveals the truth."

"I will take him to the next station," said I. "They will have to take him to the next, and so on, until he can be placed with a free Negro family in Canada."

Anneke gazed at the innocent child, drifting off to sleep in the cradle. "It will be a hazardous journey, and he is all alone in the world."

I felt tears spring into my eyes. *I will take him to Canada myself,* I nearly declared, but then thought of Joanna, and decided we should keep him with us as long as possible. Perhaps I could find Joanna and purchase her freedom before the truth about her son came out.

I thought I would have weeks, perhaps longer, but the first inquiry came in a matter of days.

The sight of Mr. Pearson coming up the road to the house so astonished us that at first Anneke and I could only stare at him from the nursery window, and I almost convinced myself I was mistaken as to the identity of the horse and rider. Anneke was the first to turn away. "I will not speak to him," said she, her voice bitter. I was even more reluctant to greet him, but my amazement at his gall and curiosity as to his purpose compelled me downstairs.

I opened the door to his knock but neither addressed him nor invited him inside.

"Good day, Miss Bergstrom," said he.

"What do you want?" said I bluntly, all pretense to politeness long past.

He promptly dropped his facade. "I understand Mrs. Bergstrom is suddenly the mother to two children."

I arched my eyebrows at him. "'Suddenly'? There was nothing sudden about it. The twins are nearly two months old. The pregnancy was of the usual length, and the labor longer than most."

"Your sister-in-law did not give birth to twins," said Mr. Pearson sharply.

"She most certainly did."

"You forget, my mother and I visited you shortly after the child was born. Anneke had only one son then."

"Mr. Pearson, I fear your memory has failed you," said I, feigning puzzlement. "Perhaps you should consult Dr. Granger."

"Don't make me out to be a fool, Miss Bergstrom," snapped he. "If I consult Dr. Granger, it will be to confirm what I already know is true. He was present at the birth, and he knows how many children he delivered that night. Despite his Abolitionist beliefs, Dr. Granger is a man of integrity. He abhors a lie, and he will not depart from his principles merely to protect you. He would not falsify birth records, and he would certainly not sacrifice his own security and that of his family to abet you in your deceit."

Just as a thrill of fear rose in my heart, I realized Mr. Pearson was utterly, entirely wrong. Indeed, Jonathan was a man of integrity and principle, but that did not preclude a well-placed lie or omission of the whole truth if he believed some greater good would be served—even if he knew he would eventually be discovered. If the fiasco with Charlotte Claverton had taught me nothing else, it had taught me that.

So I looked Mr. Pearson squarely in the eye and said, "Ask him anything you wish. I do not fear his response."

"He is not the only one who will testify as to the truth."

"On the contrary, I think you will discover a great many people will remember that Anneke had twins."

His mouth narrowed, and his eyes were bright with hatred. "I do not know whose child that is, but it is not Anneke's."

"If indeed he is not," said I, defiant, "would he be the only child to call his aunt mother?"

My words brought his threats to an abrupt and decisive conclusion.

A change came over his features as rage transformed into understanding. "Why, Miss Bergstrom," said he, the familiar smirk returning. "I knew you were no lady, but I had no idea you were a whore."

I said nothing.

Mr. Pearson laughed, and the sound was full of vengeful merriment. "I wonder if Dr. Granger is aware of this. Well, I suppose he must be. Unless there is another?" He peered at me inquisitively, but I regarded him stoically, my expression revealing nothing. "Of course not. I must say that entirely changes my opinion of the veracity of his record-keeping."

"I suppose asking you to say nothing of this would be a wasted effort."

"Indeed it would, Miss Bergstrom."

I have never seen a man so pleased with himself as Mr. Pearson was as he rode off, believing himself to be the diviner of great, scandalous truths, when in fact all he took away from his interrogation was a lie devised to conceal another lie.

ꕥ

13

June 1859 and after—in which we perfect the art of lying by omission, or, how it ended

With Dorothea's help, I sent word to Jonathan before Mr. Pearson could speak with him, so when Mr. Pearson inquired whether Anneke had indeed given birth to twins, Jonathan replied in the affirmative. More than that, he showed Mr. Pearson the official paperwork confirming that fact, and naming Hans Bergstrom as the boys' father.

Mr. Pearson knew this to be false but was entirely mistaken as to the truth. My falsehood provided him such gleeful triumph that he had no need to seek another explanation. He wasted no time spreading the tale of my ostensible shame throughout town, which, as his mother was one of the leading gossips of her era, assured that the entire county knew of the scandal within a fortnight. Mrs. Engle was careful to add that she had suspected my whorish nature long before a child was born of it, for I had often attempted to seduce her son. For Charlotte Claverton Granger, the betrayed wife, and Anneke, the virtuous woman who took in my bastard child without complaint, she had only praise, though it was tempered by disappointment that these two women had unfortunate connections to Abolitionists. In their defense, she added, they were linked to the Creek's Crossing Eight only by ties of marriage; they had not brought shame to our fair town through their own fault.

But the Creek's Crossing Eight never did come to trial, and circumstances eventually encouraged Mrs. Engle to cease her criticism of the group. The Nelsons' journalist friend was true to his word, and within weeks, our arrest and Joanna's recapture had been denounced in every Northern newspaper I had ever heard of, and several others I had not. Creek's Crossing became the butt of jokes, with the worst foibles of the worst portion of its populace exaggerated and distorted, until the town's name became synonymous with ignorance and mob rule. So embarrassed were our town leaders that they swiftly dismissed all charges against us, including the dangerous threats to the Wrights' freedom, and tried as best they could to put the terrible events in the past, but the memory of the public was long, and the reputation of Creek's Crossing never recovered. In the years to come, businessmen eschewed Creek's Crossing and brought prosperity to other towns; major roads linked nobler villages and bypassed ours, as did the commerce that traveled along them; surveyors who could make train tracks cling to the ridges of the Appalachians somehow found the route into the Elm Creek valley inaccessible. Eventually the town leaders tired of this and ruled to change the town's name to Water's Ford, retaining the original sense of Creek's Crossing while setting aside the taint it had acquired. It remains to be seen whether their efforts will be rewarded.

My reward, I admit, was seeing Mr. Pearson and Mrs. Engle

surprised and eventually undone by the consequences of their actions. I am sure I have my friends to thank for the emergence of new rumors telling how Mr. Pearson had manipulated the innocent Anneke into confessing to the authorities. If not for that, the whispered accusations told, our village never would have experienced its greatest shame. The vitriol mother and son had published in the *Creek's Crossing Informer* over the years soon came to mind, and nothing more was needed to make them the county's least popular citizens. Within a year of the arrests, Mr. Pearson and Mrs. Engle moved away; some say to Virginia, others as far away as Florida. Neither I nor any of my friends ever heard from them again, which, as you can imagine, bothers me not at all.

Before he departed, improving our town with his absence, Mr. Pearson saw to it that my own reputation was ruined entirely. The Certain Faction fought to preserve it, and each and every one of them would have sworn before the highest court in the land that she had seen Anneke cuddling twin boys within hours of their birth. But people inevitably prefer to believe the scandalous over the mundane, and so it was with me. Accordingly, the likelihood of my finding a husband, which my plainness and age had made small enough already, diminished entirely. Fortunately for me, I suppose, I never found anyone else I liked so well as Jonathan, so it did not matter.

But Mr. Pearson, Mrs. Engle, and their associates were not the only ones to receive the condemnation of the town. Although publicly we Bergstroms were exonerated and defended, privately we were lumped in with our enemies and forced to shoulder the blame for tarnishing the town's reputation. We were never quite as welcome in society as before, and over time, we accepted that the frost in our fellow citizens' address would never thaw, and we gradually withdrew into the company of our ever growing family and the warmth of the circle of our most intimate friends, which included the Nelsons, the Wrights, and the Certain Faction. We stopped attending town events, such as the Harvest Dance, and I once even overheard one gentleman respond to a visitor's questions about the "rumored scandal of years ago" with the assertion that Elm Creek Farm lay outside the city proper, so its residents were not truly citizens of Water's Ford. But although our neighbors politely shunned us, the reputation of Hans's Bergstrom Thoroughbreds had spread far beyond our little valley, and so our fortunes soared. Our prosperity might have impressed the townsfolk and increased their desire for our company if not for the Creek's Crossing Eight scandal and my ruined reputation, but instead it merely strengthened their enmity.

Jonathan's reputation, I should add, suffered little from the scandal, and within the span of a year he once again enjoyed the high esteem of his fellow citizens, while I was whispered about until I was gray-haired and stooped with age. One might say Jonathan was forgiven and I was not because he was the town's highly respected physician while I was merely a spinster of unremarkable social position, but I know it was because he was a man and I was a woman. The woman is always left to carry the burden of shame, while the man is free to go his own way. But I do not begrudge him his reprieve, for although I did not consult him before allowing Mr. Pearson to believe him my lover, Jonathan never publicly denied it, allowing the true heritage of Joanna's son to remain secret all his life.

For I am sure by now you understand what I have needed this entire history to confess: Joanna's son never went to Canada, nor did he rejoin his mother elsewhere. Instead he lived as a Bergstrom from the time Anneke first claimed him as her own.

We never intended this to happen. After Joanna's capture, finding her became my obsession, and when Josiah Chester failed to reply to the scores of letters I sent him, I decided to travel to Wentworth County, Virginia, to speak to him in person. Then war broke out, as we had all feared and expected it would, and my plans lay in ruins. The conflict forced me to set aside my search and tend to matters closer to home. Hans and Anneke had added to their family, so I had the children to think of, and the obligations and consequences of war to endure. So much I could write of that dark, unforgiving time, but I cannot divert from this history to recount it now, not when I am so near the end. Perhaps I will chronicle those events someday, if I can bring myself to do it, if I live long enough.

After the war, I immediately resumed my search, but my efforts were repeatedly thwarted by one obstacle or another. Despite my frustrations, I clung stubbornly to hope, and often played in my mind's eye a glorious and triumphant scene of Joanna's return to Elm Creek Manor and her reunion with her son. So feverishly did I believe this event would take place that I began piecing a quilt, a gift for Joanna, in anticipation of her arrival. I chose a pattern that would be easy to sew, as I had allowed my quilting skills to languish during the war, but one that had special significance: the Log Cabin, named for the interlocking design of its rectangular pieces. The design was invented, or so Dorothea once said, to honor Mr. Abraham Lincoln, and since he had granted Joanna her freedom, I thought it an appropriate choice for her quilt. The square in the center of the block was supposed to be yellow, to signify a light in the cabin window, or red, to signify the hearth, but I cut my central squares from black fabric, to symbolize that an escaped slave had once found sanctuary within our own log cabin.

Time passed, and as my Log Cabin quilt neared completion, the black center squares took on another meaning. Black was also the color of mourning, and as my relentless searches proved fruitless over and over again, I began to mourn my lost friend, who I feared would never see the quilt I had made for her.

My letters finally reached a daughter of Josiah Chester's, but she claimed to know nothing of what had happened to Joanna after she ran away. She did note that her father usually brought recaptured slaves to the home plantation for a few days of brutal punishment before selling them to family or acquaintances in Georgia or the Carolinas, to show other slaves what fate awaited them should they run off. She did not remember this happening to Joanna, but she did not know Joanna well and might not have recognized her, or so she claimed.

I might have believed her, had Joanna not told me she was a house slave and did all the sewing for the family. At the very least, Josiah Chester's daughter would have seen Joanna every time she was fitted for a new dress, and likely more often than that.

The years went by. Joanna's son grew tall and strong never knowing his real mother, and my hopes, which I had clung to fiercely throughout the war, gradually slipped from my grasp. I did not give up because I loved Joanna any less; on the contrary, I loved her more, seeing the fine young man my nephew had become, and knowing how Joanna's courage and sacrifice had brought him into our lives. No, I finally stopped searching because I believed Joanna dead. Surely if she had lived, she would have returned to Elm Creek Manor for her child. She had found her way here once as a hunted fugitive; as a free woman, she could have done so again, and certainly would have, knowing her son awaited her return. Only death could have prevented her sending word to us. I am certain of it.

But if you are a Bergstrom, Reader, you already know her son was not awaiting her return.

You may wonder why we never told him the truth about his heritage. You may question our judgment; I know I have many times over the years, ever more so as I feel my own death lurking just beyond my sight, and I know it will not be long before I must account for my life before my Creator.

At first we did not tell him because he was too young and would not understand. Then we did not tell him because we feared he might reveal the secret to strangers in an innocent remark, as children sometimes do. Later we said nothing because Joanna's return seemed increasingly unlikely, and Anneke had forbidden us to tell him. She would not see his heart broken in mourning a mother he had never known, and she did not want him to feel loved any less than his brothers and sisters. Even when he became a man, fully capable of bearing and accepting the truth, still we did not tell him, for we had discovered that granting a people freedom did not bring them equality, and we were reminded daily of the brutality of ignorant folk who would love our precious boy today but despise him tomorrow if they knew the truth. Right or wrong, we could not do this to him.

When he was still a child, Anneke pleaded with me to swear never to tell her son—for that is how she thought of him, no less her child than if she had truly borne him—about Joanna, about himself. I complied, but not without misgivings. Indeed, all my life I have wondered if in protecting my nephew from prejudice and malice we did not inadvertently perpetuate those very evils. Perhaps we should have announced the truth from the rooftops and dared anyone to treat him differently than any other Bergstrom—but we loved him, and may God forgive us if it was wrong, but we put his safety before our principles. In our defense, if we had not done so, it would not have brought Joanna back to us.

But since I did so swear, I never told my nephew the truth, nor will I ever tell him. Since I cannot tell him, I instead tell you, not only because this is part of your legacy, your rightful inheritance, but also because I could not bear to have Joanna forgotten.

Anneke has been gone these past fifteen years, and yet I think I hear her reproach me for divulging our family secrets so long and so carefully hidden. Perhaps she is correct, and whoever reads these words will despise me for what I have done. That is a risk I shall willingly take, for I do not believe, as Anneke did, that this truth will destroy us. It is the missing chapter of our family history that must be restored if we are to be whole, and if we are to truly know ourselves. Guard this, your legacy, closely, and treasure it in the quiet of your own heart.

I offer these words in memory of Joanna, whom I loved, and whom I pray found in the Kingdom of Heaven the peace, freedom, and joy she was denied in this world.

Elm Creek Manor, Pennsylvania
November 28, 1895

ꕥ

Sylvia closed the book and brushed the tears from her eyes.

Andrew had held her left hand in both of his as she read the last pages of the memoir aloud. Now he squeezed it and brought it to his lips. The compassion in his eyes threatened to bring forth more tears.

Sylvia cleared her throat and straightened in her chair, composing herself. "Well, I don't know quite what to think." And then her voice failed her, because her emotions refused to be translated into words. Her heart ached for Joanna, who had lost both her child and her dream of freedom. She was sickened and shamed that Anneke had betrayed her own family, and in so doing had ruined the lives and happiness of those dearest to her. But most of all, she was stunned. She felt as if the foundation of her universe had caved in upon itself.

"My family," said Sylvia, slowly, "was not what I believed it to be."

This time she did not mean merely that reality had failed to live up to the family legends.

"You see . . ." She sat lost in thought for a long moment. "I know David was my grandfather. And my mother's Bible indicates he had a twin brother."

Andrew nodded, waiting for her to continue.

"But Gerda does not say whether Anneke bore David or Stephen."

Andrew's voice was quiet. "I noticed."

"In fact, she quite deliberately avoids saying whose child was whose." Suddenly Sylvia remembered that odd crossed-out line earlier in the memoir, the one she and Sarah had tried in vain to decipher. They had supposed that Gerda had written the name of Joanna's child there, and now she understood why Gerda might have wished to blot it out. It was not an error, but a purposeful obscuring of the truth.

Sylvia's mind reeled. She felt as if she were swirling down a drain, faster and faster, moments away from tumbling from her safe, certain world into an ocean of unfathomable uncertainty. "Why?" she said, her voice shaking. "Why confess so much, yet hold back that last detail?"

"Maybe she was trying to protect you—you, or whoever found her book."

"Protect me?"

"She didn't know you. She didn't know how strong you are. It's quite a blow, finding out you've been lied to all your life."

"You don't need to tell me that." Sylvia felt the first faint stirrings of anger. "Then why write at all? Merely to unburden herself?"

Andrew shrugged, silent.

"She did not trust me," said Sylvia, bitter. "She did not trust me with the whole truth, so she gave me only enough to make me doubt everything I ever believed about myself, only enough to throw my entire identity into question." Even as she spoke, she felt rents appearing in the fabric of her history.

Andrew's hand was warm and strong around hers. "Your

family isn't your entire identity. You're still Sylvia Bergstrom—a strong, capable woman. A quilter, a teacher, a friend, and the woman I love. What you learned from that book doesn't change any of that."

"But it changes nearly everything else." All her life Sylvia had prided herself on being descended from Hans and Anneke Bergstrom—courageous pioneers, valiant Abolitionists, founders of a family and a fortune. She had long since come to terms with Gerda's revelations that her ancestors were not the heroes she had believed them to be, but now her ancestors might not even be her ancestors.

Sylvia corrected herself. Her parents were still her parents; their parents were still her grandparents. It was the link to Hans and Anneke that was in question, nothing more. But that was so much.

"Would it be so bad to be Joanna's great-granddaughter?" asked Andrew gently.

"No." Sylvia had responded automatically, but then she forced herself to consider the question more thoroughly. Gradually, within the dizzying mix of emotions flooding her, she recognized wonder, intrigue, and awe. "I would be proud to be that brave woman's descendant." Then, in a painful flash of insight, she realized who else she would be related to, if Joanna were her great-grandmother.

"I had not wanted to believe we had slave owners in the family." She paused, her throat constricted with emotion. "And now I discover I might be the great-granddaughter of a monster who not only owned slaves but raped and tortured them as well."

"Don't think about him," urged Andrew. "Joanna didn't when she held her son. She only thought of how much she loved him."

"I would like very much to forget Josiah Chester, but if I am going to accept part of my heritage, I must accept all of it."

"Let's not forget, you don't know for certain whether it *is* your heritage. We're jumping to conclusions a bit, don't you think? Anneke could have been David's mother, just as you've always believed."

Sylvia was about to retort that Gerda would have had little need to expose the family secret in that case, but then she reconsidered. There were other branches of the family besides her own; perhaps they were the ones Gerda had sought to protect. And there was Gerda's desire to make known Joanna's story, since the vow Anneke had exacted had nearly banished her from memory. It was entirely possible—in fact, even likely—that Sylvia's heritage was exactly what she had always believed it to be.

She didn't suppose she would ever know for certain.

* * *

Sylvia spent two days contemplating how much she would reveal about Gerda's revelations and to whom. Her friends knew only that she had finished the memoir and that something she had read there troubled her, but thankfully, rather than pester her with questions, they allowed her time alone to think.

She tried to explain to Andrew that her mixed feelings came not from rejecting her new ancestry, if in fact it was hers. It was the uncertainty that tore at her, as well as the enormous shift in her sense of self Gerda was forcing her to make. "If I had discovered the memoir decades ago, I might feel entirely different," said Sylvia. "I might have been able to embrace this change. But to have to come to an entirely new understanding of myself at my age . . . I don't think I can do it."

"You don't have to," said Andrew. "You are the same wonderful woman you have always been, and whether all those things I love about you came from Anneke and Hans or Joanna and Josiah Chester, your soul is still your own. You're not just your parents, you know. You're the sum of everything you've ever done, every wish you've ever made, every person you've ever loved, and everyone who has loved you. No one can take that from you, not Gerda, not anyone. I don't care how many darn memoirs they write."

He broke off, embarrassed, and Sylvia stared at him, amazed by his uncharacteristic speech making. His unshakable faith in her warmed her more than he could have imagined possible, but she was too fond of him to embarrass him further by telling him so.

"Perhaps I just need more time," she said instead, and Andrew agreed.

A week had passed when Sylvia realized she had come to accept the mystery Gerda had bequeathed her. She could only guess why the same woman who felt she was obligated to make the Bergstrom descendants "the heir of our truths, for good or ill," would stop short of revealing the most important secret the family had ever kept, so she decided to stop trying.

She also decided to stop second-guessing every other sentence in the memoir, trying to discern which of the two women had borne her grandfather. If a certain inflection in one sentence suggested Anneke, two paragraphs later she was sure to find a description that indicated Joanna. In attempting to puzzle it out, Sylvia had read and reread the memoir so many times she thought she might be able to transcribe it from memory, backward. When she found herself speculating that perhaps Gerda and Jonathan were her great-grandparents after all and the entire memoir was Gerda's attempt to protect her descendants from the shame of illegitimacy, she knew she had gone too far. Instead of untangling the threads of her history, she was tugging them into an ever tightening knot.

And so she gave up. Or rather, as she told herself, she acquiesced. Gerda had meant for her to know only a small measure of her history, not the whole. Since that was more than Sylvia had possessed before reading the memoir, she would accept the gift and not question the motives of the giver.

Her heart might have rested easy, if not for the image that had once haunted Gerda and now stole into her own dreams: Joanna's face as the slave catcher led her away, her silent and desperate plea. It jolted Sylvia awake at night, and before she could fall asleep again, a voice whispered in her thoughts: *My great-grandmother might have died far from here, alone, enslaved, despairing.*

She shared all her thoughts, agonizing though some of them were, with Andrew. She cried in his arms more than once, mourning her lost surety, fuming at Gerda for leaving her so many questions. Even as a child Sylvia had been proud of herself, of her family—some might say too proud. Now she did not even feel like a Bergstrom anymore. She no longer knew what it meant to be a Bergstrom.

She accepted Gerda's right to leave her an imperfect, incomplete family history, but that did not mean she had to like it. Nor did it mean that she would uphold the family traditions of silence and secrecy.

First, she told Sarah. As the heir to Elm Creek Manor and someone Sylvia thought of as a daughter, Sarah had the right to know. Even as Sylvia recounted Gerda's bombshell, she felt the burden of her worries ease as her young friend shouldered some of the anxieties weighing down her spirit.

As to the question of whether Sylvia was a Bergstrom, Sarah's firm response both surprised and comforted her. "Don't be ridiculous," said Sarah, her expression making it clear that she would not accept any self-pity or brooding from her friend—so clear, in fact, that for a moment Sylvia suspected Sarah was mimicking her.

"I didn't think I was being ridiculous."

"Well, you are," retorted Sarah. "Even if Joanna was your great-grandmother, Anneke and Hans raised her son as their own. Are adopted children any less a part of the family than one's biological offspring?"

"Of course not."

"I'm glad to hear you say that, because otherwise some of our friends wouldn't be very happy with you. Diane's adopted, did you know that? And Judy's stepfather adopted her after marrying her mother. Are you going to tell them they aren't really their parents' children?"

"I wouldn't dream of it."

"Then you shouldn't do the same to Joanna's son," declared Sarah. "Of course you're a Bergstrom. What a question."

Sylvia allowed a smile. "I suppose I am."

But what that meant, she still wasn't sure.

* * *

With a sense of recklessness, as if to spite Gerda for providing only partial truths, Sylvia set about telling her closest confidantes what the memoir had revealed. Guard these secrets in the quiet of her own heart, indeed. It was Sylvia's history, and she was free to do with it as she saw fit.

After speaking with Sarah, Sylvia next phoned Grace Daniels. To her astonishment, when she finished recounting Gerda's last cryptic pages, Grace laughed and said, "Well, let me be the first to welcome you into the family."

"I'm glad this amuses you," said Sylvia dryly.

"I've always wondered why we get along so well, and now I know."

"Why, Grace, I'm hurt. You mean to tell me we've been friends for more than fifteen years, and all this time—"

"I'm just teasing you."

"Same here," retorted Sylvia. "Although I admit I'm surprised to find myself joking about this. Gerda's memoir has my mind so twisted up in knots I hardly know what to think."

"You shouldn't blame Anneke and Gerda for keeping their secrets," said Grace. "I'm not saying our day and age is perfect—far from it—but it was radically different then. Anneke probably thought she was rescuing Joanna's son from an incredibly difficult and dangerous life."

"Was she?"

Grace hesitated. "That's not an easy question to answer."

"Please, Grace," urged Sylvia. "The whole truth. That's been too scarce around here lately."

"Well . . ." Grace sighed. "I'm torn between applauding them for adopting Joanna's son and raising him as a member of the family, and condemning them for robbing him of his true heritage. On the other hand, I don't know if it's fair for me to judge them, all safe and smug in my twenty-first-century life. The most immediate consequence of his heritage would have been slavery, and I can't wish that on anyone just to satisfy my pride. Besides, if they had sent him away with those slave catchers, he and Joanna would have been separated soon anyway, and she never would have known where to look for him."

"They might have killed him, even, rather than be troubled with a baby on the road."

"I doubt that," said Grace, with an edge to her voice. "He was valuable property, remember? Josiah Chester might have made the slave catchers pay for him."

"True enough." Sylvia sighed. "So the Bergstroms kept him safe, thinking to reunite him with his mother, although it never happened. Still, after he grew up, they could have told him the truth."

"They could have. Maybe they should have. But since he could pass, they probably thought it better to let him."

"I don't like that word, 'pass,'" said Sylvia. "It sounds like there was some sort of test, and one either passed or one failed."

"There was a test," said Grace. "And even now, in the twenty-first century, when history has provided us with innumerable lessons why it's wrong, for some people and in some places, there still is a test. To those ignorant enough to think they can judge me, I fail it every day. The ignorance of Gerda's day not only lives on, it thrives."

Sylvia did not know what to say.

Grace continued, gently. "You said you no longer know what it means to be a Bergstrom. Do you still think you know what it means to be black or white?"

* * *

Two days later, after the Elm Creek Quilters' weekly business meeting, Sylvia told them how Gerda had concluded her memoir with a mystery. Her friends took in the news with intrigued amazement—except for Diane, who claimed to have guessed it the minute she heard both Anneke and Joanna were pregnant.

"You did not," retorted Gwen, nudging Diane so hard she nearly fell out of her chair.

Diane shoved back. "I did so. I read a lot of mystery novels. Gerda's memoir wasn't nearly as complicated."

"In that case," said Sylvia, "perhaps you could put your deductive powers to work on the question of who my great-grandmother is."

Gwen grinned at Diane. "Get to work, Sherlock."

"Goodness," said Sylvia, shaking her head. "They way you two get along, I wonder why you sit beside each other every week. Maybe we should assign you chairs on opposite sides of the room."

Gwen and Diane looked at each other, and then at Sylvia, in

surprise. "Are you kidding?" said Diane. "I look forward to needling her all week."

Gwen smirked. "The way you sew, you might mean that literally."

The Elm Creek Quilters laughed, and Sylvia felt their mirth lifting her own subdued spirits. She could almost forget for a moment the loss she felt, thinking that if only Gerda had trusted her a little more, the question of her ancestry could have been answered conclusively. The more time that passed, the more Sylvia realized that the truth, whatever it was, was preferable to this empty space in her history.

Then Agnes's quiet voice broke into the laughter. "I for one hope that Joanna was your great-grandmother."

All eyes went to her. Sylvia regarded her sister-in-law, her baby brother's widow, with surprise. "Why is that?"

"She sounds like a remarkable women. Strong, courageous, proud." Agnes smiled affectionately across the circle of friends at Sylvia. "Whether she is your great-grandmother or not, I do believe I see her in you."

* * *

The next day, Summer returned to the Waterford College library and the historical society's archives, not quite sure what she was looking for. All summer she had scoured the records until she suspected she had handled nearly every scrap of paper in every file and on every shelf, and she knew the information Sylvia most wanted could not be found there. But the urgency to keep looking was too compelling to ignore. At the business meeting, Sylvia had spoken in her usual straightforward way, but Summer sensed the very real pain lingering behind her brave front. She wanted to help—all the Elm Creek Quilters did, and out of Sylvia's hearing they had all agreed to do what they could—but she did not know where to begin.

Leaving her backpack at her usual carrel, she studied the shelves and hoped her gaze would fall upon a record she had not yet examined, but all the titles were familiar.

Suddenly someone reached past her and pulled a book down from the shelf. "If you're looking for something compelling, I highly recommend this one."

Summer glanced over her shoulder to find Jeremy smiling at her. She grinned back and glanced at the title of the book he had chosen. "*A History of the Elm Creek Valley Watershed.* Sounds like a real page-turner. Does it have a happy ending?"

"The main character is really a ghost."

Summer made an exasperated face. "Now you've spoiled it for me, so I don't need to read it." She took the book from him and returned it to the shelf.

"Let me make it up to you," said Jeremy. "Last time we spoke, you said you wanted a look at the old local newspapers, the issues missing from the Waterford Historical Society's collection. Are you still interested?"

"Of course. Are they here somewhere? How did I overlook them?"

"Not here. In the *Waterford Register*'s archives."

"But they told me they couldn't spare a staff member to help me search."

"One of my students is an intern there, and he agreed to take you around after one of his shifts."

"That's wonderful," exclaimed Summer. "When can I start?"

"This afternoon, if you're free." Jeremy hesitated. "There's a catch, though."

"What sort of catch?"

"Nothing major. I have to promise him extra credit on a homework assignment. But there's something else."

"That would be two catches."

"True. But this is the most important one."

Summer regarded him with amusement. "Go on."

"You have to have dinner with me."

"I see." She hid a smile. "Do you usually have to bribe women to have dinner with you?"

"Only very rarely."

Summer pretended to ponder the matter. "I guess if that's the only way I'll get into those archives . . ." She shrugged. "Okay. But only because this friend is very important to me."

* * *

That evening, unaware of Summer's plans, her heart still warmed by Agnes's words and the comforting assurances of her friends, Sylvia retired for the night hopeful that one day soon she would be able to think of Gerda's memoir without regretting all that her ancestor had left unsaid. But first she went to the library and took pen and paper from the top drawer of the great oak desk that had belonged to her father. She wrote one letter to Rosemary, Dorothea Nelson's great-granddaughter, to inform her that her great-grandparents had indeed closed their Underground Railroad station before the Civil War began, and why they had been forced to do so. She then wrote a second, longer letter to Margaret Alden to tell her how Gerda's memoir had concluded, and to invite her and her mother to Elm Creek Manor to see the quilts Sylvia had found in the attic.

Perhaps together they could figure out how—or even if—the Bergstrom quilts were linked to Margaret's.

14

On a mid-September afternoon, Sylvia Compson stood in the library looking out the window over the front entrance to her home. On the other side of the sweeping green front lawn, the trees along Elm Creek lifted scarlet, yellow, and orange leaves to the clear autumn sky, but Sylvia scarcely noticed them. Her gaze was fixed on the road, for soon a car would emerge from the forest and bring Margaret Alden and her mother, Evelyn, to Elm Creek Manor.

Sylvia ordered herself to stop pacing around like an agitated cat. Margaret had visited before, as a camper, and her mother was likely to be a pleasant enough woman. Still, in her response to Sylvia's invitation, Margaret had expressed disappointment that the Bergstrom and Alden families did not appear to be related after all, but had not mentioned Joanna. Sylvia figured Gerda's last revelation was astonishing enough to merit some sort of response, and she didn't know what to make of Margaret's silence.

"Sylvia, do you have a moment?"

Sylvia turned to find Sarah lingering in the doorway, with Summer just behind her, carrying a large manila envelope. "For you two, I'll make time," said Sylvia with a smile. The two young women had been trying to lift her out of her melancholy ever since she had finished reading the memoir. Their jokes and diversions did not cheer her as much as the knowledge that they cared enough about her to try.

Sylvia let the curtain fall back in place as Sarah and Summer joined her at the window. "We know how disappointed you've been feeling lately," said Sarah. "We wish we could find the answers you want, but since we can't, we thought we'd at least try to find as much information about Gerda as possible."

"All that time in the library paid off again." Summer handed her the envelope. "I met someone there who managed to get me into the *Waterford Register*'s archives. They don't have all the missing back issues, but they do have many."

Sylvia was already opening the envelope. "Oh, how wonderful, dear." She removed a handful of microfiche printouts and glanced at the first few headlines. " 'Underground Railroad Unearthed! Eight Citizens Arrested.' Goodness. 'Justice and Mercy Triumph! Creek's Crossing Eight Released from Prison.' 'Creek's Crossing a Haven for Southern Sympathizers? A Righteous Nation Wonders.' My, they certainly had a gift for hyperbole, didn't they?"

"It's all there," said Summer. "The whole story, just as Gerda recorded it."

"There's even a letter to the editor from Mr. Pearson," said Sarah. "I guess the editors felt they had to show an opposing view."

"Hmph. I look forward to reading it," said Sylvia. "What does he say?"

"Exactly what you'd expect from him."

"Best of all," added Summer, "the intern who helped me at

the paper said I was welcome to come back anytime, so if you ever want to look up your father or grandmother—"

"Or your great-aunt Lucinda," Sarah interrupted, "or Claudia, to find out about those years you were away—"

"Just say the word, and I'll investigate."

"I might just do that one of these days," said Sylvia. "Thank you. Thank you both." As she returned the clippings to the envelope to read more thoroughly later, she noticed Summer and Sarah exchanging mischievous glances. "All right. I know that look. I'm expecting visitors, so whatever you two are plotting, it will have to wait."

"Actually, it can't wait," said Summer. "Because . . . some of your guests are kind of already here."

"Nonsense. I've been watching the front drive." *For the past hour,* she almost added, but decided against it. No need to let them see how anxious she was. Then she understood. "Oh, I see. This is your surprise. You invited someone else to join us, and you sneaked them in the back way. Well, who are they and where are they hiding?"

"Rosemary Cullen and Kathleen Barrett," said Sarah. "And they aren't hiding. They're having coffee in the parlor."

"Why didn't you tell me earlier?" exclaimed Sylvia. She left the library with such haste that Sarah and Summer didn't catch up until she reached the door. "Honestly, you two," she grumbled as they hurried after her down the stairs. "Haven't I taught you any manners? You don't abandon guests so you can come upstairs and have a private chat."

"Andrew is with them," said Sarah.

"That's something, at least," said Sylvia, but she gave her two young friends an exasperated shake of the head as they crossed the marble foyer and hurried down the west wing to the parlor. There she found the two women chatting with Andrew. "Rosemary and Kathleen. What a delight to see you again."

"The pleasure is ours," said Rosemary. She clasped the hand Sylvia extended to her, and to Sylvia's relief, she seemed to feel not at all neglected. "I must say, your letter has me more excited than I've been in years. It's wonderful to have so many details about my great-grandparents' lives verified. I feel like I'm getting to know them so much better, thanks to Gerda and her memoir."

"I know the feeling," said Sylvia, smiling. Of course, in her own case, as many details about her grandparents had been proven false as had been confirmed.

"After your visit, I went back and reread Thomas's letters to Dorothea," said Kathleen. "He mentions your family in at least a dozen letters."

"Does he, indeed? You're certain he meant my family?"

"Absolutely." Rosemary patted the sofa to encourage Sylvia to sit between her and Andrew. "He mentions them by name, and some of their children, too."

Sylvia's heart seemed to skip a beat, and she sat down more suddenly than she had intended. She wondered which children, and what Thomas had said about them. Surely he had been in on the secret. Even if the Bergstroms had not told him, the Nelsons had known Anneke bore only one child, and they had visited Gerda often enough to be aware that she had not been pregnant. They also knew the Bergstroms had sheltered runaways, and Dorothea's own brother had delivered Joanna's child.

"I would very much like to see those letters," said Sylvia to Rosemary.

"Usually Mother doesn't like to take them out of the house," said Kathleen, but she reached for her purse. "From what you've shared about Gerda's memoir, we knew this letter would be of particular interest to you, so Mother decided to make an exception."

With that, Kathleen placed a fragile sheet of paper in Sylvia's hand.

"Why . . ." Sylvia's voice trailed off, and with her other hand, she slipped on her glasses, which hung about her neck on a fine silver chain. She glanced at Summer and Sarah to steel her confidence, and began to read.

November 7, 1863

My Beloved Dorothea,

Dusk approaches, and finding myself with a few idle moments to spare, I improve them in writing to you. Forgive the shaking of my hand. We fought hard today, against as cunning and dangerous an enemy as I ever thought to face in my lifetime. They have entrenched themselves for the night, to wait and rest in expectation of our charge at dawn, but if I am to believe the rumors flying about our camp, we march at dusk. Since I do not know if I will live to see the sun rise, I must imagine the bright warmth of day, which always seems to surround me when I remember your smile and the fondness in your eyes.

I miss you and Abigail with all my heart. Kiss her for me, and tell her Daddy will be home soon. I tell myself the war will surely end by Christmas, but then doubt steals over me, and I fear I will never see you again in this world. But as you have often said, my dearest, I must not dwell on such thoughts, but rather pray for a swift, just conclusion to this conflict.

So, instead I will imagine you are here with me, or rather, that I am there with you, for though I know you to be a woman of remarkable fortitude, I would not wish you to look upon the scene that lies before me.

When I close my eyes and think of home, it is springtime, with the smell of freshly tilled soil in the air. It is evening, our day's work is done, and I am pushing you and little Abby on the swing your brother hung for us from the oak tree near the pasture. The sun is setting, and the baby shrieks with delight, and you look over your shoulder at me and smile, and I know that I am still alive.

I pause in my reverie to tell you I have, at last, received word from Jonathan. When he discovered one of his patients would join us here after his recovery, he bade him carry a letter to me, which I very gladly received. He wrote little about his activities, saying, in summary, that battlefield medicine is like nothing he learned at university. When I reflect on the broken bodies we send him, I cannot imagine any education that could have prepared him sufficiently.

Jonathan said he had heard from you, and that your letters gladden his heart. He also mentioned receiving word from our friend Gerda Bergstrom. Apparently Gerda has quite taken to your knitting lessons, for she sent him three pairs of thick wool socks, which, he said, he was quite glad to receive. She also sent him a book of poetry, which he confessed he has not yet opened, for at the end of the day, he is too exhausted from his labors to do anything more than remove his boots and drop off to sleep.

He did not mention hearing from Charlotte. I hope this was an oversight on his part and not an indication that Charlotte's condition is afflicting her too greatly to write, for as I recall, her confinements with the two eldest were difficult. I suspect, dear wife, that your brother had indeed heard from her, but his thoughts were so full of Gerda that Charlotte was crowded out of his letter.

When I reflect upon our friends, I cannot help but pity Jonathan and pray for his heart to find peace. I know what it is like to find one's great love, and having been married to her for so many delightful years, I cannot imagine living without her, or being married to another. I know Jonathan respects and admires

Charlotte, and I am certain he is a dutiful husband to her, but it is a pity he cannot spend his life with the one to whom he has given his heart.

I need not tell you to say nothing to your brother or to Gerda of my opinions. These are simply the ramblings of a weary mind, but I know you will indulge me and not chasten me for dallying in idle gossip. Indeed, any talk of those I hold dear, however trivial it may seem, carries great significance in each and every word when I am far from the warmth of their affection.

Now I am told I must douse my light, so I must end my letter in haste. I know you will forgive me for not sending Jonathan's letter on to you. He wrote that he sent you a letter of your own, and the cheerful tidings of loved ones are a comfort to me in this wretched place, and I would like to keep Jonathan's to read again at my leisure.

I miss you, my sweet wife, and once more I vow that when I return to the shelter of our little farm in the valley, I will never leave it again.

Kiss Abby again for me, and know that I remain,

Your Loving Husband,
Thomas

Sylvia removed her glasses and cleared her throat, blinking back a tear. "Well." She carefully refolded the letter and handed it to Kathleen. "I'm glad that Gerda and Jonathan remained friends, although it would have pleased me more to learn they had found some happy ending together." Her heart ached for them. They could have enjoyed a love as devoted and enduring as that Thomas and Dorothea shared, if only the fates had cooperated.

"But what of Hans and Anneke's children?" asked Sarah. "Kathleen said some of Thomas's letters mentioned them."

"They do," said Kathleen. "But mostly in passing, I'm afraid. He refers to gatherings at one family's farm or the other's, and recalls games the children played together."

Sylvia nodded. She longed to read any letter that mentioned the Bergstroms, regardless of how few details they provided, but twice she had asked to read them and had been rebuffed. She did not feel she should ask again.

"I do so hate to let those letters out of my sight," said Rosemary. "I'm sure you feel the same way about the memoir, Sylvia."

Sylvia forced a smile, trying to hide her disappointment. "Of course."

"So I think we ought to arrange to read together. You could bring your memoir to my house, or I could bring my letters here, and we can trade. What do you think?"

"I think it's a wonderful idea."

"Are you sure it wouldn't be an imposition? You must be a very busy woman, with your own business to run. You might not have time to sit and read on a schedule."

Sylvia glimpsed Kathleen's slight frown of worry and realized that both mother and daughter were as eager for the social aspect of their arrangement as for the information contained in the memoir. Fortunately for everyone, Sylvia had every intention of accepting their proposal. "I have plenty of time, and I couldn't think of a better way to spend it."

Rosemary smiled, delighted, and she and Sylvia soon agreed to meet every Wednesday at noon for lunch followed by an hour of reading, one week at Rosemary's home, and the next at Elm Creek Manor.

Kathleen looked pleased by the arrangements, but added, "I'm looking forward to seeing more of Elm Creek Manor myself. I might even sign up for a class or two."

Rosemary regarded her with amazement. "Did I hear you correctly? After all these years, my daughter finally wants to learn to quilt?"

Kathleen looked so embarrassed that Sylvia half expected to see her squirm like a little girl caught in some mischief. "I thought I might."

Rosemary laughed and said to the others, "You have no idea how long I tried to get that one to pick up a needle. She told me she'd die of boredom stitching together old scraps all day long."

Everyone chuckled except Kathleen, but even she managed a sheepish grin. "I've had second thoughts," she explained. "Reading Thomas's letters again helps me appreciate the Dove in the Window quilt Dorothea made for him. I thought I'd like to make one for myself, in remembrance of them."

"What a lovely idea." Sylvia recalled all the quilts Gerda had mentioned, especially those most important in her memoir—the Log Cabin, the Birds in the Air, and the Underground Railroad, of course, but also the Shoo-Fly Gerda had so reluctantly made, and the Feathered Star Joanna had pieced for her unborn child. And Sylvia could not forget Margaret Alden's quilt, which, as far as Sylvia could discern, Gerda had never seen. Yet it was perhaps the most important of all, because although its origin remained a mystery, it had compelled Sylvia to the attic, where she had found the journal.

"Our next camp session starts Sunday," Sarah told Kathleen. "We could sign you up for Beginning Piecing, if you like."

"Camp will conclude for the season soon," said Sylvia, "but afterward, I'd be happy to continue your lessons myself."

"Say yes," advised Sarah. "Sylvia's a wonderful teacher."

"Say yes," echoed Rosemary, and to Sylvia, added, "We've got to get her hooked while we have the chance."

"I heard that," said Kathleen, laughing, but within minutes

she and Sylvia had made the arrangements, and Sylvia had added another weekly get-together to her schedule. Perhaps the coming winter without the campers wouldn't be so lonely after all.

After Kathleen and Rosemary left, Sylvia fell silent, Thomas's words haunting her. Andrew put an arm around her shoulders and absently stroked her hair as lines from Thomas's letter played in her thoughts. Thomas knew what it meant to find one's great love, he had written, and he could not imagine living without her or being married to another. He had pitied Jonathan for the obstinacy that had led him to marry Charlotte when his heart belonged to Gerda. Jonathan meant to do what was honorable no matter how much it pained him, but he had wounded Gerda at least as much as himself, and he had no right to do that.

Sylvia didn't know if Andrew was her great love or if she was his, and there was certainly no question of her marrying anyone else, but she had learned from her ancestors' history and had no intention of repeating it.

She rose and took Andrew's hand. "Come with me."

"Where?"

She tried to pull him to his feet, impatient. "We're going for a walk."

His eyebrows rose. "Now?"

"Yes, now. Get up."

"What about Margaret and Evelyn?" asked Sarah as Andrew shrugged and stood.

"If we aren't back in time, you and Summer can amuse them until we return." She ignored the puzzled look Sarah and Summer exchanged, took Andrew's arm, and steered him from the room.

"What's all this about?" asked Andrew as they left the manor by way of the cornerstone patio.

"I just wanted a moment alone with you, that's all."

"I gathered that, but why?"

"You'll find out in a minute. Honestly. I'm not taking you to the far side of the moon. Have some patience."

He almost managed to stifle his laugh, so Sylvia pretended she had not heard it. She quickened her step, eager to get to the north gardens and say her piece before she changed her mind.

They sat side by side in the gazebo as they had so many times before. Sylvia took his hands in hers, closed her eyes, and took a deep breath. When she open her eyes, she found Andrew staring at her curiously. "Sylvia, are you all right?"

"Yes, I'm fine." Or perhaps she was completely out of her mind. "Andrew, dear, do you remember a particular question you asked me here, last summer in this exact spot, a very important question?"

Andrew studied her, his face expressionless. Then he nodded.

"Well, if you wouldn't mind—" She cleared her throat. "I would like very much if you would ask me again."

"Are you sure?"

"Yes, I'm absolutely sure."

He considered. "Well, okay then." He paused. "Sylvia . . ."

"Yes, Andrew?"

"What do you want for lunch?"

"Not that question," she spluttered, but her embarrassment turned to indignation in the moment it took her to realize he was laughing at her. "Andrew Cooper, you rascal, you know very well which question I meant."

"You can't blame me for teasing you after all the times I've asked and you've refused." He grinned. "Maybe I should wait for you to ask me."

Sylvia was prepared to do just that, but only as a last resort. "We're going to do this properly or not at all," she said, her voice as stern as she could make it considering how warmly Andrew was smiling at her. "So unless you're no longer interested—"

"I'm interested."

He took her hands again, and in words as simple and straightforward as they were affectionate, he told her again how much he loved her, and how he had loved her since he was a boy. He told her that he would love her the rest of his life and that he would prove that to her every day they were together. He promised to do everything in his power to make her as happy as she made him, and that he would be the luckiest and proudest man alive if she would consent to be his wife.

This time, Sylvia told him she would.

* * *

Andrew was dancing Sylvia about the gazebo in celebration when Sarah arrived to warn them that a car was coming up the drive. She had to call out over the sound of their laughter, and after she delivered the message, she regarded them curiously. "What are you two so happy about?"

"We'll tell you later," said Sylvia before Andrew could speak. She wanted to enjoy their promise in privacy a little while longer before announcing the news to their friends.

Sylvia and Andrew met Margaret and her mother at the front door. As soon as they entered, their smiles and cheerful greetings seemed to bring the crisp freshness of the bright autumn day in with them, banishing the few lingering worries Andrew's proposal had not quite driven from Sylvia's mind. By the time introductions were made, Sarah's husband, Matt, had arrived to take the visitors' bags to their rooms—except for one tote Evelyn wished to keep with her—and Sarah announced that lunch was ready.

Sylvia and Andrew led Margaret and Evelyn to the banquet hall, where they found Summer making one last adjustment to the centerpiece. Sylvia thanked her with a smile. Her young friends realized how important this meeting was to her, and they had not overlooked even the smallest detail. Sylvia only hoped that if they had any more surprises in store for her, they would wait until Margaret and Evelyn retired for the night. She took more than a little pleasure in knowing that none of their surprises could beat the one she had for them.

Matt and Sarah joined them, completing their party of seven. The cook himself served the meal, and he presented every dish in as elegant a fashion as Sylvia could have desired.

As everyone got acquainted, Sylvia used the opportunity to take her guests' measure. Evelyn reminded her of Rosemary Cullen in age and appearance, and she seemed somewhat shy and reserved, quite the opposite of her outgoing daughter. Sylvia had to hide a smile watching Margaret, for the former camper seemed so delighted to be at Elm Creek Manor again that Sylvia figured the cook could have served cold hamburgers from a local take-out joint and she might not have noticed. As they enjoyed the meal, Margaret described her camp experiences to her mother and reminisced with Sarah and Summer about the highlights of the week. She still kept in touch with all of the students in her Heirloom Machine Quilting class, and they had recently completed a row round-robin through the mail.

"We're planning a reunion here next summer," said Margaret. "We're just waiting for our registration forms."

"I'm glad you'll be back," said Sylvia, and she turned to Evelyn. "Will you be joining us, too?"

Evelyn shrugged shyly. "Oh, I don't know about that. I don't travel much anymore. I'm more comfortable in my own place."

"We'd do our best to make you comfortable here, too," said Summer, with the smile that never failed to charm the object of her attention.

"Think about it, Mom," urged Margaret.

"If you wouldn't think it an intrusion on your friends, I'd consider it, except—" Evelyn looked around the table. "I hate to admit it in such company, but I don't know how to quilt."

"What better reason to attend quilt camp than to learn?" said Sarah, and Sylvia chimed in her agreement. After assuring Evelyn she would not be the only new quilter—or "Newbie," as Summer called them—Evelyn brightened and said she would plan to come.

Andrew leaned over to murmur in Sylvia's ear. "First Kathleen and now Evelyn. Two converts in one day. Not bad."

Sylvia pursed her lips at him as if to scold him for being saucy, but she knew he saw the merriment in her eyes.

After dessert—a heavenly confection of fudge cake and white chocolate mousse that Sylvia decided ought to be added to their regular menu—the conversation turned to the memoir. Margaret and Evelyn peppered her with so many eager questions that Sylvia marveled they had been able to hold them in so long. She sent Sarah to fetch the memoir, and she read aloud from it when they asked her to elaborate on certain events she had mentioned in her letters. Evelyn and Margaret listened most intently when Sylvia read the passages in which Gerda described her unsuccessful attempts to find Joanna. Perhaps the stresses of the day had finally caught up with her, or perhaps it was sharing the journal with the woman whose startling inquires had been the impetus for all Sylvia had learned about her family, but Sylvia found herself so overcome with emotion that she frequently stumbled over the simplest phrases, until she was so embarrassed by her unusual lack of composure that she passed the book to her guests so they could read it for themselves. But no one at the table would permit it. Instead they gently urged her to read on, for they wanted to hear Gerda's words in Sylvia's voice.

Heartened, Sylvia took a deep breath and continued until the final page of the memoir. Then she closed the book softly and rested it on her lap. She imagined Gerda sitting in her room in the west wing of Elm Creek Manor, pen in hand, pouring her grief and longing into the slender, leather-bound book, never knowing who would one day read her words or how they would be received. Or perhaps she had written in the peace of the north gardens, seated in the gazebo, which Hans might have designed not to conceal runaway slaves but to preserve the memory of one, the woman who had given him his beloved adopted son. She imagined Gerda wrapping the completed record in the Underground Railroad quilt and locking it safely away in her hope chest along with the Birds in the Air quilt and the unique Log Cabin quilt, which she had been unable to give to Joanna. Then, or perhaps years later, or perhaps not until her last will and testament, she had given the slender key to Lucinda, who eventually bestowed it upon Sylvia.

After a long moment, Evelyn broke the silence. "Margaret—" She paused to clear her throat, and she removed her glasses to dab at her eyes with a handkerchief. "Margaret, dear, would you hand me my bag, please?"

Margaret nodded, and after a quick, inscrutable glance at Sylvia, she retrieved the large tote from beneath the table and placed it on her mother's lap, allowing most of the weight to fall upon her own hands. Evelyn unfastened the straps, pulled back the zipper, and withdrew a folded bundle wrapped in a cotton sheet. Sylvia immediately recognized it as a quilt, and judging by the reverence with which Evelyn cradled it, there could be no mistaking which quilt it was.

Sylvia stifled a gasp of delight as Evelyn and Margaret unfolded their own Birds in the Air quilt and held it up so all could see. What a joy it was to behold the mysterious quilt again in all its tattered, water-stained glory!

Sarah and Summer cried out in surprise, for Sylvia had told them how fragile the antique quilt was, and they had never expected to see it except in photographs. Sylvia watched fondly as her two young friends pointed out the features of the quilt to each other—the fabric held in place with careful, painstaking stitches; the worn batting with the cotton hulls still visible through the muslin lining; the delicate, cryptic quilting patterns that Sylvia had once dared think might depict scenes from Elm Creek Manor.

"Thank you so much for bringing the quilt with you," said Sylvia as all admired it. "I only wish my friend Grace Daniels were here. She would have been thrilled to see it."

"Oh, I imagine she'll get her chance," said Margaret.

"I'm afraid she's several hours away by airplane, or I'd be on the phone inviting her over at this very moment."

"Then she can see it the next time she's in town," said Evelyn.

Puzzled, Sylvia glanced at Andrew before replying. "What do you mean?"

Evelyn gazed at the quilt as if memorizing it, then sighed and passed it to Sylvia. "Just promise me you'll take good care of it."

"What—" Sylvia took the quilt, but her eyes were fixed on her guest. "You can't mean you're giving this to me."

"I am."

"But . . . but it's priceless. It's a family heirloom."

"It *is* a family heirloom," agreed Evelyn. "But not my family's."

"Evelyn—" As much as Sylvia longed to keep the quilt, she could not do it, knowing her only claim to it was the name Evelyn's mother had given it and a few odd quilting designs that could be interpreted many different and contradictory ways. "As much as I would love to, I simply can't accept this. We have no proof that your quilt has any connection to me or to Elm Creek Manor. Just because it was once called the Elm Creek Quilt—"

"We have more proof than that," said Margaret. "You're forgetting the quilt had another name. It was also called the Runaway Quilt."

Sylvia felt her reply catch in her throat.

Gently, Evelyn said, "In her memoir, Gerda wrote that she learned Josiah Chester would sell off his captured runaways to family or acquaintances in Georgia or the Carolinas."

Sylvia could only nod. She took Andrew's hand and held it tightly.

"My grandfather had a brother," said Evelyn. "That brother had a tobacco plantation in Virginia, and his name was Josiah Chester."

* * *

That evening, long after her guests and her friends had retired for the night, Sylvia lay awake in bed, her mind so full of wonder that she could not rest. Moonlight spilled in through her window, enticing her out from beneath her quilts. She dressed warmly and, with great care, took up the Runaway Quilt from the quilt rack in the corner.

Outside the air was cool and still. She crossed the bridge over Elm Creek and made her way to the remains of the cabin Gerda, Hans, and Anneke had once called home. In the moonlight the half-buried logs looked straighter and sturdier than they seemed by day, and yet at the same time they more closely resembled the tree roots Sylvia had first thought them. The night had enchanted the ruin, making it both a more solid foundation and a living thing rooted in the earth, ever growing, ever changing.

Sylvia tucked her hands into the fold of the quilt to warm them, marveling at chance and fate, and wondering if those long-ago events had not instead been shaped by a merciful providence. If Joanna had not lost her way in the storm, if she had not stumbled across the abandoned cabin and found shelter there, the lives of the Bergstrom family would have taken an entirely different, forever unknowable course. Sylvia might never have existed.

Yet she very well might have. She would never know whether Joanna was truly her great-grandmother. She had reminded Margaret and Evelyn of this, repeatedly, warning them that they might be giving their precious family heirloom to someone with even less certain ties to the quiltmaker than their own. But they insisted Sylvia keep it, saying they were acting on faith rather than proven fact.

So Sylvia accepted the quilt with a grateful heart.

She allowed her gaze to travel from the ruins of the cabin to the sky. She found the North Star, as bright and as constant as when Joanna had followed it to freedom, but a freedom that was not destined to endure. For Joanna's son, the dream had come true, although he was never to know the sacrifice his mother had made in allowing only herself to be taken away, though she must have longed to bring him with her, even into slavery, if only to hold him one last time.

A wind stirred, rustling the boughs of the elm trees lining the road to the back of Elm Creek Manor. Sylvia snuggled her hands deeper into the quilt and turned back toward home.

She passed the red barn Hans Bergstrom had built into the side of the hill, twenty paces east of what had once been the cabin's front door. She crossed the bridge over Elm Creek, and from there she spotted a light in a window. Andrew's room. He likely had heard her rise and depart, and even now waited for her safe return. She wondered if Joanna had seen a light in the window of the Bergstrom home upon her arrival so long ago, and if she had found comfort in its warm glow.

Sylvia gazed to the heavens and said a prayer for Joanna, hoping, as Gerda had, that she had at last found the peace and comfort denied her in life. For Sylvia knew by faith if not by fact that Joanna had planned to return to Elm Creek Manor for her son.

That much was evident in every stitch of the Runaway Quilt, which Joanna must have pieced by night after her day's work was done, quilting patterns to help her remember where she had traveled, how she had made her journey, so that one day she could find her way back again. In stolen moments she had labored on her masterpiece, recalling the signal she had helped Gerda make, biding her time until she could once again take flight like the Birds in the Air she created from the castoff fabric of the household, piecing a symbolic map from the discarded clothing of her owners, who must have mocked "that runaway's quilt" and the inscrutable effort of the woman who made it. Somehow Joanna had been prevented from following the patchwork cues north to Elm Creek Manor, and the descendants of those who had enslaved her had claimed her quilt as their own. Joanna would never know that generations later, her quilt would complete the journey she herself had been unable to undertake.

Sylvia climbed the stairs and crossed the veranda. She was home. This was her home, and this was her family, as it had always been and would ever be. Whoever her real grandparents were, she was the descendant of Joanna and Anneke and Gerda. The women who had shaped her origins had shaped her, and she would cherish them all as her ancestors, and accept their mystery as she had all else they had bequeathed her.

AUTHOR'S NOTE

The Runaway Quilt is a work of fiction. The debate about the role of quilts as signals on the Underground Railroad is ongoing, with the oral tradition often at odds with documented historical fact. In this novel, I have tried to remain faithful to the historical record while also presenting a plausible explanation for the evolution of the legend. For more information about quilts during the era of the Underground Railroad and the Civil War, please see Barbara Brackman's excellent resources, *Clues in the Calico, Quilts from the Civil War,* and *Civil War Women.*

ABOUT THE AUTHOR

Jennifer Chiaverini lives with her husband and son in Madison, Wisconsin, where she quilts with the Mad City Quilters.